JONNY THOMPSON

Ash and Sun

First published by Chantry Publishing House 2022

This novel is entirely a work of fiction. The names, characters and incidents portrayed in it are the work of the author's imagination. Any resemblance to actual persons, living or dead, events or localities is entirely coincidental.

First edition

ISBN: 978-1-7386660-0-3

Editing by Jessie Thompson
Editing by Laura Joyce
Editing by Leighton Wingate
Cover art by Robyn Whitwham

This book was professionally typeset on Reedsy.
Find out more at reedsy.com

To my family.

1

Jens stumbled into his apartment. He was a sorry sight for an agent. Then again, he wouldn't return to being *Senior Agent Adam Jennings* until morning, though morning could stand to hold its breath a little longer. Jens smeared a hand over his still gooey eyes, which was an unfortunate side effect from the Enzo. He was having trouble knowing if they were open or closed as he tripped over old food containers and a scattering of clothing across the floor.

It had been days since he'd been back to his apartment—he'd been on one final hurrah before his suspension would be over and he could return to work. His mind was starting its painful release from the previous hit of Enzo still in his system. What had been euphoria mere hours before was now a throbbing pulse in the center of his brain, which he knew from experience would soon feel like a nail hammering into his skull.

The highs were high, but the lows were most definitely low. It wasn't the first time he'd gone on a bender like this, but it was certainly the longest.

In the past, he found the drug scratched an itch, but this had been a complete meltdown. He'd told himself he needed the relief; his mind had been thirsty for stimulus. *But that ends tomorrow, well today, well in four hours.*

He stumbled into his room, bumping into the side table and

consequently saw the glare of the white clock resting on top of it that read "18,276 days 23 hours 16 minutes 24 sec" as it slowly flicked its way down to zero. *Christ, I should sleep.*

He silently praised himself for managing to make it to his room, where he kicked off his shoes and fell on top of his sheets just before passing out.

. . .

What began as an agonizing, monotonous buzzing turned into an explosion of sound erupting from all around the room.

"Good morning, Pittsburgh! It's another beautiful day here in the nation's capital . . ." The radio, which he reckoned he'd set before his escapades, was set to max volume.

"TURN OFF!" Jens cried out, but with no luck.

"As per your request, the radio will play out for a further fourteen minutes and thirty-six seconds," said a frustratingly calm voice before it kicked back in at full volume.

"The National Weather Station is predicting intermittent periods of rain throughout the city with some light natural rains coming in from the west overnight. Check your area to discover specific rainfall projections," said the overly enthusiastic voice.

"Can the volume be turned down, at least!" Jens said, squeezing the pillow against his ears, relieved when the volume seemed to lower a little.

As if to torment him further, the window shades began to lift automatically, revealing a blinding light which shone in harsh contrast to the darkness he'd been hiding in and burning Jens' eyes.

"Clearly, it's not raining yet, is it!" Jens said as he yanked the bedsheets up, cultivating a meager thin line of defence as he pulled them up over his head. An overwhelming shame arose for his

inadequacy at being so ill-prepared for the morning.

Still just Adam Jennings, he thought as he sank deeper into his bed. He wished he'd been excited or nervous, but he felt nothing more than relief from the overwhelming boredom of his life on leave.

That, and the searing pain still in his head, and the clamminess of his body, which dampened his sheets, despite the climate-controlled room. It was clear to him that he had not fully recovered from the previous night's adventure.

At least he was in his bed, comfortable. The bed was a luxury he maintained, and not one that everyone did.

"Another day down, and here in the Pittsburgh area we say goodbye to thirteen hundred twenty-nine community members. A full list of names can be found on our data page, and from everyone here at 88.9 Capital Radio, we wish you a happy final day!"

Jens pulled down his covers and looked apprehensively at the second clock on his table: his death clock. It was pure white, issued by the state at the request of anyone who wanted one. The data was flashing across its face, 18,276 days 19 hours 33 minutes 36 seconds. He'd started with a full cycle, twenty-nine thousand two hundred, like everyone else, and one day those would dwindle to one, as was the case for thirteen hundred and twenty nine people in the city of Pittsburgh today.

He groaned and leaned back in his bed, staring at the ceiling fan spinning softly over the bed with a slight wobble, which despite the high volume of the radio, created a constant "whopping" sound. There was a time it had annoyed him, but now its steady wobble was a comfort.

If you're not willing to fix something, then you just learn to live with it.

It was a lesson he wished he'd understood before. Before he'd noticed the malfunctioning fan, before being stuck on leave since day eighteen thousand four hundred and seventy-six.

Two hundred days of his life that he couldn't get out and do his job. He was a senior agent with the GIB, Global Investigative Bureau, the agency that dealt with high-profile cases. He was good at it, too, and of late he had missed being good at something.

"Mayor Stone refused to comment on his upcoming election campaign, commenting that he and his team are focused on the upcoming bid to host the two hundredth anniversary of the Great Mitigation next summer, saying, 'The people of this city will decide one way or another who they feel is best to lead them, but as I am leading this city now, I will do my best to bring this honour to the great city of Pittsburgh and to the Western Gale as a whole.'"

Easy to say when you're likely not going to have any threatening opposition.

Maneuvering his legs to the side of the bed, he forced himself to slide from the warm mattress.

"Please play some music! I don't need to know what's happening in the world right now, at least not yet." Jens said, his eyes closed as he stared aimlessly at the ceiling.

"The radio will continue to play for twelve minutes and forty-six seconds," said the voice from speakers throughout the room, as a female singer sang out over a low, thrumming bassline that threatened to have Jens bobbing his head.

Reluctantly hoisting himself to his feet, he tossed the sheets unceremoniously back on the bed and moved sluggishly into the bathroom. The light adjusted smoothly from one room to the other, giving him what the designer deemed optimal light to see the black-and gray-tiled space.

When he first moved in, the tile had been clean and sparkly enough for his reflection to be seen on their surface. Now, one thousand eight hundred and twenty-five days later, individual tiles were almost indistinguishable. The grime caked around the edges of the sink and

shower room, replacing his reflection with soapy mildew and old hairs he hoped were from his head.

Looking around the room, he cursed himself for not taking the time to clean it, the bitter truth being he hadn't done anything else instead.

At first, he imagined the suspension would do him some good, an opportunity to catch up on all the things he'd put off over the years. Things such as cleaning his apartment. In reality, he found himself languishing, unmotivated, and lacking any real ambition.

Without his work, he was even worse than before. At least before, he had a purpose. Now, all he had was a filthy apartment and the brutal awareness that the world continued without him.

Jens fiddled with the shower controls beside the sink, finally managing to find the setting he liked. Not that it mattered. Maybe the shower had flourished in the past, but now, what came out could barely be described as a drizzle. *Goddamned eco-showers.*

They tended to underwhelm on the best of days, but with all the buildup, the spray was dismal.

Jens pulled off his underwear, tossing it on the largest of the laundry piles, stepped into the shower, and ducked his head under the meager drainage.

Cupping his hands, he managed a pathetic collection of falling water, employing the shallow pool to bathe his body. It was a fool's task, but he needed to at least pretend to look presentable on his first day back. God knew there would be enough people in the agency who wished he had been sacked without the added ammunition of his turning up smelling like a bag of ripe fruit.

Soon he'd have access to the GIB shower rooms, with their reliable flow of water, but for now, the additional splashes would have to suffice.

To his surprise, Jens managed to feel a modicum of cleanliness,

having found a rhythm of catch and release from the water sprinkling out. It didn't hurt finding a dried sliver of body soap, which he managed to peel off the shelf. The wash was a meager triumph.

The shower shut down as he moved back to the sink, locating his bamboo toothbrush, which seemed to have all but decomposed, having likely been on its last rope seventy-five days ago, on the counter next to the final dusting of charcoal that remained in the jar beside it.

"Get a new toothbrush and charcoal," Jens said as he began to brush his teeth, shaking his head at the list now piling up in his mind of everything else he needed: socks, food, juice. *What the hell have I been doing for the last two hundred days?*

Scanning the room and finding what he deemed to be the cleanest towel, he pulled it from the hook from behind the door. Giving it a quick whiff, he opted for the more natural air dry, using the towel instead to wipe down the mirror. The steam from the shower, accompanied with the towel, helped to clean most of the muck away, the towel sliding roughly over the section of cracked mirror left by his fist the last time he'd found himself staring at it.

It had been a moment of weakness fueled by anger and frustration at the man he'd been looking at then, and he hadn't managed to bring himself back to the mirror since. Now, this time, as he examined himself, what was reflected was equally as difficult to look at, not for the same reasons.

Just shy of six foot three Jens had short brown hair and a manicured beard, and his body was thick and well cared for. But, looking at himself now, he could barely recognize who he saw. A straggly beard covered up his slightly rounded face to match his new belly, which had puffed out at some point over the seemingly endless string of Enzo-induced odysseys.

Looking at the mirror, wishing the guck would return, he felt more like a disappointment than he ever did during any of his probationary

hearings. *I wouldn't stand a chance in a chase.*

Jens had always been better at life when he was busy, though he wasn't sure what kind of assignments he would be getting now. *Maybe I won't be busy?*

Pulling out the cabinet drawer, Jens reached for a beard trimmer. Turning it on, he was shocked to find it fully charged, though with the forest currently thriving on his face, he shouldn't have been very surprised.

Working the trimmer down his cheek, he watched the clumps of facial hair fall into the sink, with each pass of the blade slowly revealing a glimpse of the man he'd once been. The mass of thick hair fell away, leaving a stubble of course hair. With a splash of warm water, he was relieved to reveal a fresh, albeit tired, face. *Little I can do there,* he thought as his hands dragged slowly down his face, attempting to smooth the dark bags beneath his eyes.

The music in the room cut out, so he knew it had been around fifteen minutes. He'd have to abandon the idea of fixing his mop of hair, opting to slick it back with a comb, and finishing it off with what he hoped was the remains of gel. The final look was less than desirable, but it would do.

Nearly dry, Jens strode back into his room and rummaged through his drawer, impressed to find a set of pressed blue trousers, white shirt, and a blue blazer, the official GIB uniform.

Even in solitary confinement, some habits are hard to break.

He put them on and felt some pride for the first time since he'd woke up, even though he had to ignore the tightness of his uniform, and the pigsty around him.

Reaching into his bedside dresser, he pulled out a silver box the size of his fist. Sliding the clasp, he opened the box, showing a well-cared-for navy blue Zen watch resting on a white pillow. It had sat unused in the box since his suspension; he'd opted to use a secondhand basic

model he'd bought, which he now carelessly tossed into the dresser. Today, like him, its full functions would be returned. He slipped the Zen watch over his wrist, the weight of it feeling good as it clicked into place.

He shot a glance back at the restless white clock ticking away and he felt revived, eighteen thousand two hundred and seventy-six, a new day.

2

The door clicked shut behind him as he rushed out of his apartment, his Zen watch making sure to lock it as he did.

Sold as the ultimate user experience, "all-in-one home-protection and digital-communication tool" with "built-in biotracking, making it nearly impossible to steal or replicate," it was the single most practical device sold around the world.

It was so convenient that many ignored its darker purposes: it tracked the whereabouts of all users, predicted trends, and captured biomarkers that could be used by agents such as him as lie detectors.

As none of this was a secret, it answered the age-old question: do people think it is better to have convenience or anonymity? The world responded: convenience.

The device provided to him was a state-of-the-art GIB Zen watch issued to members of the agency. It ensured extra security measures from near impossible to impossible to forge and most importantly, it identified them to the public. His had been restricted during his suspension but as of this morning was up and running at full tilt.

Making his way down the hallway, the doors opened silently into the sleek square elevator encased in tinted windows. Stepping inside, the doors closed just as smoothly behind him. The preprogramming in his Zen watch requested the elevator to go to level one; the default touchless system had gained popularity after several outbreaks led to

a rise of infectious disease and a massive reduction in the population. "Are you single and looking for real connections? Our residency social club gathers every Thursday night, floor thirty-four, suite thirty-four eighty-nine. Press Yes on your Zen watch if you'd like us to reserve you a spot," said the voice, which was playful over the speakers in the elevator.

"Shit!" Jens said, lifting his watch and clicking No on the face. *The damned thing must have reset to factory settings.*

Jens fiddled with the setting button and promptly removed the advertisement feature; he hated getting updates and reminders of things such as being single.

He was happy alone; partners only seemed to get in the way. Although he had tried over the years, all of them, any gender, seemed to play out the same way; they couldn't stand to be number two, and for at least the next sixty-nine hundred and ninety-five days, they would always be second fiddle.

The elevator stopped, and he stepped out into the massive and empty entrance hall. The only sound was coming from a large fountain at its center. The rhythmic rolling of water was a nice accompaniment to the lonely slapping of his shoes. It was early, and most people in his building wouldn't start work for a few hours. *Lucky bastards.*

Jens enjoyed working for the GIB, but it didn't come with the luxury of free time or time off that many jobs these days afforded.

The rain fell hard against the ground as he stepped outside. *It was sunny twenty minutes ago!*

"National Weather Station," he said, and his Zen watch loaded up the current forecast for the area.

"Rain began five minutes ago, and the current manipulated rainfall in your area will continue for twenty-five minutes," said a calming female voice. *I should have guessed given the time of year.*

10

Despite societies best effort to control Mother Nature entirely, she persisted in being better than humans, although they had managed to manipulate it a little, helping with global vegetation, urban gardens, and wet clothes.

Jens strode down the street, popping his collar up on his jacket to keep the wind at bay and the worst of the pelting water on his back as he silently cursed himself for not grabbing an umbrella.

It wasn't long before he arrived at the Inner-City Electric Rail, better known as the ICER, a localized Hyperloop rail network that carried millions of daily commuters throughout the system every day.

He stepped through one of the many archways into a screen-filled gallery, each screen paired with a particular destination and various advertisements as Jens walked toward the automated stairs descending beneath the main landing to various subterranean tube tunnels.

Locating the screen earmarked for Zone One he quickly hopped on his desired stairway, taking the steps two at a time, as he noticed the next train would depart shortly. Hopping off the platform, Jens only just managed to slide in past the closing doors of his train.

It was fuller than he'd imagined, and so Jens opted to remain standing, allowing a pregnant woman and her child to take the only two remaining seats in his section.

He'd have preferred to sit. It was early, and his body hadn't fully recovered yet. Also, not having any idea when he might get the chance to sit wasn't ideal, either. *Then again, for all I know, I'll be at the desk the rest of my life.*

That idea seemed to lighten the burden of standing, and ignoring his aching body, Jens tried focusing instead on the child seated across from him, his little hands holding an elaborately displayed 3D hologram of a tilt-a-maze.

Games. It was the reason he was selected into the GIB in the first place. He'd studied game theory and human psychology, and it didn't hurt that he also exceeded the recommended scoring in problem-solving and logical reasoning.

Though it had been some time and not having played in a while, Jens needed a refresher of the difficultly of the game. He watched intently as the boy worked with practiced efficiency, his fingers manipulating the board with skilled tranquility, as he guided the projected ball through the maze, managing to keep the ball away from the various holes scattered about the board.

Jens guessed the boy couldn't be much older than five, and was obviously a bright kid as Jens watched him make quick work of the puzzle in front of him. Jens imagine just how long the same puzzle would take him to complete.

"Smart kid," he said to the woman, who looked up from her e-book, quickly scanning Jens and deciding how best to engage. Her eyes eventually landed on the government-issued GIB Zen watch prominently displayed on his wrist, and she rewarded Jens with a pleasant smile.

"Thank you," she said politely, returning proudly back to her book. Unmoved by the comment, the boy was in deep focus, analyzing his current level in the game. The expression on his face suggested he was stuck somewhere on the new board.

Jens looked it over, understanding where the boy must be confused. Scanning the board, Jens began playing through various options in his mind, landing on the route he found the most acceptable. Proud of himself for the speediness of his solution, he prepared to propose his run, but before he could point it out to the boy, Jens watched as the boy adjusted the configuration of the board, finding the path Jens himself had seen. Before Jens could speak, the boy was off, the light cast ball moving swiftly through narrow gaps in the maze. His

youthful fingers easily maneuvered the various levels of the labyrinth, finally reaching the finish line. The boy looked reverently up to Jens.

"Nice job, kid," he said appraisingly and was rewarded with a smile from the boy full of admiration, as his eyes subtly darted from Jens to his watch. There weren't many GIB agents. It was a difficult position, and so the public still regarded his station with some respect . . . most people.

Jens nodded, used to being recognized, as the boy quickly returned to his game. Jens was still proud of himself; he may not be as nimble as he used to be, but he could still spot a pattern.

The ICER came to a stop at Zone One. The doors opened to reveal an impressively clean, white granite floor. He was in the core now, which made for more immaculate surroundings. It housed many of the city's large financial institutions and tech companies and, of course, was where the GIB headquarters was located. Working here in the core sadly affirmed two truths with the world, that neither credits nor crime ever slept.

Making his way up the granite corridor, Jens came to a metal archway and passed through. The hidden scanner in the archway simultaneously checked him for potential threats while conveniently charging his Zen watch for the fair.

Reaching the top of a long walkway, Jens stepped out onto the street, where the energy was a little more alive as more and more people walked the streets. The rain had stopped, making it a pleasant morning, as the smell of various flowers from the manicured urban gardens wafted through the air.

The respite from the rain also gave Jens a much-needed minute to dry off during the four-block walk to the GIB main entrance. He momentarily considered the idea of taking one of the automated ECars the last few blocks, which would be faster.

But something about the gardens, the air, and the well-maintained

trails that laced conveniently between buildings made him want to walk. That and his now overly pronounced stomach made him feel as if it were as good a time as any to start walking.

He hadn't been down here in one hundred and ninety-nine days, since the official sentencing, but he was happy to see that nothing had changed. It was still the envy of all cityscapes. No space was wasted, everything being used to its full potential.

Green, earthen walkways arched over the city, giving a unique elevation to it. A set of man-made rolling hills that branched outward from a central pathway like a tree, each arm weaving in and out of the various buildings. This inspired network of limbs allowed people to move readily from building to building while enjoying the outside space. Newer and wealthier areas of the city were trying to emulate the core, but few had mastered its beauty.

He walked up a tulip-lined green pathway thick with matured grass patted down by foot traffic from the morning commuters

Continuing his way up the path, the familiarity of it all came back to him as he peered down the remainder of the green arch, spotting the entranceway to the GIB headquarters.

Arriving, he braced himself for a moment, looking into the revolving doorway, which, as he was about to enter, began to spin, spitting out a large man dressed in a black suit who was leading a young woman outside.

Still easily in her first ten thousand days, she had fair skin, with light, wavy brown hair, down to her shoulders. She appeared to be struggling with her handler as she repeatedly pounded her fists on his chest.

"Let me go! I need to talk with someone inside. I need . . . ," she shouted before dropping her fists and attempting to force a more pleasant disposition before adding with authority, "Please, let me go!"

Jens had to admire her conviction, and he knew he was about to

14

regret it, even as he waved his GIB credentials to the unfamiliar guard at the door.

"Let her go. I'll take it from here," Jens said, giving the slightest of nods, acutely aware of the guard's joy at not having to deal with her anymore as he disappeared back inside.

No doubt she had just caused some sort of disturbance inside, and now here he was taking full responsibility for her. *Off to a great start, Jens.*

He reviewed the young woman in front of him, now patting herself down, washing away any signs of the scuffle she'd just been involved in, trying, with mild success, to look composed. "Thank you," she said, unable to mask the slight tone of anger.

"How can I help you?" Jens said, while glancing at his watch, checking to see how much time he had before he was officially late. But the act had the side benefit of also adding a nice indicator of who he was. It seemed to do the trick. Her demeanor made a swift shift; knowing she was talking with someone who could help calmed her down. At least she assumed he could help.

"My brother, he's missing," she said, skipping pleasantries and getting straight to the point. No doubt she had tried the civil approach early on and got nowhere and now wanted answers.

"Right, and who is your brother?"

Her blunt approach was handy, considering the time.

The trouble with missing people seemed that most often they were not missing at all, usually falling into two categories: not wanting to be found or dead.

"His name is Ryan Lilford. I haven't seen him in nearly two days." She tried unsuccessfully to mask her emotions.

"Right, and you are?" he said, keeping his tone neutral despite already making up his mind on where this mystery was going.

"His sister, Natasha," she said, her voice hopeful. Jens hated knowing that there wasn't much he could do to make her feel any better. This was neither a GIB problem nor was it a case for the police, yet. Without a body, there wasn't much he or the GIB could do.

Likely he was out and just didn't want to be found. Unfortunately, Jens didn't have the time to explain all this to her, or time to deal with her inevitable response.

"Right, well, three days doesn't seem long enough . . ."

She attempted to cut him off, but he was quicker; knowing she wouldn't be satisfied with that, he'd already formed a plan.

"Luckily, I have a friend at PPD, Constable Craig Granger. Talk to him." Jens pulled out a spare card from his rain jacket, a little damp, but it would do the trick.

"Show him the card and tell him Jens sent you." He handed her the soggy card, quickly adding, "That, unfortunately, is the best I can do for you, Natasha, and with any luck, your brother will turn up soon." He waited, praying she wouldn't respond.

Her feet shifted as she looked at the card; finally her shoulders dropped, and Jens suspected she'd gotten more than she had hoped for out of the exchange. She'd leave and get the help she'd been looking for and he could leave content that he would potentially remain on time.

"Thank you," she said after a moment, putting the card in her pocket.

Not bad for the first morning back. Maybe the rest of his day would be as good?

3

The moment Jens stepped out onto floor thirty-six of the GIB building, he became brutally aware that his day would, in fact, not be good. It had been two hundred and fifty-six days since the incident, and despite his never formally being charged with anything, there had been some "concerns" about how a man under Jens' charge had ended up with a broken cheekbone, orbital bone, collarbone, and seven broken fingers. There was also the question of one rather curious ruptured testicle.

So, it was clear that for some of his colleagues, the two hundred days hadn't been enough time to get over it. He spotted two cards placed on his desk by his fellow agents and spotted the profound differences between them. It was rare to get cards, so he was a little surprised to find two.

Looking around the room, Jens tried to make eye contact with as many people as he could. A few looked away, some avoided him altogether, and a small cohort stared back with fierce disdain. Those were the ones he'd have to watch out for. For the most part, people pretended to ignore him. As there was no way to run from his current reputation, he'd unfortunately be well known to everyone on the force in one way or another.

His age didn't help the matter, either. There was a time he would have been hated for simply being the young gun. Now he was roughly the same age as his some of the newer recruits, only he had the experience of some of those looking to retire soon. It took years of work to convince most of them that he was deserving of the position. His decision to join so young had always worked against him. Now, he'd need some time to crawl out of the crater he'd dug for himself.

Eyeing the two cards on the desk again, he picked up the one closer. Holding the first, he opened it up, the writing inside containing a simple "Welcome back" signed by a handful of names most of which he recognized—unsurprisingly, not a huge contingency of names in the "Welcome back" pile.

He placed the card down, picking up the second, acutely aware of its message. He opened it up, revealing another simple note: "Eat Shit." Unoriginal but to the point, he thought, glancing down at a smaller selection of names on the card. Clearly there'd been a large neutral party who'd opted out of either card. Jens could work with that. Closing the card, he slipped both into the top shelf of his desk.

"Hey, fat man," a voice called out from behind him. Turning, Jens spotted Agent Annette Moretti, an elegantly tall woman, with a narrow figure buried beneath her official navy blue GIB suit. Her short, spiky, auburn hair was carefully styled. As she was seventeen hundred and sixty-five days Jens' senior, he'd known her for quite some time. They'd worked a few cases together, including a particularly difficult embezzlement case awhile back. Hers had been one of the names on the "Welcome back" card.

"Fat man? Who are you calling fat, Moretti?" Jens said, happy to see a friendly face. Before he could argue, her long arms embraced him in a friendly hug. Not being much of a hugger himself, Jens had to admit the embrace was oddly comforting after his time away.

"It's good to see you. How was the vacation . . . you eat the whole west side?" she said, giving him a quick once-over.

"It's not that bad, is it?" he said, giving his belly an embarrassed pat.

"Right, well . . . define bad."

She placed her own hand on his stomach. Jens batted it away.

"You get your card?" she said, looking down on the empty desk.

"Both of them," Jens admitted, pulling out the drawer, showing them off, a detailed pile of shit depicted neatly on the uncovered edge.

"It's a hell of a picture, very comprehensive," Jens said, musing, then shutting the drawer and the cards along with it.

"The bastards," Moretti said, glancing around the room. "Don't mind them. They wouldn't know a good agent if one took a comprehensive shit in their mouths." Her booming laugh was infectious, pulling in looks from passersby. Letting the moment settle, her voice dropped just above a whisper. "For what it's worth, there are a few of us who think you did the right thing," she said, giving his arm a supportive nudge.

"I didn't do anything," Jens said, his voice unintentionally matching her conspiratorial sound.

"Right, of course not." She said, giving him with a wink. "Best just let the whole thing blow over," she concluded with a good slap on the arm.

As Jens looked around the room, people appeared busy enough, but their eyes stole the occasional glance at the returning pariah. A crackle of energy filled the room, a palpable buildup of tension. Everyone was expecting or hoping for some kind of reaction from him.

Jens, not wanting to let the people down, climbed atop his unnaturally bare desk. With two hundred days away, it seemed only natural to take advantage of his stage. Standing on his desk, he cleared his throat. If the room wasn't looking at him before, they certainly were now.

"I just want to thank all of you for your cards," he said, emphasizing the word *all*. "I'd like to make a few things clear. First, I'm excited about getting back in to do my job. Second, I'm well aware of how much weight I've gained in my two hundred days, so please get the jokes out now while you can." He took the opportunity to look around the room, which for a moment remained silent; then an unknown voice called from across the room.

"You look like a puff pastry" got a few laughs from the gathered agents.

"I'm surprised you fit through the door," Angelia Danbrook called out from her desk a few rows back. The roar of laughter was getting louder around the room.

"I liked that. Any more?" Jens said, taking a final spin around the room. In his experience, the best way to clear the air was to sacrifice yourself to the wolves to let them know you couldn't be bothered with their bullshit.

"If you ask me," a voice called out from the gathered crowd. People stepped away, revealing Andrew Zhang, one of the names Jens spotted from the "Eat Shit" card and Jens' resentful ex-partner. "Two hundred days wasn't long enough, you piece of . . ." He didn't have the chance to finish, but the room was in no doubt of where it was heading before Captain Rollins interrupted the whole display.

"This isn't a goddamned zoo, Jennings. Get your ass off that desk. Two hundred days away clearly didn't teach you manners."

She looked angry. She didn't have time for immature bullpen jungle rules. She was running a division and needed her people ready and willing to work.

Dana Rollins was a fair and decent captain, coming up through the ranks with grit and determination. She was the best of the best, and Jens could see from her face that she understood what was going on despite the disapproving tone in her voice.

Jens had seen her come out of her office; she'd watched him make the play in front of the other agents, something he figured she would appreciate. By giving it a moment to play out before she spoke up, it was clear Jens was correct. But it was her job to make sure things never got out of hand, and Jens understood she'd be damned if she was going to let it happen this morning.

"Briefing room: five minutes," she said before leaving the room. It was only then that Jens noticed a new face beside her. A fresh face, she must have been new to the department; she certainly hadn't been here before he'd left.

Not surprising, as new recruits were often coming in. It was an honour to work for Captain Rollins, who was as fair, reasonable, and loyal as anyone as long as said person was prepared to work hard and get shit done. Not everyone had that kind of commitment.

The unknown face turned around and followed Captain Rollins back into her office, her eyes briefly meeting Jens' before disappearing.

Jens hopped off the desk, happy for the captain's intervention. Sure, she may have called him out, but she set the tone for the rest of the day. Playtime was over.

"Smooth moves, Jens." Moretti smiled knowingly at him. She was no idiot, and Jens was happy she'd been in his corner.

"Who was that with Captain Rollins?" Jens asked before she had the chance to run off.

"Not sure," she replied with a shrug before walking away.

A new recruit on the first day he returns from his suspension—something in his gut told him this was no coincidence.

4

"Welcome back, Jennings," Captain Rollins said, getting a mixed review as expected from the room. Jens, to avoid another outburst and more importantly anyone seeing his face when he was inevitably selected for an unimportant assignment that would place him at a desk and would almost certainly underutilize his talents, took a seat at the back of the room.

Agent Zhang predictably did not bother to look his way, and Jens knew it would likely be some time, if ever, before some of his colleagues would look at him the way they used to. Once a young rising star, he was now branded as a traitor.

"Glad to see the suit still fits, more or less," she added, receiving a round of laughter, before she continued with a short briefing.

Her attention now shifted, giving a slight nod to the new woman Jens saw her with earlier, who promptly stood.

She was young, certainly younger than Jens. *So, a new recruit or a transfer?*

"This is Agent Ali Hantsport—she's a transfer from the Tkaronto District," Captain Rollins said, confirming Jens' assessment.

"Looking forward to working with you all," Hantsport said, taking a moment to scan the room, her eyes finally settling on Jens. He looked back. Her features were sharp, her dark hair falling just below her shoulders, framing her olive-skinned face. Her deep-green eyes were piercing, even from across the room. For a brief moment Jens could have sworn she was looking directly at him.

"Thank you, Ali."

She took her seat at the front of the room, confirming Jens' suspicions as she turned her head once more to look at him. A soft smile appeared on her face, as if she knew something he didn't.

The pleasantries over, Captain Rollins ran through open cases and progress reports. Apparently, the Global West and the city of Pittsburgh didn't slow down while he was on holiday. She divvied up the casework until a single file remained with only a few senior agents left. Jens looked at the room, trying to figure out his chances of getting on a case his first day back. It didn't look great.

"Lastly," said Captain Rollins, looking around the room. "We have an abandoned warehouse in River Bend, Zone Thirty-Six. It appears that a few of our little drug boys got into some trouble last night." Her eyes peered about the room, finally landing on Jens. "Jens, I know you just got back, but do you feel up for a fresh case?" Jens covered his shock with an overly committed nod.

"Yes, ma'am," he said, watching as she typed in his ID code to the screen; the data from the open file linked immediately to his Zen watch. A short vibration on his wrist indicated a new message. Turning his watch face up, he saw a Halo projecting the message *do you accept* above his wrist. He accepted, and the watch silently scanned him, reading his biosignature. Another swift buzz completed the transfer, and the details of the report appeared before him.

"Perfect, you'll take Agent Hantsport with you on this one," she said coolly, causing Jens' mood to drop. He knew he shouldn't be surprised by a catch; it was too good to be true. He'd routinely worked his previous cases on his own, partnering up only on major projects, and he preferred it that way.

He found it difficult to explain to people how his mind worked through the problem, and in time he found it best to simply avoid it. Before the incident, the captain would have never assigned him a partner, especially not for something that by all accounts seemed to be a simple gang hit.

"Sorry, ma'am . . . ," he began saying, but was quickly cut off.

"That's all, everyone. Ship out and catch us some bad guys." She was off, ignoring his protest.

When he finally looked over at Agent Hantsport, he noticed her eyes were firmly focused on him. She knew this would happen, having likely received some warning that Jens would be difficult. *Was it punishment?*

Ali started to walk over to him. Ignoring her advance, Jens left the room, making his way toward the captain.

"Excuse me, ma'am," he said, now only a few steps behind. Captain Rollins, unperturbed, walked into her office, took off her more formal jacket, and hung it on a hook beside her desk.

It was a simple office—neat, beautifully designed, and encased by windows. The back window prominently displayed the Pittsburgh skyline, giving the room an airy feel. Not much in the way of personal effects, save a picture of her sister with her family beside her. Captain Rollins was one of those who had sacrificed a family for the job, not ever wanting to complicate things. Rumour had it she kept a steady string of young people close to her for companionship, but Jens would be damned if he ever asked her about that.

She now sat calmly at the large steel desk, which must have weighed a ton and seemed bulletproof. She pulled up her data display, beginning to type away, completely disregarding Jens' intrusion. Jens stopped at the door, knowing how unhelpful it would be to his cause to enter uninvited, giving Ali a moment to catch up, now just behind him.

He looked at her and tried hard to give what he imagined to be a friendly smile, but it likely looked more like a grimace. He wasn't used to playing nice with others.

"Come in," she said, finally glancing up to the doorway, "both of you."

Jens would have preferred to speak to her privately, entering the room with Agent Hantsport directly on his tail. But if she were going to insist on her being there, he'd willingly oblige.

"Right, what seems to be the problem?" Captain Rollins asked, placing her elbows on the desk, her body suggesting this better be over quick. "You don't want the case?"

"It's not that," Jens said, speaking more nervously than he'd intended. Truthfully, he couldn't have been happier about getting a case on his first day back, eager to jump back in. But he just didn't know how to tell her, in a polite way, that this Agent Hantsport would only slow him down.

Opting to try a more tactful approach to the situation, the last thing he wanted was to sound ungrateful.

"It's just . . ."

He was immediately cut off by Captain Rollins. "Shut the door, Agent Jennings," she said, her eyes flickering toward the door, the request catching Jens off guard. He turned, shutting the door, and as soon as it was closed, she was off again.

"I suppose you came in here to give me some bullshit about working alone?" She paused, leaving nothing but dead air in the room. Contemplating a response, he knew, deep down, it was a trap. He remained silent, his better judgment taking over. "Well, tough shit. You're a damn good agent, Jennings, but frankly, thanks to the little stunt you pulled, you're not exactly back to the big leagues. Shit like that doesn't really instill confidence to let you get out there on your own and fuck up another investigation. I wanted you back out there as soon as possible. Why? Because you're not a complete shit, and your record speaks for itself."

"If I may, ma'am, you say my record speaks for itself?" he began, rewarded with a sympathetic nod from his captain. "Then why slap me on babysitting duty?" He said this, looking over at Agent Hantsport. It wasn't meant to sound as harsh as it came out, but it was true. He didn't have time to watch over someone else.

To his surprise, this brought a laugh from the captain.

"You think you're with Agent Hantsport to babysit her?" she said incredulously.

"Why else would you stick her on my case?" He was looking a little closer now at Agent Hantsport, who kept alarmingly silent through all this exchange, almost as if she knew what was happening.

Jens suddenly got the impression he was missing something. He was right, as Captain Rollins began to laugh at him again.

"Good God, I thought you'd be smarter than this, Jennings. You're not babysitting her. She's babysitting you. Some of my commanders don't feel you can be trusted on your own . . ."

It was Jens' turn to get angry.

"That son of a bitch was guilty!" he yelled, causing Captain Rollins to get to her feet. Although four inches shorter than Jens, she appeared to tower over him.

"I could give a shit what you think happened. In the eyes of the law, he wasn't guilty. He was in the hospital for twenty-six days!" Her face was growing hotter with each word. "So, you don't get to lecture me on what you think is right! If it wasn't for my recommendation, you would be sitting on the third floor pushing goddamn papers for the rest of your career!"

Jens knew she was on his side with the case, but she was also a GIB captain and thus had to remain as neutral as possible. He also hadn't imagined just how hard she would have had to fight for him to be allowed to come back. This reevaluation silenced him.

"Now, that's in the past. This is the future. You may have got to work on your own in the past, but here, now, and most likely for the future, you don't get to pick and choose. You've lost that privilege. So, Jennings, are you going to play nice with Hantsport here? Or are you going to fuck off to the basements?"

Whether he liked it or not, that seemed to end the conversation, as she took her seat calmly, never breaking eye contact.

"No, ma'am," Jens said, being the first to break his gaze, realizing he wasn't going to win this battle.

"Good. Agent Hantsport, I'm sorry you had to see that. I'd say he's not usually this big a prick, but I can't." She looked back down at her files. "As to your point, Senior Agent Jennings, the cartel involved in the fire? They're believed to be part of the Scorpion crew. As it happens, Agent Hantsport has some history dealing with them. I figured her input would be useful." Her point made, she returned to her work. "Anything else?" she said. Agent Hantsport shook her head. Jens followed suit.

"No, ma'am," he said, the words coming out a little more quietly than he intended.

"Good. I believe you have some policing to do," she said, settling back into some data fragments on her Halo screen. "Close the door on your way out."

Jens, realizing there was no more to discuss, gave a curt nod before exiting the room. A nervous Agent Hantsport shut the door behind them, keeping a short clip from his heels as they left the bullpen.

It didn't take long to pull up an ECar once they got to the street. Normally Jens would have just taken the ICER to a crime scene to give himself a little more time to think about how he wanted to handle the situation he was in. But now, he had a partner, and that meant talking out loud. Or at least he assumed that's what it meant.

So far, Agent Hantsport hadn't said a single thing to him, which didn't surprise him. She was likely scared of him and had probably been told he was a pain in the ass. Jens wouldn't know. He'd never worked with himself.

As they hopped in the back of an ECar, Jens uploaded the desired address from his Zen watch into the car's data box. It would cost more, but this one was on the GIB, and he needed to get to know his new partner.

He sat in the back and pulled out the Halo of the case file, popping it up on the screen in front of them. All files were encrypted, so he wasn't worried about being hacked, although he wouldn't normally be displaying files like this.

"ID marker," Jens said as he started reading over the file. Agent Hantsport looked at him for a moment, then quickly realized what he was asking for. As she placed her thumb on the Halo, an upload bar showed the transfer to Agent Hantsport's Zen watch.

"In case you need it for reference," Jens said without looking at her. She nodded. At least he thought she did; he didn't bother to look.

She was shifting back and forth attempting to get comfortable. Jens realized that she was sitting on her words, wanting to say something but unsure how.

"Say it," he said, causing her to stop shifting, clearly thinking about how she wanted to broach the situation.

"I think we got off on the wrong foot," she said, looking at him, her hand jetting out for a shake. "I'm Agent Ali Hantsport." Her outstretched hand waited for the customary shake. Jens hated formalities, but he understood people needed them.

"Agent Adam Jennings," he said, clasping his hand around hers. He was impressed she had a firm handshake, a sign of confidence. This was surprising, given her other behaviours.

Releasing her hand, he resumed his focus on the case. After a moment, he realized she was staring at him, clearly more on her mind. He looked at her expectantly as if giving her the permission she needed to speak.

"I know you're not happy with me as a partner."

"Let me stop you there," Jens said, putting a hand up between them. "It's not you. I'd have an issue with having any partner." His eyes went back to the screen to continue reading the file on the Halo. "Go on," Jens insisted.

"Right," she said, rethinking her approach. "Well, I know you're not happy with a partner, but I wanted you to know that I've admired your work for some time now, and I'm very excited to have the opportunity to work with you," she said, the words spilling out of her. Jens stopped reading and looked at her, unable to hide his surprise. This was not what he had imagined her saying.

"Even up in Tkaronto, people know who you are," she added, getting her points in now while she had his attention. "That said, I'm good at my job, and I can help you if you give me a chance."

Jens wasn't used to dealing with people's emotions. Most of his interactions were either with criminals he didn't give a shit about or brief. Electing to establish a comfortable formality with the people he worked with, he wasn't sure what this was, and he wasn't sure he liked it.

He stared at her for a long moment, trying to decide how to approach it.

The reality is I don't care about you being good or bad at her job. You're a member of the GIB. If you weren't good, they wouldn't have hired you. So that's irrelevant to me. It's also irrelevant that you feel the need to tell me to give you a chance. If you are, in fact, any good, then it wouldn't matter what I think about you.

At least that's what he would have said had he not come to the realization that he didn't care to have that particular conversation with her.

"What do you think about the fire?" he said instead, changing the talk to work and not personal. However, he noticed a release in her body; clearly, she was relieved by the outcome despite Jens not fully being aware of what that meant to her.

As far as he was concerned, he was still stuck with a partner, which he hated, and he was forced into having a weird conversation that had nothing to do with the case, which he hated. He hoped this wouldn't become a regular occurrence. At least now, she was focused on the case file and no longer worried about getting his approval.

"Well, according to this, there were seven bodies inside the building, six of which were known Scorpions, and one is still waiting to be identified, likely by the time we arrive." She looked pleased with herself, although Jens wasn't exactly sure why. All she had done was sum up what was already known. *Is this what a partner was good for? Why would anyone want one, then?*

"Well, thank you for that insight, agent," he said. Going back to reading the file, he saw her face dripping with disappointment.

"What do you think?" she said, with more aggression than he would have suspected.

He had read over the file and given it some thought, but he didn't have all the information in front of him.

"I hate making assumptions without all the information," he said, turning back and reading quietly.

"Well, give it a shot," she said. "Clearly, my insights weren't up to snuff."

She looked at him expectantly. He'd angered her. It was common enough when people were around him. He could handle groups, but one-on-one he was like a cheap wine, better kept in the cold away from everyone.

"Right, well," he said, thinking for a moment—"seven people in the fire, six Scorpions, and one unknown assailant, as you said," he added, turning away.

"That's exactly what I said." She was looking at him confusedly. "So . . . what else do you have?" she asked, leaning back and crossing her arms. She'd obviously not be satisfied with his attempt to moderate the situation.

"Well, like I said, not enough information, but based on the current facts, I'd say . . ." He stopped for a moment, trying to think, wanting to make his wording as precise as possible. "Six Scorpions, no other known cartel, means it wasn't likely a gang-on-gang crime. There are no signs of any weapons or drugs in the building, which leaves me to believe it wasn't a weapons or drug deal gone wrong." He was in a steady rhythm now, with his mind firing through miniature bits of information, slashing away things it deemed irrelevant.

"As you said, we're still waiting on the body to be identified, but if there are no drugs or weapons, that leaves us with a final conclusion that the seven people at the party were in some way connected to the Scorpions through credits." He heard a sharp inhalation, but before she could speak, he barrelled on, not wanting to stop.

"They weren't tied up, and by all accounts appeared to be there of their own free will, so we can count out kidnapping." This appeared to answer her thought, her mouth shutting, as she listened to him speak.

"However, a possible gunshot wound to the head suggests that whoever they were, they'd done something wrong. My best guess as the person was alone, thus implying that what they were doing was in some way a secret, history would suggest credit laundering." He finished, finally looking at Agent Hantsport, who appeared to be processing his information.

"However, this leaves us with two questions that need to be answered: Who killed the cartel? And why? My best guess would be to examine the ownership of the warehouse. They clearly knew it would be empty, but how? It would suggest some link between the two parties." He stopped for a moment, thinking.

"That all?" Ali said, looking up at him.

"Well . . . personally I find this case offers more questions than answers at this point, but like I said, we don't have enough information." He concluded his thought and went back to reading the file on the Halo in front of him. He could sense Ali beside him staring, the moment lasting a little too long for him as he began to feel uncomfortable. Eventually she spoke.

"That makes sense."

It was his turn to stare. *Of course, it made sense.*

The two of them rode in silence, which was perfectly okay with Jens. But despite feeling a sense of confidence in his initial assessment and wanting desperately to agree with his partner that everything did in fact make sense, he couldn't shake the feeling that none of it did. *Maybe I've just been away for too long.*

The ECar pulled up to the ashes of an old warehouse, its solid steel skeleton somehow managing to remain erect despite its smouldering joints. Jens and Ali stepped out of the car, greeted by five uninterested Pittsburgh police constables standing around having finished taping off the area in yellow do-not-enter tape. Jens still found it shocking that in three hundred years, the best thing they'd found to hold people back was physical tape.

The tape was wrapped around the steel pipes framing the sidewalk, blocking access to the main building and its crime scene. Inside, an IT spec analyst, someone tall, features hidden by the white bio-suit, was still working away on-site. To Jens luck, the person appeared to be finishing up, now turning to lift the yellow tape and meet them on the other side.

With the touch of a button, the facemask of the helm rolled back, revealing IT Specialist Dr. Jamie Nazari. Her face glistened from the combination of the suit and heat from the recently burning building as she greeted them both with a smile.

"Jens," she said, putting him on the receiving end of yet another uncomfortable hug.

Jamie was a few hundred days older than him, Jens had known her since his days in the Pittsburgh Police Department. She released him and gave him a playful tap on the belly.

"Two hundred days will do that to you, I guess," she added with an affectionate smile.

He knew he had gained a little weight, but this was starting to be a little ridiculous.

"Good to see you, Jamie," Jens said. It seemed the appropriate response to her larger show of affection. She looked at him expectantly, her eyes glancing over at Ali.

"Who's your friend?" she said, giving Jens an annoyed look.

"I'm agent Ali Hantsport," Ali said, holding out her hand. "His new partner."

This last bit got an eye raise from Dr. Nazari.

"Partner, eh? What did you deserve to get that punishment?" She laughed at her own joke as she reached for Ali's hand and said, "Dr. Jamie Nazari, pleasure to meet you."

They shook hands, holding on a little longer than Jens would have found comfortable, but then again, that was a severely low bar.

Clearing his throat, he broke the moment between the two women, causing Dr. Nazari to blush.

"Right, what do we have?" Ali said, forcing herself to take a professional step back and looking around the area.

"You're kidding, right?" Jens said, looking at her. He waited for a moment, but he was greeted with a confused expression on Ali's face.

"What?" she finally said, crossing her arms.

"We've just read the file, and we talked about it in the car . . . I would say it's fairly clear what we have here," he said, moving away from her.

"I know, but I thought it would be helpful to get it from Jamie's . . . Dr. Nazari's perspective," she said, giving Dr. Nazari a warm smile.

"Right, then, what's your perspective?" he said, putting her on the spot.

"Right, well, it was a fire killing seven people . . ."

"Have you identified the seventh body?" Jens asked, jumping in, deciding quickly he didn't need another person to tell him more nonessential information.

"Right, yes, the seventh body was a . . ." She pulled out her Zen watch, a Halo screen appearing in front of her. She scrolled through a couple of pages before landing on an image of a middle-aged man in a suit, with short brown hair and an ugly little mustache. "Nigel Eriksen, forty-six, worked for the Global Lottery. Wife and two . . ." Jens had heard enough; it was rarely important about family history. He found typically that would be a catalyst for why people did the things they did. He was less interested in why, and just interested in catching everyone involved. He turned and walked away, leaving the two women looking confused.

"Don't you want to know about the victim?" said Ali, her arm reaching out to stop him but thinking better of it.

"I'll leave that in your very capable hands," he said, giving her a smile and turning away. "Have you analysed the crime scene?" he asked, not looking back at Dr. Nazari.

"Yes, just before you arrived," she said, apparently scrolling through her Halo, finding a file. "Data is being sent to your Zen watch."

He felt a light tingle on his wrist, indicating the file had arrived.

"Thank you," he said politely and walked away.

"Is he always such a dick?" Ali said when she thought he was out of earshot. He was unfazed by the comment; he'd been called much worse.

"Yes," Dr. Nazari replied. "But you get used to it," she said with a smile in her voice.

"What if I don't want to get used to it?" Ali said, turning back to watch Jens maneuver through the wreckage.

"Then I'd say get out while you can. But you should know that while he's definitely hard to work with, there really is no one better."

Jens could almost feel the eyes of the two women watching him as he examined the area, quickly turning away when he glanced back in their direction, sharing a snicker between the pair.

Jens went back to examining the site. He could never understand the sensitive nature of most people; it seemed tiresome, and a waste of time.

He was aware of how smart Dr. Nazari was, but that was why she wrote reports, so she could share them. He didn't need to talk with her about it.

It had been some time since Jens had been with someone. His last relationship, with a young PPD constable, ended in a yelling match, and a transfer to a new city. Since then, he decided he would no longer try for relationships.

It was always more of an informal practice for him, anyway, as many people in his position had tried to have relationships in the past, and they never seemed to survive the long hours. *Why would I put himself through all that again?*

Instead, Jens found other, less socially acceptable ways of stimulating his mind and his body.

He looked around the ruins and pulled up Dr. Nazari's file on the fire. It was detailed and precise; he admired that about her.

Scrolling through, he paused on the probable cause of death. The bodies showed signs of suffocation presumably from the smoke inhalation and loss of oxygen, but they all seemed to have expired within a ten-meter radius of one another.

Looking around, he found the described area, and he was perplexed to see that they all died in the center of the warehouse.

He was still processing it all when Ali approached from behind, startling him and bringing him back from his thoughts.

"Strange," she said, taking in the charred building around her.

"Why's that?" Jens said, dropping his wrist, the data files vanishing as he did. He looked up, unable to hide his annoyance at being interrupted, but was also interested in her thoughts, because he also found it strange.

Ali must have felt on the spot, as Jens watched her brows tighten up on her forehead.

"Well," she said, taking a dramatic walk around, carefully stepping around various debris. Jens' stare must have rattled her slightly, because she seemed to lose all train of thought, which became obvious as she spoke. "It seems strange to me, is all."

Jens shook his head and turned away.

"They're all trapped in the middle of the room. Why?" she said quickly.

Jens turned to face her, giving a slight nod as if to say, "Go on."

"It's just if I was in a burning building, I think I would make my way toward an exit, not huddle in the middle of the room. They all appeared to have died from the smoke, but even if the smoke was thick, they would have likely seen it first and tried to run, but they didn't," she said, and he smiled at her.

"Not bad, agent," he said ,walking around. "You're finally asking yourself some good questions." Ali smiled, her newfound courage giving her permission to press on.

"My guess is this is a murder."

Jens stopped for a moment. He simply stared off into the decrepit space, finally looking toward her.

"Why?" he said suspiciously. Ali assumed the fact he was neither mocking her nor giving an outright denial meant she was on the right track.

"Because it's the logical conclusion. If you have seven bodies in a warehouse with no explanation as to why, you should rightfully assume foul play, no?" She shrugged. *This is the most natural course of action. Isn't it?*

"What is it, 'oh great wise one'?" Ali added sarcastically.

Jens had been looking around the warehouse.

"Nothing, I agree. I'll have Dr. Nazari do a full tox run on the bodies and see what she comes up with," he said, reaching for his Zen watch but was stopped by Ali.

"No need," she said, putting her hand out and blocking his Halo. "While you were busy doing your little lonely walk-around, Dr. Nazari and I were discussing the layout of the building. She assumed the same thing as me, so we set up a toxicology report, and we should have it in the next couple of hours."

She seemed surprised by Jens' anger.

"Why wouldn't you tell me this?" he said, looking at her.

"Because I wanted to see the look on your face when I told you. You see, sometimes it pays to have a conversation with people, Jens." She turned and walked away.

"Agent Jennings," he said, trying to regain what little control he could muster.

"You got it, boss," she said, giving him a cool smile as she walked across the ash-laden remains of the building toward the road.

Jens wasn't used to people undermining him; then again, he wasn't really used to working with anyone. The conversation had filled him with a mix of emotions, and he didn't like them. He lagged behind Ali, making his way toward the road. A scattering of people had congregated around where the PPD had set up its tape.

Jens didn't want to deal with any questions, so he slid off to the side, leaving Ali to deal with the gabs.

By the time Ali realized Jens had sneaked off in another direction, it was too late. She was bombarded with questions from the media. She turned, waving to Jens to come over, receiving instead a cool smile as he sat down on a small bench off to the side of the old warehouse.

Jens almost felt guilty, but he also thought she would be fine, and he needed a quiet place to think, not the media yelling at him for answers.

He pulled up the Halo from his Zen watch and started to read. He'd got halfway through the report sent over by Dr. Nazari when a thin woman took a seat beside him. She had dark skin, and her eyes were a deep-brown. Her jet-black hair was short and spiky. Jens put her somewhere in later end of her first ten thousand days.

He closed the Halo as she sat beside him. For a moment she didn't say anything, just sat there looking forward as if he weren't even there. But as Jens was about to leave . . .

"What happened here?" she asked, turning to face him. Jens didn't say anything. He wasn't in the habit of talking with colleagues, so he wasn't about to talk with a stranger. She grabbed his arm as he stood to leave.

"This have anything to do with Mayor Stone?" she asked, now standing up beside him.

"You're a gab?" Jens asked and when the woman looked confused he added, "a reporter?" She didn't respond to him, giving him everything he needed to know. "Well, then, as my partner over there is likely explaining to all your colleagues, I suggest reaching out to the GIB information bureau if you want answers."

He started to walk away, but her hand stayed on his wrist. It was soft, not forceful, and suddenly he wasn't entirely sure of her motive.

"I'm aware of the Harold Act," she said softly.

"Then you would be aware getting any information from me isn't going to happen," Jens added sharply.

"I'm not here to spread my opinions. I'm here about the truth."

"Aren't we all," Jens said, looking around to see if anyone was watching him. "I know what your kind wants, but what I want is to never have another Jeffery Flinn on our hands."

"You think I'm here to spread false information to the public under the misguided presumption of 'free press'?" she said hotly.

"Honestly, I don't know what the hell you want," Jens said, getting to his feet.

"The truth," she said slowly. "I want you to have the truth."

Jens began to shift uncomfortably in his shoes. He knew he should be walking away, cutting ties with whatever this was, but something about the way she was gripping his wrist and looking at him gave him pause.

"You know I can't tell you anything," Jens said a little more softly.

"I know," she said, meeting his eyes.

"Then why come and try and talk to me" he said, realizing he was now talking with a reporter, an act that could get him fired. "I have to go," he said as he pulled his arm away and started to walk.

"Please, I'm not looking for much and certainly not for an article, but I need to know. Is Mayor Stone involved." *Mayor Stone again? Why would she think that Mayor Stone would be involved?*

"What would the mayor of Pittsburgh have to do with what's going on here?" Jens asked her. "What do you know?"

"You mean what would a millionaire philanthropist, who's up for reelection in a city that reveres him, be doing in a place like this?" she said, standing up to meet his gaze.

I mean why in the world would he have anything to do with the warehouse murder of six Scorpions and one mystery man?

"I can't speak with you!" *My first day back, and I'm already breaking rules.*

"Look at who owns the building," she called after him. "He's not everything he seems to be." Her voice trailed off as Jens walked toward Ali, who'd already started making her way toward him.

"Thanks for that," she said, pulling up her Zen watch to read a message. "Goddamn gabs, they're all vultures. You'd think by now they would just give up."

"They'll give up when agents stop giving them information," Jens said nonchalantly.

"Stupid bloody loophole—all it does is prey on agents so they can make a quick buck selling it as a 'quote' for the next cycle." Ali's words came out hot.

Jens wasn't surprised by her sentiment; it was shared by most agents. Jens, on the other hand, had never cared. He just simply refused to talk. *At least I always used to.*

"Who was that?" Ali said, looking over and noticing the young woman walking away from the bench.

"I'm not sure," Jens said, still playing the meeting over in his mind, unable to shake the feeling she seemed scared. *If she is, by who or what? The mayor?*

"Any updates?" he said, looking at Ali and trying to deflect the conversation. She'd been reading a message and was giggling, not something Jens was used to seeing when reading a data entry.

"What's so funny?" Jens asked, looking at Ali, who stopped laughing abruptly and was trying to suppress a smile. Whatever it was, she clearly didn't want to tell Jens about it.

"Just a personal message from Dr. Nazari," she said, swiping the message aside, showing another data entry.

"Personal messages should be read on personal time," he said in a dull tone. Ali started to smile, thinking he was joking, but quickly realized he wasn't.

"Right, yes, we have the tox report coming in soon and the information on Nigel Eriksen, the seventh body found. It appears he works for the Global Lottery Foundation . . . accounts department." A smile on her face indicated they were clearly on the same page.

"Looks like we should pay the GLF a visit," Jens said, processing an ECar request through his Zen watch.

"Looks like your credit-laundering theory might be correct," she said, opening the side door of the car.

"We'll see," Jens said dispassionately.

"Are you always this optimistic?" she said, sliding into the back of the ECar.

"Yes," he said she sat down beside her. She looked at him awkwardly. "That was a joke," he said, pulling up a file on his Zen watch.

"Is that what that was?" she said, smiling.

5

They pulled up to the front entrance of the Global Lottery Foundation headquarters. It was the largest and most ornate building in the Western Gale, taking up an entire city block, and was just over two hundred stories tall at its highest peak. It was a marvellous display of spiralling towers linked together by a spiderweb of connective walkways. The entire structure seemed to act as a beacon of power nestled in the heart of Pittsburgh.

Unlike generic lotteries, no one had to buy a ticket, and everyone in the world was entered to win. Each day ten thousand winners were named, each receiving roughly 1.5 million credits.

The GLF affected millions of lives every year, and with estimates of fifty trillion of alleged assets, it was easy to see where someone such as Nigel Eriksen might find some potential extracurricular opportunities.

Jens and Ali stepped into the entranceway of the tower, which was bigger than most tenant houses up in Zone sixty-five. The colossal and bright open space was punctuated by a particularly ingenious mirror display dangling from the center of the ceiling. The effect gave the illusion of sunlight showering in from the ceiling, filling the space with a warm glow.

Thousands of people were walking around, busying themselves throughout the building. Jens had found himself in there only once, and unfortunately it was not because he won the lottery.

"You okay, boss?" Ali asked.

"Fine, I just haven't been in here in a while," Jens said a moment later.

"You won the lottery?" Ali asked, trying to mask her excitement.

"No, far from it," Jens said as he let out an awkward laugh.

"What was it?" Ali asked, looking at him expectantly.

It had been a long time since this particular case had burrowed itself back into Jens' mind, but now that it had, he remembered just how frustrating the whole ordeal had been.

"It was one of my first cases at the GIB. I was young, maybe a little less than twenty-one thousand days. There was some suspicion around the disappearance of a lottery winner. I was convinced it had been the parents behind it."

The memories began to flood Jens' mind along with all the oddities from the case; something had always bothered him about it.

"But it wasn't?"

"No. They'd apparently been away on a trip with no idea their son had been missing until they got home."

"Could they have been lying?"

"Maybe. But when he was finally presumed deceased, I saw them at the boy's funeral, I have to admit they played the parts of grieving parents fairly well."

"So, what happened?"

"Nothing, the case went cold. I was told to drop the investigation."

"That's such horseshit. Given what we have access to these days, no investigation should ever be unsolved." The bitterness in Ali's voice matched that of Jens' own feelings.

"Easy to forget that as we get better at solving cases, people get better at covering their tracks," Jens said, wishing he could rid his mind of the awful memory. "It seems they sent us a child greeter," Jens said, gesturing to the fresh-faced intern somewhere in the twenty-two thousand's, approaching them from the elevators. Jens guess was confirmed when he felt a buzz on his wrist as the young man's credentials appeared on his Zen watch.

"A little hypocritical, don't you think? Didn't you just say you were in your twenty-ones on your first cases with the GIB?" Ali asked.

"Yeah, but I thought we've established that I'm a little odd?" Jens said, garnering a laugh from his partner. "I assume kids these days would be traveling, not trying to put in their fifteen thousand days."

"Only fourteen thousand six hundred days," Ali said, receiving an annoyed look from Jens. "What?"

"I rounded up," Jens said.

"Right, well, I wouldn't feel too sorry for them. Unlike the GIB, most of these people are working twenty-five hours a week. I'd hardly say they're being challenged." Ali laughed.

"Agents!" said the young man wearing blue dress pants and white button down dress shirt as he approached he stuck out a hand for them to shake. Jens ignored it, instead looking around the building.

"Agent Hantsport, GIB," Ali said, taking his hand.

"Charlie," he said, giving them a big smile. *This is a waste of time, he knows who we are, he came out to meet us, for Christ sakes.*

"It's an amazing building, isn't it?" he said, taking in a deep breath before looking at Jens, who was still scanning the room.

"Sure," Jens said curtly.

"You know interesting fact," Charlie began to say.

"Nigel Eriksen, he worked for the GLF as an accountant," Jens said, watching the obvious look of disappointment on Charlie's face for not being able to share his knowledge about the building. "We'd like to see his office," Jens said, watching the disappointment turn to nervousness as Charlie's left eye began to twitch.

"Please," Ali said quickly, giving him a warm smile.

"Right, well, actually . . . yes, I can . . . follow me, please," he said, turning to walk back toward the elevators.

"What? Do you just enjoy making people feel uncomfortable?" Ali whispered as she followed Charlie. Jens found it amusing, especially when he caught Charlie wiping a sweaty palm down his pant leg.

"Yes," Jens said simply as Ali stifled another laugh.

6

"The elevator is state of the art. It's the latest in high-speed, zero-gravity vacuums," Charlie said, the twitch still quivering away in his eye.

Looking through the four glass walls surrounding him, Jens couldn't tell what the big deal was; they appeared to be travelling at a normal speed.

"We're moving a little bit faster than a bullet," Charlie added nervously.

Jens was impressed by the information, giving a slight bob of the head, which Charlie seemed to take as an acknowledgment that he should continue.

"The effect when you first get in can make your stomach queasy, but they are certainly efficient," he added quickly, just as the elevator made it one hundred and sixty-seven floors up in no time at all.

Stepping out from the elevator, Jens couldn't help but notice the entire floor was littered with hundreds, maybe thousands, of data screens. *This must be where the credits handlers work.*

"The lottery predates the Great Mitigation, which has allowed us a certain level of . . ."

"The Great Mitigation?" Ali asked, giving Jens a sly wink when he turned to give her an incredulous look. Ali tried to suppress a smile when she saw Charlie become visibly flustered. Jens shook his head at her as he realized she must be playing a little game with their new friend. Charlie, like a good schoolboy, began laying out what Jens hoped would be the condensed version.

"Well, the Great Mitigation refers to the people who the world powers gathered to create the Big Five. Supercontinents, that were formed to protect themselves after the devastating impact of World War Three and the Silent Death, which decimated sixty-two percent of the global population," Charlie began saying. Jens wanted to jump in with alternative figures, as the topic was widely debated, but decided it wasn't worth the effort.

"The world followed the lead of the then-European Nation who had banded together to combine resources to protect one another and form The Central Stone." Charlie gestured to a blue flag with a circle surrounding a ten-pointed gold star. It hung on the wall next to four others.

"From there we formed The Southern Moon." Charlie gestured to the green flag with a silver crescent moon with a diamond between its tips. Then his arm moved across to a red flag with three three-pointed green stars at its center. "The Eastern Star, The Northern Sun," he said, pointing at a black flag with a red dot at its center. "Lastly our own Western Gale," he said as his hand rested on the yellow flag with a purple soy flower in its center.

"Where is Nigel Eriksen's office?" Jens asked, as he was beginning to grow weary of the history lesson.

"Just down this way," Charlie said a little more confidently now that it seemed he was giving more of a tour than he was breaking the rules.

"And you run all the currency transfers for each of the Big Five through this floor?" Ali asked, appearing to still be enjoying the brief history listen.

Charlie smiled at that.

"This is Nigel's office here." Charlie said directing them into a small relatively bland looking square office, before continuing on with history lesson. "What a great question. Most people assume we handle currencies from all the Big Five, but like everyone else, we heap our holdings in Central Stone and dispense the winnings in the currency of the individual," Charlie added, seemingly happy to share his knowledge of the building with someone. "Obviously this is just one of many floors that handle currency conversions. However, this is the floor that approves the final expected payouts."

Jens' ears perked up at the last bit, noting it for later. Charlie must have sensed he'd said more than he should have because he suddenly stopped talking.

"Fascinating," Ali piped in, "and you say the lottery is older than the Big Five?"

Charlie nodded and had started talking again when Jens noticed the name tag on the door just up ahead of them and jumped in.

"What did Nigel do, exactly?" Ali asked Charlie, who pulled up a file on his Zen watch. *Another pointless question, it was all in the file.*

Jens, taking the time to look around the room beginning to wonder if Agent Hantsport even read the files.

"He was . . . ," Charlie started to say, before Jens cut him off.

"Financial auditor for the GLF. His job was to check over the details to make sure the credits were sent to the right people," Jens said, not looking up from around the desk.

He noticed nothing special, just a family picture of them on a vacation, someone Jens supposed was a friend, their arms wrapped around each other as they looked into the camera after what appeared to be a difficult hike. Nothing that screamed, "I launder credits for the cartel."

"What he said," Charlie said, looking at Ali.

"Right, well, we're going to need access to what Mr. Eriksen was . .

"

"Mrs. Choi," Charlie said, his face going a pale white as an angry-looking Mrs. Choi entered the office. She was in her middle days with light-brown skin, and although she seemed younger than Jens, he would have suspected her commanding presence was certainly felt in the room.

"What exactly are you doing in here?" Mrs. Choi shouted.

"We're with the GIB . . . ," Ali started to say.

"And you!" Mrs. Choi said, pointing at Charlie. "You can't just bring anyone in here without permission. It is against protocol."

"I'm sorry . . . ," he started to say, but she pointed to the door, sending Charlie on his way. Jens almost felt bad knowing he likely cost the kid his job. But he should know protocol; he could consider it instead a free lesson. He was young and would bounce back.

"I'm sorry, but who are you?" Jens asked quickly.

"Angela Choi, head of Global Lottery West," she said sternly before eyeing the two agents up. "As for you two, I understand you're with the GIB, but that gives you no right to come into this building without proper permission. Now I suggest you get the hell out of here before I send your details to your commander."

Jens looked around the room one last time and wordlessly exited, with Ali close behind him.

As they walked back to the elevators, the doors sensed their arrival. They stepped in, and the automated system assured their smooth transition to the main entrance and out of the building.

They had remained silent since they'd left Nigel's office. But that didn't stop Jens from feeling the wrathful eyes of Ali on his back the entire way. Now finally, they were alone on the street as an ECar turned the corner heading their way.

"You knew that would happen?" Ali said, looking at him with a sliver of hope that her assumptions were wrong.

"Yes," Jens said, not giving her the response she appeared to crave. The car stopped short of where he was standing.

"Then why did you do it?" she said, trying hard not to yell.

"Because they would have had time to go through his office before us, and what good would that do us," he said bluntly without a hint of remorse in his voice.

"But how did you know he would let us in?" she said curiously.

"I didn't, we were lucky." He shrugged. "Sometimes people get lucky," he said, opening the door to the car, but Ali put out a hand to stop it. Jens let out a sigh. "His ID badge said he'd started only a couple of months ago. I hedged my bets that he wasn't up to date on GIB protocols."

"But that kid? Likely lost his job because of us," she said, removing her palm from the door.

"Or did we just teach him a valuable lesson in learning protocol? It depends on how you want to look at it," Jens interjected, and despite her anger, Ali smiled.

"You really are a prick, aren't you," she said as her hand returned to the door, stopping it from closing. "What's the plan?" she asked, Jens looking at her, forgetting that no one could read his mind.

"Well, I'll put in the request for the GLF, and we will likely have access by tomorrow morning," he said, trying to shut the door.

"What can I do?" Ali asked.

Jens suddenly remembered the conversation with the woman at the scene of the fire. He knew he should let it go, but he couldn't shake the feeling something was off.

"Find out who owns that burned-down warehouse," he said.

"Why?" she answered, looking at him curiously.

"I'm interested in it—that's why."

He made his way to shut the door, thinking the conversation was over, but Ali grabbed the top of the door again and stared him down.

"What?" he asked, giving her an exhausted look.

"Eriksen's office, what did you see?" she asked.

Jens, remaining silent, looked back at her.

"Come on, why waste your time on a stunt like that if you didn't think it was worth it." She was hunched over, her arm pinned to the door. Jens knew there was no use trying to avoid it.

"Everything," he said thoughtfully.

"Really? Because I saw nothing," she said, releasing the door.

"Exactly."

7

Jens walked in his front door. The search request for Nigel Eriksen's office arrived during the ride back to his apartment, which meant he'd have the evening to relax and get some sleep.

His Zen watch, sensing his return, adjusted the room to his preferred settings. He looked around the space, noting that the past two hundred days had been a lazy version of himself, and he wasn't prepared to go back to that now.

A hired cleaning service would be faster, but this was one mess he had to clean up himself. He hated the person he'd become during his suspension and was so thankful to be back on the job—even if it came with a partner. Ignoring the pang in his stomach, he told himself he needed to tackle this project before he could eat.

One hour into the clean, he had tackled most of the main living space, but was in no mood to start cooking. Pulling up a Halo screen from the kitchen island, Jens began scrolling through various menus before deciding on Jing's Southern Chicken. But giving himself a once-over, he opted to go for the side salad with the chicken. *Progress has to start somewhere.*

After placing the order, he entered the bedroom. He had purposely saved it till the end for fear that if he started there, he would have fallen asleep. Reprogramming the lights to full, he stared open-mouthed at the space. *It's even worse in the light.*

He started with the obvious pile of dirty underwear, which he picked off the floor. Noticing a pair of jeans crinkled up within the pile, he had a difficult time imagining the last time he had worn jeans. At the moment, he was contemplating simply throwing them all away and getting new clothes, a fresh start. He didn't have that many clothes to begin with. *Waste not, want not.*

He'd tossed the underwear in the laundry bin and was about to do the same with the jeans when he felt something in the pocket. Digging around the inside of the pocket, he found a familiar object—no, two. Jens pulled out the two tiny glass vials, each filled with a deep-purple sand. *Enzo.*

The vials rolled around in his palm, their glass surfaces clicking together, toying with him. He watched, mesmerized by the display, as the purple sand fell from one side to the other. *Hello, friend. All I need to do is break a vial and breathe.*

The vapour released was a neurotoxin that temporarily manipulated select neuropathways, resulting in a rush of endorphins unlike anything a human could experience on their own.

It had been Jens' habitual pastime since being released from the agency. *These can't be here, not anymore.*

The night before had been the last night, because the consequence of getting caught using it as a GIB agent would mean immediate expulsion. *But how good would it feel now! No!*

He'd get rid of them when he had the chance. He pulled out an old mint tin from the drawer of the bedside table that his grandfather had given to him before he died and placed the two vials inside. The tin wasn't important per se, but it was one of the only things he felt resembled an heirloom in his life. He placed the tin back in the table drawer. *Out of sight, out of mind.*

He picked up the jeans and the other clothes from the floor and tossed them in his laundry cycle just as a message appeared on his

Zen watch. "Your delivery has arrived."

The timing couldn't have been better, as Jens tucked in the final corner of his bedsheet. Heading back to the living room, he opened the delivery drawer and found the meal waiting for him inside.

The food was still hot, and a thick cloud of steam rose as he unwrapped the bio plastic lid.

As if the restaurant could sense he'd just sat down to eat, a message appeared on the Halo. "Are you happy with your delivery? Please rate service here." Jens clicked the Halo, giving them five stars.

"Play the news," Jens said as he leaned forward to take a large bite from his chicken. The spices caused his lips to tingle almost immediately. He chased the bite with a few bites of salad, which he found oddly satisfying.

"The bodies of seven people have been found in a warehouse fire in Zone Thirty-Six near River Bend. PPD was on-site, though the investigation is being headed up by the GIB. No word as to who the people in the fire might be or why they were there."

At least no one seems to be talking yet.

"We had two winners of the lottery today in the Pittsburgh area, bringing the grand total to ten this month. Will you be next? What would you do with one point five million credits? This reporter would likely visit the jungle cruise on Mars, something with a little fresh air and some sun. What about you?"

"I'd probably try to solve this murder," Jens said, his mouth full of chicken.

"I'm sorry, but your request could not be submitted to the station for review," said a gentle voice from the radio.

"Good," Jens said as he swallowed the last bit of chicken.

"Are you tired of being alone . . . ," the radio began saying.

"Switch the music, now!" Jens said before the ad could finish, "and no more ads!"

"Your request for 'no ads' has been denied unless you wish to pay for a premium account. Would you like . . ."

"No. Stupid bloody machine."

Jens leaned back in the couch as low, thrumming music played in the background. He began going over the events of the day and his thoughts on Agent Hantsport. He wasn't used to working with a partner, but he had to admit she had surprised him at times. It wasn't often, but it was clear she paid good attention to detail, even if she did talk a little too much. *Maybe she wouldn't be such a pain in the ass?*

Then his mind flashed back to the mysterious woman. He'd got Ali to investigate the building's ownership. It wasn't an odd angle to take, and Jens had even thought about it himself. But the fact that this stranger was interested in it caught him by surprise. *She must have more information on the fire than she's letting on. Why didn't I get a name?*

Not that it would matter—if she were smart, it would be a fake. It had been a huge risk coming to Jens like that. As an agent for the GIB, he would have been well within his right to tag her right there and take her in. *But I didn't, why?*

Replaying the conversation in his head, there was just . . . something about the way she asked him. It wasn't forceful; some might even say it was sad. *Had she even said she was a journalist?*

Jens had been the one to bring it up. She just didn't deny it, adding to the increasingly more bizarre encounter.

Jens put a note in his data log, reminding himself to look into this mysterious woman when he had a free moment. But for now, he was more than a little tired, as he moved toward his room, took off his clothes, and tossed them in the home cleaner, which was currently working on overdrive with his recent cleaning. By morning, he hoped everything would be done and pressed for him, though he'd never tried it with so many clothes at once. *For all I know, this will break it.*

Ignoring that thought, he climbed in bed as his Zen watch adjusted his room to sleep mode; the blinds dropped down, drowning the lights from outside the window and dampening the outside sounds. It wasn't long before Jens was out cold.

. . .

He felt as if he'd just lain down when the blinds lifted; the light began to shine through the windows. His Zen watch cueing the room to wake him up, he was thankful the radio hadn't been programmed back into the routine. He hadn't slept that well in months.

Hopping out of bed, he made his way to the bathroom. Turning on the shower, he was proud of the almost-generous flow coming from the shower head, courtesy of the cleaning from the night before. The steam was billowing out from the shower as he stepped inside. Warm water caressed his face, helping to wash the sleep away.

By the time he stepped out of the shower and dried off, he had a message waiting for him on his Zen watch from Agent Hantsport, details on the warehouse, no doubt. He was impressed she was up and already sending him files. *Another tick.*

He scanned the files quickly, not seeing anything out of the ordinary. *Most importantly, there is no link to Mayor Stone.*

Probably for the best—not likely to get a lot of enthusiasm if the first thing he did was link everyone's favourite mayor to an alleged murder and some sort of potential drug-trafficking scandal.

He signed off, sending a reply request for Ali to meet him at 9 a.m. in the bullpen. Looking for a quick bite to eat, he realized he didn't have much in the way of food. He grabbed a questionably ripe banana and made another note on his data list. *Go shopping on your way home.*

It was 8:45 a.m. when Jens entered the GIB headquarters, surprised at how quickly the ICER had been that morning. Despite the best updated tech in the world, it still managed a delay occasionally, often fanning the debate of technology versus human error. Jens leaned toward the human side. *To err is human.*

"Bullpen is bustling this morning," Ali said, sneaking up on Jens, causing him to flinch. She handed him an extra coffee, which he took gratefully.

"Bullpen's always busy, Agent Hantsport," he said, taking a sip, happy to discover it wasn't the usual coffee made in-house. "Thanks for this."

"I only mean it's a little different here than back up in Tkaronto," she said, taking a sip of her own coffee.

"Well, I'm not sure how days are structured up your way, but with most shops in the city on split times and open only five or six hours a day? It basically means every agent has to work some overtime," Jens said as he approached their desk. He took off his blue blazer and hung it on the back of his chair.

"Same up north, but I guess it's true. More people mean more crimes. Are you in the city, Agent Jennings?" she asked, taking the seat across from him.

"Why?" Jens said warily.

"Figured if we are going to be partners, we should get to know each other," she added with a shrug.

"Yes," Jens said after a moment, "unlike some of these new fools coming up through the ranks, who think they can start a family with no more than eight thousand days on them and still be good agents."

"You don't think you can do both?" Ali asked, and to Jens' surprise, she seemed to be asking honestly. That gave Jens a good laugh.

"No."

"Well, I think it's great people are starting families so young. Not everyone needs to give their commitment as early as you," she said, waving away Jens' laugh. "Not when you can break up your commitment, a few years here and there. Not like you, straight through, I bet," she said, musing. "How many days you have left? Five, six thousand? I bet you're one of those renegades who would rather get shot on the job than forced into senior subsidies," Ali said, laughing at her own joke.

Jens didn't say anything. Ali was talking about society's contributions, in which everyone who wanted to collect youth and senior subsidies had to put in a minimum of ten thousand nine hundred and fifty days of work contributing to society.

She was also spot-on with her assessment. Jens dreaded taking the senior subsidies. He had hated youth subsidies when he took those. Getting credits without doing anything felt useless to Jens. He understood why it worked, but he wasn't sure it worked for him.

"I'm sorry," she said, stumbling, "I didn't mean to offend you or anything. It's just you're older and . . . I mean you're not old," she said, correcting herself, seeing Jens' brows jump up. "It's just young people know how to do things differently, and your way isn't wrong. . . it's . . . I'm sorry," she said, finally shutting her mouth and finding interest in whatever was on her Halo.

"That was fun," Jens said, trying his best to sound sarcastic. "We should do it again soon." He smiled at the look of shock on his partner's face. Frantically typing on her Halo, she looked up at him, all embarrassment seemingly forgotten.

"Did you get my message?" she asked, her voice suddenly breathless, as if she'd been running. Jens looked at his Zen watch, which had a new message flashing on its face.

"You've hardly given me time to miss it," he said jokingly.

"Sorry," she added excitedly "It's just I was going over the files for the building, and something strange came up."

Whatever she found she was obviously bursting to tell him. Jens nodded, letting her know to get on with it.

"Well, I looked at the file, and the building is owned by a group called Titus Manufacturing."

"Right, I read your report," Jens said, sitting down, opting to leave out his criticism that Ali seemed not to like getting to the point.

"Right, I figured you had," she said with a smile, "but I couldn't figure out who owned Titus Manufacturing, so I did a little digging. It turns out Titus Manufacturing is a shell company owned by Temple Corp., which is owned by, and you'll never guess . . ."

Jens got a worried feeling in the pit of his stomach

"Stone Industries," he said glumly, seeming to suck the wind out of Ali's sails.

"Yes! How did you know?" she asked, sounding more than a little confused.

"That's not important," Jens said, dismissing her. She'd obviously put a lot of work into discovering this information, and Jens had ruined it by knowing the punch line.

The woman on the bench was right. Mayor Stone was connected to the murders. Well, at least on paper he was. *Dammit, this would definitely complicate things.*

By the excited look on Ali's face, she clearly hadn't reached the same conclusion. Jens almost felt guilty having to rain on her little parade.

"What's wrong?" Ali asked, taking the empty seat beside Jens' desk. "This is good news—we've tracked down the owners! We're one step closer to finding out what happened there." She gave him a big smile.

Jens suspected this was her first major crime and decided she had every right to be excited, despite the fact it was quickly becoming a higher-profile case. Considering the news runs were already popping up about the deaths, they were officially on the clock to solve it.

Linking the building to Stone Industries was also not something that they could sit on for very long without informing the media about it, which meant figuring out what the connection to the mayor could be before some idiots decided to start to speculate. Essentially this whole thing just became a ticking time bomb, and here was his partner smiling.

"Try not to look so excited," Jens said, tapping the desk in front of him.

"Why not? A link to a running mayor, up for reelection—this could be huge," she said, her youthfulness starting to show. She may be only twenty-nine hundred days younger than Jens, but her time in the agency had been brief, and from what Jens knew about Tkaronto, it was likely a little tamer than here in Pittsburgh. She'd need to keep her head on a swivel if she wanted to keep on the right track, one on which Jens needed to get her back.

"Which means we will be put under a microscope moving forward. Everything we do will be watched and scrutinized. Mayor Stone is the most respected mayor this city has seen in a long time, and everyone, I mean everyone, likes him," Jens said, giving a noticeable glance over toward Captain Rollins' office.

"So, when we go in there and tell her that we need to investigate him, we better be ready to play by a new set of rules, or else you may find this is your first and last in major crimes. And I'll be looking at more than two hundred days out of the office."

Jens saw the smile disappear from Ali's face, with the sudden realization of the gravity of it all.

"I'm not sure what people told you about me and why I was on leave, but I can assure you, if this went south, it would make what I did look like petty crime." Jens was trying to put a little fear into her heart.

She was excited, and if Jens was honest with himself, he was excited, too, but they had to be realistic about the expectation of a conflict like this. It wouldn't be easy on either of them.

"Do I make myself clear?" he finished, secure that the fear of God had been firmly instilled in her.

Ali sat thinking about it rationally, which Jens appreciated, and he was happy to see her come out the other side with her youthful determination relighting the fire in her belly. Jens gave her a knowing nod, and the two of them got up and made their way over to Captain Rollins' office, stopping short before entering.

"Maybe for right now, let me do the talking," Jens said, still seeing the fire.

"Yeah, that's probably best," Ali said, patting him on the back. "Boss," she added before they walked through the door.

8

If he were being honest, Jens wasn't sure exactly what he was going to say to Captain Rollins as they entered her office. He couldn't simply blurt out that there was a connection from the warehouse murders to the mayor—not without some immediate kickback.

He'd had only a few seconds to think about it all, and it didn't help that it was first thing in the morning. When the dust settled, Jens would be hit with the reality that his days just got a whole lot longer.

Captain Rollins was sitting at her desk reading through a Halo data screen.

"Shut the door," she said without looking up at them from her file. Ali closed the door, turning back to the silent room.

"Am I reading this request right?" she said, finally looking up at the two of them, putting her arm out, signalling them to take a seat. *How the hell could she know about this request already?*

Unsure, Jens didn't want to say anything. *Maybe she could be talking about a different request?*

"Ma'am?" he said, taking a seat in one of the steel chairs in front of the desk. They were ergonomic to provide maximum support, but Jens always felt they were made to be purposely uncomfortable, as he wriggled around the chair.

Ali sat in the one beside him. From the shimmy she was doing on the chair, Jens got the sense she was feeling the same way.

"You want to look into Stone Industries?" Captain Rollins said, glancing between the two of them. Jens shot Ali a look, her face reddening. *Clearly, she forgot to mention she'd already put the request in.*

For another moment, the three of them sat in silence with no one wanting to be the first to speak.

"You do understand that for me, this request looks bad—like no one in their right mind would want to touch it bad," she said, her eyes passing between the two of them.

"Luckily no one has ever accused me of being in my right mind," Jens blurted out.

"Is that a joke, Jennings?" she asked, and he quickly shook his head and cleared his throat.

"We've put the request into the system based on a series of shell companies. For all we know, it has nothing to do with Mayor Stone," Jens said, trying to crawl back.

"Bullshit. It's got his damned name on the front of it. Bloody gabs won't let that go. But it's already in the system, so we can't move backward, only forward. So, how worried do I need to be?" she asked, clearly trying to figure out just how much she wanted to be involved.

A case such as this could ruin careers, and Jens suspected she was in the process of trying to mitigate all potential fallout.

"At this point, we have the link, that's all," Jens said, hoping it sounded reassuring.

"Right, well, do we all understand how difficult this is?" she said, continuing, though Jens suspected it was a rhetorical question. "How confident are we in the information?" she added. Ali looked toward Jens nervously and was about to speak. *Dammit!*

"I'd asked Agent Hantsport to look into the building, ma'am. We've double-checked—it appears accurate."

He was superior on the case, and like it or not, he had asked Ali to investigate the building knowing what he might find. *Not that they need to know that.*

"Well, then. As the line of inquiry is linked to Stone Industries, we should start there. Your request has been approved." Captain Rollins entered a code on her data screen, and Jens felt a slight buzz in his Zen watch.

Jens opted not to press his luck as he got up from his chair with a respectful nod.

"Yes, ma'am," he said, turning toward the door and hearing the light squeak from Ali's chair as she got up and followed close behind.

"Jennings?" Captain Rollins said, stopping them before they left the room.

"Yes, Captain?" Jens said, turning to meet her gaze, the heaviness in her eyes telling him everything before she spoke.

"Please don't mess this up." It was genuine—a simple plea from a captain who cared and who understood the severity of an inquiry such as this one. It was a warning, something that didn't warrant a response as Jens and Ali turned and left the office.

They made their way straight to the elevators, Jens wanting to get out before anyone tried to talk with them. A few minutes later, they were finally in some fresh air, standing wordlessly beside each other.

Stone Industries was nearby in Zone Two, and only a twenty-minute walk. Despite the doom and gloom Jens felt, it was a pleasant day, the sun was out, and the sunlight crashing down on them. Ali, who was not her usual chatty self, must have been feeling the weight of it all as well.

"Come on, it's not far. A walk will do us good," Jens said to Ali, getting a simple nod in return. "God knows I could use the steps." Jens joked as he tapped his belly, getting a chuckle out of his partner.

Jens tried to kill the time on the walk by reading over the paperwork for Stone Industries. He suspected he might find something in the paper that would make their lives a little difficult, though nothing seemed off about it. *One good thing, I guess.* Jens felt a quick buzz thrumming on his wrist from his Zen watch. He glanced down to find a message from Dr. Nazari.

"Did you ask for a toxicology on the other six bodies?" he said, looking over at Ali. She looked away nervously as the data now streamed into her Zen watch as well.

"I just thought, it was too strange to be nothing. All of them trapped in there like that. I thought it would be smart to at least test one of them." She wouldn't meet his eye, likely after seeing where her most recent request had landed them.

Jens was mad, but not because she requested it without telling him—because he hadn't thought of it himself.

"Smart thinking," he said with a nod. "Give it a read and let me know what you find," he said, and a hint of a smile returned to Ali's lips as she pulled up the data from her Zen watch.

"However, in the future, next time you make a request like that, tell me. You're not the one who gets burned if something goes wrong," Jens added, wanting to be clear that he was in charge. She had broken the chain of command, and now, with the way things appeared to be going, he wanted her to know that she couldn't just go rogue on him.

"Sorry, sir," she said, pulling up the report, though it didn't take long before she'd found something interesting.

"Sir." Ali sounded excited, though she quickly wiped the look away. "I think we were right. The tox report on Mr. Eriksen was clean. Nothing in his system out of the ordinary," she said, her voice rising with excitement. "But it appears the other men had high amounts of Flunitrazepam in their system. They wouldn't have been able to move even if they tried."

She looked expectantly at Jens as he processed the new information.

"Which means they were set up in that building to die when it burned down," Jens finally said.

Ali nodded her agreement.

"Right," he said quietly.

"This is a murder," Ali said, closing the data pad.

"Let's not jump to conclusions," Jens said, running scenarios over in his mind. "We don't know that for sure."

Ali appeared more and more convinced.

"You have to admit, though, this whole thing seems a little strange, doesn't it?" Ali said distantly.

"True," Jens agreed, feeling a twinge of excitement at the thought. "What could connect the mayor, the Global Lottery, and a drug cartel?"

"Credits," Ali said quickly.

"Seems too obvious," answered Jens. His hands moved over his face as he thought. "Maybe you're right. But a case like this can make or break a career, Hantsport. Last chance to get out unscathed." Jens gave her a stern look.

Ali thought for a moment before answering, which Jens appreciated; this wasn't something that one should take on lightly.

"I'm in," she said confidently.

"Well, at least if we're going to go down, we might get to have a little fun doing it," Jens said with a smile.

9

"I imagined a company that just found out seven people, including six cartel members, were killed in one of their buildings would be a little more . . . frantic," Ali said, looking around at the seemingly undistracted faces of the various workers pacing through the front entrance hall. "Even just losing a building worth hundreds of thousands of credits might warrant something."

Jens agreed as they made their way farther into the large, inviting entrance hall.

It was ornately decorated with four granite pillars in the center bearing the words "All Life's Greatness Begins with a Strong Foundation." It had a welcoming vibe to it.

"What did you learn from the report, Hantsport?" Jens said while he scanned the space, looking for whoever was signalled to greet them.

"Right, well, Stone Industries was one of the newest, major manufacturing companies in the Global West. It was impressive. They seemed to build their success up quickly—a success that everyone attributed to their fearless leader, Allan Stone, who, by all accounts, is an impeccable human being and pleasant to work with. A little over eighteen hundred days ago, he stopped his work here and ran for mayor, won, and is now running for a second term and is favoured to win," she said, giving Jens a shrug. "He also has a beautiful smile, though that's not actually in the report and merely an observation I made," Ali added with a wink to Jens.

"More importantly," Jens said, shaking his head, "he's virtually untouchable."

Jens and Ali were cut off by a buzz in their wrist. A set of credentials flicked across Jens' screen as he noticed a woman who Jens guessed couldn't have used up more than twelve thousand days and had piercing green eyes, which seemed to welcome everyone in, appeared. She had an open data pad, which she shut down as she approached.

"Agents," she said. Her voice was soft and had a rhythmic quality with an accent likely from the North. "My name is Lillian Shogunov. I'm your liaison here at Stone Industries while your investigation is ongoing. I'm your personal direct link, if you will," she said, this last part with a smile. Jens couldn't help wondering what she had done to be stuck with this job.

"We would like to speak with Allan Stone. If you could help with that, that would be wonderful," Jens said, a little smirk on his face. It was a joke, knowing full well they would never actually talk with Mr. Stone. He looked at Ali expectantly, who looked back confusedly. *At least I think I'm funny.*

"Unfortunately, Mr. Stone no longer handles any of the many responsibilities here. He had to relinquish his position when he ran for office. But I've set up a meeting with Ms. Purchase. She runs the day-to-day operations. She's agreed to meet with you, at nine forty-five a.m.," she said, looking down at her Zen watch—"if you don't mind waiting the fifteen minutes."

Jens hadn't been surprised Mr. Stone wasn't in. He assumed as much but figured with his name being on the building still, he would want to be the one who answered the call. It had been a stretch.

"It's so nice of her to agree to meet with us, Lillian," Jens said, giving her his best smile, despite feeling like a wolf in a henhouse.

"Lily, please, Agent Jennings," Lily said. Jens realized now that the data file she was reading before must have been on the two of them. So, Stone Industries was told who exactly would be coming.

"Right, well, Lily. Is there a place we can sit and wait for Ms. Purchase?"

This statement received another smile, which Jens had to admit was very disarming, as she waved them to follow her toward the elevators.

Lily led them into a spacious waiting room with an assortment of couches and chairs for them to choose from. It felt strange for them to be the only ones in the massive space. Jens took a seat in one of the big faux-leather chairs that looked out over the surrounding city, and Ali took the one beside him. Lily was busy working away on another data screen, shutting it down.

"Coffee, tea, water?" she asked politely.

"I'd love a water," Ali said beside him.

"Absolutely, Agent Hantsport, and anything for you, Agent Jennings?" she said with another large smile.

"Coffee, thank you," he said, Lily giving a nod and quickly turning, leaving them alone.

"Pretty amazing building, isn't it?" Ali said, looking out the massive window in front of them, giving a great view of all Pittsburgh's south districts. Jens nodded absently but remained quiet; he was too busy looking around the room at the data cams in each corner—*pretty heavy stuff for a waiting room.*

"Did you know Mr. Stone wouldn't be here?" Ali asked, her finger tapping away on the edge of the chair, waiting patiently, clearly becoming aware of Jens bouts of long silence.

"I had a suspicion," Jens admitted to her. Ali pulled up a data file again and started to read.

"So, what's the plan?" she asked, reviewing the data.

Jens hadn't put very much thought into it. In his experience, nothing was likely to happen on their first visit. They would claim to know nothing about it, tell them they would be happy to help, and then take their time giving them any relevant information.

It was standard with large corporations that didn't want to appear as if they weren't helping but also didn't actually want to help. He made no assumption this would be any different.

Ali must have taken his silence as a sign he didn't want to talk about it, which, of course, he didn't. But looking around the room again, he couldn't help thinking the data cams were put there on purpose, leaving him with a little suspicion he shouldn't be giving very much away. *No, better to wait and see how they wanted to play this out.*

Lily walked into the space a few moments later with a coffee and a glass of water, with a lemon in it.

"Here you are," she said, handing them each their drinks. Jens looked at his Zen watch, the time reading 9:44 a.m. as he took a sip of his coffee. Lily must have noticed him glancing at his watch.

"It shouldn't be too long now . . ." She was unable to finish her sentence before a well-dressed woman stepped out the door and walked over to them. It must be Ms. Purchase. She had long red hair draping down her back, bangs cut in straight angles framing her face, highlighting her pronounced jawline. She looked formidable with a narrow gaze and high cheekbones. The latest Zen watch wrapped around her wrist in custom gold, paired nicely with matching earrings and necklace. Her overall appearance wasn't by any means flamboyant, but she could certainly be pointed out in a crowd.

She gave the distinct impression of someone who felt comfortable in a room of powerful people and wouldn't be afraid to express herself.

"Agent Jennings, Agent Hantsport, please come in. I'm sorry to have kept you waiting." She turned and walked back into the office.

Lily stepped forward, putting her arm up, accompanied with a gracious smile, guiding them into the office. It was a large, square

9

room with a steel desk in the center. It was simple and practical and by no means flashy. She took her seat in a very old but well-maintained, high-back leather chair. Jens couldn't help noticing how impressive she appeared.

"You look surprised, Agent Jennings," Ms. Purchase said, before gesturing for them to take the two steel chairs across from her, both in stark contrast to the chair she had for herself. Lily stood attentively at the back of the room by the door, her smile never leaving her face, which Jens found remarkable.

"I have to admit I was expecting someone . . ."

"Older?" Ms. Purchase answered for him.

"Yes," Jens said, trying to hide the red burning in his cheeks. "I bet you haven't even hit fourteen thousand six hundred days."

"Well, I am fortunate to have some time before my half life, but I assure you I am an old soul," she said, giving him a thin smile. "So, what can I do for you?"

"We were hoping we would get a chance to speak with Mr. Stone directly," Jens said, shifting in the chair and trying to find the most comfortable position, doubting there'd be one.

"You and the rest of the world," Ms. Purchase said, pulling up a data file on her screen.

"He's a busy man, as you can imagine. Even so, he doesn't have much to do with the company anymore and likely wouldn't even know about the building in question if he were here, as we purchased it," she said, looking over the file, "seven hundred days ago, as part of a merger. He was on the council at the time, and he really keeps only an honorary position on the board," she added, sending the file over, entering a code on the computer. Jens could feel his Zen watch vibrate.

"That is all the information on the warehouse that we have along with footage on-site, which I'm sorry to say isn't much. It had been

71

abandoned, so we don't keep very many records on it." She sat back in her chair, giving yet another one of her tight smiles.

Jens had to admit, as he scanned the file, that the information provided was certainly convenient and surprising. Not at all what he'd suspected would happen. *So why do I feel as if I'm missing something?*

"Thank you for being so . . . efficient," Jens said, looking around the room. The chair was very uncomfortable, so he got up and walked over to the window. It was an extension of the one in the other room showing the south city. If he squinted, he could likely see his house. He didn't try.

"You don't get to sit where I'm sitting without being efficient, agent," Ms. Purchase said, leaning forward to pull up another file. "I have been informed by Mr. Stone himself that we are to do everything in our power to assist you on this case," she said, gathering up files.

"Well, Mr. Stone is very kind," Jens said, turning back around.

"Thank you," said a man who'd walked in through a side door Jens hadn't even noticed.

Allan Stone was a large man with jet-black hair and a tanned face hidden beneath a well-manicured beard. His smile was huge, and his eyes were soft; it was easy to see why people trusted him. He walked over to Ali, putting his hand out to greet her.

"I'm Allan Stone," he said, Ali's hand meeting his, while his other hand cocooned her hand as he shook it. "You must be Agent Ali Hantsport—a recent transplant to our city, so I'm told, possibly a future voter?" he added with a wink.

"Possibly, sir, thank you," Ali said, stammering.

"It's a pleasure to meet you," he said, releasing her hand before turning to look at Jens. "Which means you're Senior Agent Adam Jennings." He put his hand out once again, only this time offering it to Jens. Taking it, Jens was impressed, it was firm but gentle, with an unseen quality to it that Jens guessed had a way of making people feel special. Even his eyes lingered longer than necessary. *Ever the politician.*

"Nice to meet you, sir, though I have to admit this is a surprise," Jens said, as the man released his hand and turned toward Ms. Purchase.

"I didn't expect you to be here today," she said coolly as he moved and gave her a cordial kiss on either cheek.

Behind Mr. Stone was a mountain of a man now blocking the doorway. *Mr. Stone's bodyguard.*

His dark complexion matched his suit. He silently moved to his post against the back wall, giving only the slightest nod to Ms. Purchase.

"I hadn't planned on it, but I had a small opening in my schedule and thought it would be a sign of good faith to show our friends at the GIB that we are intent on helping them one hundred percent," Mayor Stone said, moving closer to the window, now standing very close to Jens. "Which we are, Agent Jennings." He continued without looking at Jens.

"Ms. Purchase, I assume, has given you the files you need on the warehouse? Is there anything else we should know about?" he said, finally meeting Jens' eyes, and giving one of his award winning smiles.

Jens remained quite still while he looked at Mayor Stone.

Finally, Ali jumped in.

"We have reason to believe it may have been a murder," she said, casually taking a sip of her water.

Jens shot her a look but remained silent; he'd not wanted to share that with anyone quite yet.

"Murder?" Ms. Purchase asked.

"Well, Agent Hantsport and I are looking into various possibilities. But it does appear to be suspicious," he said, looking directly at Ali, who must have realized she'd made a mistake as she took a big gulp of water.

"I'm sorry to hear that. As Mr. Stone has said, anything we can do to help, please let us know," Ms. Purchase said, composing herself after the momentary emotional hijack.

Jens looked around the room, giving Ali a nod to leave, which she received. Promptly getting up, she started toward the door with Jens right behind.

"This should be more than enough to get started, thank you," Jens said, stopping before leaving the room.

"Lily here can be your contact person if you need anything else. Please don't hesitate to contact her," Ms. Purchase added, and as if on cue, Lily pulled out her data pad and scanned it over to Jens' and Ali's Zen watches. Jens felt his wrist vibrate; Lily's contact details now linked into their watches.

"Thank you. If you think of anything else, let us know," Jens said, turning to leave. To his surprise, he was stopped by Mr. Stone.

"Now that you mention it," he said, looking over at Ms. Purchase, her face once again a mask of emotions. *It must be a gift to stay that composed.*

"Yes?" Jens said, turning back, now looking at Mr. Stone, who'd started pacing across the floor.

"It's likely nothing, and I don't want to point the finger at anyone," he began to say. Jens was happy enough to stand there in silence, waiting for him to finish, but Ali jumped in.

"All information is helpful, sir." Jens would really have to chat with her about what she could and couldn't say in meetings. In fact, the conversation may be rather short.

"Well, we've been under attack. The company, I mean, but also myself. As the face of the business, I'm used to it. But this has been different," he said, looking out the window again.

"How so?" Jens said, taking a step back toward him, the conversation starting to get a little more intriguing.

"I've given my life to this city. I wouldn't expect everyone to understand why, but the truth is I care about it. The person sending us messages seems to think I'm destroying it and threatens to burn down what I've built." He turned back to look at Jens.

"It may just be a coincidence, but if people got hurt because of me, I feel I should do everything in my power to help find out who's responsible," he said, looking right into Jens' eyes.

"I'm going to need anything you have regarding these threats," Jens said in an even tone, trying to take a page from Ms. Purchase's book.

"I'm afraid it's not much, just some messages from a moniker. They go by Ash and Sun, but everything we have, I'll have Derris send over." He looked over at the man by the front door, who pulled out a shiny black Zen watch. "He's my head of security and handles all the threats," Mayor Stone added. Derris pulled up the needed files, entered in a code on his Zen watch, and Jens' own watch vibrated. "I hope this helps," Mr. Stone said as they turned to leave.

Jens stopped and turned around.

"You've been incredibly helpful. Thank you for your cooperation."

Jens turned and left with Ali in tow, with Lily leading them out, guiding them through a maze of a building until they finally got down to the street.

"If you need anything, agents, you have my information" she said with another smile before heading back inside.

Jens stood for a second, watching her leave.

"They were helpful," Ali said, turning to the street as she hailed an ECar with her watch.

"Yeah, really nice," Jens said, his brain playing over the sequence of events in his mind.

"What's wrong?" Ali asked, looking back at him.

"Nothing," he said, lying, unable to shake the feeling that something was wrong with that whole situation, as if they were being played somehow. "Maybe I'm just being cynical. You ever heard this name before?" Jens said, pulling up the file marked "Ash and Sun" before looking over at Ali.

"No," she said as the ECar pulled up. She opened the door and hopped inside. "You coming? It looks like it's going to rain," she said expectantly, making a show of looking at him, then up at the sky. It was starting to get dark.

"I think I'll walk," Jens said, shutting the door before she could respond. Rain or not, he needed a few minutes alone with his thoughts. The ECar pulled away as he pulled up all known data on Ash and Sun he could find.

10

The walk back to the station did nothing for Jens in the way of clearing his head. In fact, he was more confused than he'd been when he left Stone Industries, and he was also wet. It didn't make it any easier when he returned to see Ali in Captain Rollins' office. *I thought I'd made myself clear—it's my ass on the line.* Ignoring the meeting, he sat at his desk, grabbing a retro Rubik's Cube from out of his drawer, mixed it up, and began to solve it.

He'd solved the thing so many times he no longer needed to think about it, which made it the perfect distraction when he needed his mind working on other puzzles.

"Cool, what's that?" Ali said, stepping up behind him, watching as his fingers wrapped efficiently around the cube.

"It's a Rubik's Cube," he said, absently.

"A what?"

"A turn-of-the-century puzzle," he said, finishing up another row.

"How did you get that? It's got to be like . . ."

"A few hundred years old? Yeah, it was my grandfather's, I guess, though, to be honest, I'm not sure how he got it."

"So, it's like an heirloom of sorts," Ali said as she watched curiously while Jens turned the pieces, arranging all the colours neatly around the sides.

"It's just a toy," Jens said, having never thought of it as anything more than a child's game, though he guessed in some ways Ali was right. "I got nothing on Ash and Sun, you?" Jens said, tossing the finished cube up in the air, where Ali snatched it and began turning it over in her hands.

"Nothing yet. Oh, I almost forgot, the captain wants to see you," Ali said, nodding over to Captain Rollins' office. "Think you can teach me how to do this?" Ali asked, holding up the colourful cube.

"No," Jens said evenly as he walked off.

"Fine, I'll figure it out on my own," Ali said, scoffing as she began mixing up the cube again.

"Good luck," Jens called back with a smirk.

"Captain," Jens said, standing in the doorway of her office. Captain Rollins shut down her data screen and offered him a seat.

"How are you doing, Agent Jennings?" she said, her hands resting on the desk in front of her.

Jens wasn't sure what she meant by the question. *Is this some sort of trick?*

"Good, Captain. This case is . . . interesting," he said, not knowing how much she'd heard from Ali.

"So I've heard. Becoming a little higher profile than I would have liked for you on your first case back," she said, trying to get a rise out of him. "I was thinking I would transfer the case to another team, give you something a little lighter," she said, leaning forward. Jens could feel his eye twitching; he certainly had some choice words he'd like to say but refrained.

"I think that would be a mistake, ma'am. With respect," he said, watching as she leaned back in her chair. *If this were a test, I just passed.*

"Why's that?" she said, her hands wrapped together. The fingers on her right hand tapped a little too calmly for Jens over her left knuckles.

"Well, I believe . . . ," Jens started to say and noticed the tapping stopped. He'd made a wrong move. "That is, we believe, Agent Hantsport and myself, that there is more going on here than meets the eye."

He finished, and Captain Rollins resumed her tapping. *Test two passed.*

Jens had worked it out; she was clearly trying to get a sense of his willingness to take commands, keep calm, and play nice. *This is about trust; can she trust him on her team?*

She'd not completely yelled at him, so likely Agent Hantsport didn't say anything terrible, meaning now was a good time to return the favour.

"It was actually Agent Hantsport who asked to run the toxicology on the remaining bodies in the fire. It was smart thinking," he said, his gesture rewarded with a smile from the captain—though he kept to himself the fact that he would have eventually done the same thing.

"You understand my predicament, don't you, Agent Jennings?" She left space for an answer, but Jens knew better than to take it. "You see, many people don't believe you should have been invited back, that you're burned out and a liability to the GIB and what we stand for."

Had the situation been different, Jens might have admitted that he was burned out in a way. *Who isn't after so much time as an agent?*

Jens had snapped, letting the pressure build up too much, and he paid the price. But he was given his two hundred days' leave, and if he realized anything during his time off, it wasn't that he'd been burned out. He was an addict.

Addicted to the danger of the job, letting it fuel him. But he also discovered that if he wasn't getting it here at work, he would find it elsewhere. *Surely one of these is better than the other.*

"I think you're a good agent, you've had an impressive career, but for the time being, you have a watchdog," she said, glancing up through the window at Agent Hantsport.

"And if you do anything to fuck up this investigation, you'll be out of here faster than a shit down the drain. Do you understand me, Jennings?"

Jens remained silent, opting for a nod of the head instead.

"Good. Because I've put my neck out for you to get you back investigating, because frankly, I'm not sure what you did was wrong—but that shit stays between you and me."

Jens allowed himself the tiniest of smiles.

"However, if you think for a moment I'm going to go down with the fucking ship, you have another thing coming. So let me spell this out for you. If you overstep—you're gone. If you step on the wrong toes—you're gone. If you do anything to jeopardize this investigation, you're fuckin' gone. Frankly, while fighting to catch the bastard who did this, you're going to have to work very hard not to be gone. Understand me?"

As it had served him well so far, Jens nodded.

"If you don't think you can do these things, tell me now and I'll remove you from the case. This is your only chance," she added, but Jens remained quiet.

"Good, well, then, do me a favour and catch the bastard."

Jens got up from his seat, suspecting the warning and/or a pep talk—likely both—was done. Jens left the office knowing the message was clear; if anything went wrong, he'd be the one to be blamed.

He remained silent as he returned to the desk and found Ali still fiddling with the cube. Seeing her sitting there now, he wished he'd asked to go at this alone, if all screwups were going to be on him. *Shit!*

Damning himself for not thinking about that sooner, he snatched the Rubik's Cube out of her hand.

"Hey!" she said, looking up at him.

"Shouldn't you be doing something?" Jens said, spinning the cube in his hands.

"I was, trying to figure that thing out," she said with a grin. Jens looked at the cube and started spinning it; with a couple of precise moves, he had the bottom row complete.

"Neat," Ali said, amazed. "Sure you can't teach me?" she asked.

"I never said can't. I'm saying won't," Jens said with a smirk. "We need to learn more about Ash and Sun." It had been more to himself, but if he were forced to work with a partner, he would have to get used to talking out loud, if only to pretend to use her.

"Right, about that . . . ," she said hesitantly.

"What?" he said, looking up from the cube, not stopping his movements as the cube edges spun around.

"Well, I don't know about you, but I couldn't find anything in the database about Ash and Sun . . . ," she started saying, leaving room for a possible response, but nothing came, so she continued. "Anyway, I have a friend up in Tkaronto who works in cybercrimes, and he said he would have a look at the moniker and see if anything came up. He might turn up empty, but I figured it was worth a shot."

Jens saw that she was smiling, clearly pleased with herself.

"Good work," he said, setting the cube down. "But do me a favour and stop doing things without telling me first. I'm not sure how they do things up in Tkaronto, but here we tell our senior agents what we are doing—because in case you haven't noticed, I'm the one they're going to slaughter if we fuck this up." He got up to leave. "Message me when you have any information."

"Where are you going?" she asked, calling after him.

"Out," he replied. "I need time to think," he said, slipping his jacket on and walking toward the elevator.

11

John had walked his dog along the river every day for the past five years. It was quiet, unlike so many other parts of Pittsburgh, and he felt as though he could relax more with Cricket, his seven-year-old black Labrador retriever. He also enjoyed the fact that Cricket could go off leash and run and jump in the cool waters without the scrupulous eyes of non-dog lovers.

It was hard to have a dog in the city. They took up space and pooped, and over the years, fewer and fewer people kept them. They were a rural luxury. But when John came to the city eight years ago, he was alone and in a new place. Cricket became his partner, and the two of them took care of each other.

Most people wouldn't come down by the waters because it smelled like fish. The concrete cityscape made the area a little warmer, giving the smell a nasty ripeness, not like the waters back home in Montana. They were clear and clean; the openness of the country gave everything a fresh earthiness.

It was hard to keep city water clean, regardless of the city's treatment facilities. They were sterile—John knew that—and safe to be around, but they were not "natural." *It's such a shame.*

From the water's edge, he could see the high buildings across the river which had been designed perfectly, but in Johns view lacked any natural beauty. He'd moved to the city for work, which is also how he knew the waters were clean, having worked for Enviro-Tech, which helped cities and large communities integrate green tech into their designs.

Since arriving, he'd dreamed of finding a way to clean up the river and give it back its natural beauty. It was one of the many water veins in the city, and he felt as though it was his mission to rejuvenate them all.

He watched as Cricket ran headlong down the path jumping into the water, his bark echoing off the high stone walls. John chased him, hoping he wouldn't go too far into the water. That's when he noticed Cricket heading toward something.

It looked like a floating log bobbing in the water. That was strange, because trees would be picked up in treatment plants and used as biowaste for urban agriculture, one of John's more ingenious ideas.

Cricket reached the bobbing vessel and started to drag it in. As he came nearer, John's heart sank as the dark image in front of him took shape. Cricket pulled the bloated body up on the rocks; its young form must have been dead for a while, its head bashed in.

John's first reaction was to vomit, which he promptly did, splattering his morning breakfast over the rocks. Cricket, seeing his owner kneeling on the rocks, left the mangled body and moved to comfort his John. *Always the faithful companion.*

John instinctively looked down the river at the series of tall bridges along its route, silently imagining how the body could have arrived here.

Looking at the lifeless form only a few feet away, John pulled up his Zen watch.

"Police," he said somberly into the watch, his voice low and crackly. Kneeling on the ground with Cricket's wet body resting against him, John was unable, despite his best efforts, to take his eyes off the poor thing that lay dead in front of him.

12

Jens didn't know where he was walking, only that he was frustrated by the conversation with the captain and couldn't exactly figure out why. *Maybe it's Agent Hantsport?*

He'd never wanted a partner, though she seemed to be the only one coming with good ideas. *Maybe I've lost my touch. I'm just not as good as I used to be? Bullshit! Maybe a little rusty around the edges, but I'm not bad. What I need is a win, something to light the fire again. It's just this damn investigation, leaving me more questions than we have answers? None of it makes any sense. Who was the woman on the bench, and why can I not find any record of her? Who burns down a building filled with drugged-up members of the cartel? So many damned "whos," and none of them looking as if we have the answers.*

Jens wanted to scream, and maybe he would have, had his wrist not began to vibrate from his Zen watch, happily rescuing him from his spiralling thoughts. *Unknown caller?*

He pulled out a set of ocular pads and placed them behind his ears. It was the best way to have a private conversation.

He connected to the call. A weak voice appeared on the other end of the line; whoever it was had most certainly been crying. Her first words came through as more of a sob than anything else

"He's dead," she said mournfully, the voice shaking from the effort of talking.

"I'm sorry—who is this? Who's dead?" Jens was confused, unsure who this was or how she had his number, but frankly he didn't have time for any of this.

"Natasha Lilford," she said quietly. "You gave me your card the other day. I was looking for my brother." Each word was barely coming out between sobs.

Jens vaguely remembered giving his card to someone and kicked himself as he recalled telling her he could help.

"Right, Natasha, this is really . . ."

"He was murdered—I know he was! Please, you have to help me. . . I have no one I can go to." The line was silent for a moment, and Jens was thinking about how he wanted to handle this. The last thing he needed was to drag himself into someone else's problems. His life wasn't exactly perfect at the moment, and any more distractions would only hurt his chance of solving his case.

"Please," she said. Jens sank his face in his palms, sighing deeply.

"Meet me at the Dan's Diner on Washington Avenue in twenty-five minutes," he said. "I can't promise anything," he added quickly.

"Thank you, Agent Jennings, thank you!"

Jens closed the link and put the ear pad back in his Zen watch. *What the hell have I just got myself into?*

Jens arrived at the diner, and it didn't take long for him to recognize the woman he'd seen a few days earlier who he now knew as Natasha. However, the woman he saw in the diner was not the same woman he had remembered from outside the GIB station.

Then she had been worried, flustered by the situation, angry for being brushed aside, but completely together.

The person he saw in front of him now as he approached the table looked as though she hadn't slept in days. Her hair was tied in a messy bun, and although he couldn't be sure, she appeared to be wearing the same clothes.

Stepping closer, his suspicion was confirmed as the smell wafting off her hit him. Now only a few paces away, she began to look as though she'd aged, her face a series of deep creases, large bags under the eyes, with red lines streaking her face from tears.

Jens couldn't help feeling sorry for her. Turning his attention to the waitress, he ordered two coffees and a couple of waters before sitting down across from her.

"Natasha?" Jens said. Natasha looked up slowly from the table. She was weary; her movements were dragged out and strained.

"Thank you for meeting me," she said softly. Her hysteria seemed to have dissipated, or maybe she was just trying to keep herself together long enough to see him.

"I'm sorry about your brother, Ryan."

Jens had called his friend Granger at Pittsburgh PD for information. The two had gone through the academy together, and Granger was one of the few people who still got along with Jens after he'd left the PPD.

He'd confirmed that Ryan Lilford was a probable suicide assumed to have jumped off one of the nearby bridges. As far as the police were concerned, the investigation was open and shut. Clearly Natasha didn't feel the same way.

"I know what you're thinking," she said softly. "The police told me they think it was a suicide, but I know it wasn't. Ryan would never do that. He wouldn't leave me alone like this. We were the only family we had." She spoke quickly, not giving Jens any chance to jump in. Not that he wanted to. But still he felt bad because she was right; it was what he'd been thinking.

Suicides weren't uncommon, despite all the advancements in mental health. People always slipped through the cracks. People's problems were difficult to see when family and friends didn't always know what to look for. Jens glanced at his watch, knowing he shouldn't have come. *I don't have time for any of this.*

"He wasn't suicidal," she continued saying, happy to fill the empty space with anything but silence. "He loved life, and he would have done anything for me." She reached out and grabbed Jens' hand, which had been resting on the table. "Please, you have to believe me," she said, as she stared pleadingly into his eyes.

"What makes you so sure it wasn't?" Jens said, pulling his hand back. Touching someone on a case under any circumstance was not okay. He noticed her face suddenly drop at the gesture, then quickly transform into a fierce defiance. *She was expecting resistance.*

"His wrists," she said, as if it was all Jens needed to know. She must have recognized his confusion, adding, "He was beaten up, his head was smashed in, and he had cuts all over his face, arms, and chest," she said, trying absently to spit out all details of his brother's body. Jens was now more confused than ever.

"I went in to identify the body . . . like I said, I'm his only family." Her speech broke for a moment.

"What about his wrists?" Jens said, unsure how much time he could spend with her before getting the call from Ali wondering where the hell he'd gone, so he wanted to get to the point.

"They said the bruises and cuts were from the water. Fine, I could have bought that. But when I held his hands, I saw bruising on his wrists. Why would he have that? It didn't make any sense. They tried to tell me it was likely something else, but I knew my brother. Who ties themselves up and then jumps off a bridge? None of it makes sense."

Tears began rolling down her face. Jens reached into his pocket, pulling out a tissue and handing it to her, and she wiped her eyes.

Jens looked at her for a moment, his brain jumping around. He had to admit that it was weird. It was unlikely to have had anything to do with the death, but it certainly raised some alarms.

"Do me a favour," he said, calmly trying to remain as neutral as possible. "Go home and have a shower, get cleaned up, and get some sleep. I know this is a lot for you to take in, and I also know you're stressed that nothing will be done."

Jens closed his eyes, taking a deep sigh, silently beating himself up for getting involved in anything other than the warehouse murders. It was clear that his ass was on the line. *Am I really thinking of piling more shit on my plate?*

Not to mention if the PPD had already looked into it, he'd be stirring up trouble if he overstepped and examined the body.

He felt terrible for Natasha. It was obvious she loved her brother. *No, dammit, Jens, you can't run around trying to solve everyone's problems. You can barely solve the ones you have!*

"I'm sorry, but I can't help you," he said before he had time to talk himself out of it. "This is a PPD matter, and I can't just . . ." Natasha stood up.

"So, you're not going to help me?" she said with a hiss, any veil of calmness disappearing into rage. Jens had wanted to do this in a public place to prevent this from happening. *Clearly, I've underestimated how angry she is.*

"Please, calm down." He tried putting his hands up in a soothing gesture.

"Calm down?" she cried out. His gesture had backfired. "My brother was killed, and the police are being too lazy to look into it because it's inconvenient. And now you're telling me you won't do anything because it's not your job?" Her face turned red, her tears replaced with rage.

"That's not what I'm saying . . . ," Jens said, trying to get back on track, but it was too late. He'd lost her.

"Your job is to protect people, and right now I'm telling you there is something horribly wrong about the way my brother died, and you want to brush it off like everyone else! You're not an agent, you're a pansy!"

Her point made, she stormed off from the now-silent diner, as everyone was watching the show.

Jens wasn't one for embarrassment, but he felt his face go red, quickly realizing from the chatter around the room that he was the bad guy.

"Listen, I can't . . ."

She turned on him. "You can't, you can't, you can't! You can GO TO HELL! I'm tired of hearing what people can't do. How about you do your fucking jobs and find out who killed my brother!"

She stormed out the door, and Jens swiped his Zen watch at the table, paying for the drinks he'd ordered but not received, before he rushed out the door after her, but she was gone.

"Goddammit," he shouted. "Why the hell did you come here in the first place? What did you think was going to happen? You'd just talk her down, try to make her feel better about her brother's death?!" He kicked the dust off the sidewalk as people stared at him as they wandered by.

As if on cue, his Zen watch went off with another call. Reaching for the ocular pad, he placed it behind his ear.

"What?!" he said angrily to the other person on the line. It was Ali.

"Sorry, sir, it's just . . ."

He was still fuming from his idiotic interaction with Natasha. "Spit it out, Hantsport," he said, being more disrespectful than she likely deserved.

"Sorry, sir, the captain has requested we go and talk with Nigel Eriksen's family."

The news snapped him back to reality. It was the last thing he wanted to do, but he needed to get back to the matter at hand.

"Right. Send me the details, and I'll meet you there," he said passively.

"Now, sir?" she said. Jens looked at his Zen watch and realized they would be off soon. Weighing it in his mind, he knew this would not likely be a welcomed visit, and with his day going the way it was, he certainly wanted to get it over with as quickly as possible.

"Yup, no time like the present," he said, signing off and letting out a deep sigh. Feeling the Zen watch vibrate on his wrist, he pulled up the data screen and hailed an ECar, hopped in, and readied himself to ruin another person's day.

13

"Sorry I'm late," Jens said, approaching Ali, who had been waiting for him by the front gate. She greeted him with a nod, no doubt still ticked off from being dragged out here so close to the end of the day.

"Pretty nice-looking spot," Jens said, looking over the gate at the collection of tiny town houses that all wrapped around a central courtyard in a giant U.

"Maybe if you ask politely, they will give you a tour," Ali said coldly as she pressed down on the number six of an old retro buzzer machine.

"Is there a problem here?" Jens asked.

"I don't appreciate being talked to like that," Ali said, not bothering to look at him.

"Look, I'm sorry, it was bad timing," Jens said as he spotted various data cams around the perimeter of the gates. *Obviously not everything is retro.*

"Where were you?" Ali asked, pretending she didn't care about the answer.

"Personal stuff," he said, lying, not wanting to let it be known he was talking with Natasha. He had made up his mind not to get involved, and the last thing he needed was rumours going around that he had talked with her. He was still kicking himself for going in the first place.

"Who is it?" said a soft voice from the other side. Jens assumed it was Mrs. Eriksen.

"Mrs. Eriksen, we're with the GIB. We have some questions about your husband."

There was no reply, just a click and a loud buzz as they pushed in through the gate.

The center of the courtyard was large and appeared to be shared by six different homes. Each one had its own little garden—some growing vegetables, some just flowers. In the center was a large patch of grass like a small park. Jens assumed if someone had kids, as the Eriksens did, this was the type of place they would want them to have.

He knocked on the front door. Mrs. Eriksen answered; she was wearing her husband's housecoat, and her red and puffy eyes showed she'd clearly been crying. She didn't invite them in but just turned around and walked in, leaving them to follow behind her and shut the door.

"Mrs. Eriksen . . . ," Jens started to say softly.

"The police have already been here," she whispered. "Can I get you anything—water, coffee, or something?" Her eyes were soft, as if she were simply looking through them, trying to keep her emotions in check.

"Water would be great. Agent Hantsport, why don't you grab us all some waters. I'll talk to Mrs. Eriksen."

Ali didn't look impressed, but she didn't object.

Mrs. Eriksen sat in one of the chairs in the living room, and Jens sat on the couch across from her. An electric fireplace hummed off to the side, giving the room a cozy feel. On top was a steel mantel with the images of a happy family—some on vacation and other scenes of various adventures, hiking, fishing, canoeing. *They'd certainly been the outdoorsy type.*

"You have a beautiful family," Jens said, looking around.

"Had," Mrs. Eriksen replied, blowing her nose and stuffing the tissue into one of her pockets.

"Can I ask you where your kids are?" Jens said, looking around and noticing the pictures, but not hearing any sounds in the house besides Ali in the kitchen with the tap on.

"They're in their rooms. They haven't come out much since they found out. I don't blame them. They likely need some . . ." She had to stop as her eyes started to tear up. She seemed to be trying to be dispassionate about it but appeared to be losing her hold.

"I don't understand. There has to be something going on here. Nige was a good man. He would never . . . he could never do what they said he did—embezzling credits for a drug cartel. If he were doing that, do you think I'd be working the extra job to help give us these vacations, this house?" she said, gesturing to the pictures on the wall.

Jens started to shake his head, unsure of what to say.

"You bet your ass I wouldn't! It's ridiculous and a bold-faced lie. Whatever was going on there, Nige—MY NIGE—had nothing to do with it." Her tears were steeped in rage.

Ali's return with waters and a pot of tea was perfect timing.

"He was a good man!" she went on again, grabbing a water and taking a couple of tiny sips.

"I'm sure he was," Ali said softly, as Jens gave her a shake of the head. He didn't have all the information, and he also suspected something strange, but right now, all the evidence they had showed Nige was working with the Scorpions. That was what they knew, and they couldn't afford to get caught up in the emotions behind it. *Dammit, how do I keep finding myself in rooms with people yelling at me for not believing their stories?*

"If Mr. Eriksen didn't have anything to do with this, Mrs. Eriksen, then can you explain what your husband was doing there?" She gave him a dirty look and finished her drink of water. Ali also shot him a look, and Jens replied with one of his own. *She may not be happy with the question, but it's a valid one.*

"No," she said softly. "The last time I saw Nige was on a data message he'd sent saying that he found something at work, and that he wouldn't be home till late." She slumped back in her chair.

"Do you have the message, Mrs. Eriksen?" Jens asked, trying to be as polite as possible. His day hadn't been going very well, and once again he'd regretted the position in which he'd put himself. But he was here and would be damned if he didn't get everything he needed the first time.

Mrs. Eriksen looked at him for a long moment before tapping her Zen watch, and a Halo popped up in front of her. She scrolled for a moment and slid it across, linking the data entry to Jens' Zen watch.

He felt his wrist vibrate; it would be a great resource, but he decided to save watching the video for later, not wanting to subject Mrs. Eriksen to watching it again with them.

"I can't explain to you why he was there. But I do know my husband, and he was a good man who wanted to help people. That's why he worked for the lottery in the first place. Did you know if you work for the lottery, you abdicate from it? He was never interested in being rich—he wanted to be fulfilled. So, ask yourself why a man like that would launder credits for the cartel."

Ali asked a few more questions while Jens looked around the house. By all accounts Mr. Eriksen seemed like a happy man with two kids and his wife. But Jens knew that sometimes in life things were deceptive, and not everything was as it seemed.

Even if he wanted to believe that Nige was a good family man, in the back of his mind Jens couldn't shake the feeling that Nige was as bad as anyone else, especially when it came to credits.

Jens heard a creak from above him and then the soft footsteps of a child walking down the stairs. Jens recognized her from some of the pictures he'd seen; it was Mr. Eriksen's youngest daughter.

She couldn't have more than thirty-seven hundred days on her. She looked over the railing from the stairs and stared at him.

"Who are you?" she asked as politely as she could with only a hint of fear in her voice. Jens tried his best to give her a warm smile, but he was afraid it might have done more damage and stopped.

"I work for the GIB," he said, hoping she was old enough to know what that meant. If she did, it didn't seem to matter to her. Jens could tell she'd also been crying.

For some reason, Jens was suddenly aware of the relationship he had with his father. *Would I have had the same reaction?*

"Are you going to find out who killed my father?" she said, her soft voice carrying him back into the moment.

He didn't know what to say, battling with something between honesty and a half truth.

"I'm going to try," he said with a conviction that surprised himself. It wasn't a lie; it was his job to find out what happened, after all. He decided she didn't need to know that she might not be happy with what he found. Either way he appeared to have satisfied her with the answer, as she gave Jens a tiny grin, showing a gap where her big tooth would soon fill in.

"Thank you," she said, leaving him at the bottom of the stairs. *It might be a little premature to thank me.*

After a few more insubstantial questions, the pair finished up at the Eriksens' house and soon enough left the apartment compound.

It was set to rain in twenty minutes, though it would have been nice to walk home. Today had been harder than he would have cared to admit. Ali stood on the curb waiting, having already hailed her ECar.

"What do you think?" she said, looking at him. Jens, who was used to sitting on his thoughts and not talking with anyone about them, couldn't bring himself to say anything. "Come on, you must have some idea," she said, prodding him.

"I would like to believe her, that he was a good man," he said, choosing his words wisely.

"But?" Ali said impatiently, as the car pulled up in front of her.

"I've been around too long to believe everyone is what they seem. The facts are he was there—our job is to find out why," Jens said, turning to walk away.

"You have to admit, though. Nothing about this case seems to line up," she said, as Jens turned to look at her. "What about the message? Anything useful?" she added.

Jens pulled up the video. The face of Mr. Eriksen popped up in front of them. He was dressed in a suit and tie, but the first thing Jens noticed as he pressed play was the smiling, happy man from the family photos had been replaced with someone slightly on edge.

"Hi, Lovie, I'm so sorry, but I found something in one of the files at work that doesn't quite add up. I'm sure it's nothing, but I need to get it sorted before I get home. I'm not sure how long it will take, so don't wait up. Tell the kids I love them. Bye-bye." Mr. Eriksen's face faded away as Jens closed the video. Ali stood with one foot in the car and her face in deep concentration from what she'd just listened to.

"It's not a lot, but we should probably talk with his colleagues—see if he was working on something," Jens finally said, turning to walk away.

Ali snapped out of her daze.

"You want a ride? I'm heading back your way," she said.

"No," Jens said, and kept walking, hearing the door close behind him. *After today, I deserve a little rain.*

Jens was drenched from head to toe by the time he'd made it home. He couldn't be sure the exact moment it had started to rain, and if he was honest, he didn't care. His mind was too preoccupied with everything; each unending conversation seemed to lead to the same disappointing question. *Have I lost touch with what makes me a good agent?*

He was tired and wet and desperately wanted to collapse in his bed. His entire body was exhausted, and his mind badly needed a break. What he really hoped for was sleep.

But even as his body sank into the mattress and he could feel his body settle in, his mind was racing.

Jens' frustration was building up until he remembered the two vials of Enzo in his bedside table. One of those vials would rid his mind of everything that was troubling him. *I could be better by morning.*

Jens leaned, opening the drawer as he looked down at the old mint tin inside. Lifting it out, he opened it and looked over the two vials. *One crack is all I need to put my mind at ease.*

"No," he said, getting out of bed and pacing the floor, the purple vials on the table staring back at him. "I can't. I can't," he said, shutting the tin and reopening it, as if expecting to see they'd somehow magically vanished but finding them there, taunting him.

"FUCK!"

He tried to ignore them as he went into the living room, his mind incessantly telling him it would be fine, as the rest of him cried out to ignore the craving and do something, anything else.

"Activate bio gravity machine," Jens said absently as he hurried back into his room, ignoring the vials, and began rummaging around his closet for some exercise clothes, which, like his shoes, had been tucked away deep into his closet.

He heard the machine unpack itself in the other room as he changed, and by the time he returned, a small section of the apartment had been filled with the BGM, a round omnitrack pad about six feet in diameter and encased in glass. The BGM was a unique combination of treadmill and high-gravity training modules and allowed the user to train while putting their body under continuously changing conditions to maximize a workout.

Reducing the output, Jens hopped on the pad and began to run, immediately feeling the pressure building in his chest.

He started to wonder if it was a bad idea when the pressure began to loosen, and he managed to find a rhythm as the omnitrack adjusted its design beneath him.

"Activate thought board," Jens said between heavy breaths as the glass case around him lit up.

"Thought board activated," said a soft voice above him.

"Topic, Nigel Eriksen," Jens said as the former's name appeared on the screen. Various data entries Eriksen had collected, including his video to his wife, appeared on the board.

"By all accounts he is a good husband and a good father. He seemed happy. Even his daughter seemed upset by his death, and maybe that's my own bias, though I have to put that in the not-a-complete-piece-of-shit pile. So why was he with the cartel?" all these thoughts Jens was saying began to fill up on the screen around him. "Why was he the only one not drugged? What was he working on at the office—did it have anything to do with this? Is that why he'd been targeted? What makes a man like him do something like this? Was it his family? Does the Global Lottery know anything?" Jens said, sweeping his hand across the screen as everything on the glass disappeared.

Jens ran and let his mind wander as the track below him adjusted beneath his feet, his body forced to follow its ever-changing movements as the pressure around him strengthened.

"Topic, Ali Hantsport," Jens said, watching the screen around him light up with various details about his new partner, though he had only one question on his mind. "Is she a good partner?" he asked as the words appeared in front of him. They seemed to follow him around as he turned on the track until he eventually waved them away as well.

He was getting tired, though he still had questions on his mind he wanted to get out. These he had been dreading because he wished they would leave him alone.

"Topic, Natasha Lilford," Jens said. A small set of notes appeared before him.

"How can something I have so little information about be cumbersome in my mind?" he said softly, though the words still appeared in front of him.

"What can I do that will actually help her?" Jens asked, feeling the pressure beginning to build up again in his chest. His breath suddenly felt shallow as his feet pounded heavily against the track under him. The words on the screen in front of him seemed to blur, but he had one last thing on his mind, something he needed to get out.

"Do I think helping her will make me feel better about what I did?" he said as his legs buckled. The machine shut down, and Jens fell to the ground. On his knees, he began to vomit.

Taking a few moments to catch his breath and wipe his mouth with his shirt, he left the BGM waving around the final topic as he did.

Tossing the now-dirty shirt in the auto clean, he heard the BGM being packed away, and he felt fortunate for its self-cleaning feature. Maybe his body wasn't entirely ready for such a heavy workout, though he had to admit it felt good to empty his mind.

He was about to hop in the shower when he noticed a flashing light on his Zen watch—a missed message from Ali.

"We found him! Anton Preston, aka Ash and Sun, is here in Pittsburgh. I'll send details in the morning."

Jens smiled, already feeling better about the day. This was icing on the cake. *Ali's contact in Tkaronto panned out, and I've avoided falling back into old habits.*

Jens closed the mint tin and shut the vials away in the drawer, kicking himself for coming so close to taking the easy way out, all to forget about his problems.

14

"Rough night?" Jens said, handing her a coffee.

Jens had arrived early to the location Ali had sent him that morning. He'd never been great at apologies, but he figured being early with coffee would be a great place to start. She looked at him suspiciously and took the coffee, taking a long sip.

"Do you actually care?" she said, looking at him. He thought for a moment and shrugged.

"What you do on your time is your business. I just assumed that was what partners did." He tried to smile, but it wasn't his best feature, and he quickly aborted when he saw her face.

"We're partners now?" she said, sarcastically.

"I admit I wasn't keen on working with you, but we wouldn't be here without you, so credit where credit's due, I guess."

She looked at him, possibly trying to figure out if it was all genuine or not. He'd hoped she'd accepted it for the honesty, it was meant to be.

"Well, thanks, and thank you for the coffee. As to your question, yes, late night and possibly one too many drinks," she said, rubbing her temple before fumbling around in her pocket, pulling out a small pill and ingesting it.

"A date?" Jens asked, which got a smirk from Ali.

"Let's leave it at too many drinks," Ali said, letting out a deep sigh;

the pill must have helped a little. "How about you? Do anything special?"

"I tried to work out again," Jens said casually.

"And how did that go?"

"I vomited," Jens said, taking a sip of his coffee. Ali, who'd been mid sip, nearly spat up her coffee as she began to laugh.

"Stop," she said, wincing as the sudden laughter must have spurred her headache. "You're joking?"

"You asked. Though I have to admit I feel a lot better this morning, a little refreshed," Jens said, taking a deep breath.

"I bet you do," Ali said, musing. "So, what's the plan this morning? You got the details I sent?"

"Yes, although I have to admit I'm grateful your contact up north was able to help out. It feels . . . ," Jens said, pausing while he searched for the right words.

"Too easy," Ali said for him.

Jens nodded.

"I feel the same way. Though my guy is great, maybe it was just a little slipup, or maybe we just got lucky."

Jens didn't want to say it out loud, but he wasn't a firm believer in getting lucky.

"I called in a favour from the PPD, and they have a couple of uniforms and an IT person coming down. Should be here any minute," Jens said, looking around. Ali still didn't look great, but she seemed a little more human now after the mysterious pill and coffee.

"People owe you favours?" Ali said with a laugh. "Doesn't that normally involve playing nice with others?"

"Constable Granger and I used to work together at PPD. He's one of the few people I still talk with."

"You mean one of the few people you haven't completely pissed off?" Ali asked.

"Yes," Jens said. "As for the favour, you're looking at it. A high-profile arrest in conjunction with the GIB goes a long way in the PPD. They get credit, and we get access to Ash and Sun without stepping on anyone's toes."

"Seems like you're almost being generous. You must like this guy," Ali said with a wink.

"I tolerate him," Jens countered.

"I'm sure you do," Ali said, laughing.

"With any luck, this will be in and out, and we can find something to help us on this damned case," Jens said, ignoring Ali's gibes. Ali gave him a nod of agreement as Granger and three other uniforms Jens didn't recognize pulled up beside them, getting out of their ECars.

"Jens, you awkward piece of shit, how are you?" Granger said casually as he stepped out of the ECar. He was a tall man, classically handsome, fit, smart, and had a particularly engaging personality.

"Agent Hantsport, meet Constable Craig Granger, one of the best damn agents I know," Jens said, his comment receiving an exasperated look of Granger. "At least he would be if he ever decided to leave the PPD," Jens said, musing, the two friends laughing as Granger approached and gripped Jens' forearm, a sign of trust in the PPD.

"I like my little slice of heaven," Granger said, turning then to look at Ali. "Besides, we get to have all the fun," he said with a wink as he pressed his arm forward to show her respect. Ali embraced it.

"Great to meet you," she said, her face cleared of all the regrets from the night before, no doubt not wanting to show weakness to the anyone in the PPD.

"Thanks for inviting us to the party," Granger said, giving her a winning smile. "So, what did you do to deserve a punishment like this?" he asked, his head tilting toward Jens and giving a hearty laugh in the process.

"I requested it. You want to be the best—you work with the best," she said, with no hint of sarcasm and never looking over at Jens.

If she had, she'd have noticed the slight surprise on his face. This was the first time he'd heard this version of the story, having assumed this was a punishment for both of them. *Maybe I'm wrong about you, Ali?*

"You got everyone I asked for?" Jens said, looking at the three others with him.

"Two triggers and a disc jockey," he said with a smile to his people.

"A disc jockey?" Ali said, looking around.

"An ironic name the PPD uses for people who work on IT," Jens said.

"A throwback to the glory days of computers, if you will," Granger said, stepping up to a small woman whose Zen watch was a little larger then Jens own, no doubt to accommodate the backup data drives she would need in processing wireless tech.

"Plus, we like to play with all things tech," she added, trying to embrace the nickname her fellow coworkers had given her. "The name's Tia Fields" she said, giving them a warm bow. Her accent suggested she was originally from the Central Stone. Granger introduced the rest of his team as Constable Harold Tong, a bulky man with an athletic build, and Constable Victoria Wilson, a tall woman with piercing green eyes who had the look of someone Jens wouldn't want to mess with.

Constable Tong was clearly on hand to provide protection, although Jens got the distinct impression Constable Wilson might have been a surprise contender. With everyone having arrived, it was time to get the party started.

"Ali, since it was your contact who got us the lead here, you take point," Jens said, noticeably shocking not just Ali but Granger as well. Ali recovered quickly, giving Jens an appreciative smile.

"The building is a small, abandoned warehouse with only two exits save the windows. This should make it easy. The objective is to bring in Anton Preston, aka Ash and Sun. I'll lead the Alpha team with Granger and Wilson through the main entrance of the building, with the Beta team, Jennings and Tong, coming in from the rear. Fields, you'll be the Gamma team. You'll run coms and cover the east windows in case he decides to get tricky," Ali explained smoothly. "Any questions?" When no one spoke, Ali initiated the coms. "Let's do this."

The teams divided up, though Jens managed to give Ali a nod of approval before he ran off with Constable Tong behind the building.

"Everyone in position?" Jens heard Ali through his coms.

"In position," he said after getting an approving nod from Tong, who was tight on his back against the wall.

"Enter on my count, three, two, one," Ali said, finishing as Jens kicked through the back door.

. . .

"Uneventful" would likely be the one word Jens would use on the paperwork when describing the raid on Anton Preston; the prep work took longer than the raid itself.

Anton Preston, aka Ash and Sun, seemed calm, as if expecting their arrival. When the unit had entered the room, Anton had been typing away on his data pad, and not even the sudden burst through the doors distracted him from his work. The oddness continued when rather than putting up any type of struggle, Jens watched in disbelief as Anton calmly raised his hands and dropped his knees to the ground.

All in all, getting to the address and confiscating all his hardware took less than thirty minutes. The only confrontation had been between Anton and Granger, who seemed to know each other. Anton briefly lost his temper, and Constable Wilson retaliated with a short electro-pulse, sending him to the ground. This seemed rather excessive, but Jens kept his mouth shut, enjoying the rather easy collar.

Jens and Ali followed Granger and his team back to the PPD station, where they quickly had Anton set up in one of their newer interrogation rooms. Jens and Ali hung back as Granger and his team got Anton settled.

"Been here before?" Ali asked, noticing Jens glancing around the building as they waited.

"Zone Fifty-Four was my first station after leaving the academy," Jens said with a hint of a smile.

"Shouldn't we be with them?" Ali asked, obviously bored with waiting around.

"Best to let them get him settled. This is their territory, and it goes a long way to not be the hovering agents trying to take the lead," Jens said, leaning back in his chair as if expecting to be there awhile.

Ali laughed.

"What?" Jens said, taken aback.

Ali shrugged.

"I don't know, I guess I wouldn't have expected to you 'sit back.' From what I heard, it's not really your style," she said.

"And what exactly have you heard?" Jens said, his tone even. He'd also heard what people said about him, and although he agreed with some of it, like most things, much was usually drastically overstated.

"Top of your class at the academy, one of the youngest recruits in GIB history . . ." Ali stopped when Jens shot her a look.

"Youngest recruit," he said, correcting her. "And all that's fine and good but doesn't say much about what you heard," he said, almost challenging her to speak.

"Okay, doesn't work well with others, a possible superiority complex, refuses to listen to authorit—"

"Only when they're wrong," Jens said, cutting in. Ali laughed. "You knew all this, and yet you requested me as a partner?"

"I meant when I said I wanted to work with the best," she said.

Jens smiled despite himself.

"And look, the bad guys just let you arrest them," Ali said, giving Jens a pat on the shoulder.

Jens' eyes furrowed at the thought. Something about the whole arrest hadn't seemed right. *Why was Anton so calm?*

"I'm thinking the same thing," Ali said, as if reading Jens' mind. "It doesn't make sense. Why would he just roll over and let us bring him in?" Ali pulled up a Halo, and Anton's information appeared in front of them.

"Look at this, pretty bleak-looking document for a data wizard" she said, using the playful term giving to people who make technology look like magic. "Child prodigy, private schools, then his parents die, and he becomes one of society's children. Then an underground conspiracy blogger?"

"I read through his file. Underground activist, charged for assault on a security guard before he burned down a manufacturing plant. He fits the bill for our warehouse fire and seems like a perfect fit for our perp," Jens said, wishing he'd sounded more confident.

"A little too good, though, right?" Ali said, lowering her voice to a whisper. Jens remained quiet. "I know you think there is something else going on here. He's no popcorn hacker. He's been underground for what? Thirty-five hundred days? All that time, he's left no hits on our data cams. He was a ghost," she said, shutting down her Zen watch and turning to Jens. "Now suddenly he's in one of our cells . . . seems a little too convenient."

Jens sat in silence for a long moment.

"If it hadn't been for your contact in Tkaronto, we'd have nothing," Jens said more to himself than anyone. Something about this was wrong. Jens got up and walked down the hall.

"Where are you going?" Ali said, struggling to catch up.

"Time to start hovering," Jens said, turning to smile at Ali.

15

Anton was relaxed his hands resting calmly on top of the desk, with his wrists wrapped in mag cuffs, a device that magnetically sealed an assailant's wrist together. As Jens and Ali walked in, Anton's hands moved awkwardly as he struggled to lift a glass of water.

"Agents," he said smoothly. Jens took the seat across from him while Ali stood in the corner, her foot propped up on the wall, arms crossed, trying to look as comfortable as possible for someone utterly in the dark.

Jens hadn't told her anything before they stormed in, but he was hoping she would stay quiet, and for now, at least, it looked as if he would get his wish.

"What's your game?" Jens said after a moment's silence.

"I don't know what you're talking about," Anton replied, allowing a hint of a smile.

"Someone like you doesn't just get caught. So, what do you want?" Jens said, slowly trying to spot anything he could in Anton's face but found nothing.

"My hardware, you brought it in, I'm assuming?" he said, ignoring Jens' questions. Jens in turn ignored his. "Of course, you did, it's protocol." Anton's face was disturbed. "You'll find enough information on those drives to finally shed light on Firefly," Anton said, taking another sip of water.

Jens didn't think Anton was insane, so clearly, he believed whatever he was telling himself.

"Who is Firefly?" Jens said slowly.

"I only know it exists, and that Allan Stone is one of its key members. But I don't think anyone knows how deep it goes," Anton said.

"Sounds convenient for you," Ali said from the corner.

"She's right," Jens said, his eyes never leaving Anton.

"I know who you are, Agent Jennings. I know what you've done, and I want you to know that what you did was the right thing," he said.

"I don't . . . ," Jens started to say before Anton rolled on.

"Captain Dooley, it was the right thing to do." Anton said this part so quietly that even Ali had trouble hearing him. The entire time his eyes never left Jens.

Jens didn't say anything, so Anton didn't stop, as if he were reading Jens' mind. "The same way I know about the Enzo." He looked at Jens and winked, leaning back into his chair.

Jens had no way of knowing how he could possibly have known that information. Jens wasn't a fool; he was careful. Even the Dooley information shook Jens, all of it having been swept under the rug, known only internally. He assumed people must talk. *But who talked to Anton?*

"Ali, go check on the hardware data," Jens said, not turning to look at her, too afraid to break his connection with Anton, still smiling at him.

"Sir?" she said, bewildered.

"Now, Hantsport, that's an order." She was about to object but stopped herself. This was lucky for Jens, because he really didn't have any good reason for sending her away. He just knew he needed to be alone with Anton. Ali threw open the door and left the room in obvious frustration. No one spoke until the door closed.

"What are you playing at?" said Jens the moment they were alone.

"You're a good agent. You care about people. That's why I chose you." Anton began settling into his chair.

"What do you mean, chose me?" Jens asked incredulously.

"You think it was an accident your partner got my information. Or that this is your first case back? I needed someone I could trust." His voice was steady and direct, clear. Had he played this moment out already?

"You don't know me," Jens said, flustered by Anton, and hating to admit he seemed to be losing control.

"We don't have much time. You can either stay in the dark or you can be enlightened . . . up to you. But decide quickly," Anton said, looking up at the clock on the wall. Jens sat still for a moment.

"Enlighten me."

. . .

Jens stepped out of the room, his mind racing, still unsure of what had just happened . . . Anton's so-called "enlightenment."

There was no way he could be telling the truth. Even the implication of the information he gave Jens would be . . . unthinkable. Jens had started to believe this case was strange, but this was taking it to a new level. Jens wasn't even sure how Anton could know about the body, but if it turned out to be a murder, then what did that mean about the rest of this case? Had Jens' understanding of the events really been so wrong?

Jens noticed Ali coming down the hallway, her face a mix of confusion and concern.

"I have good news, and I have bad news," she said, trying to sound calm. Jens shook his head. He knew what she was about to say but prayed to whatever entity was out there watching over him that she wouldn't say it.

"The son of a bitch put a burn drive in his system. The moment the tech team tried to start it up . . ." Jens cut her off.

"All the data on the drive was deleted?" he said, not looking at her, his feet continuing forward, Ali struggling to keep up.

His mind was racing now. *What the hell am I supposed to do? What can I do?*

"How did you know?" Ali asked.

Jens was barely able to look at her as he made his way toward the door, desperate for some fresh air.

"Where are you going?" Ali shouted as he was leaving the building.

"I need to check something," Jens said.

"Wait! Don't you want the good news?" Ali shouted, but it was too late; he'd left her stranded in the PPD headquarters. If Anton's intel was accurate, then Jens suspected he already knew the *good news* Ali thought she had. He'd explain himself later, but for right now he needed to check something, alone.

Jens got outside and into an ECar, going over everything that Anton had just told him, trying to sort out what, if anything, he should believe.

Ali's update about the malware in the data files was the first clue. Anton could have been lying, sending Jens on a wild-goose chase, but he had no reason. Anton wasn't a pawn in the game; he was the queen, and by all accounts, he was about to sacrifice himself to the game.

Jens ran over the data log until he found them—the death records of Ryan Lilford. He scrolled through, reading the entire report. Nothing seemed off about it, but he had to see for himself.

Jens felt his Zen watch vibrating. He ignored the call, and a data message popped up. It was Granger.

"I've got good news. Not all the data has been deleted from the file. Some of it is still viable, including a video of Anton outside the warehouse the night of the fire. He also just so happened to be carrying a can of ethanol. It should be enough to convict him on the arson charges."

Jens read the message twice before getting another message from Ali, saying she was going to follow through with the arrest of Anton unless he had anything to add.

There were a few other embellishments, clearly making it known she was not happy about his running off in the middle of an investigation. Jens didn't have time to explain, and even if he did, he couldn't be sure Ali would believe him. *I'm not sure I believe Anton!*

No, he had to do this one on his own, and she could have the collar. After all, Anton did start the fire. He said as much in the interview. It was everything else he'd told Jens that shook him to his core, and Jens would be damned if Anton was going to drag anyone else down with him.

And with this, Natasha Lilford would get what she wanted—Jens to investigate her brother's death. Because if Anton were telling the truth, there was a hell of a lot more to Ryan Lilford's death than a suicide.

"I need to see the body of Ryan Lilford," Jens said, approaching the lanky man who currently stood behind the main desk. He froze for a moment, seeming a little taken aback by Jens' abrupt arrival.

"And you are?"

"Senior Agent Adam Jennings, GIB," Jens said, flashing his watch. "Now I need to see Ryan Lilford's body."

"The GIB? I didn't realize that body was needed for another investigation," the man said, looking nervously around the room.

"Well, he is now, so will you please check."

"Right away, sir," he said, running off into the back room, the swinging doors sending the hint of sterile air into the main room. The harsh odour of bio-rubbers, chlorine, and ammonia attacked Jens' nose.

Jens hated being here, the house of death that held all the early sleepers and everyone not fortunate enough to get their 29,200.

People were meant to go out in style, parties, jumping out of planes, swimming with sharks, a celebration of death on their death day—not end up in here. This place seemed to serve as a reminder that the world was still flawed. All people should live out their days peacefully, every one of them provided income, housing, and food, and yet somehow humanity still managed to find the same old ways of sabotaging itself.

"What's taking so long?" Jens shouted, and a moment later the doors flung open again and the man returned.

"I'm so sorry, but that body has already been through the cremation process. I'm afraid you're too late." It wasn't difficult for Jens to tell he was lying; he was sweating despite the frigid condition of the room. Jens remained silent, quickly assessing the man, looking him up and down, noticing his name tag, Dr. Atkins.

"Why do I get the impression you're lying to me?" Jens said coldly.

"I'm not, sir. It's just his body was scheduled for removal yesterday."

"Listen, Dr. Atkins, I'm going to give you one chance," Jens said, now noticing how Dr. Atkins kept looking back into the cold room.

"You can't go back there!" the man said, though he sounded far from confident, as he attempted to step in front of Jens, but Jens was faster as he pushed his way through the swinging doors.

"You're lying to me, and I want to know why," Jens said, as frustration began to build up inside him.

The first thing he noticed was a body on the slab covered by a white blanket. Jens lifted the blanket. It wasn't Ryan Lilford, Jens knew as he'd he seen a picture in Ryan's file. He covered it back up.

"I told you the body is gone! Now please leave. I'm having words with your captain, Agent . . . ," he said, waiting for Jens to show his GIB ID while he pointed toward the door.

"I know you're lying, and I swear to God when I learn what's going on, you can bet your ass I'll be back here to bring you down, you lanky piece of shit." It was harsh, but Jens felt as if the world around him were unravelling, and from what he could tell, everyone was hiding something. He was tired of it.

Jens waited, hoping that Dr. Atkins might crack, but they were in his world now, so he was much more confident. Jens sighed as he began to pull up his GIB credentials and leave, knowing that the moment he did, he would most likely be fired. He was furious. *What the hell was this? A wild-goose chase set up by Anton to fuck with me. But why? It didn't make any sense.*

Jens' mind spun; he needed to get out of here. That's when he noticed one of the fridge doors ajar. He was about to tell Dr. Atkins but stopped; something seemed off. He looked around at the rest of the room, immaculate, clean, everything in its place. *Why would a guy who clearly cares about the organization of his room forget to close a door?*

"Your fridge door is open," Jens said, turning back around to face Dr. Atkins. It had been slight, but Jens had seen it, a flinch, a sign of distress. *He was hiding something.*

Without skipping a beat, Jens was off, pulling open the fridge door. He grabbed the stainless-steel bed and slid out the table. There in front of him was Ryan Lilford. Jens faced Dr. Atkins, who didn't stand a chance of stopping Jens after he'd made his move. Now he stood defeated, his face a mess of emotions, clearly kicking himself for making such a silly error.

"What the hell is going on?" Jens shouted, looking down at Ryan's cold body. Nothing had been done to fix up the damage on his body, and he would likely have been cremated immediately after Jens had left, had he not stopped it.

Dr. Atkins was trying to mutter something behind Jens, who ignored him. Jens had what he'd come for, but even as he stood over the young man's lifeless body, he was suddenly afraid by what he might find. He had come here to see for himself despite every ounce of his being telling him to run.

Even now, a part of him wished he'd been wrong and that Ryan's body had been destroyed. It would be easier. As Jens folded back the sheet covering Ryan's body and pulled out his left arm, he knew they would be there, just as Natasha and Anton had said. There it was, clear as day, the bruising around his wrists that had been left out of the report.

Jens looked up at Dr. Atkins, who still seemed in shock, unable to put words together, his face draining of colour after seeing Jens expose Ryan's wrists. The man was looking more like one of the many bodies on his tables every second.

"Why wasn't this in the report?" Jens asked, pointing to the obvious discolouration around Ryan's wrists. Dr. Atkins looked as if he might either try to run or vomit. Jens needed to play this smart before the good doctor could think of any more convincing lies.

"Were you paid?" Jens said. Dr. Atkins remained quiet, but eventually he slowly nodded his head. It was taking every ounce of willpower for Jens not to grab the man's skull and bash it in. He didn't have time for these games; he needed answers, and he needed them now.

Jens grabbed his collar, his fist pushing uncomfortably against Dr. Atkins' throat just enough to still allow him to speak. Despite having three or four inches on Jens, it was clear this was not a man built for conflict. It didn't take much threatening for him to roll over and tell Jens what he wanted to know.

"Nothing. I swear I was sent a message telling me what they needed me to do along with credits and a picture of my wife and kids, at home." Dr. Atkins began to cry. "And at school. I swear I don't know anything else."

Jens didn't say anything even as the man began whimpering, clearly shaken up and scared.

"He should have been cremated over the weekend. I planned for my night manager to do it. It should have been taken care of. Is my family in danger now? Are they safe?" Dr. Atkins cried out as he collapsed to the floor. Jens looked at him, almost feeling bad for the man despite his involvement in trying to cover up a potential murder.

"Let me see the data log," Jens said to Dr. Atkins, now crumpled up on the floor.

"I can't—it's gone," he said softly.

Jens pulled up his Zen watch, which got a look from Dr. Atkins.

"What are you doing?" he said, his voice starting to rise a little.

"This is a murder investigation. This body needs to go back to our team," said Jens, completely surprised when Dr. Atkins jumped up at him and nearly knocked him over.

"YOU CAN'T," he shouted, pinning Jens up against the wall. Jens still wasn't in the best shape, but he was stronger than this man. Dr. Atkins had height on his side. His long arms clawed away at Jens' face.

"They'll kill my family! You can't, you can't!" Jens pulled out his electro-pulse and placed it on Dr. Atkins' kidneys, pulling the trigger, sending a brutal shock through his body. Dr. Atkins dropped to the ground, convulsing.

Jens couldn't understand what the hell had happened to him. What would make a man such as him try to attack a GIB agent? As Dr. Atkins' body shook on the ground, Jens saw tears streaming down his face, and he couldn't help feeling a little sorry for the man.

16

"Shit!" Jens said, unsure of what to do next now that he had just electro-pulsed a grown man. *I was defending myself.* The data cams would show Dr. Atkins attacking him, though none of that explained why Jens was even there in the first place. By definition, this was a closed investigation, and even if he said he was doing it as a favour, he now had a tall, crying morgue doctor mag cuffed in the back of an ECar.

"Shit!" Jens cursed again. *What am I doing?*

"If this was some sort of weird cover-up, would that mean that the PPD was in on it?" Jens said, mumbling to himself.

"What are you doing?" Dr. Atkins said between sobs.

"Shut up—I need to think!" he said, turning on the man. It was the PPD's people who found the body. Jens could call Captain Rollins, but she had made it very clear he needed to stay within the lines on this one. *And I'm fairly sure I've just triple-jumped those lines.*

He tried to remember everything Anton had told him, hoping that something new might come up. At the very least, he needed to figure out who he should trust. *Could Ash and Sun be the one behind all this? Is Anton even who he says he is?*

The whole thing was starting to get complicated, making it so much worse when Jens' Zen watch started to vibrate. Ali's name popped up on his screen.

"Shit!" He forgot he had left her alone to take care of Anton at the PPD, and she would likely be looking for some answers, answers he didn't have. He knew he should ignore it, but the last thing he needed was for her to go to Captain Rollins.

"Go for Jens," he said as he placed his ocular pad behind his ear. He didn't need Dr. Atkins listening in on his conversation.

"Help! I'm being kidnapped!" Dr. Atkins started to shout into the pads. Jens knew his voice would be muffled but not completely.

"What the hell was that?" Ali said on the line.

"Long story. What's up?" Jens said, trying his best not to show just how stressed he was. He hadn't realized it before, but his heart was pumping. The heat of the moment was beginning to wear off, and what was left of his anger was quickly becoming a sinking feeling that he was in trouble. At least the doctor had shut up, obviously understanding the principles of the ocular pads' function. He'd resorted instead to crying.

"Well, I'm not sure why the hell you ran off, but after you did, Anton Preston stopped talking with everyone. The funny thing was when I went over the video . . ." Jens didn't think his heart could beat any faster, but the word video certainly helped push it to the max. The last thing he needed was for more people to know what he said. It was odd enough him running around like this.

"What about the video?" Jens blurted out.

"Well, there was some sort of encryption on the recording device." Jens didn't say anything. He had basic ideas of how the tech worked, but this felt beyond him.

"Basically, it means it was hacked. So, there are about seven minutes where only you and he know what was said. Care to explain?" She must have assumed it had something to do with why he ran out on her.

"No," he said bluntly, letting her know it wasn't up for discussion.

"Right, well, it didn't matter, because our tech crew was able to retrieve some of the data lost on the device," she said, her voice showing a hint of pride.

"That's lucky," Jens said. Ali must not have known Granger had already told him about the retrieved data, but he knew what was coming next, because it was what Anton had told him was going to happen.

"Some of the data showed Anton, aka Ash and Sun, in the warehouse with an accelerant. I've already talked with a prosecutor, and it's enough to link Anton to the fire and the murders." She was obviously excited by the news. This was an open-and-shut case and no reason for anyone to think otherwise.

Then again, no one else had spent seven minutes in the room with Anton. Jens couldn't say any of this to Ali, because, like it or not, he didn't know her, and frankly, everything about this was getting a little too weird.

"Jens, you there? I said we got the guy." Ali was clearly looking for a little praise, but Jens was having trouble focusing.

"So, you got everything handled there?" Jens said maybe a little too abruptly.

"Yes, but . . ." Ali was obviously taken aback by his lack of enthusiasm at solving the case. She started to question him but was cut off.

"Good, you take care of things there. I'll be in touch." Hanging up before she could respond, he realized that he gone officially off the rails.

As the ECar drove quietly down the darkened road, Jens still had no idea where he was going. The only thing he knew was that whatever he did next, he needed to be careful.

It wasn't just that he seemed to be breaking too many GIB rules to count, but also that everything Anton had told him seemed to be steeped in truth.

Jens had almost forgot about the crying doctor beside him, he'd grown so quiet.

"What do you know about the man you were paid to dispose of?" Jens said, leaning back in his seat.

"I honestly don't know anything," Dr. Atkins said between sobs. Jens pulled out his electro-pulse and pointed it at him threateningly. He wasn't going to use it, but he was short on time and needed the doctor to start talking.

"Please, you have to let me go," Dr. Atkins said quietly. "You don't understand," he pleaded.

"Help me understand," Jens said, turning to face his captive.

He shuttered his face and began to shake his head vigorously.

Jens thought back to his seven minutes with Anton and how since leaving he'd been accurate about everything Jens would find. He'd admitted to being at the warehouse and to wanting to burn it down. But he'd stopped when he found it hadn't been empty. He told Jens that he'd caught it all on video and how that video would be mysteriously deleted.

Jens wouldn't have believed any of it, if he hadn't brought up Ryan Lilford's so-called "suicide." It had been too random for Jens to ignore and now he was here, holding a man captive because of it. There had been only one other thing he'd mentioned. It can't be.

"Firefly," Jens said almost imperceptibly under his breath. But if he thought the word had been meaningless, he would be wrong as he watched the grown man before him quiver and once again cry uncontrollably.

"They're going to kill me and my family if you don't let me go. It was a suicide . . . why can't you just accept that?" he said, the tears streaming down his face.

"Because Ryan's family deserves to know the truth," Jens said, looking at him defiantly. That's when it dawned on him. "You've done this before?" Jens said, demandingly, and when he didn't reply, Jens held the electro-pulse up to his side. "How many others have you covered up?"

Jens was genuinely angry now, feeling as though the weight of everything he'd discovered was crushing him. When he still had no reply from the doctor, Jens set the electro-pulse to low and pressed it into the doctor's side.

Dr. Atkins screamed in pain as the electric currents ran through his system. If Jens had been off the rails before, he might have just derailed the whole fucking train.

"Who is doing this?!" Jens shouted, as Dr. Atkins let out another cry, only this time the shock never came. Jens simply stared at the man. He had nowhere to go, and he couldn't simply drive around aimlessly all night.

"You know who it is! Firefly," Dr. Atkins said, his voice strained from his cries, but it didn't stop the malice from filling each word.

"But they're not real," Jens said.

"Maybe they are, maybe they aren't. But they pay well, and no one ever comes to ask questions, no one," he said, his eyes meeting Jens.

"I'm the first person?" Jens asked. Dr. Atkins nodded aggressively, clearly afraid he would get zapped again. "Tell me what you know."

"This is illegal!" Dr. Atkins cried out. He wasn't wrong, and Jens knew it. But so was everything else that was going on, and no one seemed to want to talk about it. The only person who would was a criminal. Dr. Atkins was simply following someone blindly, but he must know something. Jens lowered the electro-pulse with a heavy sigh.

"Please, something is going on here, and it's not right. Help me make it right," Jens said, removing the currents from Dr. Atkins' body. Jens was finished hurting this man. He would either talk or he wouldn't, but Jens wouldn't torture him again. After a moment, Dr. Atkins looked over at Jens and nodded.

"I can tell you everything I know," he said, his voice barely above a whisper, but Jens had heard it loud and clear. *Maybe I'll finally get everything I need?*

That was when Jens noticed the massive steel waste collector driving at full speed into the side of their ECar.

It was too late to do anything but brace himself for the impact as the truck smashed into the side of the car, flipping it over. The windows shattered as the car toppled side over side before finally grinding to a halt upside down on the road.

Jens could hear only ringing and the pounding of blood in his ears. He knew he must have been cut somewhere, because he could see the blood dripping down his arm, moving slowly toward his fingers. His body dangled upside down still strapped to his seat.

Looking over, he saw Dr. Atkins, his body completely limp, and he hoped the man was just unconscious. But he didn't have high hopes, seeing that the truck collided with his side of the car, slamming him with the worst of the impact.

Through blurry eyes, his head still rattling, Jens saw a figure reach into the ECar. *Someone is here to help him.*

But he was wrong. As Jens watched, a pair of black-gloved hands gripped Dr. Atkins' neck and snapped it with cool efficiency.

Jens felt powerless to do anything to help. He tried again to move his arm, realizing as the sharp pain shot through it that it was likely broken; blood covered his eyes, making it difficult to see.

"Stop," Jens said, though his voice barely came out as a whisper. Jens struggled in his seat, fearing he would be next, terrified as he watched the black-gloved hands pull away from Dr. Atkins' neck, the hint of a black Zen watch peeking through from under the attacker's jacket sleeve.

Jens tried desperately to escape, blood now dripping freely from his fingers. His one good arm struggled to reach the seat belt. When he finally clicked the release, he plummeted downward, his head and injured arm smashing against the metal roof of the car. The pain coursed through Jens' body as consciousness slipped away.

17

Jens awoke to the rhythmic beeping of machines hooked up to his body. He was unsure of how long he'd been out. All he knew was that his head was throbbing in agony, which seemed only to get worse as his eyes adjusted to the bright lights in the room, sending another flaring pain through his head. He instinctively tried to put his hand on his head, but when it didn't move, he realized his arm had been frozen in place and there was a sling tied around his neck.

Only the slightest twinge indicated his arm had been broken. *I was in an accident.*

Jens' mind began to flood with the events in the ECar, Dr. Atkins beside him, his neck snapped by the unknown assailant. Jens was suddenly aware of his own danger. He tried to make mental notes of his situation; it wasn't the first time he'd broken his arm, although this situation had been a first. Right now, nanobots in his arm would be reopening the tissues and cells in his muscles and using collegenetics to fuse the bones. *Which explains why I can't move. They must have thought I would rebreak the bone if I woke up early.*

As he surveyed the room, he could see a box to the side. He knew his Zen watch and the clothes he'd been wearing were inside. He understood protocol insisted he stay where he was. *What the hell did protocol know about what had just happened to me?*

Luckily, when he tried to move his legs, they worked, so he got up, doing his best to keep his arm in the sling, as his buttocks popped out from beneath his gown when he crawled out of bed.

He began to regret the decision when the room began to spin around him, and even with some freezing, his ribs began to hurt like hell. No doubt at least one or two had broken, and he winced in pain. *Possibly some internal bruising?*

If he stayed tight, the doctors would sort him out in no time. But the doctors hadn't witnessed a rogue waste collector being rammed into them.

The level of technology required to do something such as that was so astronomically high that whoever was behind it would be damn sure not to get it traced back to them.

It had clearly been no accident. Though Dr. Atkins couldn't say much now, Jens suspected he likely never would have, considering Jens had him bound in the back of the car—all things that would surely come back to bite him in the ass. *So much for staying under the radar.*

He moved over to the box. Noticing the condition of his clothes, he saw they wouldn't be better than the gown he was wearing. Some of the feeling was beginning to return to his good arm now, and though he struggled, he managed to pick up his wallet and Zen watch. The rest he would leave for the burners.

Struggling to latch his Zen watch with one hand, he finally managed to wiggle it on and lock it shut using one of the side monitors which light up as he pressed it. It was his data report, with the list of injuries he received from the accident. Reading the list made him want to collapse back in the bed and sleep, but he forced himself to read through until he found what he wanted.

"Dr. George Atkins," Jens said, reading the name out loud, unable to remove the image of the man's neck being snapped in front of him. Jens' eyes settled for a moment on the details of the man's family, his wife, and daughter.

Jens forced himself to remember why he had done what he did, silently hoping Dr. Atkins' family was safe, that his death would be enough to save them. *His death.*

Jens scrolled farther down the document, and according to the assessment, Dr. Atkins supposedly broke his neck on impact. *Lies.*

Whoever had planned this either knew what they were doing, or were so confident with their ability to bury the incident that they didn't feel the need to kill him, too. Either way, it didn't look good for Jens.

He took one last look around the room and noticed a tube of pills on the desk across from the bed. *Painkillers.*

He winced as he snatched the bottle off the table. *They have my name on them, after all.*

He was almost to the door when the nurse walked in, startled to find her once-comatose patient, once in a bed, now standing bare-assed in front of her.

"You shouldn't be up, you need to . . . ," she said, stammering and trying hard to remain calm. Jens stopped her there, not wanting to listen to all the reasons she thought he should stay. He slapped his Zen watch on the data report.

"Adam Jennings, release form," he said, the automated response calling back from the report.

"How would you like to proceed?" it asked in a calming, mechanical, central accent.

"I confirm my release," Jens said, as he hobbled his way past the young woman still stunned by his behaviour. He knew what she had to say, but he would be damned if he stayed here any longer. His list of questions was getting longer, and his list of people he could trust was getting shorter.

Jens wasn't sure if he should be excited or nervous to see Ali walking up the hall to see him.

"Jens?" she called out. Jens attempted to turn around to go back the other way, but it was useless; he was injured and by no means making a hasty getaway.

"What the hell are you doing? You should be in bed," she said, easily closing the gap between the two of them, her eyes shifting down to the Zen watch wrapped around his wrist.

"I was just walking around, stretching the legs," Jens said, looking back and seeing the young nurse he'd pushed past, now standing a little more confidently with a large muscular orderly by her side.

"He's just released himself from the care of the hospital," the young nurse said to Ali. He'd not played this well, and the reality of his situation began to sink in. Outnumbered, and in pain, he had only one option.

"Ali, you don't understand. Something is going on here." His words sounded more like a plea than anything, but at this point he felt screwed.

"Maybe it is, but for right now, Senior Agent Adam Jennings, I'm placing you under arrest for the kidnapping of Dr. George Atkins," Ali said, snatching the pain pills from him, before grabbing his good hand and wrapping it in a mag cuff.

"You're making a mistake," Jens said, flinching as she placed the other mag cuff around his injured arm before locking the two cuffs together. He was just thankful she didn't break the arm again by putting it in the cuff. He wagered he'd feel it when the freezing wore off.

Ali dragged him out of the hospital, and they got into a waiting ECar. *Straight to the GIB headquarters to a waiting seat in front of Captain Rollins, no doubt.*

"What were you thinking?" Ali said when they were finally alone in the ECar. "Do you have any idea how mad Captain Rollins is right now?"

Jens ignored her questions; he was too preoccupied with trying to understand what happened himself. Maybe some of it he could explain, but certainly not all of it.

Someone had killed Ryan Lilford and Dr. Atkins and likely tried to kill him, too. And the only person who might be able to shed light on any of this was currently being charged with arson.

Ali did not seem happy about the silent treatment.

"Why are you so hell-bent on doing everything on your own? You know I'm here to help you," she said as his mind started to come back. He looked at her blankly.

"Sorry, what were you saying?" he said, looking at her for the first time since getting in the ECar.

"For the love of all things holy, I want to help you. What the shit is your problem?" she said, leaning back in her seat, looking out the window. He hadn't noticed it before, but it had started to rain heavily, creating a rhythmic tapping on the car's hood. The sound was soothing.

He was fortunate that Ali had taken the mag cuffs off in the ECar; the freezing agent in his arm was starting to wear off, and he figured soon enough he would be in an immense amount of pain as the nanobots tried to repair again what was just damaged.

"I think the freezing is beginning to wear off," Jens said dryly.

"Bet you'll wish you had these soon," Ali said, smiling as she waved the pain meds in his face.

Jens looked outside, recognizing one of the buildings as they drove by.

"We're not going to headquarters?" Jens asked, turning to look at Ali.

"No, I'm taking you to your house," she said, not bothering to look at him.

"Why? You know that's not protocol," Jens said, looking at her, suddenly becoming more concerned for his life.

"You're my partner, and you got hit by a car—not to mention your ass is hanging out. The least I can do is get you into a good set of clothes before you get your head ripped off," she said, continuing reluctantly while still not looking at him.

"Thank you," he said quietly. "Why did you transfer to Pittsburgh?" Jens said after another few moments of looking at Ali. Jens really hadn't given her a chance before, realizing now he didn't know anything about her.

"I didn't," she said softly almost to herself out the window.

"What? The captain said . . ." Ali cut him short.

"That's what my file says. But the truth is I was forced to relocate." She stopped. This appeared to be all she wanted to say on the matter. Jens sat, uncharacteristically patient, while she chose her words.

"I was helping out on a case watching a small-time drug gang," she said finally as the floodgates seemed to open up.

"It was my job to find out who they were working with and report back. I had planned to do that, but I saw a chance to move in, so I called in a team, and rounded up the gang and four of the suppliers. But one of the guys recognized me. The agency thought it would be safer to get me out of town for a bit. Then this opportunity opened up here." She looked over at Jens, who was suddenly very interested in the fact she'd worked with the cartel in the past. *Was it a coincidence that Ali showed up just after the Scorpions got to town?*

Jens didn't believe in coincidences.

"It's a good transfer. It's a shame you got stuck with me," he said, giving her a light smile. Not much was said after Ali's story. Jens was still trying to understand if it all meant anything.

"I told you already. I didn't get stuck with you." Ali said still peering out her window.

By the time they reached Jens' apartment, he'd decided to give Ali a chance and trust her. *What do I have to lose?*

Jens would tell her everything and would let her decide if she wanted to go down with the ship or get off now. But first he needed to figure out how to tell her without sounding like a lunatic.

They walked into the apartment, and Ali made herself comfortable on one of the sofas in the living room while Jens went back in his room to find some fresh clothes. Neither seemed concerned that his ass had been sticking out the whole time.

"I'm not sure what's going to happen when you take me in," Jens shouted from the other room, "but I wanted you to know that, for what it's worth, you're not terrible."

"Wow, such high praise from the great one," Ali said, mockingly.

"I mean it. You're a good agent. And you're not the worst partner," Jens said, sticking his head out from around the door, giving her a nod.

"Well, I imagine a worse partner would have taken you in ass cheeks and all, ready for the wolves to tear you apart."

"Yes, I imagine they would," said Jens as he donned fresh underwear and the customary GIB blue trousers. Putting pants on had been a much larger ordeal than he had imagined. His arm was throbbing with pain as the freezing wore off. He stood staring at the shirt and jacket he laid out on the bed, not at all confident he had it in him to get the whole uniform on.

The shirt lay there taunting him. The only thing going through his mind was that he would be damned if he was going to spoil the opportunity Ali had given him to present himself with a little dignity.

Jens grabbed the shirt and tripped out into the living room as he tried squeezing his arm through a long-sleeved, white button-down before all of the numbing solution wore off.

His teeth chomped down on his lower lip in pain as he slowly worked his arm in.

Ali watched in stunned silence from her spot on the couch.

"Not one to ask for help, are you?" Ali said, casually pulling out his pain meds from her pocket and tossing them at him.

"Thanks," Jens said, quickly popping one of the pills into his mouth. Well as quickly as one could with one good hand. He took a deep breath, knowing relief would follow soon.

"It was a setup," Jens said, looking over at Ali, trying to gauge her response. None came, and she looked content to simply hear him out.

That was all he needed for the floodgates to open. Jens told her all about his discussion with Anton, leaving out a few of the more "bizarre" details that even he was having trouble understanding. He chose instead to stick to the case in front of them, which was weird enough on its own.

He told her how Anton believed there were people in the PPD who helped cover up the murder investigation and put the blame on him as the arsonist. How he claimed he didn't put in any data virus to wipe out his system, that PPD had wiped out all the evidence he had on them. Jens added in his own doubts about what he could and couldn't believe.

Finally, he told her about Ryan Lilford and how he had to go along to see if what Anton said was true. How Ryan's murder was also covered up with the help of the PPD and Dr. Atkins, and that's why Jens had been there.

To his surprise, Ali just sat patiently and listened, not saying anything until he got to the part about Dr. Atkins.

"Why did Dr. Atkins have marks on his body?" she asked, leaning forward. Jens had forgotten about his momentary lapse of judgment, resorting to electroshocks.

"He was being difficult, and he attacked me. Why?" Jens said, convincing himself that wasn't necessarily a lie. Jens watched as Ali stared intensely at him, likely trying to decide whether she should believe him.

"How much proof do you have about any of this?" she said after a moment, her body relaxing back into the couch.

Jens thought for a moment, realizing he had Anton, who was now in prison, Dr. Atkins, who was dead, and a few other dead bodies that he was positive would be burned up by now. And all their documents would be purged; it was a short and futile list.

"Basically? None," he said, slumping down into the seat across from Ali, his shirt still dangling from his limp arm. For a long moment, Ali simply looked at him.

"Right, well, you said Anton had another copy of his stuff somewhere, which means there is a chance we could find it. Assuming he's not completely trying to fuck with us," Ali said. Her use of the word *us* surprised Jens, having half expected her to put him back in mag cuffs, call him any number of names, and truck him down to a mental health complex. But despite the odds, she appeared to be on his side.

"You believe me?" he said apprehensively. Trusting people was still not in his nature.

"You're my partner. I should give you the benefit of the doubt," she said, lifting his shirt so he could place his injured arm more easily through. "Besides, if you were going to make up a story, I doubt even you could come up with something this messed up. It doesn't seem your style," she said as Jens finally slipped his shirt all the way on, and Ali took the time to button it up for him as well. "And I happen to agree with you. Something about all this doesn't make any sense. It's complicated and yet a little too easy," she added before handing him his sling and retaking her spot on the couch.

"Walk me through what happened at the morgue," she said, pulling out her data pad and scanning. Jens, feeling grateful for the help, wrapped the sling around his neck.

"Why does it matter what happened at the morgue?" Jens could not understand why, after everything he'd just told her, she would be choosing to focus on that.

"You're under investigation for the apprehension of an innocent person with the use of force that led to his death." Her voice remained steady despite the severity of it all.

"What good are you to me if we can't find a way to sort that out before they send you to jail or worse, fire you?" Ali said before putting her attention back on her data pad. Jens watched as she pulled up images on the screen.

Jens had never had anyone be on his side before. He wasn't sure what he'd done to deserve it and was ashamed to admit that had the roles been reversed, he'd never be as forgiving. He realized just how grateful he was that she was.

"Thank you," he said sincerely, realizing it might have been the first time he'd ever said it so genuinely to anyone in his life.

"Don't thank me yet. By all accounts you're still pretty fucked," she said so bluntly that it took him by surprise, making him laugh and causing a sharp pain in his sides. *Damn, I hope these pills kick in soon.*

"Now tell me what happened," Ali said once again.

18

It took the better part of an hour for Jens and Ali to finally arrived at the GIB headquarters, both feeling a little better prepared for Jens' meeting with Captain Rollins. Jens was still a little apprehensive about the whole thing, but he had to admit that with Ali's help, he almost felt as if he stood a chance.

Jens hadn't told Ali everything, and he had some regrets about it, but it was one thing to share information and an entirely different one to spread conspiracy theories.

Maybe he was wrong, but knowing that he wished he hadn't heard some of what Anton had said made himself feel better. Perhaps she was better off not knowing, at least right now.

"Okay, so we've got the data from the morgue," Ali said, taking a deep breath as they stood in the elevator heading up to the bullpen. "Not that it makes you look all that good. The electro-pulse was a little difficult to watch, I admit."

"Is this supposed to be helpful?" Jens said. "I told you I felt bad about that, but he did come after me, and I wasn't exactly in a good headspace."

"Just stick to what we talked about," Ali said.

"You look nervous. I'm the one in trouble here, not you," Jens said and hoped that it was at least a little comforting.

"I took a risk taking you home. She'll know something is up and . .

„
.

"Don't worry, I won't let you go down for this," Jens said, the words seeming to calm Ali, if only a little. "Now you're positive I should bring up Ryan's body? You can't really see the details on the footage." "The important thing is he was hiding the body from you. We've already looked, and he had credits paid in regular intervals from an unknown source. It's enough to think he was up to something. All you need to do is say you got a tip. Just maybe leave out who and where and most of the other details you told me about." Ali finished as the elevator door opened up to the bullpen.

Word had obviously gotten around about the accident and his coming in with his arm in a sling, and a heavy limp must have backed up, to some degree, the rumours going around. Based on their faces, Jens felt as though the story wasn't a good one for him. The sinister smile on Zhang's face amplified Jens' uncertainty.

"Ignore them," Ali said as she led him back toward Captain Rollins' office and knocked on the door.

"Come in" came the captain's voice from the other side of the door. Ali opened the door, and she and Jens stepped in. The captain didn't even look up to greet them. Her eyes darted over her data screen, clearly frustrated by its content as she shut it down and finally peered at them standing there.

"It's you two? Fantastic." Her voice was a little more sarcastic than Jens was used to. "Shut the door and have a seat."

Ali shut the door and took the seat beside Jens in front of the captain's desk. The two of them remained quiet until they were asked a question. Jens knew he would need to play this one right if he planned on getting out unscathed.

"How's the body?" she said, eyeing the sling around his shoulder.

"I'll survive," Jens said as he wriggled uncomfortably in his seat. Looking at Captain Rollins, Jens quickly understood he was not well positioned to receive any form of sympathy from his captain despite her relaxed tone. He was right.

"Then would you mind telling me why the hell you had a civilian, Dr. Atkins, locked up in an ECar?" she said, not quite yelling at him but certainly coming close. He needed to stick to the plan that he and Ali had come up with at the house.

"I was there as a favour to Natasha Lilford, who was asking about the death of her brother. I told her I would look into it. When I found him, the doctor became violent and started to attack me, and I defended myself. I had him in the ECar in order to bring him back here for questioning. It appeared that the documents on Ryan Lilford's death were inaccurate, and I had reason to believe that Dr. Atkins was paid to cover up his murder and make it look like a suicide. Then we . . ." Jens wasn't sure just how much of the story the captain would need, but she ended it there, putting her hand up to stop him.

"What does Ryan Lilford's death have to do with Anton Preston?" she said passively. It was Jens' turn to be confused.

"Sorry, ma'am. Why do you ask?" Jens said, trying to buy himself some time. He wasn't sure how much she knew and didn't want to throw him, or now Ali, under the bus.

"Well, you arrested Mr. Preston, aka Ash and Sun, did you not?" She turned her focus on Ali, now who answered.

"Yes, we found evidence linking him to the fire, ma'am," said Ali.

"But why weren't you there, Agent Jennings? As the senior agent in charge of the investigation, I was surprised to learn that you had spoken with this Ash and Sun and then left for no apparent reason. To go, as we are aware now, to a morgue and assault a doctor because you were doing a favour for . . . a friend?" Her eyes drilled into Jens. Obviously, she'd heard more details than either Jens or Ali had mentioned.

"So would the two of you stop pissing around and tell me what the hell is going on!" she said, slapping her hand on the desk, emphasizing her frustration with them.

"I'm sure you've come up with a pretty good story, considering you were released from the hospital over two hours ago. So do me a favour and just get to the point." *So much for the plan.*

Jens hadn't realized he'd been holding his breath until it all fell out of him in an exaggerated sigh. His head fell into the palm of his one good hand as he raked his fingers down his face.

"Well?" Captain Rollins said, her arms now folded at her chest as she leaned back in her chair expectantly, waiting for them to speak.

"Anton Preston informed me that he was there to burn down the building but didn't when he saw people inside. He told me that he didn't believe Ryan Lilford committed suicide and that he had proof saying how someone at the morgue had falsified documents to cover up evidence that could be found on the body. I went to see for myself, leaving Agent Hantsport in charge of Mr. Preston." Jens watched the captain's face as she played around with the idea for a moment.

"Do you believe him?" she asked quietly.

"I believe he was telling the truth about Ryan Lilford. I saw the body—it wasn't a suicide."

The captain shook her head.

"No, it wasn't," she agreed, taking Jens and Ali by surprise.

"Ma'am?" Jens said, now awaiting his own set of answers.

"Thirty minutes ago I received an email from Ash and Sun with the images from the coroner's office. I had them checked for alterations, but the report said they were authentic," Captain Rollins said.

"That's impossible. We have Anton Preston in custody. There's no way he could have sent you that file," Ali said. The whole room suddenly fell silent.

Was this proof they had the wrong person in custody? Jens had taken his word that he was Ash and Sun after he'd admitted as much in the room. *Was there a chance he was lying? Why would anyone lie about being a criminal? What's the return on that?*

"He could have automated the message. Isn't this guy some sort of genius tech wizard?" Ali said after a moment.

Jens shook his head.

"Maybe, but I'm pretty sure not even a wizard could have timed this out so perfectly," he said, leaning back, his good hand brushing aside his hair. Jens wasn't about to say it out loud, still unsure of where he sat in the captain's eyes in terms of punishment, but something was definitely going on here.

"What else did he tell you, Jennings?" Captain Rollins said, leaning forward.

Jens looked at Ali, who gave the slightest shake of her head. She knew what he was going to say and knew it was a gamble, but maybe they needed a little gamble.

"He said he saw Ryan Lilford in the building, and that he was there meeting with Allan Stone." He blurted it out before he could persuade himself not to.

It was Ali's turn to drop her head in her hands, no question she was having some doubts about putting her trust in Jens.

Jens stayed focused on Captain Rollins and was shocked by her poker face. He had no idea what was going on in her mind but wished he did. *Is she nervously processing the information implicating the city's favourite mayor in this little game? Or planning the best way to tell me to never set foot in the building again?*

"Does he have proof?" she asked, sucking in a deep breath when Jens nodded.

"He claims to have a backup of all his data, and footage of everything," he said slowly, feeling a glimmer of hope that she may just believe him.

"So why don't we have this data?" she asked with a hint of anger in her voice, as if fearing she knew the answer even before Jens spoke. "He doesn't trust us. He believes there are people in the PPD and here at the GIB who work for Stone. He believes there is more to this than it appears." Jens tried to keep his tone neutral but felt very uneasy about how freely the words came out about his fellow agents being in someone's pocket.

"It appears to be a nightmare," said Captain Rollins, getting up from her seat and moving toward the window. "Dammit! Do we trust him?" she said almost to herself.

"Whatever it is he's got, he's prepared to go to jail for it, ma'am," Jens said quietly. Captain Rollins stood quietly thinking as she looked out over the city.

"Nothing!" Ali said excitedly, all eyes suddenly turning to look at her.

"Say that again, Agent Hantsport?" Captain Rollins turned around to look at her.

"Nothing. He isn't asking us to do anything more than our jobs. So far only the three of us and Anton know anything about Allan Stone. But Stone Industries are already a part of our investigations." Ali was starting to build up momentum as her logic puzzle pieced itself together.

"So, we just do what Anton says and follow the threads, which we've already been doing. If he's right, we will find whatever it is we need, and if we don't, then it's on him to either trust us or we leave it alone," she concluded.

It wasn't the best plan, but Jens had to agree it was the path of least resistance. In fact, it was no resistance. Ali's words pinballed through his mind, and try as he might, he couldn't find fault in her logic—it was perfect.

"So, let's just say we do this," Captain Rollins began saying, as much to herself as the others. "We're basically putting a target on our backs if this goes south in any way. I'm not sure about the two of you, but I like my job and would not want to see that happening."

Her statement garnered a collective nod from Jens and Ali, who leaned in, keenly waiting to hear her out.

Jens silently prayed for the opportunity to come out of this unscathed.

"I'll take care of Dr. Atkins' death. It was a shame, but you're right—you had nothing to do with it. It was just bad timing and wrong place, wrong time," Captain Rollins said.

Jens was in utter disbelief at her reaction and nodded his appreciation so as not to jeopardize his sudden change of fortune.

Jens began to feel a little guilty, having opted to neglect telling Ali or Captain Rollins about the mysterious set of hands that broke the neck of Dr. Atkins. As far as they were concerned, his neck snapped in the accident.

Jens wasn't sure why everyone seemed to believe him about the conspiracy behind the death of Ryan Lilford and the bodies in the warehouse. He couldn't bring himself to push his luck. *Maybe I don't need to share everything.*

For all he knew, he was being kept alive because they thought he didn't see anything. If there was a traitor in the GIB, he didn't want word getting around, and possibly getting either of them hurt.

"Who was the constable on the suicide?" Ali said, looking over toward Jens, who was ashamed to admit he hadn't looked it up. *Great question!*

Presumably whoever was on the case was the one in some way or another covering it up. Captain Rollins pulled up a data log and began scrolling through case files before landing on the right one.

"Constable Wilson," she said, as Jens' stomach sank into the floor beneath him. *Shit!*

The warning bells were blaring in Jens' mind as he and Ali shared a gutted look.

"Would someone please tell me what the hell just happened?" Captain Rollins said, having sensed the shift in the room.

"Constable Wilson was one of the PPD constables with us on the raid of Anton Preston," Jens said slowly. Ali was thoughtfully shaking her head.

"She seemed loyal," Ali added, more for herself than the rest of the room.

"Explain to me again why you used PPD to go in after this guy?" the captain said, leaning back in her chair. She was obviously attempting to remain calm with this new knowledge, whilst leaving everyone else on edge with the current line of inquiry.

"I have a friend on the PPD. Technically it wasn't a GIB matter, just a tip. Rather than turn it into a big thing, I called in a favour—we use their resources, since he was in their territory. It was an olive branch. Obviously, hindsight's twenty-twenty," Jens said. Unsure of just where to look, he finally settled on the back wall, unable to meet the captain's eyes.

"If you need to blame someone, blame me," Jens added. *How many times can I dig myself out of one hole, only to get buried in another?*

"Trust me, Jennings, I do," Captain Rollins said with a sigh. "Well, it creates a link, which is good. How well do you trust your person down at PPD?" Captain Rollins asked. Jens was once again surprised by the understanding she was showing.

He had to admit it was a tough question. Inherently it wasn't in Jens' nature to trust anyone. In fact, the last two hours had seen his biggest act of trust with anyone in recent memory.

"I've known him a long time, ma'am," Jens answered, "but honestly, I don't know who to trust right now—present company excluded." He added this last bit more out of respect, but he still didn't know who to trust.

He'd been back only three days, and so far, he'd been dragged through the mud, been hit by a waste collector, and was being investigated for civilian abuse. He knew from experience that none of this was likely to go away any time soon, even with the captain in his corner. Internal investigations would be on him like a hawk, especially with his history.

No, despite everyone's help, he wasn't sure who he could trust now, but so far, Ali and Captain Rollins were his best bets; both seemed to believe his story of what Anton told him. *Why? I'm not sure, just another mystery.*

"Right, well, see if you can't get any information from him about Constable Wilson, but dammit, Jennings, be subtle about it," she said, pulling up her data pad, running her fingers over some files before presumably finding the one she needed. Tapping the document, she fired it over to Jens, who felt a light buzz on his wrist.

"Open," Jens said, happy to have the voice commands on his Zen watch with his arm out of commission for at least the next thirty-six hours or so. "What's this?" he asked, looking at the file displayed in front of him.

"You two still have jobs to do, and one of those jobs is to figure out what the hell Nigel Eriksen was doing with the Scorpions. Those are search requests for his office at the lottery, which reminds me, Jennings . . ." Captain Rollins' eyes fell heavily on Jens.

"Next time you want to try and pull a fast one on the lottery, maybe do me and the rest of us a favour and don't. I've had three calls from people I don't like getting calls from about your tactics," she said, closing down her data screen and signalling the end of their conversation.

"With respect, ma'am, all I did was ask, and they showed us around . . ."

"Dammit, Jennings! I don't care. Frankly, I'm not sure why the hell

I don't just fire you now. The amount of shit you cause isn't worth the trouble. Now get the hell out of my office, and for the love of God, find out what is happening here."

Captain Rollins finished with the two of them, and she buried herself in new files, ignoring their exits.

Ali stood first, giving a polite nod before leaving the room. Jens couldn't help being impressed by Ali's ability to keep her mouth shut and listen—something Jens hadn't picked up on yet. She's going to go far here.

"Why do you keep me around, ma'am?" Jens asked, suddenly wishing he could be more like Ali.

"I'm not here on this planet to stroke your damn ego. Now get the hell out of here," Captain Rollins said, not bothering to look up, as she continued to read over her data pad. Jens turned to make his way to the door, but hearing a deep sigh before he left, he turned to find Captain Rollins with her face buried in her hands.

"Shit! You're a good senior agent, but you need to learn to trust people, or else this world is going to get very lonely very quickly," she said, giving him a wave of her hand. "Now fuck off."

Jens wasn't sure what he'd expected and didn't know what to make of her comment, so he left quietly, turning around to follow Ali out of the office.

Jens was still pondering the captain's comment and barely noticed a smiling Agent Zhang sitting with his feet up on Jens' desk.

"Three days must be a new record for being fired, Jennings" he said, his smile somehow getting even larger.

"Who's fired, Zhang?" It was Jens' turn to smile. "Not me, in fact, if you'll excuse me, I have an investigation to get back to—something you wouldn't know anything about, I'm sure." By the look on Zhang's face, he was more than a little rattled by Jens' jab. Clearly, he'd been under the impression Jens would have no chance of surviving this one. Flustered, Zhang stood up, getting so close to Jens' face that Jens could have given a detailed description of the man's lunch.

"I'm not sure what kind of horseshoe you have shoved up your ass, but your time is coming, you arrogant piece of shit."

The last words came out more as a hiss as he bumped past Jens, intentionally aiming for his wrapped arm. Shooting pain went up Jens' arm into his chest.

Jens winced from the pain, silently thanking Ali for the pain meds. He turned, unsure of what he was going to say, but knew it wouldn't be good. That's when he noticed Ali, with stunning accuracy, kick Zhang's back foot as he walked past. His one foot now entangled with the other, and the momentum of his stride carried him forward as his body tumbled heavily to the floor. His cry echoed throughout the bullpen.

Ali was the first to laugh, but soon, everyone was laughing as Zhang struggled to get himself off the floor as quickly as he could, meeting Ali's eyes with a devil's stare.

"You better watch out, Hantsport. You're on a sinking ship. Don't let that son of a bitch take you down with him," Zhang said, venom dripping from every word. Ali met his glare unflinchingly.

"Tuck your shirt in, Zhang. It's embarrassing." She laughed as she looked him up and down. "Ready?" she said, turning now to Jens and walking toward the elevators before he could even answer, leaving Zhang embarrassed, looking around the room and quickly tucking in his shirt.

But the damage had been done. Zhang had been humiliated, which meant the lines had been drawn, and it was clear to Jens that Ali was on his side.

Jens got the satisfaction of watching Zhang hurry across the room to the washroom, his hair still dishevelled from the fall and his hands still tucking frantically at his waist.

As Jens looked over at a still-smiling Ali, he felt for the first time as if things were looking pretty good for him.

19

Jens and Ali were still laughing about Zhang's little mishap when they reached GLF headquarters. They were unsure of what to expect walking into the imposing atrium of the head office as Jens felt a buzz on his wrist. Ali must have felt it, too, as the ID badge and information for their fresh-faced new greeter, who wielded an approachable, yet cautiously guarded, smile, appeared on Jens' Zen watch. He'd barely had time to glance at it before they approached.

"Hello, I'm Chris. I'll be . . ."

"Our chaperone?" Jens offered.

"So to speak," Chris said as they read over the data file in front of them. "I have been authorized to take you to Nigel Eriksen's office to have a look around. We do not have authorization to access his computer or its contents, though I'm told all necessary documents have already been copied and will be provided to you. Any questions?" Chris said, looking between Jens and Ali.

"What happened to Charlie?" Ali said.

"Who's Charlie?" Chris asked.

"Guess that answers that." Jens smirked "Lead the way, Chris."

Chris, a little confused, led the way toward the elevator, though thankfully was not nearly as chatty as their previous host.

Nothing but a few shared looks between Ali and Jens occurred on the walk, and even the elevator ride seemed to take longer. *He might have been annoying, but least Charlie knew how to make time pass.*

"I see you've had the chance to go through the office," Jens said as the group stepped into the now-immaculate-looking room.

"We've had the room cleaned, of course. All Mr. Eriksen's things have been left as they were," Chris said, clarifying.

"So just all the information he was working on with the lottery has been moved?" Ali asked.

"All classified documents pertaining to the Global Lottery have, of course, been removed. You can understand our predicament," Chris said as they began typing away on their data pad. *I guess they're no longer interested in us.*

"Yes, I'm sure whatever Mr. Eriksen was working on had nothing to do with why he was burned to death in a building," Jens mumbled under his breath, catching a smirk from Ali.

"Sorry, what?" Chris said, looking up from their screen.

"Nothing," Jens said as he looked around, noticing that a couple of the sticky notes on the desk had been tossed away. *Final links to what he'd been working on, no doubt. How the hell can we be expected to do our jobs like this?*

Jens looked over at Chris, who was busying away on their data pad.

"See anything?" Ali said, looking through the shelves. Some paperback books and an e-frame with images of Mr. Eriksen's family were scrolling slowly past her.

"Nothing," Jens said. "Excuse me, Chris?" Jens said, looking at Chris in the corner. They stopped typing for a moment to look up, annoyed by the interruption. The friendly greeter had disappeared. They didn't say anything, just stared at Jens waiting for more information.

"Can you override the data log so we can see what Mr. Eriksen was working on before he died?" Jens asked, tapping the shiny black sphere on the desk. Chris didn't even bother looking down at it.

"No, I can't. As I said, I'm not authorized to do that. And even if I were, only senior management has the ability to override an individual system," Chris said, going back to whatever they were working on. Jens knew that last bit to be a lie. *Obviously, Chris is smarter than some of their other companions.*

"Can we bring someone from senior management in to do it?" Jens said to Chris, who looked up, once again annoyed.

"No need," said a high-pitched voice coming from the doorway. Jens turned to see the woman who was clearly important enough for Chris to drop what they were doing and give her their full focus.

"Angela Choi, head of Global Lottery West. I believe we've met before, Agent Jennings and Agent Hantsport." Her confident tone reminded Jens immediately of the woman who'd kicked them out on their last escapade through the lottery headquarters.

Mrs. Choi's eyes narrowed on Jens, giving him the impression she was always trying to be one step ahead. Jens tried unsuccessfully not to feel insecure and inadequate compared with the woman in front of him.

As Mrs. Choi tapped the data pad on her Zen watch, a catalog of files popped up in front of her. She scrolled through them, her finger finally resting on the one she needed.

She flicked her finger toward Jens and Ali, who promptly received a buzz on their own wrists.

"No need to access the data pad, as we have already sent over all the proof you will need. It turns out Mr. Eriksen had in fact been using the lottery to funnel credits through our system. He was doing a fairly good job at it, too, which is why we were unable to catch him at the time. Clearly, it just got away from him," Mrs. Choi said with zero hint of emotion in her voice at the death of her colleague.

Jens didn't bother looking at the file, noticing Ali had already opened and started reading it. *No doubt, every page of it was just what we need to put Mr. Eriksen's guilt to rest.*

"Any reason why?" Jens asked, trying to get a sense of the man, not the problem.

"Credits, adventure, does it matter? The point is he was doing it, and it proves why he was there and what he was doing," Mrs. Choi said, her eyes meeting Jens', and for a moment her dark eyes remained unflinching.

"Something doesn't add up," Jens said quietly, looking around the room again, painfully trying to spot something he knew wouldn't be there.

"I thought you didn't know his motives," Mrs. Choi said with possibly a hint of interest. Perhaps she was interested in solving the mystery of how her employee died.

"Not his, the cartels," Jens said casually.

"He owed them more credits than he could get his hands on. Best guess they got mad and killed him," she said, her voice still oddly calm for someone who just discovered mass corruption and the death of her colleague.

"Then burned themselves down in a building?" Jens said mockingly.

"I thought you'd already arrested someone for burning down the building?" Her tone was a little harsher than before, obviously surprised by Jens' candor.

Jens ignored the tone, more stunned by her knowledge of the case.

"Where did you hear that?" Jens asked, looking toward Ali, whose brows had shot up, as she was clearly thinking the same thing.

"News is a commodity we enjoy staying on top of, especially when it pertains to one of our own," Mrs. Choi said evenly.

"None of this explains why . . . ," Ali started to say.

"I'm not an agent, and I wouldn't try to tell you how to do your job. All I can do is try to help. That's why we here at the Global Lottery have done our best to be cooperative." Her statement came off like a news release.

"Now if you'll excuse me, I have work I need to do. Chris, if you wouldn't mind showing the agents out." And with that, she turned on her heel and exited the room, leaving Jens, Ali, and the not-so-lovable Chris alone once again. Chris' head immediately dived into their work on the data pad. *I wonder if losing Charlie had doubled their workload.*

After another minute of worthless meandering, Jens was itching to get out of there. The introduction to Mrs. Angela Choi made it clear enough to him that this place wasn't going to be very generous with its insights into the death of Mr. Eriksen.

As they walked through the open-concept office, with its multitude of screens all displaying various numbers flickering by in constant flux, Jens couldn't help thinking that despite all the action in the room, all eyes were on them—although only a couple of people dared meet his eyes, giving him his last, stupidly brilliant idea for the day.

"I know you're all busy," Jens said, stopping in the center of the room, everyone turning to look at him and Ali. Even Chris stopped what they were doing looking shocked.

"I'm Senior Agent Adam Jennings with the GIB. We're looking into Mr. Eriksen's death and would love some help understanding the man." Jens looked at Ali, giving her a wink. She was the only one not surprised—after her day, how could she be—and had a smile despite shaking her head at him.

"We would just like to get a sense of the man and understand why he would have done what he did. Clearly all of you know by now of his . . . transgressions . . ."

Jens was immediately cut off by a high-pitched shout by Mrs. Choi from an office down the hall.

"Agent Jennings, we have been more than helpful in your case, and I assure you our internal team continues to be vigilant on this, but if you would please stop distracting my employees, we have a business to run," she said from the other side of the room.

Jens looked down at his Zen watch, and with a click, he sent his details to all watches in the room, a special tech to allow agents to hand out mass contact details to any number of people at one time. *Maybe one of them will reach out anonymously.*

It might be a waste of effort, but he had a sneaking suspicion that some of the people who couldn't even look at him knew more than they were letting on. *Hopefully one of them would have some courage.*

The action, however, did little for Jens' relationship with Mrs. Choi, who currently stood red-faced and angry.

Chris, who perhaps could feel their job on the line, practically shooed them down the hall toward the elevator and didn't stop until they were entirely out of the building.

"I hope you have everything you need for your case and might I add so boldly that we do not see you again," Chris said with a smile before turning to head back inside.

Ali and Jens stood on the side of the street, Ali flagging an ECar while Jens pulled up the file from Mrs. Choi and began reading it.

As he suspected, it was perfectly processed, with all its crossed t's and dotted i's, but that's where the problem was. How could someone go over eighteen hundred days under the radar of a company that now had meticulous records of his transgressions? No one was that clever.

"Pretty ballsy stunt you pulled there, Jens," Ali said as she pulled the door to the ECar open, letting Jens hop in; Ali followed.

"It's our job to understand why. 'Facts,' or at least the way they're presented to us, don't always make sense. It's not always about what people do, but why they do it," Jens said, shutting down the data pad and looking over at Ali. *All I did was cast a few lines; all I need now is a nibble.*

"You look worried," Jens said.

"You're not?"

"In my experience, most people are not helpful. They tend to have something to hide that they don't want people to find out. So, I find that generally, when they are trying to be 'helpful,' people tend to either make something disappear or add things to distract you from finding the truth. Follow?" Ali nodded along in understanding, patient enough to let Jens continue—one more thing Jens admired about her.

"This document paints a great picture of what Mr. Eriksen was doing, and how he was doing it. He is clearly guilty of a crime, and we would be well within our rights to close this case up, and nobody would blame us for that." Jens looked closely at Ali trying get a sense of what she was thinking, but she remained silent.

"What it doesn't tell us is why he did it. He had a happy life, a loving family, so why would he risk it all to get into laundering credits? It doesn't make sense, not with the information we have. That means one thing to me," Jens said, assuming that Ali knew where he was heading, and now was the time to voice her concerns. To his delight, Ali remained steadfast in her silence.

"This is the second time a big corporation has come out and handed us everything we apparently need to solve our crimes. That seems a little too convenient to me."

"I was thinking the same thing." Ali sighed. "Things are about to get complicated," Ali said as she started to giggle.

Jens began to join in. Eventually the laughter subsided, leaving Jens with only one thought on his mind. *Have we both just gone mad?*

20

Four hours of sleep were all Jens could manage, despite double-dipping into his pain meds. He'd struggled to calm both his mind and his body for very long.

In the end he'd simply called it quits despite his alarm being set for hours after he woke.

"Play music," Jens said as he winced to stand up, his arm still braced tightly to his chest.

The music was much more upbeat than he was feeling, though he suspected that was on purpose.

He managed to get himself ready in less time than he expected, given how long it had taken him the day before. His arm was still being a hindrance, though manageable, as he slid it through the blue suit jacket before strapping it back up. *Must be getting better.*

He was surprised to see his Zen watch lit up this early in the morning and more surprised that he'd had two missed messages.

"Play messages."

"From Agent Hantsport: Jens, PPD has officially charged Anton Preston with the warehouse fire. I gave support to proceed. Without anything new, I don't think we can stop them or that we should. I know it should feel like a win, but it's bittersweet. We can talk about it in the office, and I wouldn't worry. I'm sure it's all just a formality. Message complete." Jens didn't know what to make of that last bit, but didn't have long to wait as the second message played.

"From Captain Rollins: Jennings, Chief Constable Furland has requested you and Agent Hantsport come in this morning nine sharp, for a meeting. They wanted to discuss the warehouse murders. I don't think I need to tell you how important it is that you don't fuck this up. So do what you need to—when you get in this morning, you have a good head on your shoulders. End of message."

"Good thing I'm so well rested," Jens said jokingly as he stared at himself in the mirror and pulled the bags down from under his eyes. "Coffee." He sighed.

Jens actually managed to have a nice morning, finding a new coffee place on his walk, and was even surprised to find the ICER hadn't been delayed.

The city was peaceful as he strode through the nearly empty streets, giving him ample time to commiserate over the events of the last few days.

He knew he should be happy; since he'd been back, they managed to catch an arsonist and a thief, and six members of a dangerous drug cartel were no longer on the streets of Pittsburgh. But somehow, he still managed to feel robbed of the truth—that all their so-called great work was a lie.

What great work had he really done? Someone served this up to us on a silver platter. Begging the question, who and why?

Jens took his time getting to the GIB headquarters, giving himself the space to wallow in self-pity while he could. He knew that the moment he stepped into his meeting with Chief Furland, he would need to have his wits about him.

He was beginning to feel almost normal as he kept a good clip up the sidewalk toward the main entrance of the GIB headquarters when his Zen watch began to pulse. Thinking it was Ali, wondering where he was, he slipped on the ocular pads and answered, immediately regretting it.

"Did you see him? Did you?" It was most certainly not Ali's voice he heard, but that of Natasha Lilford, sounding more than a little crazed and frantic. Jens desperately wanted nothing more than to hang up and ignore it.

"What are you talking about?" Jens replied, knowing exactly what she was talking about.

"He's dead! But you knew that because you were with him." Her breath was heavy over the line. She must have just read the article about the car crash and the death of the good Dr. Atkins.

"You saw Dr. Atkins! I know you did, which means you saw my brother. I told you! I told you he was killed." There was a hint of vindication in her voice, which was muffled between sobs. "Why didn't you tell me?!"

"Look, I can't talk right now, but I'll get in touch with you later today," Jens said, knowing he wasn't able to say the things she wanted him to say. Not right now. "I promise I will be in touch," he said.

"But there is something I need . . . ," she began to say, but Jens disconnected the line before she could argue. He was looking into it, and she would have to trust him. And had he not been rushing into a meeting with the chief constable, he might have taken the time to try to explain that. But as it was now, he didn't have the time.

Jens made it up the stairs with a minute to spare with both Captain Rollins and Ali already there waiting for him.

"Dammit, Jens, you're cutting it a little tight, aren't you? Chief Furland is not someone you want to piss around with. They run a tight ship, and please, for the love of God, don't . . ." Captain Rollins wasn't able to finish her thought as the door swung open, and Chief Sandy Furland stepped through. They were large, not just in girth but in height, as they stood at nearly six feet five. Their mountainous frame and stern but relaxed expression looked intimidatingly down over all of them, though Jens was taken aback by their high-pitched voice, which cut through the air, a little more singsongy than Jens would have ever imagined.

"Welcome, I appreciate you all coming in to see me this morning on such short notice," Chief Furland said, greeting them, as Jens caught the slightest hint of a smile tucked away in the side of their mouth. *Maybe a good sign?*

Jens had never been introduced to the new chief, as they'd arrived during his suspension. But Jens immediately understood why they were sitting on the other side of the table and not him.

"Captain Rollins, a pleasure to see you again," they said, putting their hand out in greeting as Captain Rollins accepted it, giving them a slight nod of additional respect.

"You must be Agent Ali Hantsport, which makes you Senior Agent Adam Jennings," They said, giving a nod to Ali and Jens in turn, and both again remained obedient and quiet.

"I'm Chief Sandy Furland, Agent Jennings," they said, taking a seat in the large leather-back chair.

"We've not had the chance to meet, as you were suspended for . . ." Chief Furland looked at their silver Zen watch and made a show of reading a file of which they most certainly knew the contents.

"Attacking the former chief of the GIB," they said, appearing to bait Jens into a response.

"Allegedly, Chief Furland," Jens blurted out. He could see Captain Rollins shake her head, no doubt wishing he possessed Ali's skill of remaining quiet.

"Of course, alleged," Chief Furland said, gesturing for the three of them to take a seat and leaning back, resting their hands on their chest. "All that's in the past, and as we have seen, you've certainly not lost your touch," they said, praising them all with a full smile.

"It was a team effort, Chief Furland," Jens said, signalling to Ali beside him.

"So not a bad week for your team, Captain, capturing an arsonist, murderer, and a thief. All in record time, I might add. I would say you've got yourself a crack team." Chief Furland chuckled as they seemed to be the only one relaxed in the room.

"Thank you," Captain Rollins said, looking apprehensively to her team as if they might jump in at any moment and ruin the it all.

Jens had to admit, he was starting to get a little uncomfortable and not just because the seat was so unbearable. He knew he should sit quietly and take the praise, but it didn't feel right. They all knew there was more to this story than met the eye.

Jens tried desperately to ignore the conversation, and instead focus on the room around him, trying to get a sense of his new chief, though it wasn't much to talk about.

It was still more or less empty and entirely ordinary. The perfectly square room seemed to give nothing away, leaving the chairs as the only thing left on which to focus.

Would the chairs have been less comfortable if this were a lashing and not congratulations?

"You all right, Agent Jennings?" Chief Furland asked, leaning forward in their chair.

"Yes, Chief Furland, I'm just . . ." *Dammit, just say it!* His mind's eye looked over at Captain Rollins, picturing her giving him the death stare.

"Nothing, I'm sorry, bad sleep last night. The accident did a number on me," Jens said, not entirely lying. He was in discomfort from the accident, and he was still working through his pain meds, but right now it was hardly the problem. He needed to end this meeting and tell Ali and the captain about Natasha and her call.

"Right, well, I'm sorry you had to go through that. I've read the report submitted by Captain Rollins, and it sounds like a terrible accident," the chief said, emphasizing the word *accident* at the end, which seemed to encompass their high level of political prowess. "I just wanted to say good work and finally put some faces to the names," they said, standing up as a signal for them all to leave. "I suppose I should let you all get back to doing such great work and thank you for, indulging me, this morning."

Jens let out an inaudible sigh and turned to make his way for the door.

"Thank you, Chief Furland. It was great to meet you," Jens said politely before turning toward the door—although he barely had a chance to turn the handle when his Zen watch began to vibrate.

Jens' stomach sank as he turned around to see his wasn't the only watch that had gone off. Jens was the last to look down, though the only one likely to recognize the distraught face of Natasha Lilford displayed on the icon.

21

"I told them he was murdered." The room filled with a voice that Jens recognized immediately as Natasha Lilford's. It had been Chief Furland who'd opened up the data screen first.

Jens pulled up his own display, seeing the image of Natasha Lilford sitting in a comfy chair along with images of Dr. Atkins, Ryan Lilford's dead body, and the falsified autopsy reports signed off by Dr. Atkins.

"But they wouldn't listen to me," she said, continuing. "I saw the body and the marks, and the coroner at the time told me it was normal. He lied to me. He was trying to cover up my brother's death, and I want to know why."

"Who was the doctor who told you it was normal?" asked an anonymous voice that was much more calming, contrasting with Natasha's hysteria.

"Dr. Atkins, who was recently killed in a car accident, or at least that is what they are calling it. I don't know what to believe anymore." Tears continued to fall down Natasha's face as Jens began to fear just where all this was heading. *So much for all that praise.*

"This is being streamed on all open networks," Ali said, her head gesturing to the people in the main office, who appeared to be watching the same thing.

"How far can they stream this openly?" Jens asked quietly, but Ali only shrugged.

"Who did you tell about your brother?" the stranger asked innocently, though to Jens it felt more like a dagger being slowly pushed into his chest. *Why the hell did I hang up the damn phone?!*

"Senior Agent Adam Jennings with the GIB, he was in the car with Dr. Atkins when he died," she said, now looking directly into the feed as if she must have known Jens was watching. *Son of a bitch!*

"None of this should be common knowledge," Jens whispered to Ali, as Ali stuck him with an elbow, fortunately on his good side, as she pointed to the bottom of the data screen.

Jens felt as though he might vomit after reading the source of the stream. Yet there it was clear as day in front of him—the streamer was Ash and Sun. *How is that even possible?*

"I've already checked. He's still in custody—he's not the one streaming this," Ali whispered in his ear as if she'd been reading his mind.

Jens didn't bother listening to the rest of the interview, as he shut down the data screen and mentally prepared for the barrage of questions that was sure to follow, already knowing he would have zero answers.

When it finally ended, everyone including Captain Rollins was silent, everyone waiting for Chief Furland, though they, too, seemed content to let the air around them still.

"How much of this is accurate, Sergeant?" Captain Rollins ventured to say as, after a moment, it was clear the recording linked to a page that seemed programmed to loop the video on its private site.

"That's what I was attempting to find out, Captain, but for the moment . . . all of it," Jens said quietly. There was no point in hiding anything now that he was in so much hot water that he could boil a lobster.

Ali, who Jens had regrettably kept in the dark as well, seemed distracted as she busily typed away on her data screen. *Probably trying to find the best way to separate herself from this situation before it came back to destroy her career, too.*

"When were you planning on telling us?" Captain Rollins asked, crossing her arms and pulling herself up to her full height.

"I spoke with Natasha on my first day back. She was trying to get someone to help her find her missing brother. I gave her my card and a name at the PPD who could help and told her we don't normally deal with missing persons. She thanked me and left." It was easy once he'd started to tell them all about the following encounter with Natasha after discovering her brother's body. How she believed he'd been murdered. Then about the conversation with Anton Preston, aka Ash and Sun, and how he informed Jens that Ryan Lilford's body wasn't a suicide and how since then he'd being trying to figure out exactly what to do next.

The room was silent after that. Chief Furland, who hadn't even appeared to be listening to Jens' story, shut down the data screen and stared at Jens. Their face was a granite slab, as they paced back and forth, neither Ali or Captain Rollins saying a word for fear one of them might fall into the path of hell that was surely heading Jens' way.

"So . . . Ash and Sun, aka Anton Preston, is in jail for arson," Chief Furland finally said, getting a nod from both Ali and Jens. "He is also broadcasting a rather embarrassing story about the GIB across Pittsburgh and possibly the entire Global West?" they said, nodding toward the glass windows that now revealed numerous people throughout the office watching the clip on their own data screens. *It had been a larger hack.*

Jens couldn't help noticing the number of eyes glancing their way despite the hideaway windows preventing anyone from the outside seeing in.

"Correct," Jens said uncomfortably.

"Do you understand, Agent Jennings, that this organization can function well only if we know all the facts in order to prevent fallout like this?" Chief Furland asked in a tone clearly not meant for a response, and yet Jens couldn't help himself

"I do, but with respect, I've been back for three days, and a convicted felon told me an outlandish story that would likely have gotten me laughed out of my position. I needed more proof before I brought it up with anyone. I felt it was the responsible thing to do," Jens said, leaving out that he had shared the information with Ali so that when he was inevitably fired, she could deny everything. *I owe her that much.*

"He shared the knowledge with me as well, Chief Furland. I was the one who helped understand what happened during the accident. I admit I don't know anything about Ms. Lilford, but I suspect if Agent Jennings did find the proof he was looking for, he would have immediately gone through the appropriate channels," Ali said, as Jens only stared blankly at his now-soon-to-be ex-partner.

She could have been safe, and now she was throwing her towel in with him. The captain looked as though she might say something but waited. Chief Furland still paced the room slowly, though Jens found it disturbing how calm they appeared.

"What you both need to understand here is that this is unacceptable behaviour. You just can't go around investigating on your own, especially not on our time. The shitstorm you've dropped on us isn't about to go away any time soon, and you've put me in a difficult position. Despite my deep desire to do so, I can't fire you." Jens and Ali each let out an audible breath.

"Oh, please don't underestimate just how deep a desire that is, but not now, after they've called you out on a national broadcast. Even if I wanted you gone, the people would have my head. This is clearly an attempt to undermine our system and play on the people's fears," Chief Furland said.

"Throwing you off the case now would land us with a shitload of difficult questions to answer," Captain Rollins added absently. *Had that been the point of this little stunt? Could someone be trying to manipulate things for me?* "I need you to be honest with me, Jennings. Is any of this true? Is there a cover-up going on, and was this boy's body somehow involved?" Chief Furland looked desperately at Jens,

who suddenly realized this was likely not something the chief wanted so early on in their position.

From what Jens knew of Chief Furland, they'd had a long and difficult career to get here, and now it was in falling to shambles. Jens couldn't help feeling bad for them. More than anything, he wanted to say no, but everyone answered to someone.

"Yes. There is a high possibility there is more going on here than we are being told," Jens said as Chief Furland's head sank low, as they collapsed back into their chair. For what felt like an eternity, nothing was said.

"Obviously this is not what I wanted for my first one hundred fifty days," they said with a sigh. "Like you, Agent Jennings, I haven't always been the most popular with my superiors, though I can confidently say I've never found myself in a mess like this," they said, giving Jens a curious look, before peering out the window for what seemed like an eternity.

"I'm going to regret this, but I want the two of you to continue to look into this, secretly. You report only to Captain Rollins and me. No one else on the GIB is to know what you're up to. Do I make myself clear?" Chief Furland said in a low, conspiratorial voice, as if anyone in the building could hear them. "You've all but tied my hands on this one, and from where I'm sitting, the only way out of this mess is to barrel straight through. We seem to be caught up in a game of chess, and up till now, there has been only one player making moves.

I suggest you figure out who that is and quickly before we all find ourselves out of a job."

Jens hated the idea of being a pawn in someone else's game, though Chief Furland was right—someone did seem to be moving the pieces around them. *Still, better to be in the game than not playing at all.*

Jens looked to Ali, now silent as ever. She didn't appear to have received the memo about this being a difficult task; she grinned from ear to ear—the naivety of youth.

"Now, get the hell out of my office, and for the love of God, I hope you're all wrong about this." They finished with a definitive turning of their chair. The meeting clearly was over.

Captain Rollins, Jens, and Ali left the office not saying a word until they'd reached the elevator.

"I hope you know what kind of shit you two just put us in," Captain Rollins said as they stepped onto the elevator. "Agent Hantsport, wipe that stupid grin off your face. You just put a target on your backs in the office. I suggest you avoid the bullpen and take the afternoon to regroup. Your lives are about to get complicated," she said, as the elevator stopped on their floor.

All eyes in the bullpen shot toward them as Captain Rollins stepped off. She turned back, took a deep sigh as if to say more, but decided against it. She let the doors close, with Jens and Ali still onboard heading for the main lobby.

For a moment the silence lingered, before Ali prepared to speak. Jens held up a finger to stop her, his eyes flicking to the data cams in the corner. Ali wanted to protest, but at another shake of his head, she stopped. They got off and kept the silence until they reached the street.

"What was that about?" Ali asked, still looking confused.

"You don't understand, do you? We've just been entrusted to root out whoever the hell is covering this up!" Jens said, with a slight frustration in his voice at a still oblivious-looking Ali.

"Yes, I know, and it's a good thing. Why are you acting like it's not?" she said with an edge to her voice.

"Because I've done this before, and trust me, you don't make friends. Whoever is covering this up is powerful. Powerful people have powerful friends. We go about this the wrong way, well, let's say two hundred days might be lucky."

Jens stating the facts seemed to bring Ali back down to earth. The high of the project quickly lost its steam.

"It's a lonely job looking into our own. You're sure you're up for it?" Jens asked, looking at his young partner.

"Do I have a choice?"

"All we ever really have are choices," Jens said.

It had been only a few days, but Jens was really starting to like her. She was resourceful and eager, all the things he used to be. But he knew what that type of attitude got people and unfortunately it wasn't friends.

"I'm in," Ali said confidently.

"Good, well, first things first. We never talk about the investigation in the building—too many cams. We meet outside and go in to talk only with Captain Rollins or Chief Furland, understood?" Ali nodded. "Good. I want you to go look into Nigel Eriksen's theft accusations and find out what exactly he was doing, and if he was making credits, where the hell was it going?" Jens said, feeling a sudden rush of excitement at the act of giving out orders.

"Got it. What are you doing?" Ali asked, the thrill of the job rushing back to her.

"I'm going to the PPD. I need to talk with Granger about Constable Wilson and find out why he never talked with Natasha Lilford," Jens said, remembering Natasha's comment about going to the PPD. It had been Granger Jens had sent her to, and he wondered why he hadn't helped her. Secretly, though, he also wanted to speak again with Anton Preston.

"Jens," Ali said, stopping him before he could run off. "If I'm going to trust you on this, I need to know you're being honest with me. I want to trust you, but so far all you've done is lie and keep things from me. I'm running out of reasons to stick around."

"Why are you sticking around? You could have gotten out and no one, including me, would have blamed you," Jens said.

"Because nothing seems to add up here. I can see that, and I want to know what's going on as much as you do. But dammit, Jens, how am I supposed to be an effective partner if you don't tell me what's going on?"

Jens knew she was right. He'd kept her in the dark for so long, but right now there were still too many unknowns—such as how Ash and Sun are broadcasting that video and who was interviewing Natasha. But one thing bugged him more than all that, and for that he needed to talk with Anton, alone. *Because, if I'm a pawn, what did that make Ali?*

"I understand, and right now you know everything I do. I promise," Jens said, lying and feeling a wave of guilt wash over him as he did so. But he squashed that down quickly. *This is for the best.*

"We will meet up tomorrow," Jens said, finishing and turning to leave, but Ali grabbed his arm, stopping him again.

"I can't tomorrow," she said quietly, which took Jens by surprise. *Only a few minutes ago she was excited, and now she can't even meet?*

"Why not?" he said, not hiding his disappointment at his partner's sudden change in mood.

"I've had the day booked off since I joined. I have things I need to do," Ali said, not looking at all like her confident self. Whatever it was, the thought of it had somehow changed her.

"What?" Jens said, pressing.

"Things! Okay, just please, I will be in touch tomorrow night with anything I find, but tomorrow I can't meet you," Ali said hotly and turned to leave, not bothering to wait to hear what Jens had to say. *Obviously, she doesn't trust me with everything, either.*

22

It was just before noon by the time Jens walked into the PPD station back in Zone fifty-four, where he was greeted by an older, heavyset woman with short dark hair and blue eyes, looking as though she'd just sat down with a cup of coffee.

"How are you this morning?" Jens said, offering her one of his not-so-famous smiles. He wasn't usually in a chatty mood, but he wanted some questions answered, and no one knew a station better than dispatch.

"I'm busy, so I would like it if you got to the point," she said, barely looking up at him as she blew over her coffee.

Jens decided to drop what he assumed was social protocol, take her advice, and get to the point.

"I wonder if I could ask you a couple of questions about one of your constables." It was blunt, and Jens hoped she would appreciate that.

"Who's asking?" she said, eyeing him up and down as if she were trying to figure out just how important he really was.

"Senior Agent Adam Jennings, GIB. I'm not here to get anyone in trouble, just wondering about . . . people's characters," he said, thinking hard about this last part, not wanting to come off strong with the local PPD, especially on a case like this. Though he had the advantage of not lying, he did want only to get a better understanding of Constable Wilson.

"Right, the fella from the feed," she said, sipping her coffee casually. *Shit! Apparently, the feed of Natasha had covered the city.*

"Yeah, that's me," Jens said, waiting to see just how bad it was all going to be. The woman eyed him suspiciously before talking.

"Who do you want to know about?" she said, sipping her coffee, no cream or sugar—a straightforward kind of woman.

"Constable Wilson, know her?" Jens said. He'd already done a little more research on Wilson before arriving. By all accounts, she was an upstanding member of the PPD who'd moved quietly up the ranks with no real blemishes—though Jens knew she'd deliberately lied on one of her crime reports.

It seemed obvious to Jens that if something were going on here, the PPD wouldn't be the ones releasing it. No, Jens' only option was to go straight to the source.

"I know everyone, sweetie, including Constable Wilson," she said, leaning back in her chair, letting the mug of coffee rest on her stomach.

"How would you describe her?" Jens asked.

"Normally I wouldn't think about her," she said, staring at Jens. "So, you're the one who brought in that Anton fellow for the arson case," she said, her eyes narrowing slightly.

"I am, Constable Mullen," Jens said, reading the silver nameplate shining prominently in the centre of her well-maintained desk. Jens hoped his honesty would help avoid going into any unnecessary details on the matter.

Constable Mullen, with all her casual astuteness at the front desk, might offer up some help in understanding the constables in the PPD, but she was also likely to be the number one cause of rumours spreading throughout it. Jens would need to be careful about how he handled the line of questioning.

Constable Mullen sat patiently waiting for Jens to say more, casually sipping her coffee as other constables passed by greeting her: the perennial face of the building.

"Well," she began, unaware of Jens' unnerving ability to happily stand there in silence. "I can't say too much about Wilson. She's good at what she does, at least in the books. Her only real weakness is that she would do anything for Constable Granger," Constable Mullen said with a coy smile.

Jens didn't have too many friends in the agency, Granger being, to his knowledge, the only one, and it bothered Jens immensely that his name continued to be brought up in the surrounding cases. *Was he a blind spot? Does he have anything to do with any of this?*

"What do you mean anything?" Jens said, trying to avoid any hint at his relationship with Granger.

"Well, it's all speculation, and you didn't hear it from me."

Jens was confident he wouldn't be sharing whatever she said with anyone, but he gave her a reassuring nod to ease her mind—which she seemed to appreciate.

"Rumour has it they're sleeping together," she said, her grin growing as she leaned back in her chair, her eyebrows going up for increased measure.

Jens sighed, not caring what they were doing romantically. He needed to know if either of them was the type of person to lie. What they did in their free time was not his concern. But to other members in the PPD, a secret love affair was likely the star of the rumour mill.

"I'm less interested in her personal life and more wondering if she was the kind of person who would ever lie on a report?" Jens asked bluntly, having felt he'd already wasted enough time here. The question seemed to hit Constable Mullen hard. People don't normally admit to suspecting that sort of thing.

However, watching her squirm, if only slightly, in her chair, Jens got the distinct impression that she was actually a little scared.

"If you know anything . . ." Jens prodded, and for a moment she looked as if she might say something, but as her eyes shifted across the room, she stopped abruptly, as if what little air she had in her had been sucked away.

"Jens?" a familiar voice called from behind him. Granger walked over in civilian clothes, putting his hand out casually to greet him. "What the hell are you doing here? I assumed you'd be in for a promotion after your success yesterday. Solving the town's two biggest crimes is no easy feat," he said with a hearty laugh. *Can you actually solve a case that is practically gift wrapped for you?*

"Constable Mullen here was just telling me how to find you," Jens said, lying, an act that obviously put Constable Mullen at ease. Whatever it was she might have said, Granger's appearance had unnerved her. Her reaction was by no means a confession, but it was enough for Jens to reconsider just how closely he needed to think about his old friend.

"Well, here I am. What do you need?" Granger said.

"Thank you for your help, Constable Mullen. I appreciate it," Jens said, as the woman remained quiet, providing only a slight nod before linking up her data pad to her main desk, happy to bury herself in work.

"What brings you back here, Jens?" Granger said, leading Jens farther into the building before entering a smaller side room. Granger took a seat at one of the long waiting benches normally reserved for visitors.

"It seems pretty quiet today," Jens said in a sad attempt at small talk.

"You remember what it's like at headquarters—not usually anyone here. Not much needs to come to us after they bring it up with their zone committee," Granger said, his tone shifting to confusion. "But why am I telling you all this? You already know."

Jens sighed; it had been a stupid question, since he'd gone through the program himself. He knew each zone had an oversight committee that acted to moderate the PPD and ensure constables followed the official health and de-escalation program. It was essentially a way for the community and PPD to protect the people in the community jointly.

"Natasha Lilford," Jens said, his sober tone presumably saying the rest to his so-called oldest friend.

"I saw that," Granger said, looking down at the floor. "I'm sorry about that, Jens, and I assume I know why you're here," Granger said. Jens was almost certain that he didn't, but he didn't say that. It would be good to know what Granger was thinking as his friend let out a heavy breath.

"You're mad at me for not processing her request to look into her brother," Granger said, shaking his head and looking every bit the remorseful friend. Jens felt a little guilty that his first thought was that his friend was a great actor, before the possibility that he could be telling the truth.

"Listen, you know the procedure. It is not up to me. We need more then a sister who hadn't talk to her bother in two days before we can do anything. He's an adult. We can't jump to conclusions until we know more. I was just following procedure, and I feel terrible for how it ended up, but you have to know I didn't want that to happen." Granger could barely look up, and Jens was unable to figure out if he was just a really good liar or genuine.

"No, I understand. It's a shame about how it ended up," Jens said after a moment.

Granger met his eyes, bouncing back quickly from his rather emotional display.

"I'm glad we got to the bottom of that," he said, his casual grin returning as he made his way to get up before Jens could stop him.

"That's not why I'm here, Granger," Jens said quietly, as if to hide his next words from anyone who may be passing by in the hallway. Granger cautiously sat back down beside him.

"I don't understand," Granger replied in a tone to match Jens', while his eyes instinctively darted toward the entranceway of the still-empty room.

"The feed: Natasha was right. The marks on his body showed clear signs of a struggle, yet it was never in the report. Why?" Jens said, trying to catch any slipup from his friend, but nothing came.

"I'm not sure. I wasn't the constable on that case," he said, his head shaking slowly as if thinking.

"I know, Constable Wilson was." Jens paused to let the new information sink in before asking, "Do you know why she would have lied about it?"

Jens still wasn't sure who to trust, but at least he knew Granger; he didn't know Constable Wilson. Unfortunately, what he needed right now was information, turning on the one man he knew in the department was unlikely to get him anywhere. *Better the devil you know than the devil you don't.*

"She's one of the good ones," Granger said.

"One I hear you're sleeping with," Jens said. This time Granger's silence said more than enough. "Listen, I don't care what you do—that's your personal life—but if there is more to this, I need to know what's going on. The fact is, Wilson lied, and I can't imagine that will go over well. Do you understand what I'm telling you?"

Granger remained silent but nodded his understanding.

"What can I do?" Granger said after a long moment.

"Find out what you can about Wilson and the autopsy." Jens pulled out his data pad. "If you can find out anything about Dr. Atkins, that would be great, too. He was being paid. I know that much. I don't know by who or where all those credits are. This case isn't technically GIB territory, and I have no right to go in now and stir it up. I'm relying on you do be discreet about this," Jens said, opening his data pad, hoping he'd given enough information to convince Granger that he had complete faith in him.

"Anything I can do to help," Granger said, as his hand flinched at the vibrational pass of information.

It was Jens' turn to be silent, as he debated whether to ask his second request, the one he'd been battling with all morning.

"I'm glad you said that," Jens said after a moment, "because there is one more thing I need from you, and you're not going to like it."

23

Jens watched Anton Preston sit comfortably in the center of the room despite his current predicament. His hands were relaxed, resting unrestrained on the interview table. Jens was hit with another burst of silent aggression coming from Granger as he shut the door to the tiny interview room, leaving Granger perplexed and angry, outside.

Jens had been right. His friend did not like his request, not that it mattered. What Jens needed was answers, and Anton was the only one who could give them.

"You seem a little too happy for someone heading to prison for arson and possible murder charges," Jens said, gesturing toward Anton's smile. Pulling out a chair, Jens took the seat across from him.

"Maybe, but I knew what I was getting into when I turned myself in," Anton said, tapping his finger rhythmically on top of the table.

"In case you forgot, we caught you," said Jens, looking around the room as if this highlighted his point, making a show for the data cams.

"Let's be clear. No, you didn't, and you can rest assured no one is listening in," Anton said. "You can say what you came here to say." Another warm smile.

"How could you . . . How?" Jens asked while he found himself slowly hating Anton's arrogance as he watched him shrug. He seemed to trust Jens, but not enough to give away all his secrets. "All right, fine. You were right, I saw the body, and I watched as our good friend the doctor got his neck snapped because of it. You care to explain why?" Jens asked with only a hint of annoyance. For a moment there was silence before Anton shook his head, and the smile faded from his lips.

"I'm sorry about Dr. Atkins. He wasn't a bad man. He just had weaknesses, and that's what Firefly does—they exploit those weaknesses, taking advantage of good people." Jens heard a genuine sadness in Anton's voice.

"Who is Firefly?" Jens asked quietly, still not convinced of Anton's ability to block an entire room of its security from a prison cell.

"No one knows exactly. I've managed to link a few people together, but nothing is solid. As I mentioned before, Mr. Stone is involved somehow. I just don't know specifics." This last part seemed to grind away at Anton a little; clearly, he wasn't a guy who enjoyed being in the dark.

"And you say you have proof of this?" Jens said, shifting in his seat uncomfortably. *Why in the hell can't I, just once, get a comfortable seat?*

"You do have proof, don't you?" Jens added quickly. Anton's silence was beginning to stress him out.

"Yes. And no." Anton shrugged, as if admitting this wasn't such a big deal.

"What the hell does that mean?" Jens said with a bark. "I'm putting my neck on the line for you." His voice began to rise, as Anton's finger pressed to his lips and his eyes darted toward the door, as if someone might be trying to listen in from the outside.

"Actually, I'm putting my neck on the line for you. In case you're forgetting, I'm the one with a real chance of dying here," Anton said, his manner remaining light, but Jens sensed some deeper emotion in his voice. It was true he had no reason to help.

"So why do it?" Jens asked him, his temper having settled back down.

"We get only twenty-nine thousand two hundred days to live on this earth. What's the point in that if we know that someone out there is inherently controlling it for us? What does that say about life? People may choose to ignore this, but at the very least, they should know it's happening. Let them decide what to do with that knowledge," Anton said. His body was present, but Jens couldn't shake the feeling his mind was somewhere else.

"And that's worth your life? You're still young."

"I have to act while I can, and right now, I can."

"With no evidence," Jens asked incredulously.

"I didn't say no evidence. I have enough. It may not be perfect, but it should expose at least some of the truth," Anton said dismissively.

Jens didn't understand what that meant, and maybe that was the point. He hated riddles, and he would have only a limited amount of time with Anton before he was taken away. It was time to stop pissing around and start getting down to the real questions.

"Fine, say I believe you . . . ," Jens started to say.

"Thank you." Anton said it with an obvious attempt at humour, bringing a smile back to his face, the darkness of where he'd been vanishing. Jens, on the other hand, wasn't having any of it yet.

"Say I believe you . . ."

"I believe you," Anton said with a rueful smile. Jens frowned at the childishness of the joke. "Sorry I haven't had much in the way of 'joking around' the past little while. I couldn't help myself."

Anton laughed as Jens let out a big sigh and continued.

"Who are you working with? You can't be doing this all on your own. You broadcast a video nationwide, and you expect me to believe you did it from a jail cell?"

This little trick was still fresh in Jens' mind. Anton remained quiet, perhaps thinking the question was irrelevant.

He'd already mentioned he'd given the video proof to someone he trusted. *So, he's obviously not working alone. Don't be so stupid, Jens! Think!*

"Why can't you give us what you've found?" Jens asked, trying again.

"We've told you what we know. In my experience, it's better to guide people to find it out for themselves rather than tell them everything. This is a deep rabbit hole, Senior Agent Jennings, and as you're here, I'm willing to guess you're starting to realize that. If we simply told you what we found, you wouldn't believe us."

There's the confirmation I need that he's not working alone.

It was a start, albeit an incredibly frustrating one.

"So, you're saying there is a connection among Global Lottery, Stone Industries and Ryan Lilford's death?" Jens asked. Anton rewarded him with a nod before glancing up at the clock flashing on the wall beside them.

"You have only two minutes left, so choose your next question wisely, Agent Jennings, because I doubt we will get another chance to chat."

Anton relaxed back into his chair, suddenly making Jens feel as if he were the one being questioned.

Jens had been debating about what he wanted to ask Anton, who had made it clear he wouldn't answer things he wanted Jens to find it out for himself. *What would be the most effective thing to know?*

"You chose me specifically for this task, right?" Jens asked. Anton nodded his affirmation.

"Agent Hantsport. Did you also choose her for this?" Jens asked. Anton smiled. It must have been the right question to ask, Jens thought.

"I'll admit she was not in our original plan," Anton said coolly. Jens expected him to say more, but he remained quiet

"Dammit, can I trust her?" Jens smacked the table, tired of playing this little game; he needed answers now. But if his sudden show of aggression affected Anton, he didn't show it.

"Trust is an interesting game, Agent Jennings. It has to be earned. We don't know if we can trust you to do the right thing. Me personally, I'm allowing you the opportunity to earn my trust. I'm willing to risk it all. Agent Hantsport, like you, came with her own . . . history. It's up to you to decide if she is someone you can ultimately trust, not me. But I will say this. Everyone is hiding something. Time's up," Anton said, his eye on the clock, just as the door to the little interview room swung open.

But it wasn't Granger who stormed in. To Jens' surprise, it was Constable Wilson, along with the constable who'd brought in Anton.

"He's doing something to our systems. I thought you should know!" Wilson said, shooting Anton a dirty look, no doubt mad to be undermined again in her own house.

"Everyone," Anton said, glancing back at Jens as he put his hands up to be bound.

"Good luck, Agent Jennings," he added before the braces wrapped around his wrist as Jens got up and left the room, Constable Wilson in tow.

"Agent Jennings, was everything all right in there?" Wilson said, trying to keep up.

"Where is Constable Granger? I was hoping to talk with him. Wilson, is it?" Jens asked, feigning ignorance and knowing exactly who she was, but desperately needing her to think she was not on his radar.

It didn't help that Jens' mind was also racing through his conversation with Anton and what it all meant. *Why the hell does it feel as if every time I'm getting close to answers, I get rocked by a whole new set of questions?*

"Constable Granger got called out. I heard you were talking to Mr. Preston and thought I would check in. Figured you'd want to know when I found out our system was down," she said, struggling to keep up with Jens down the narrow hallways.

"Well, I appreciate your letting me know, Constable," Jens said, making his way to the elevators, needing to get home and process everything he'd learned.

Jens was happy that Granger was gone. He would have wanted to know what was said, and Jens couldn't afford to tell anyone.

"Do you mind me asking what you two spoke about, sir?" Wilson asked.

Jens hadn't noticed she'd climbed into the elevator with him, so her presence surprised him. He turned to face her.

"Yes." He'd taken a breath as if to say more but thought better of it.

"With all due respect, sir, he is our prisoner," Wilson said, her voice taking a more forceful tone.

"You're welcome to go in and talk with him, Constable Wilson," Jens said, wishing the elevator would get to the main level so he could get the hell out of this place.

"We would, but he seems to want to speak only with you. Why is that?" she said, not hiding her suspicion.

"Must be my winning personality," Jens said, musing, as the elevator doors slid up to

freedom. Wilson put her hand out to stop him.

"Why won't you tell us what he said? This is the second time you've spoken with him, and our systems have been down. One would say that is curious," she said, her eyes narrowing in on him.

Jens had had enough. Stepping off the elevator, he turned, stood his full height up, his good arm bracing the door as he glared at Wilson.

"If you have something you want to ask me, Constable, you ask me. But I would be careful about what you are insinuating. I am a senior agent for the Global Investigation Bureau. You are a constable for the PPD." The intimidation game seemed to work as she hesitated, if only for a split second. "If I were you, I would be less concerned about my conversation with Anton Preston and more concerned about how I broke my arm. I was visiting your friend Dr. Atkins down at the morgue—the one who processed Ryan Lilford. I'm sure you recently saw the video his sister released."

Wilson's face paled.

"Those images were falsified," she said, her voice stumbling through the sentence.

"I saw the body," he said sharply. Constable Wilson was visibly shaken as she backed away, now only to find herself trapped in the elevator.

"But you know what? I will share with you something Anton said to me. You may find it enlightening. He said everyone has their secrets. So, tell me, Constable Wilson . . . do you have secrets?" Jens removed his arm from the door, and it slid shut, leaving the pale-faced Constable Wilson on the other side.

24

All Jens wanted to do was collapse on the couch and devour a sushi burrito that he'd picked up from the ICER terminal. But despite his best efforts to ignore his conversation with Anton, he'd ended up, as it seemed to be these days, with many more questions than answers.

With a reluctant sigh, he forced himself to set the meal aside.

"Activate Bio Gravity Machine," he said as he slipped off his suit and tossed it into the Auto Clean, before grabbing a fresh pair of shorts and top.

The machine unpacked itself from the wall, and Jens was happy to see the vomit from his last attempt had been washed away.

He checked his arm, testing it first by rotating it slowly. It was stiff, but it appeared the nanobots had done their jobs despite Jens not taking the suggested rest period.

He still had to be careful with it, though, but he should at least be fine to do some light training, and light it would be.

"Reduce intensity by fifty percent," Jens said before stepping into the omnitrack.

"Activate thought board," Jens said as the screens surrounding him began to light up. Jens began to run as the track below him moved beneath his feet.

It took him a little longer to get into a rhythm as he adjusted the pressure to accommodate his recent injury. But after a few minutes, his body had steadied as he trotted along the track.

"Topic: Adam Jennings," he said as the board lit up with all the previous information he'd ever asked about himself, his eyes landing on the last post: "What do you plan on doing about it?"

"Hide all previous notes," Jens said as all the files zipped away into a little folder in the corner before he gave his mind the opportunity to collapse back into a more dangerous headspace.

What he really needed to do was focus on the here and now, and if he were going to do that, he would need to work through major questions.

"Are you being manipulated? Initial analysis is yes. So, by whom? Who are all the players in the little game you've been sucked into, and what does each side want? If you can't answer these questions, then you will never know who you should be helping. Can you trust Ash and Sun? Can you trust Anton? Is the other side Firefly? Is Firefly even real?" The board began to fill up with the questions and statements as Jens expunged all his inner worries about his so-called "solved cases."

As he rambled, threads of thin light connecting various phrases branched off, linking some obvious and some less-obvious connections to one another.

"What is Anton keeping from me? What could be so important he would risk his own freedom just so that I would pay attention? What does it all have to do with me?"

Jens began uploading topics on the wall, as thin lines of light began linking various topics together in different categories. Slowly he began to add in all the additional information he had about Ryan Lilford, the PPD, Nigel Eriksen, the Global Lottery, and lastly:

"Topic: Ali Hantsport."

Documents jumped up on the screen, linking Ali to various details of the investigations, including the big unknown question in the middle.

"Can I trust her?" Jens read.

"Ali has had previous dealings with the Scorpions. Is that a coincidence? She happens to come to the city at the same time that six are found dead? What is she hiding from me?" The new question popped up in front of him before attaching itself to the web of other information.

"Topic: black Zen watch. Who owns it? Why didn't they kill me when they had the chance?" he asked, rubbing his arm despite the fact it felt fine.

"Topic: Everyone has secrets."

He watched as light branched out across the web into all his recent categories, including his old files still tucked away in the corner.

"Deactivate." Jens sighed as the thought board vanished from his sight and the BGM slowed to a halt. He'd had enough for one night, though his mind still felt a little heavy.

But at least he'd managed to train without vomiting, which meant one thing. *Dinner!*

His stomach growled as he slumped down in the couch and unwrapped his burrito. It was cold, but at least now the contents might actually stay in his stomach. But just as he was about to take a bite, Jens' Zen watch began to vibrate. *Unknown caller?*

He slipped on his ocular pads and answered. A short breath came from the other end of the phone, as if the caller wanted to speak but didn't. Jens gave the phantom breath another moment.

"Hello?" Jens said after a painful beat of silence, but the now heavy breathing remained voiceless.

Then, just when it seemed the breath was preparing to speak, the line went dead. For a few minutes afterward, Jens waited, half expecting the person to call back, but whoever it was didn't call. *Weird.*

Jens woke early the next morning unrested. Despite the thought board he was unable to shake one topic from his mind. *Ali.*

He rolled out of bed, moving slowly toward the shower, his body sore from the BGM.

Jens let the steam fill the tiny space before stepping into the shower. The hot water felt good on his aching body. He rotated his previously broken arm back and forth, clenching his fist repeatedly. It was still tight, but it had healed well.

So, it was no surprise that it took him much less time to get dressed than the previous day as he took joy in the fact he now had use of both arms again.

What he didn't take joy in was his decision that he needed to speak with Ali. He was aware she'd requested the day off, but that had been with someone else, not him.

Jens needed to come clean with everything; if he were going to do this, she was right, he had to trust her. Besides, Ali had been his biggest ally, and he couldn't see himself going forward without her. But the only way to do that was to have no secrets, and if that meant asking her outright, so be it.

Jens almost felt guilty for knowing so little about his partner. He started to read her file, which he found to be surprisingly vague, but it did show some helpful information, such as where she lived.

Jens had considered sending her a message but thought better of it. *Better to catch her off guard.*

Jens had planned on catching her at her apartment, but when he reached Zone thirty-five where she lived, he was surprised when he saw her rushing into the same ICER terminal he'd just come out of.

Ignoring his luck and the potential ramifications of breaking all levels of trust and friendship, he abandoned his previous plans and followed her.

As Ali moved through the crowd, Jens kept his distance, telling himself that what he was doing was fine. *It's uncomfortable because it's important.*

Eventually she slipped onto an eastbound train. Jens hopped on after, taking a seat a couple of cars back with a clear view of Ali.

He started to doubt if she would see him, her eyes appearing to be fixated on the floor and distracted. *She doesn't seem at all worried about being followed by a paranoid partner.*

Jens shrank back into his seat, especially as the cars began to empty and he feared it might end up just the two of them on board—which was unlikely to end well.

Luckily Ali finally got off at the Hyperloop transfer system. *Is she planning on leaving the city?*

Jens followed her discreetly down the path. The station was busy with various commuters and travellers, which made it a little easier.

Jens glanced at a map of the Hyperloop system, suddenly aware that Ali might be travelling anywhere in the Global West.

But he didn't need to wait long to see her pass through the archway for the Charlottesville loop. *She requested a day off to go to the beach?*

Jens stepped through the archway; he was committed now, though he couldn't help wondering if this was one of his more expensive wastes of time as he watched the credits adjust on his watch.

Jens tucked himself into the back corner out of the way. Unlike the ICER, which made frequent stops, this loop would be direct, which gave Jens thirty minutes to dive into some work.

He pulled up the file Ali put together on the lottery, feeling more than a little silly that he couldn't just walk over and talk with her. But it was too late for that; he'd committed, no matter how much he wished he could decommit.

Because if Jens were being honest with himself, she didn't look as if she were being sneaky—she looked sad.

To Jens' surprise, at some point along the trip he'd dozed off, waking up with a start as the loop began to slow. He stole a glance toward Ali, who was in the same place he'd seen her last.

Ali got off the loop, making her way out of the station toward Main Street. Jens stayed close behind, hoping she wouldn't hop into an ECar. *It would be a shame to lose her now.*

But she skipped the line of ECars and made her way down the main strip toward the waterfront district.

Jens hadn't been to Charlottesville in a long time. His last memory was coming here as a kid with his grandfather, before his parents left for their "trip."

Jens watched Ali walk briskly toward the waterfront, pausing briefly to glance down the miles of man-made beaches that hugged the water's edge. Ali spun around curiously, forcing Jens to duck behind one of the large monuments to avoid being seen.

He waited a moment, catching the plaque in front of him, which read, "In memory of those who lost their lives in the rising." Atop the monument was a wave crashing over a city.

Jens tried to remember the stories of the rising from school, the two catastrophic waves that hit the eastern shore of the Global West, each one obliterating the old coast and changing the landscape forever. Jens glanced at the quote under the plaque and could almost hear the voice of his grandfather in his mind as he read it.

"The waters rose to remind us they can, so we may humble ourselves in its presence and take our rightful place as nothing more than the stewards of this earth."

Jens risked poking his head out from around the monument and found Ali walking up the beach. Taking one last look at the monument, and shaking off the forgotten memory, Jens caught Ali strolling up along the boardwalk. It was nearly empty; this time of year was not nearly as popular with the tourists.

Which meant Jens had no issues keeping well enough behind, and it wasn't long before Ali stopped, taking a seat at one of the empty picnic tables set up around the pathway.

Jens, not wanting to get too close, spotted a nearby café that didn't look very busy and would be a good place to watch without being too obvious.

"What can I get you?" asked a young waitress with a colourful apron with Fiona's Café printed across the front and a name tag that read Tara.

"An Americano, please, Tara. You mind if I sit over there?" Jens asked, pointing to a set of tables that seemed to have a good view of the beach.

"If you can find room," Tara said with a smile, gesturing to the nearly empty café. "I'll bring it over to you," she said as Jens moved over to take a seat.

He noticed Ali still hadn't moved. *Is she waiting for someone?*

Jens scanned the beach, not seeing anything out of the ordinary save a couple of families on vacation and a few Death Day parties.

Jens had been to only one Death Day party, and it was his grandfather's—though it hadn't been like the extravagant parties he'd heard of other people having.

He'd done a few traditional things, jumping from a plane, swimming with sharks, and on his final day, he'd been with Jens and some of the members of his staff. Not even Jens' parents had bothered to show up, and the next day he was gone.

Jens had never really understood how a man who'd dedicated his life to the service of society as the head of the GIB, then as a successful politician, could have found himself so alone at the end of his life. Jens had practically had to force himself into the man's life, though once he was in, he found nothing more than a kindhearted old man—nothing like the man his parents had described to him as a child. He'd told Jens once that he was happiest alone, but for whatever reason, Jens had never believed that about his grandfather, certainly not after the way he embraced Jens in his life. It was as if he were hiding, which was made even more real when he'd asked Jens to keep their relationship as *their little secret*.

Tara arrived with his coffee, and Jens, who couldn't remember the last time he'd sat down and simply enjoyed a coffee, suddenly felt relaxed. *I suppose I should thank Ali when this is all over.*

But Ali didn't seem nearly as relaxed as Jens, and by the time he'd finished his coffee, he'd developed a heaviness in the pit of his stomach.

"Can I get you anything else?" Tara asked.

"Yeah, could you make it two more coffees, and would you mind holding this table for me?" Jens asked.

"I'm sure I can, as long as you don't run off," she said with a laugh before turning to head back inside.

Ali's back was toward him when he approached the table where she'd been sitting. If she heard him coming, she didn't move, though she did seem distracted.

"Hi," Jens said, waiting for her to recognize him before taking the seat beside her. Ali was startled at first, which quickly turned to anger.

"You followed me?" she said, turning her focus back to one of the Death Day parties. There were about thirty people there surrounding an old man who was laughing and playing horseshoes with a little girl who Jens suspected was likely his granddaughter. There was a barbecue set up, and people seemed to be having a good time. It was in odd contrast to the angry, brooding woman beside Jens.

"Yes," Jens said, having no reason to lie. "The truth is I didn't know if I could trust you." The words came out slower than he'd hoped.

"I'm not surprised," Ali said. "Doesn't play well with others, abandonment issues. You're a genius unless it comes to human interactions. Then you're basically a small child," Ali said, not bothering to look at him.

"Is that what my file says about me?" Jens was a little surprised at the blunt rational assessment of his file.

"It's not verbatim. I added the small-child bit, but yeah, that's the gist. Haven't you ever read your file?" she asked, stealing a quick look. Jens shook his head.

"It's people's perspectives about me. Only I need to worry about me," he said as if that absolved him of any responsibility.

"You do realize that's your problem, right?" She laughed. It was a geeky laugh accompanied by a snort. It was an honest human response, he thought.

"Come on," Jens said, getting up from the table.

"I'm going to stay here, thanks," Ali said defensively. She wasn't going to leave, but then again, Jens already knew that.

"We're not leaving, Ali. I know why you're here," he said, a hint of disbelief on her face.

"I've got a table at the café over there and an Americano with your name on it. Looks like they've got some good food, too."

"Coffee?" she said, still a little apprehensive about leaving her spot. Jens nodded.

"On me," he said, which was enough to at least have her follow him.

Jens and Ali headed to the café, where Tara had just dropped off the two coffees.

"I managed to keep the hordes off it." She laughed. "Anything else for you?"

"A menu, please," Ali said before Jens could say anything.

"Of course," Tara said, flicking her watch as the menu popped up on Ali's Zen watch.

"Thank you. And thank you, boss," Ali said, scanning the menu.

"Eggs Benedict, with hash browns," Ali said.

"Great choice."

"What about you, boss, anything?"

"Same," Jens said.

Tara smiled, then returned inside.

No longer needing to spy on Ali or have an interest in the DD party, Jens took the seat opposite, giving Ali a view to watch the party.

"How did you know?" Ali asked.

"I'm not a terrible agent, you know."

"Just a terrible friend," she said, taking a sip of coffee.

The dig hurt Jens more than he would have admitted; it was also brutally accurate.

"I admit it isn't my finest moment, and you have every right to be mad. It's just this case. . . ," Jens started to say.

"It's fine. I guess I understand. I read all your files once I heard back from the lottery," she said, her eyes never leaving the party behind him.

"You heard back?" Jens asked. Ali nodded. "What did you learn?" he added. Ali, for a moment, remained quiet.

"Don't you want to know why I'm here?" she said, finally looking over at him.

Jens wasn't sure if it mattered anymore. She was clearly here for the DD party. But he could see from her expression that she wasn't interested in talking about the case, at least not right now.

Jens had also broken down their trust when he was willing to follow her across the country on the loop, and although she may have wanted to be alone, Jens got the feeling she was happy he was there. Jens felt as though now might be a good time to try to be a friend, or at least try.

"Who is it?" he said slowly.

"My grandfather," she said, looking back at the family playing.

"So why are you over here? And not over there?" Jens asked, more than a little confused. Ali sighed; whatever this was, she had been holding on to it for a while.

"I told you I worked that Scorpions case," Ali finally said. Jens nodded. This seemed like the time for a friend to listen.

"It's one of the reasons I was partnered with you in the first place. I didn't move down here because I liked the city. I got transferred because the Scorpions found out who I was and threatened to kill me and my family." Ali's head sank down into her chest. "The little girl, there," she said, pointing to the girl Jens had seen playing horseshoes with Ali's grandfather, "is my niece. I would do anything for her. Even leave." Tears began to fall down her face, and Ali didn't bother to wipe them away.

"But now here I am wrapped up in the same mess as I was before, only worse, because I can't see my family." The words were barely coming out.

"This is your secret?" Jens said softly and suspected this is what Anton must have.

Ali had been forced away from her family because she tried to do the right thing. Now she was forced to watch her grandfather's Death Day party from a café stool with someone who couldn't even trust her. Jens felt ashamed.

"What?" Ali said, Jens not realizing he'd said anything.

"Something Anton said to me—'we all have secrets.' This is yours," Jens said while Ali looked away.

"It was to protect them," she said defensively.

"You don't have to explain," Jens said quietly.

"Clearly," Ali said as she turned to glare at him. He cringed at the jab.

"I deserve that," he said, trying to hide as much of the shame as he could.

"Yes, you do," Ali said, finishing her coffee. "Which is why you're buying more coffee," she said, setting her nearly empty mug back down on the table. Jens dared a smile.

"Is that why you're on this case?" Jens asked, signalling Tara for another coffee.

Ali looked at him, her face giving away everything.

"If the Scorpions go down, then you're free to see your family. You can go home?" Jens asked.

Ali's fresh tears streamed down her face as she nodded. Jens wasn't much for sentiment; his family had never done that sort of thing except for maybe his grandfather near the end.

Seeing Ali there crying, he thought how supportive she'd been of him, even when she had no reason to be. He realized just how good a partner she was.

Picking up his chair, he moved beside her, then placed his arm around her shoulders vowing, "I promise I'll do better."

"You can start by moving back over there." Ali laughed, and Jens' face flushed. "The food's here," she added quickly, saving Jens from some of the embarrassment as Tara returned with a couple of plates of food and another coffee for Ali.

The two of them laughed as Jens moved back to the other side of the table. *Maybe I'll have to work up to hugs.*

They continued laughing as Jens listen happily to Ali share stories about her family and her grandfather. And after an hour or so, Ali got up and left the table. Jens watched her walk across the pathway to the bathroom standing just off the beach. She stood patiently outside; Jens wondered just what she was doing when her grandfather stepped out of the restroom.

Ali was shielded from the rest of the party, and Jens watched as the two of them stood staring at each other as if trying to figure out if either one was real, until Ali's grandfather embraced her in a hug, Ali burying her face in his shoulder.

They spoke briefly, and Jens realized this would be the last time Ali would ever get the chance to see her grandfather. He would be dead tomorrow, and Ali would have only her memories of him. Jens guessed that this had been her plan all along, a chance to say goodbye.

One final hug, and Ali turned to head straight for the loop. Jens quickly scanned his Zen watch, paying Tara, before racing to catch up with Ali.

It wasn't until they got on the loop and were making their way back to the city when Jens felt a familiar buzz on his Zen watch. He'd opened his data pad, and there were the details Ali had got from the Global Lottery search she had done.

Jens read through them slowly. There was so much information he didn't exactly know how to process it, but the more he read, the worse it seemed to get.

"Does this mean . . . ?" Jens couldn't even bring himself to finish, knowing what the ramifications of this information could mean.

"Yes," Ali said, "the Global Lottery is a scam."

25

"What do you mean the lottery is a scam? What exactly am I looking at?" Jens said, still struggling to make sense of what Ali was showing him. It was years' worth of data sitting before him, but in bold letters on top of the page were the words "the lottery is a scam."

"It's stranger than it looks," Ali said as Jens began to comb through some of the highlighted areas, each one for the moment meaning nothing to Jens. Ali's family seemed to be a distant memory as she flung herself back into the work.

"This data must go back . . . ," Jens began to say.

"Nearly fifty-five hundred days," Ali said, cutting him off. "This content proves that the Global Lottery, possibly through Nigel Eriksen, were using its position to mask various credits being moved in and out of the charity.

"fifty-five hundred days? Why the hell would the lottery provide us with records going back that long?" Jens asked, scrolling through the highlighted passages, recognizing some recurring anomalies in the files. "Sure, they're given a little more flexibility with their position with the UN, but could it really be this easy for them to get away with something like this? Even if the good they do offset the bad, this has to be worse, much worse."

"The lottery didn't give us these records," Ali said, not meeting Jens' eye. It took Jens a moment to let that information sink in.

"These were hacked. Ali, please tell me these files are not illegally hacked lottery files?"

"Okay, these files are not illegally hacked," Ali said with much less conviction than Jens would have preferred.

"Ali."

"Jens, these records date back fifty-five hundred days. Nigel Eriksen worked for the company for only half that time," Ali said, allowing the gravity of the words to land.

"They gave us only what we needed to pin it on Eriksen," Jens concluded as Ali nodded vehemently.

"So, whoever has been doing this had been doing it for a lot longer," he said, still trying to navigate the idea of having illegally obtained data.

"This is just the tip of the iceberg," Ali said, pulling up her own files.

"The thing about icebergs, Ali—they have a history of bringing down the ship that encounters them," Jens mumbled to himself as he scrolled through the data.

"It's a lot, I know. But . . ."

"Ali, I should tell you something," Jens said, jumping in. "I spoke with Anton Preston yesterday."

"Again?" Ali said. Jens was happy that she sounded more intrigued than concerned. "What did he say?"

"Not much. But he was clear about one thing, that he needed us to unravel the threads of this case. He insisted it was the only way anyone would ever believe what was going on," Jens said.

"Given this bombshell, I'm not surprised," Ali said, laughing.

"So far, he's been right. Even with this proof, I'd say we're crawling up a steep hill. No way anyone in their right mind would let us go after the lottery," Jens said, scrolling through the mounds of data. "This doesn't happen without people knowing about it," he said, pointing to the files. "Which begs the question, who can we trust? Constable

Wilson has already shown it's in the PPD," Jens added.

Ali lifted a quizzical eyebrow at that.

"Wilson's covering this up?" Ali asked in confusion.

"I know for sure she forged the examination of Ryan Lilford. Who knows what else she's done?" said Jens.

"But she can't be doing it alone—she would need help," Ali added.

"I agree," Jens said, shutting down his data screen and looking around the loop, making sure they were alone. A couple was near the front of the train, and a young mother and her baby were off to the side, though none of them seemed interested in Jens or Ali.

"Ali, there is something else you should know." Jens had held off on telling anyone about this, unsure if he believed it. But with everything going on, he owed it to Ali to tell her everything.

"When I was hit the other day, it wasn't the impact that killed Dr. Atkins. Someone wanted to make sure he was dead," Jens said, trying to gauge Ali's reaction.

"What?" Genuine shock appeared on her face, then confusion.

"Someone broke into the car and snapped his neck. And I assume they must have thought I was already dead," though even as he said it, he wasn't sure he believed it, and neither did Ali. "What?" Jens asked.

"It's just . . . ," Ali began to say, seeming unsure of her words. "Only what if they knew you were alive? What if they wanted you to see it? To show you what they are capable of."

The skin on the back of his neck began to prickle. *Had it been a message?*

"Either way," Jens said, trying to disguise his own worry, "you understand what I'm saying?" Jens said calmly. "Anyone who could hijack a city waste collector and kill a man in front of a GIB agent in cold blood is clearly dangerous. Meaning from this moment forward, we have to assume our lives are in danger."

The two seemed to let that sobering reality set in even as they pulled into the transfer station.

"What's up?" Jens asked as they made their way up the stairs back toward the ICER.

"I've just been thinking about all this, and there is one thing I still don't understand," Ali said.

"What's that?"

"Well, according to the lottery, Nigel Eriksen was a thief. We have proof of that. And the fire at the warehouse was started by Anton Preston, and we have the proof of that, too."

"I know all this," Jens said, confused.

"I know you do. It's just what does that mean you and I are doing? What is the case we are working on? On paper we have solved our caseload, and I can't imagine anyone is going to put the project with the lottery or Mayor Stone on the books. So, what exactly are we telling people we are doing here?"

"To mind their own damned business." Jens smirked.

"I'm being serious, Jens."

"I know you are. I've been thinking about that, too. But we have the support of Captain Rollins and Chief Furland."

"Right, but that's only the case until we don't. I think it's great they have given us support, though I can't help thinking that will last only as long as what we are doing doesn't step on the wrong toes."

"I think you're right. This might be the biggest case the GIB has ever had. But you and I could stop now, and I don't think anyone would blame us."

"I'm not sure I could do that," Ali said.

He nodded his approval.

"You okay?" Jens asked when they reached the ICER.

Ali nodded absently.

"I think I just need some time on my own. Been a long day," Ali said, a sad half smile on her lips.

"Fair enough," Jens said quietly. "Ali, I'm sorry about today, but for what it's worth, I had . . . fun, spending time with you."

"Adam Jennings admitting to having fun? Here I was thinking today couldn't get any weirder." Ali laughed. "I had a good time too, boss—though do me a favour and never follow me again?"

"Deal. See you tomorrow, partner," Jens said.

"See you tomorrow, boss," Ali said before hopping on the ICER home.

. . .

By the time Jens got home, he hadn't managed any real progress in what the connection might be among the lottery, Mayor Stone, the cartel, Nigel Eriksen, and Ryan Lilford.

That was if he were going to believe Anton Preston had been at the warehouse the night of the fire, but other than his word, there was no actual proof linking Ryan to any of that. Yet someone had gone to some serious trouble trying to cover up his death, which meant it couldn't be meaningless.

What Jens really needed was to talk with Anton again, though as of today, he was officially transferred to one of the community's rehabilitation sites, where he'd be kept for six months without leave, and it would be impossible to request time with him without some serious string pulling.

Jens unbuttoned his jacket as he sank down into his couch. His eyes felt heavy, and given the events of the day, he wasn't surprised. *What I need is a hot shower and sleep.*

"Play music," Jens said, and a series of low thrums filled the room.

Setting his watch on the bedside dresser, he tossed his dirty clothes in the Auto Clean and grabbed a clean towel from the banister. He'd almost reached the shower when he heard a faint buzzing coming from his bed.

"Incoming call from *Unknown*," said a soft voice as the music cut out. Jens spotted the Zen watch glowing as it went off, and he desperately wanted to ignore it.

"Access seventeen forty-two" Jens said as the call's audio linked into the home speakers. For a moment there was only an eerie silence, followed by a shallow inhalation that filled the room, giving him the impression someone was in the room with him.

"Hello?" Jens said cautiously, his body suddenly very tense. "This is Senior Agent Jennings. Who is this?" He heard a sharp intake of breath. Then the line went dead. Jens scanned the room unable to shake that feeling that whoever it had been might pop out at any moment.

This was the second time he'd received contact from his voiceless caller. Once was odd, but twice was no coincidence. *Whoever this is is trying to reach me, but why?*

26

Jens woke early and had already sent Ali a message to meet him at a café near Natasha's home in Zone forty-six. It wouldn't do them any good to go into the GIB headquarters now. They agreed that there would be too many questions that they didn't have answers for, and the coffee was terrible.

It had been Jens' idea to see what Natasha might know about her brother; after all, he was the biggest wild card, and besides wanting to cover up his death, there was no reason why he died. It wasn't much, but for the first time in a while, Jens liked that they were actually investigating something—which felt good.

Jens, who'd been too excited to stand around, arrived fifteen minutes early for their meeting and probably shouldn't have been surprised to see Ali stepping out of Troy's Café holding two black Americanos.

"Thanks for the coffee," Jens said as Ali handed him a cup.

"Figured you'd be early," she said, taking the lid off hers to give it a couple of cooling breaths.

"Should have guessed you'd be earlier," Jens said, musing.

"So, Natasha Lilford. What do you think we're going to get out of her?" Ali said, taking a cautious sip.

"Maybe nothing. Whatever Ryan was doing probably didn't involve telling people. But we seem completely in the dark on him, so frankly anything would be helpful at this point," Jens said.

"Did you get the file I sent?" Ali said, pulling up her data pad.

"I did, but I wanted to hear what you thought," Jens said.

"Who are you, and what have you done with that other prick?" Ali said with a laugh.

"You going to joke or get on with it?"

"Fair enough. According to reports, Ryan was last seen Monday, October ninth, leaving work. He was not due back in until Wednesday, and only Natasha found it strange that she didn't see him Tuesday. By the time he didn't show up to work Wednesday, well, she'd talked to you." Ali gave him a playful nod.

"No data footage of him leaving his house once he arrived home Monday night, but his body was found in the river fifteen miles from his apartment seven days later by a John Cooney, who was out walking his dog."

"No footage found? What do you think of that?" Jens asked.

"Besides a face modulator, which, by the way, are a hundred percent illegal, not to mention expensive, I don't see how it would be possible for him to have gotten out."

"Agreed, though I imagine money and tech might be two things that whoever is covering this up might have," Jens said. "You think your friend up north could go over the footage? Discreetly? They've been helpful so far."

"It's a lot of data, but I'm sure they could," Ali said, sounding not the least bit optimistic about their prospects.

"That everything?" Jens asked.

"Pretty much—it wasn't much information, considering it was an assumed suicide," Ali said, closing up her data file.

"Right, what do you say we get this over with?" Jens said, taking a last sip of coffee and tossing the cup into the compost.

Ali followed suit, and as a little coffee dribbled out the side of her mouth, her face flushed red with embarrassment.

"Smooth," Jens said, letting out a hearty laugh, surprised that he couldn't remember the last time he'd really laughed like that.

The laughter was soon forgotten when Natasha Lilford opened the door to her tiny tier-two, one-bedroom apartment. It was filthy and smelled as though she hadn't let anyone in to clean in days.

"Natasha, are you okay?" Ali asked, though it felt unnecessary as she stepped around old food containers and clothes.

Natasha didn't say anything. Her eyes were red and swollen from all the crying, and discarded tissues were scattered throughout the apartment.

"Why don't I make us some tea?" Ali said, moving to the kitchen, piles of dirty dishes in the sink.

"Maybe I'll clean a little of this up while I'm at it?" she added, getting nothing more than a shrug from Natasha.

Natasha brushed off a spot on the leather couch, knocking a huge pile of clothes on the floor along with a half-eaten slice of pizza. Jens took a seat cautiously on the couch. Natasha found her seat on a well-worn portion of the couch, which she also seemed to be using as a bed. Jens heard the tap in the other room turn on and the sound of glasses being shuffled around carefully. He may not have known what he was sitting on, but he thought the kitchen had to be worse.

"I'm sorry about your brother, Natasha," Jens said.

Natasha's stare was no longer angry, just empty.

"I want you to know I believe you," Jens said, looking at her with what he hoped was compassion.

"A little too late for that, don't you think?" she said, a little fiery, but that quickly vanished.

"It's not too late to figure out what happened to him. That's what we are trying to do." Natasha continued to stare at him, not saying a word.

"We know it wasn't an accident, and we know someone wanted to cover it up. What we don't know is who or why," Jens said.

Natasha's eyes focused on the floor, knowing what was coming but looking helpless all the same.

"Do you know anything?" Jens asked, and Natasha shook her head even before he'd finished. *Of course, she didn't know anything—she'd obviously thought about it every day and night since it happened. If she'd known anything, she would have told me.*

"I've thought about the days leading up to it and after he went missing. I should have known something was wrong, but I thought he was just being weird."

The words came out softly. She clearly hadn't spoken to anyone in a while. Her voice was slightly hoarse, making it difficult to hear. Jens leaned in so as not to miss anything.

"What do you mean weird? Honestly, any details would help," he asked, as he watched her shaking her head as if desperately trying not to relive it again.

"He just kept saying that he took care of it, that I would be okay. I would be taken care of. I thought he was just being strange and that maybe he'd gotten a new job, but he wouldn't say anything else. Then he was gone. I certainly don't feel taken care of."

She began to cry. Jens found a half-used tissue box and picked it up and held it for Natasha to grab. She took a bunch and blew her nose.

Jens let the words percolate in his mind. It was a weird thing to say before one disappears and ends up dead. *But the theory he left on his own seems more likely, but why?*

Ali entered the room with a couple of cups of tea and handed them to Natasha and Jens. He wasn't a big tea person, but warm drinks tended to soothe people enough to help make them more comfortable.

"We are going to do our best to find out what happened to your brother," Jens said softly.

"He wasn't my brother," Natasha said softly, "not exactly. We were society born. Ryan and I were paired together when he was two. We chose to remain paired as we got older—better to have someone than no one, we thought."

Natasha never looked up, but had she, she would have seen Jens' shocked expression. *How could I have missed this in the file?*

"You stayed matched this whole time?" Jens asked, getting a nod from Natasha. *So, both Natasha and Ryan were orphans? Interesting.*

"He must have cared for you a lot," Jens added remorsefully. Fresh tears began to fall down Natasha's face.

"Do you have any siblings, Agent Jennings?" Natasha asked as she wiped her eyes.

The question had taken Jens aback; he hated discussing his personal life with anyone, let alone a stranger, and to make matters worse, he could sense Ali looking at him, too.

"No," Jens said, hoping his voice showed just how little he cared to discuss the topic of his childhood. On paper his life might have even looked good, but he'd never had anyone who cared for him as Natasha seemed to care for Ryan.

"I'm sorry," Natasha added softly.

"Don't be. Your brother sounds like a good man. You were lucky that you had each other," Jens said sincerely.

Natasha gave him a sad smile before blowing her nose in her tissue and wiping her nose.

"Everyone deserves their full cycle," Ali said, her voice trying hard to suppress the anger in the sentence. Everyone nodded in agreement, Jens glancing down at his own watch displaying his own fourteen thousand two hundred and ninety-one days remaining.

Jens hadn't been expecting to feel so emotional talking with Natasha; in the past, he'd always been a passive observer on his cases. But this case seemed to be getting under his skin. Each step forward seemed to lead to a bigger injustice, and he hated it.

"Natasha," Jens said quietly. She looked up at him, her hands wrapped tightly around the warm mug of tea that she hadn't even sipped.

"I need you to tell me about the stream." He noticed the flicker of light in her eyes.

"I was wondering when you'd ask me about that," she said, a hint of a smile appearing on her lips. "You have to understand I was desperate. No one was helping me. So, when I was contacted by someone saying they'd help me tell my story, I did. I tried to call you before. . ."

Jens put a gentle hand up to stop her.

"You don't have to explain yourself, Natasha. You wanted to give us a little nudge," Jens said, softly.

"More like shove," Ali said playfully from the side of the room, causing Natasha to chuckle, if only for a second.

"Well, either way it worked. But we need to know who contacted you," Jens said calmly. For a moment, Natasha just looked at him, then let out a deep sigh.

"Truth is, I have no idea. I received a message asking me if I would tell my story, saying that the world needed to hear it," she said, her hands fidgeting around the mug.

"Do you still have the message?" Jens asked. Natasha nodded as she pulled up her Zen watch and sent it over to Jens. No doubt the encryption on it would give them nothing, but anything helped at this point.

"Is that everything?" Jens asked, trying to read Natasha as best he could but getting nowhere.

"Only that the person I spoke with was gentle. She actually seemed to care," Natasha said, that last part to Jens, and her words stung him.

"I'm sorry for your loss, Natasha, and I promise we will do everything we can to discover who did this to your brother."

Jens meant every word, and yet they still felt hollow. The damage had been done; she would never get her brother back.

Ali and Jens let themselves out, leaving Natasha once again alone on her couch. The pair didn't say anything until they reached the street.

"Well, that was awful." Ali was the first to speak up. "I didn't even think it was possible for someone to live like that."

"Apparently if someone tries hard enough, they can," Jens said, trying to imagine just how Natasha managed to get into such a state of disrepair.

"Do you think we should inform the community council to see if someone should intervene?" Ali asked skeptically.

Community councils were designed to help families in need, and for the upkeep of schools and rec centers. Essentially, they oversaw the success and failure of a community.

"You know GIB agents aren't supposed to get involved in community affairs," Jens said, turning to face Ali, clear disappointment in her face. "However, anonymous calls happen all the time," he added with a wink.

"They do, don't they," Ali said, giving him a smile before adding, "what do we do now?" as she hailed an ECar.

Jens had a sudden spark of inspiration as he began to think about his own experience with anonymous calls.

27

It wasn't long before the ECar arrived at the GLF entranceway, and Jens was cautiously optimistic about what they might find. They were met at the door by Chris; it was good to see they hadn't lost their job after Jens' last visit.

They were as distracted as ever looking over their data pad and clicking frantically away at something, though they had the decency to smile at Jens and Ali when they walked in, however insincere it was.

"Oh, you're back," Chris said with an uncomfortable sigh. "I thought we sent you all the information you required," they said, looking back at their work. *I wonder if they're messaging their boss?*

"Yes, well, funny thing about police work is we keep doing it when you're not around," Jens said, receiving another curt smile from Chris.

"We need to talk with your boss," Ali said, flicking through her own data pad. "Mrs. Choi?" she added, finding the name again in her notes.

Jens smiled at the tactic, *as if we haven't been talking about her for the past twenty or so minutes.*

Mrs. Choi was the one who provided them with the misleading files. But thanks to Ali's digging, they knew there was no way Nigel Eriksen, if he'd actually had anything to do with this at all, could have done it alone.

"Right, well, she's in a meeting," Chris said, looking around the room, nervously.

"That's all right. We have nowhere to be, we can wait," Jens said, taking a seat on one of the plush chairs in the front lobby. Jens noticed a pile of *Lottery Life* eco-prints on the table and picked one up.

"It will give me time to see what our winners have been up to," Jens said in mock excitement.

"I've been wondering what the best twelve ways to manage my credits are," Ali said, taking the seat next to Jens. "Do you know if your counselors are only for the winners? Or can anyone request their services?" she asked, opening to a random page.

"You'll have to read more and find out," Chris said, forcing a smile as they turned away, head sunk back into their data screen.

"All jokes aside, I think it's wonderful they assist winners. Could you imagine getting that kind of credit?" Ali said with a laugh.

"Yes, I can," Jens said slowly.

"Holy shit, you won the lottery?"

"No. My grandfather did fairly well in his life."

"Oh. But I thought the state took seventy-five percent of all inheritance funds," Ali said skeptically.

"They do. I guess I should say he did really well," Jens said with a smile.

"Wait! Are you trying to tell me you're rich?!" Ali asked, unable to hide her excitement. "How am I just finding out about this now?"

"I'm not in the habit of telling people—it's not like I use it."

"What? Hold on, you have all these credits, and you spend your time working overtime with the GIB, Mr. No Vacations, Mr. Five Thousand Days Left."

"Firstly, I didn't earn those credits. They were just given to me. Secondly, I happen to enjoy my job, and thirdly, I have fewer than four thousand days left. But I'll happily stick around for another ten thousand if we don't royally mess this up."

"You really only have four thousand days left?" Ali asked, shocked. "I thought you said . . ."

"No, you assumed I had more days. I just never corrected you. And as for the lottery, I agree, they provide aid and resources for hundreds of thousands of people every year. Whatever we end up finding here, I have to believe it's just people's greed, who somehow believe they are above the law. They're not. But the reality is the Global Lottery is our seventh nation, and without it, well, I'm not sure anyone could predict what might happen," Jens said, leaning back in his chair looking at his eco-print.

"You truly are an enigma, Jens." Ali laughed as she leaned back in her chair. "So do you have a plan?" she asked quietly.

"I'm working on one," Jens whispered back.

"Should I be worried?" Ali's brows shot up. "What makes you so sure the call was even coming from here?"

"I got the impression they want to talk to someone, or else they wouldn't have called, and this is the only place I sent my number out."

"That's not really a strong case," Ali said.

"Well, if you have any other leads that you're not telling me about, then now would be a good time to bring them up. If not, then I think I'll stick to my plan."

"What plan?" Ali said as Jens got up from his chair. "Jens, what plan?" Ali said with a hiss as Jens walked over toward Chris.

"Is there a water closet I can use?" Jens ask, setting the eco-print back on the table. Chris pointed absentmindedly over toward the elevator.

"Just past the elevators on your right," they said between typing. "Do you need me to go with you?" they asked, briefly eyeing up Jens, but quickly distracted again by the data pad.

"No, I should be fine," Jens said, turning back to give Ali a little wink as he made his way toward the elevator. Ali shook her head at him as Jens slipped into one of the open elevators. *Plan seems to be working well.*

Jens didn't have much time to figure out the rest of his plan before the doors opened on the familiar scene of groups of people huddled around working and flashing screens displaying the trading of global currencies.

Jens had no idea if the plan he'd only just made would actually work. But he hoped that whoever it was that had called him didn't have their ocular pads in. Lifting his Zen watch, Jens called back the unknown caller hoping. He waited a moment trying to listen for any sound of a call coming in, which was harder than he thought with all the beeping and buzzing in the background. Jens heard nothing on the first attempt, and he tried calling back again, but again he didn't hear or see anything strange. *Maybe they have in ocular pads? Or maybe your little gambit didn't pay off and you were wrong?*

Jens ignored his doubt and called back again. This time it was answered, though they didn't say anything into the line.

"Hello," Jens said, as he scanned the room trying to catch a glimpse of anyone with a set of ocular pads in. He saw a few, but they all seemed to be talking. *Maybe they aren't here?*

"It's Senior Agent Adam Jennings," Jens said into the phone, breaking the stalemate as he continued to scan the room. The voice remained silent, but Jens could hear them breathing. Whoever it was wasn't hanging up, which was a good thing.

"I know you're scared. Does this have anything to do with the lottery? About Nigel Eriksen's death?" A chair squeaked, and Jens frantically looked around for the sound. He saw a man looking around nervously.

"Are you in the lottery building now?" Jens watched the man scan the room and then start to walk away. He still hadn't seen Jens, who approached him quietly from behind. But as the man in front of him turned, Jens noticed he wasn't wearing ocular pads.

"Can I help you?" asked the very confused man, who was obviously unnerved by Jens' close proximity. The man, catching a glimpse at Jens' Zen watch, said, "The GIB? Am I in trouble?"

Jens waved him off, and the man happily moved away, pretending to refocus on his data pad.

Jens spun around, scanning until locking eyes on a little man with pudgy cheeks and dark skin. His terrified eyes looked fixed on Jens. The line Jens had with him went dead, and the little man turned to move away. Jens could have caught him had he not felt a strong hand on his shoulder, a large hand attached to a wrist accented with a black metallic Zen watch, which emitted a white light in the room. Jens was turned around abruptly to meet the large stature of Derris Harding, who maintained a firm grip on Jens' shoulder.

Behind him was Maggie Purchase, looking as uptight as ever with her pencil skirt and narrow eyes. There was something about her that made Jens feel uncomfortable. Jens noticed there was no Mayor Stone. It was odd to see the head of security nowhere near the man he was sworn to protect.

"Agent Jennings, I'm surprised to see you up here," Ms. Purchase said, her eyes burrowing into him.

"Not as surprised as I am to see you," Jens said, trying to hide his confusion. Why would the head of Stone Industries be anywhere near the lottery?"

"You're the one who shouldn't be here. I'm Mr. Stone's representative in all his affairs. One of those things includes a seat on the board here at the Global Lottery," she said with a well- curated smile. All this was news to Jens, who silently berated himself for not knowing this tidbit of information sooner. "Now, I ask you again, why are you here?"

"Would you believe I got lost," Jens said, trying to play it off as a joke.

"No," Derris said as he spun Jens around and led him over to the elevator. It wasn't the ideal situation, but Jens had learned one thing from this little research assignment. There was someone in the lottery who is willing to help us. *And I know his face.*

They reached the bottom on the elevator, with Jens being closely followed by Derris and Ms. Purchase, who quietly walked behind. Jens noticed Mrs. Choi talking with Ali, but it was Chris who noticed who was behind Jens first. He had to admit that their expression was priceless as Jens got to watch the colour slowly drain from their face.

"Is there a reason why I found Agent Jennings unaccompanied on the thirty-fourth floor?" Ms. Purchase said, looking to Mrs. Choi first, who turned to glare at Chris. *Sorry, Chris, it was a good run.*

"I got lost, and I remembered seeing a bathroom up on the thirty-fourth floor when we were here last. I didn't think anyone would have a problem with me being there," Jens said, lying, but he felt bad for throwing this kid under the bus.

"I'm sorry, Ms. Purchase, it was my fault. I should have kept a better eye on them."

Mrs. Choi's remarks cut into Chris as they shut down their data pad to pay closer attention.

"We just had some questions about the files you gave us and were wondering if it would be possible to get them going back to before Nigel Eriksen was in his position," Ali said, cutting through the tension with the matter-of-fact police work she seemed good at.

"Why would you need those?" Mrs. Choi shot back, clearly still reeling from losing control.

"Well, we want to rule out the possibility that someone other than Mr. Eriksen was involved with moving those credits around," Ali continued saying.

Jens noticed a look of concern on Mrs. Choi's face. She no doubt hated the good name of the lottery being pulled through the mud like this.

"We've done an internal investigation, and that was all the data we found relevant to this investigation," Mrs. Choi said, trying desperately to regain her composure and failing.

"So, you're saying there were other investigations?" Jens asked, prodding her a little to see if she would break, as she was visibly upset by all this. *No more upset than he was.*

Perhaps it was seeing Natasha that morning, and her brother's death was still on his mind. But he hated that this organization was lying directly to their faces, and what was worse was that they felt as though it was completely normal.

Even their own employees were afraid to come out and say anything. *And why wouldn't they be? Look what happened to Nigel Eriksen.*

Mrs. Choi remained silent and bit her bottom lip. She took a deep breath and waited a second before responding.

"We have no reason to believe that anything was done before Mr. Eriksen arrived," she said, looking to Ms. Purchase, who was a cooler example of stoicism.

"So, you wouldn't mind us looking?" Ali asked politely, trying to take the lead as she recognized Jens' building anger.

"Look, as we said . . . ," Mrs. Choi began saying, but it was Jens who snapped first, fed up with all the skirting around.

"Cut the crap. We know the transactions go back nearly fifty-five hundred days, likely even longer. So why don't you and your little team of specialized liars go back there and get us those damned files!" he shouted. The outburst took everyone, even Ali, by surprise. She'd not seen this side of Jens, and frankly, he'd only seen it once. *People need to stop stepping on the little guy—too many innocent people have already died!*

"Even if any of this were true, which it isn't, what makes you think you know any of this?" Mrs. Choi asked, her fist clenching so tightly her knuckles had turned white.

"Who gives a shit how we know? The fact is at least ten people are dead because you won't tell us what the hell is going on. And one of them barely got eight thousand days, and for whatever reason, you're trying to protect whoever killed him." Jens was heating up. He stepped toward Mrs. Choi as he spoke, his pointed finger pushing her back.

"Now are you going to tell us what the hell is going on here? Or do I need to come back with a warrant and arrest you all for impeding justice?!" Jens said with a hiss, and for a brief moment, he lost himself and saw the terror in Mrs. Choi's eyes.

Immediately, Jens knew he had made an error; rule number one was to never physically engage with a civilian. Right now, Mrs. Choi, although a known liar, was not at fault for anything.

Ali had got the files on the lottery in secret. In the eyes of the world, the lottery was fulfilling their obligations to help the police, whilst also catching a thief in their company. It was all good news for them. But Jens knew it was all a lie and was fed up with the games.

Based on the expression on Ali's face, what Jens had just done was not the right tactic. In fact, she looked pissed. But to his surprise, the final blow came from Ms. Purchase, who once again stepped in, brushing Jens' hand from Mrs. Choi.

"Mr. Jennings," she said, her omission of "agent" said it all in the moment. His position of power had been lost, but he didn't care. He wanted them to know they were onto them, and they should be afraid. Yet, Ms. Purchase didn't look afraid—she almost looked, pleased.

"We've done everything you have asked, and I'm not sure what source you got your information from, but I can assure you that we have checked our files, and there is no trace of any illicit activity before Nigel Eriksen joined that division. Furthermore, you do us all a disservice by laying down baseless accusations on this organization. I can assure you that there isn't a judge in the West who will support your claims to look into us." She was all but on top of Jens now.

"We've given you all the information you have required, and if I'm not mistaken, you have caught everyone responsible. I suggest you take the win, and you leave this building before I ask Mr. Harding here to forcefully remove you from the premises." Her tone was suddenly laced with pity. "You disappoint me, Mr. Jennings. Now please leave." She turned and started walking away. Mrs. Choi and Chris followed closely behind. Jens was left standing there with a still-rattled Ali.

"What the hell was that, Jens?" Ali said, shaking her head. "We caught them in a cold lie. We could have found a way to get the records, but now, even if we did, you've told them we know. No doubt they will be able to cover their tracks. I mean, goddammit, Jens, we had them." Ali turned and stalked out of the building, leaving Jens alone.

In the moment, he'd been so sure he could swing around and get them. But he'd been naive to think the most powerful company in the world would just bend to him.

"Ali!" Jens said, chasing after her. "Look, I'm sorry. I'm just so tired of them thinking they can get away with whatever they want."

"Well. Because of you. They will," Ali shot back. Taking a deep breath as she reached the sidewalk.

"Look. I know I messed up . . ."

"Messed up? Jens, you broke rule number one. You cannot touch or threaten a civilian."

"I pushed her with a finger."

"IT DOESN'T MATTER!" Ali said, stepping away.

Jens knew she was right, even if he didn't want to admit it. GIB agents were supposed to be calm and collected, yet he'd just lashed out at a leader of the biggest corporation in the world.

"You could have just messed up the entire operation," Ali said, opening the door to a waiting ECar, but she turned on him as he went to get inside.

"I strongly suggest you get your own," Ali said, getting inside and shutting the door. *Have I messed up this whole operation?*

As if he'd needed a further slap in the face, Jens' Zen watch began to vibrate.

"MY OFFICE NOW!" read a message from Captain Rollins.

"Shit!"

28

Jens didn't waste any time getting back to headquarters, and although he tried multiple times to reach Ali, she wouldn't answer.

For the second time in under a day, the bullpen was eerily quiet as Jens walked out of the elevator, all eyes seemed to find him. Muted whispers crept in from people as he walked by; everyone in the room at least pretended like they didn't have some idea why Jens was there.

Only Zhang and his little posse watched Jens unapologetically. Zhang was smiling broadly. He held back any remarks as Jens passed by, though. *Likely saving those for later.*

Not even Moretti could look at him for more than a second, offering a half-hearted smile as he passed.

Jens spotted Ali already in with Captain Rollins, standing arms crossed as she clocked him through the window, turning away when he met her eye.

Jens suddenly felt as if he were walking up to the gallows. Sucking in a deep breath, he stepped into the office.

The room had a somber feel to it and was permeating with anger from Captain Rollins. She was standing in the corner of the office squeezing a stress ball, which seemed ready to burst.

"What the hell were you thinking?" Captain Rollins asked, turning on him, her eyes narrowing in. "You understand what you've done, don't you?"

Jens knew it was a rhetorical question. He'd been getting so many lately, and he knew he should stand there, hoping she might take it easy on him. Unfortunately, he wasn't used to standing there being yelled at.

"We know they're lying! We caught them in the act. What the hell was I supposed to do . . . ," Jens argued.

Ali shook her head as she stood in the corner.

If I'm going down, it will be with no word left unsaid.

"You were supposed to do nothing!" Captain Rollins chastised him, the glass shimmering as she pressed a button activating the colour-corrected glass so no one on the outside could peer into the office—only they could look out, giving Jens a great view of a laughing Zhang.

"Your job was supposed to be to find the proof and bring it to us to deal with it. You were just supposed to be looking into the possibility that they were hiding something. NOT FUCKING TELLING THEM WE ARE INVESTIGATING THEM!" she shouted, highlighting her point by throwing the stress ball against the wall.

"They needed to know they're not above the law," Jens replied, each word another nail in his coffin.

"Well, that's fine work, Agent Jennings. Tell the largest damn organization that we suspect something. What do you think is going to happen? They're going to turn themselves in. If something is going on, they've already figured out a way to cover their tracks." She was no longer yelling, but there was still venom behind her words.

"Something like this doesn't just go away!" Jens shouted. "They may be big, but they're not magic." Maybe it was too soon to be making jokes as the room fell silent for a few moments.

"Five fucking days," the captain said quietly. "That's how long it took you to come back into my department and completely destroy our credibility." Her voice was eerily calm and direct.

"You managed to jeopardize all the arrests made on this investigation, on the belief that a criminal is telling you the truth. Maybe we were wrong—maybe he is playing us the fool. Did you ever think of that, Jennings?"

"He's not," Jens said as much to himself as to the others.

"Really? While you were off trying to prove this little theory of yours, I took the time to look into your little friend Anton." Captain Rollins pulled up a file on her data pad, sending it over to Jens, his wrist vibrating.

"Let me save you the reading time, agent. Your boy apparently has had it out for the lottery for some time now. Covert hacking interrupting their data streams. No doubt he planted all this to send us on his little vindictive witch hunt," Captain Rollins said calmly.

"So, he's hacked them. He's a hacker. We know that. But even the best hackers couldn't alter financial records covertly for fifty-five hundred days," Jens countered.

"Maybe not, but he's got motive. Turns out the lottery mistakenly assigned his parents winning funds. Thinking they had won, they moved houses, which put them in debt, only to have the lottery claim an error on their reporting and take the credits away. The family never recovered, and his father eventually took his own life. His mother did the same a few years later, at which point the state waived their debt, and he and his sister became society's children. No doubt our little hacker blames the lottery for the death of his parents. Still willing to put our credits on him, Jennings?" Captain Rollins said, taking a seat in her chair, her elbows perched on her desk as she let the information sink in.

Jens felt like a fool for not looking into Anton himself. It should have been the first thing, to know who's leading him through the fog. But even now this information did little to change Jens' mind about who the real enemy was. *Sure, he has a grudge, but he couldn't do what the captain was suggesting, could he?*

"This doesn't change anything," Jens said, protesting. "They are hiding something, and we all know it. Why are you so content for us to not investigate them?" Jens asked, pointing a finger at Captain Rollins.

"How dare you, you ungrateful prick! I stuck my neck out to get you back. I supported you to follow this lead! You're the stupid son of a bitch who overstepped his role." She was back on her feet. "Don't you dare put that on me. You want someone to blame? Look in a mirror. Then on top of all that, you broke the cardinal rule, Agent Jennings. Under no circumstance are you to physically touch a member of the public who is not under arrest. Seeing as you have no legal evidence to support your claims, you royally fucked yourself." *No more playing around.*

Captain Rollins pulled up her data pad and typed away on it. A moment later Jens felt a buzz on his Zen watch. He didn't need to look to know what it was. Ali, on the other hand, did. Jens shook his head; he was the one who should be punished, but apparently that wouldn't stop the captain from tearing down the people around him as well.

"Excuse me, ma'am, what's going on?" Ali asked as she saw the restricted access on her Zen watch.

"It's standard operations during an inquiry like this. I'm sorry, Agent Hantsport, but your partner is being held on suspension until the inquiry can be considered. As his on-site partner, you're also under investigation until we can clear this all up."

Jens could feel the burning of Ali's eyes on his back. She didn't deserve this, and he felt so ashamed he couldn't even meet her eye.

"How long, ma'am?" Ali said through gritted teeth.

"Two to three days without pay. But I have no doubt you'll be back. I can't say as much for your partner," Captain Rollins added for Jens' sake.

"May I be excused, ma'am?" Ali asked, getting a nod from the captain before she stormed out of the office.

Jens desperately wanted the chance to have her on her own to apologize, and maybe try to explain, although he couldn't see that helping him much. Instead, he stood there waiting.

"Agent Jennings, you've disappointed me." Captain Rollins sat down at her desk. "Get the hell out of my office." He'd expected another rant, but all he got was the disappointment speech.

Jens hadn't felt this deflated in a while. He may not have ever been a "great" partner, but Ali had been different. *She was willing to support me on this crazy witch hunt, and how did I repay her? By getting her suspended.*

He felt sufficiently terrible about Ali, who had already vanished by the time he left Captain Rollins' office. So, when Andrew Zhang stepped into his path, he was unwilling to have any of it.

"So, shit-for-brains, heard you screwed up another case," Zhang said. Jens wanted nothing to do with him, and attempted to step around him to avoid the whole confrontation.

Zhang, on the other hand, had other plans, stepping in his way and placing his fingers on Jens' chest. It was not altogether threatening, but certainly not the time and place.

"Get the hell out of my way, Zhang," Jens said, trying to keep himself together.

"Not enough, eh, to ruin your own career, but now you're bring others down with you?"

Zhang was talking quietly, but it didn't matter; the place was quiet enough to hear a pin drop. Jens could feel his blood boiling over; he needed to leave. He tried again to move around him but was stopped.

"I'm serious, Zhang. Get the hell out of my way." Jens could feel his pulse quickening.

"When are you going to learn—stop pissing in other people's backyards." The words were a threatening whisper meant for only Jens.

Jens looked up at Zhang, who was staring into his eyes. Zhang's face didn't bear the usual smug smile he wore, as if he were God's gift to the GIB, but it was dangerous. Jens had heard the warning loud and clear. Stop. Now.

For the third time in Jens' life, he felt as though his being here was a sign. Jens was onto something, and he was digging it up fast enough to rattle the right cages.

Normally this might have made him feel vindicated, that he was digging in the right spots, but now it infuriated him.

Which is why it wasn't a surprise to him, although maybe to the rest of the room, when his fist slammed into Zhang's jaw, dropping him down to the floor. There was a collective "ew" from the onlooking GIB agents in the room. Jens knelt beside Zhang, who lay stunned on the floor, clearly surprised by the attack.

"You tell whoever sent you to scare me that they should run and hide. Because I'm going to find them, and I'm going to tear down their whole fuckin' world," Jens whispered as he stepped over his body and walked out of the bullpen.

Jens looked back and saw a few of Zhang's followers scurry in to help him up, but he waved them off. Moretti was standing off to the side, smiling, giving him a subtle thumbs-up.

Apparently, whoever was behind this had friends in the GIB, but so do I.

Jens stepped onto the elevator; all eyes turned to watch him. Little did they know the storm that was about to come their way.

Jens slumped down on one of the benches outside the main building. The flowers growing up around them were bright and cheerful, everything he was not.

Once again, he'd missed Ali, who was likely avoiding him for obvious reasons. *I'd avoid me, too!*

Jens had no idea how long exactly he'd been sitting on the bench, but when he finally looked back up again, the sky had darkened, and now rain had begun to pour.

Jens didn't budge, even as the slow trickles of rain turned into a steady pour, his blue suit soaking up the wet.

"You idiot."

Jens barely felt the tingle on his wrist from his Zen watch, which had lost all its GIB functions. *So, who has access to its standby mode?*

The screen flashed as he lifted the watch to see the message. "Go to Memorial Hospital quickly. They've attacked him and will kill him. They're going to kill Anton Preston."

There was no sign-off address, no number, just the message warning Jens that someone would kill Anton Preston. Jens looked around as if half expecting whoever it was to be nearby when he spotted a single data cam, which seemed to be turned toward him.

Standing up slowly, he moved around, watching as the data cam tracked him. *Someone is watching me.*

"Why the hell should I care about Anton Preston?" Jens said, looking into the camera lens. Happily, no one was out in the rain watching his odd display. "He's a criminal, and he's safe in a rehabilitation facility."

His wrist vibrated again. "He's not safe. They found him."

"Who? Who found him?" Jens pressed.

"Go now!"

Jens wanted to shout, but whoever had hacked the data cam must have left as the data cam began swivelling around on its normal track.

"Goddammit!" The outburst received an odd look from a passerby running through the rain. "Shit!" he said as he hailed a nearby ECar, hopping inside when it arrived.

Jens hated hospitals, having released himself from one just a few days ago. The memory was still fresh as he started to rub his arm;

the nanobots had done a good job of repairing the arm tissue, but it would likely feel tender for some time. Something med-bots couldn't do was heal the psychological pain behind all of it. The memory was too fresh to forget and Jens assumed that's why he was so quick to answer this message. Whoever had tried to kill him, was apparently after Anton now. Anton should be safe at a rehabilitation site, but then again who knows what these people were capable of. *But if Anton is in a rehabilitation site, who is sending me these messages?*

As if on cue, a new message arrived, "room twenty-two, now." Jens looked around, noticing no one else in the hall, just a data cam in the corner of the room.

He walked quickly up the stairs to the second floor, then walked down the hall following the signs leading him toward room twenty-two. He hadn't known what to expect, but with the urgency of the messages, he felt as if he might walk into the room and find someone standing over Anton's body. But since exiting the stairwell, he'd seen only a single nurse walking around. There hadn't even been a guard posted at the door.

Jens began looking around, feeling some hesitation as he walked in. *Was this really Anton?*

Jens began to believe he'd been played, with some embarrassment washing over him as if some unseen spectator were having a laugh at his expense.

But as he approached the lone bed in the middle of the room, what he saw shook him to the core.

"Anton?" Jens said in a hushed whisper, as if the body lying before him had any hope of answering him. Jens stepped closer, and with each step, he took in the tattered body of Anton Preston.

Anton had been beaten to a pulp. His face was puffed up, and the bruising around his eyes was black. His jawbone looked to be shattered. Jens could tell the medical team had injected the nanobots,

and they were likely working double time to clean it up, although Jens knew from other crimes like this that Anton might never look the same—not without a little help from a doctor. Facial bones had too many nuances, making them more difficult to repair than larger bones. They were small and precise, so any alteration would likely show up during the healing process.

Unlike his arm. Once it was reconnected, it would still be an arm. *I'm sorry, Anton.*

Jens heard footsteps behind him, and he found himself hoping it was Ali so he could talk with her. But it was Granger who stepped in from the hallway.

"Jens? What are you doing here?" he asked, momentarily taken aback by seeing him.

"I heard Anton was attacked. I wanted to see for myself." It was a big lie, but he figured telling him about the random messages would be too weird. "What are you doing here?" He was suddenly concerned by his friend's arrival.

"I'm one of the arresting constables. When I heard what happened, I wanted to come and check on him. Poor guy, no one should have to deal with that." His voice was soft as he noticed Anton's face.

"So, you came out of protocol?" Jens asked suspiciously. That got an unusual look from Granger, who took a step forward.

"Yes, not to mention the fact that you told me there might be a leak in our department. So, I thought that if anyone were going to come and check on him, it should be me," he said, looking at Jens. "What is this, man? You think I'm some evil bastard trying to kill him? I told you I would help you," Granger said with a little force.

Jens sighed, taking a step back and finding a seat in the corner of the room. His head dropped into his hands. He was exhausted, and this cat-and-mouse game was getting to him.

"I'm sorry. I just . . . I don't know what I thought." Jens was looking

down at his shoes. "I'm back on suspension, not sure how long," he said, looking up at Granger, who had moved in to take another look at Anton's face.

"Holy shit, why?" Granger said, looking back at his friend.

"Let's just say I broke the no-contact rule with a group of people you don't break a no-contact rule with," Jens said. It wasn't as though he hit anyone, but law enforcement had zero tolerance for laying a hand on anyone without a person's permission unless they were under arrest.

"Holy shit, of course you did," Granger said, shaking his head while simultaneously amused.

"I'm glad you find my situation funny," Jens said irritably.

"Hey, don't get mad at me 'cause you can't follow the basic rule of engagement," Granger said, holding his hands up in defence. "Knowing you, it was either a minor infraction, or you beat the living shit out of someone," Granger said with a large smile. "The former, you'll be back in a day or two—the latter . . . well, you won't," Granger said, letting out a laugh.

"It was minor. But it didn't help that I may have punched another agent in the face as I was leaving," Jens said, his mouth betraying a hint of a smile. At that, Granger doubled over with laughter.

"Jesus, Jens, why the hell would you do that?" Granger finally asked.

"It's a long story, man," Jens said, moving closer to Anton.

"You know what you need? A drink," Granger said, putting his arm around Jens.

"What about Anton?" Jens asked. "He's still in danger."

"Danger?" Granger replied confusedly.

"Another long story," Jens said, regretting he'd said anything.

"We may need more than one drink," Granger said, musing. "I'll have one of my guys stay with him and make sure no one comes in or out other than the medical staff. Sound good?" Jens looked around

the room and nodded.

"Then a drink sounds good." Jens laughed as he followed Granger out of the room. Before they left, Jens noticed Granger tap away on a data pad, and another constable stepped into the room. Jens hadn't seen her before, but she gave a respectful nod to Granger and Jens as she walked by.

"Room twenty-two, got it?" Granger said, pointing down the hall. Another nod and she was off.

"Quite the loyal team you've got there, Granger," Jens said, watching the constable leave wordlessly.

"You spend as much time on the PPD as I do, big guy, you can get that reputation." He laughed, leading Jens down the stairs.

It had been a long time since Jens had gone out for drinks with a friend—well, with anyone, really. During his suspension, he rarely left the house, and when he did, it hadn't been to drink.

So, he had to admit the company was nice. Granger was an easy guy to talk with; he oozed confidence and could keep any conversation alive—not in an exhausting way, but with a genuine desire to listen to what people had to say. He certainly didn't monopolize the conversation as some people might have. He was a great listener. Jens understood why people liked him and followed his command.

Jens, on the other hand, blunt and to the point, was not one for small talk. He was beginning to understand that there is a time and place for it, and maybe, if he were still a GIB agent when all this was over, he would make more of an effort with some of his fellow agents. *What would I do if I wasn't a GIB agent?*

"What's on your mind, Jens?" Granger asked as he took a long swig of beer from his glass.

"Wondering what I would do if they didn't let me back into the GIB," Jens said honestly.

"Forget that, man, they are lucky to have you. You're a born agent,"

Granger said with more confidence than Jens felt.

"This is my second offence, and honestly, with everything going on," Jens shook his head, "I'm not sure . . ."

"Remember when we were in the PPD academy together?" Granger said, cutting Jens off before he could finish his thought.

Jens nodded, unsure of where his friend was going.

"You were the worst person there, so frickin' young and cocky it was like you wanted a target on your back to get smacked," Granger said, half laughing.

"Is this supposed to be helpful?" Jens said, unsure whether he should be amused.

"My point is none of that mattered. You were good at what you did, and you knew then that you wanted to be an agent, unlike the rest of us, who were happy to stay in the PPD," Granger said, gripping his beer in both hands. "What I'm getting at is that you can't not be you, Jens. You're a know-it-all who gives a shit about helping people. To a fault," he added seriously.

"I guess we can't all be handsome, confident PPD constables," Jens said, trying to evade the sudden wave of compliments.

"You forgot rich. I'm also rich," Granger said with a sad smile.

Jens knew little about Granger's family, but what he did know was a similar story to his own—a wealthy family that cared little for him no matter what he did. Even more so than himself, Granger likely didn't even need to contribute to society. The fact that he did always impressed Jens.

Granger slammed his finished drink down in front of Jens, who noticed his own glass was still half-full. Granger gave him a wink as Jens attempted to finish the remainder.

Jens wasn't a big drinker, and Granger was. Jens made a mental note not to try to keep up with his old friend.

"Jenny! Another round, please." Granger gave the petite girl behind the bar one of his winning smiles and turned to Jens. "I forgot how exciting it was to drink with you," Granger said, slapping Jens on the back as Jenny dropped off the two drinks with a wink to Granger. He handed one to Jens. "Come on, then, let's hear it," he said, sipping from the glass.

"What do you mean?" Jens ask skeptically.

"Come on, what were you even doing at the hospital? You beat me there, and I'm the senior constable on the case," Granger said, taking a big gulp from his mug.

"I thought Wilson was," Jens said, confused.

"Let's just say I volunteered after our little chat about her," Granger said, the words coming out in hushed tones.

"You okay with that?" Jens asked, taking a little gulp of his beer, his stomach still bloated from the last one. Granger shrugged.

"Look, I don't know what she is up to, and I'm not going to point fingers quite yet. But if she is doing something, then I owe it to the community to step in." Granger continued his reassuring words, doing little to convince Jens. Jens suspected Granger cared for Wilson, so what he was doing for Jens was difficult.

"I'm sorry," Jens said after a moment.

"Don't be. So, you going to tell me what's going on?"

"You wouldn't believe me if I told you," Jens said, spinning the beer glass on the table and watching the moisture drip down the side.

"Try me," Granger said, giving Jens a calm slap on the back before propping his elbows on the table ready to hear what was coming next.

For a moment Jens considered it, but he knew that Granger was definitely not ready to hear what he was about to say. He sat for a moment contemplating what to do.

Granger didn't move, just waited there, giving no signs of moving until Jens told him what was up. Finally, Jens let out a big sigh and turned to his friend.

"Fine, but I'm telling you, you're not going to believe me."

Granger gave Jens a slight nod and a smile. Jens proceeded to tell him about the fire and the bodies inside, the shady information the lottery was giving them, how he'd caught them in the lie, and how he'd ruined it by overstepping his position.

Jens told him about the connection to Stone Industries and the mayor and how they were linked to all three cases, finishing off with Anton Preston and Kyle Lilford, who were now dead or nearly dead for no apparent reason.

By the time Jens had finished, he and Granger had finished their second drinks and were making good headway on their third. Jens had forgotten about his note not to keep up with his friend. To his surprise, Granger didn't question anything Jens told him; he simply sat and listened the entire time, only occasionally jumping in for clarification.

Jens wasn't sure if it was because he believed him or because he was trying to figure out just how crazy he was. But it didn't matter; by the time Jens finished, he'd said all he needed to say and set his drink down in front of him, nodding slowly as if even he had a little trouble believing what he'd just said.

Granger, on the other hand, didn't move except for his eyes, which darted around as if placing the sequence of events, trying to see how they all fit in.

Jens knew he was smart. He'd known that since they were stationed together on an assignment in the PPD. Up till that point, Jens hadn't made very many friends, and for whatever reason, he was paired with Granger despite his request to be alone. As expected, they stepped on each other's toes when they started out, each wanting to make a name for himself.

Jens had eventually realized that Granger was by no means just a smooth talker. He was bright and had an uncanny ability to think twelve steps ahead.

"What are you thinking about?" Jens finally asked.

"The scenarios. Just sorting through them in my mind."

"And?"

"That's quite the story, Jens," he finally said, taking a long sip from his glass.

"I told you you wouldn't believe me," Jens said, a little deflated.

"No, I believe you. To an extent. But I believe it was you who always used to say that without the right facts, all you have is beliefs, and beliefs don't catch criminals." Granger laughed, using Jens' own words against him.

"Damn your memory." Jens laughed. "But true enough, I can't believe you remember that."

"Of course, our first case together. As I recall, it was a pretty good team effort." Granger laughed, putting his hand up for another round.

"I really shouldn't," Jens said, looking at the quarter-full glass still in front of him.

"Come on, what do you have to do tomorrow?" Granger said, the dig creating a fresh wound in Jens, but he wasn't wrong. *I won't be going back into work any time soon.*

"Fine, one more. But that's it," Jens said before reluctantly sighing.

"Jenny!" Granger shouted, putting up two fingers, getting a nod from Jenny behind the bar.

"Right, so tell me what you think is going on," Granger said, the conspiratorial voice coming out as the two of them played out scenarios together.

29

Jens woke the next morning with a splitting headache. As it turned out, one more beer to Granger is never just one more beer. Jens vaguely remembered taking a pill that was supposed to help with the hangover before bed, which seemed to be useless.

He went into the bathroom trying to find anything that might cut the edge a little; he found nothing. *I remember now why I don't drink very much.*

He briefly toyed with the idea of going back to bed, but he decided it would do no one any favours to sulk in his bed. Not after the night he'd had with Granger, which turned out to be more rewarding than imagined.

Granger certainly knew how to lay out a puzzle and fiddle around with it. Although many of the pieces were still missing, Jens believed they may have found a possible working story line. So instead of lazily dropping back into his bed, he opted for the Bio Gravity Machine.

It never hurt to try to sweat out the demons, and God knows he had a few of those right now. He geared up and started low to ease himself in.

After a few minutes, he pushed it up a little higher, only to realize his body wasn't having any part in the game he was trying to play. More than once he had to stop himself from vomiting, after which he decided not to push it. It took a good fifteen minutes on the machine, but he finally found his rhythm.

"Activate thought board," Jens said, the case around him lighting up.

"Topic: connections."

One conclusion from the night was that it was no coincidence that all this was connected. In every case there is something hidden.

"The hidden lottery files and questionable transfer of funds. We know Stone Industries and the lottery are connected, but does that mean Mayor Stone is? What does he have to gain from any of this? The PPD is linked to Dr. Atkins, who is linked to Ryan Lilford. The glaring question is who is pulling all the strings?"

Though it had been only a short time, Jens felt the sweat dripping down his back.

"Action-Breakdown," Jens said as all the categories and subcategories broke off into small chunks as a web of information appeared on the board. "Assess data, find possible connections."

"Assessing data now," said a soft voice as various snippets of information began to flash on the screen all too fast for Jens to make out. "Data points to two possible connections, though neither is conclusive."

"Show connections now," Jens said, feeling as if he knew the answers before he even asked.

"Data suggest connection with Ash and Sun or Firefly, though neither has enough information to be certain."

"Shut down," Jens said, no longer feeling as if he could run. It was the same conclusion Jens and Granger had managed the night before, and like the program, they couldn't decide one or the other.

Jens' Zen watch flashed, sending a short pulse through his wrist.

"You failed us," Jens read. It was short and confusing, all the things Jens hated, especially right now. *What the hell does that mean?*

"Deactivate Bio Gravity Machine," Jens said, walking over to the miraculously clean island separating the kitchen and living room. He plugged his Zen watch in, activating the built-in Halo projection in the island.

"Let's see if we can't find out who sent this," Jens said as the GIB access portal popped up in front of him.

"Damn." Jens was locked out of the GIB. He wished he could call Ali and her friend in Tkaronto who could help, but she was more likely to tell him to piss off than help.

Jens lamented the fact he'd somehow managed to make a friend and ruin the friendship in in under a week. *That has to be some sort of record?*

He needed to fix this, if he had any chance of getting to the bottom of what was happening. *I can't do this alone.*

Later, he waited outside her building, holding a coffee. It took some time, and unfortunately the coffee had gone cold, but eventually Jens saw Ali leave her building, heading toward the market. She spotted him right away and pretended not to see him. He chased her down holding the apology coffee.

"The hell do you want?" Ali said, not bothering to look at him when he reached her.

"To apologize," Jens said, hoping it sounded as sincere as he wanted it to. He wasn't used to this and was finding it very weird. He held up the coffee, and Ali reluctantly grabbed the cup and took a sip.

"You wanted to apologize with cold coffee?" she said, tossing it in a bin as she passed.

"In my defence, it was hot when I bought it," Jens said, attempting to joke, but if she heard it, she ignored him.

"Look, can you just stop for a moment?" Jens was struggling to keep up, and he stopped. To his surprise, she stopped a couple of paces ahead of him.

"I understand you're pissed off. I didn't mean for you to get into trouble, too. Fuck, I didn't mean to. I just . . . it doesn't matter." Jens had rehearsed what he'd wanted to say all morning, and yet, despite all his practicing, he was failing miserably.

"But it does matter, Jens? What the hell were you thinking?" Ali said, turning on him, taking a step in, and putting a finger up to him, her gesture careful not to touch him.

"This is okay," she said, keeping the finger away from him. "This is not!" she said, giving him an aggressive stab in the chest. "You know the rules! So, why the hell would you do it, not to mention telling them we were looking into them. An unsanctioned operation on the biggest company in the world, and you blow up on them in a goddamn tell-all?" she shouted as people around them were now giving them a wide berth.

"I know, I'm sorry, but don't you want to know why Ms. Purchase was even there? Don't you find that strange?" Jens asked. He'd known why she was there, or at least why she claimed to be there, having been a member of the board.

But Jens hadn't had the chance to tell anyone yet, not even Granger, despite their endless banter around the case. But even knowing the why still made her timing very strange. Ms. Purchase was now directly linked to two of the companies in question, which in Jens' mind made her a prime suspect.

"Of course, I do!" Ali yelled back. "But thanks to your stupidity, we won't know. Don't you understand that?" Jens dropped his head. "Seriously, what the hell got into you? I was told you were a sensible human being, but all I've seen you do is push people away. It's like you're trying to sabotage yourself. The only problem is you're bringing me and everyone else down with you!" Ali's face was red. She was upset and had every right to be.

She didn't know much about him, and Jens never shared much. But he realized if he were going to gain her trust back, he would have to explain some things to her.

"Come with me," Jens said, turning to walk away without waiting to see if she was following. At this point, she was either willing to trust him or she wasn't. If she were, he would explain everything to her.

30

As it turned out, Ali's curiosity must have outweighed her anger as Jens now found himself in an awkward silence, neither of them having said anything since leaving Ali's apartment.

Jens occasionally looked over at Ali as she peered absently out the window. Jens couldn't be sure what Ali was thinking about, but he was feeling nervous about the whole thing. A steady rotation of rubbing his hands together made them become annoyingly clammy, then he switched to twiddling thumbs before getting irritated and repeating the process over again. In the moment, shrinking into himself, Jens felt like a little boy again trying to come clean about some childish foolishness.

But it wasn't either of those things, as the pit in his stomach kept reminding him. Jens hadn't been out here in forty-seven days. He wasn't supposed to be anywhere close to here, but he always stayed the appropriate distance away and never got out of the car.

Eventually, they pulled off the interstate and into a secluded community. People here had lawns and big homes; families ran around, others outside for walks. It was by all accounts an ideal place to live. The car stopped on one of the side roads, a yellow, stucco-sided bungalow beside them, matching the theme of the neighborhood.

Jens knew this house well, because it was ten feet from the legal cutoff before his Zen watch would send to the local enforcement community.

From here his view was clear to the two-story, redbrick house that stood at the end of the cul-de-sac. It was a nice home with white shutters on the window, an old colonial style. Outside a woman worked her garden. Jens thought she was had less then eight thousand days left on her clock, although one wouldn't guess that just by looking at her. She looked happy and healthy out in her lawn planting flowers. There would have been three kids in the house at one time, but Jens knew they were also gone. It was just she and the large man with thinning red hair Jens could see through the window. He looked to be making dinner and laughing with someone off the data screen. The image of the man made Jens want to jump into the house and beat him up again.

He'd obviously been to the doctors and received some med-bots to fix up his injuries. Jens rubbed his own arm, taking comfort in his own discomfort, knowing that man would feel the same thing. Med-bots were good but not perfect.

"What the hell are we doing?" Ali finally asked, looking around the area. Her eyes settled on the redbrick house at which Jens was staring.

"You want to understand why I lost it? There he is."

Jens assumed she would have known the story; someone must have told her. But from her expression, Jens could see she had no idea what he was referring to.

"That's Chief Daniels." Even saying his name agitated Jens slightly. Ali must have heard some of the stories, a spark of recognition in her eyes.

"Why are we here?" she asked quietly, possibly fearing another outburst from Jens.

"He's the reason I'm like this," Jens said quietly.

"You're going to need to explain more here, Jens, 'cause right now you're doing a piss-poor job," Ali said, turning to face him.

"I heard accusations that Chief Daniels was part of some . . ." the words were difficult for Jens to get out, but he forced himself, anyway. "He was trafficking women and possibly sexually assaulting them as well. I tasked myself with finding out."

Jens caught a hint of a smile on Ali's lips at that.

"It took some time, but eventually I was able to link him to some of the attacks."

"Sounds like a dirtbag," Ali said quietly.

"It gets worse. I found out he, ummm, he preferred children," Jens said, feeling the rage build inside as he said it out loud. "That guy," Jens said through gritted teeth, pointing toward him, "is a real shit bag."

"So why is he out here?" Ali asked again, obviously fearing the worst.

"Exactly." Jens shook his head, the answer being more for himself than Ali. "He used his position to pull some strings. The scandal attached to him was too big, and someone wanted it to go away."

"You had proof, though?" Ali asked.

"I did. A number of the women were ready to testify against him. But then suddenly they were afraid to do it. Some of them even recanted their statements, and by the end of it, it looked like he would get away with it." Jens could barely look up from his lap, and his hands knotted together reliving the frustration.

"Are you sure you had the right person?" Ali asked after a moment, her voice trying to remain sympathetic.

"A hundred percent. That asshole did it," Jens shouted, his eyes focused fiercely out the window at Daniels from a distance.

"Fine. But it still doesn't explain why we're here," Ali said after another moment, her impatience creeping through in a make-your-point-or-take-me-home kind of way.

"I have an issue with supposedly good people who use their position to do bad things. They are not bigger than society. Chief Daniels may never go down for what he did because why? He was in power? That's bullshit." Jens turned to look Ali in the eye.

"We're not allowed to look into the lottery killing innocent people because why? They help people. The organization is designed to do good. Not the individuals. If individuals are out there getting people killed, we need to expose them. I'm sick of trying to do the right thing, only to have someone tell me to stop because they don't want to ruffle any feathers." He grabbed Ali's hand, shocking her with the gesture.

"Doesn't it piss you off to know something is going on here, and we were asked to stop looking at it?"

"Yes, but it's our job to follow orders," she said, defensively pulling her hand away.

"No, it's our job to provide justice to the people. Not some of the people. All the people," Jens argued.

"So, what would you do?" Ali snapped back.

"Get justice for what they did! Make sure that Ryan Lilford, Nigel Eriksen, and Dr. Atkins didn't die for nothing. Even those piece-of-shit Scorpions deserve a little justice," Jens said pleadingly. It was hardly a rallying cry, but he knew he needed to rebuild her trust. Jens knew he needed to connect with her, she'd let him in on her secrets, and it was time he did the same.

"Captain Daniels didn't fall down the stairs. I pushed him."

Jens thought back to the little girl. He'd seen her immediately being taken in through a side entrance. They weren't even trying to hide it. Jens had known about the building but never actually seen anyone go in.

He been following him now for a little over three hundred days and all the while knew what was going on and felt helpless to stop it. So, watching this scared little girl with tears streaming down her face, alone, being pulled by the larger man, something in Jens snapped.

"Hey!" Jens said, stumbling into view as the both the guard and the girl turned to face him. "Are you okay?" Jens said, his words slurring slightly, though he found it difficult to hide his rage when he saw the bruising on the girl's body.

"Mind your damned business, ya filthy drunk," the guard said, taking a step toward Jens.

"Why not pick on someone your own size," Jens said, but the oversize man laughed.

Pretending to stumble, Jens fell into the giant, who put his arms out to stop the collision. Taking advantage of the outstretched arms, Jens pulled the man into him, kneeing him square in the balls.

"You thought this was a fair fight?" Jens said, slipping behind the man's back while locking his arms around the man's neck and choking him.

"You're a dead man." The guard wheezed as he stepped up to his full height, Jens wrapping his legs around the man's chest to stay in place.

The little girl began to scream as she hid behind a dumpster.

"Shush, you're going to be okay," Jens said to the little girl as the guard smashed him into a wall. Jens managed to stay locked even as his head collided with the wall.

"Go down!" Jens said with a hiss as he tried to pinch his legs around the man's lower ribs to help stifle his breathing, which was beginning to sound ragged.

"I'll kill you." The words came out as mostly a series of gargles. The man attempted to throw Jens into the wall again, though with much less effort than before, which was good, because Jens didn't know if he'd be able to hold on after another full blow. His head was killing him.

Finally, the man collapsed to his knees and then to the ground his body limp as Jens laid his head softly on the ground.

"Night, night," Jens said, his arms now like jelly. He caught his breath quickly before looked around for the little girl, who was huddled in the corner hiding beside a nearby eco-bin.

"Are you okay?" Jens said softly. The little girl nodded. As Jens got closer, he realized she wasn't as young as he thought, just very small. Jens figured she couldn't have more than forty-seven hundred days on her.

There was a silver band around her wrist, the oval plate showing the two hands with a heart between them. It was the mark of society's children, and she would be forced to wear it for six thousand days unless legally adopted.

"Why are you here?" Jens asked her.

The girl was hesitant as she stared at the big man on the ground.

"He told me he could find me a home," she said quietly after a few moments.

Jens was trying to suppress his anger, knowing Daniels had been lying to these kids, tricking them into . . . whatever the hell this was.

"I'll tell you what," Jens said. "I'll help you find a home, but you have to do me a favour. Okay?"

She nodded.

Jens tapped his data watch, scrolling quickly down a list until he found the number he was looking for.

He sent it to the young girl's beat-up data watch. It looked as if it barely worked, but when he had her test it, it did.

"Go to that address and tell them Agent Jennings sent you. Can you do that?"

She nodded, still seeming unsure of everything.

"Okay, go, she will help you find a home—I promise," Jens said, and for a moment the little girl looked as though she would break down again. But instead, she turned around and ran off, stopping briefly to turn back.

"Thank you," she said meekly, and off she ran.

Jens would have preferred to take her himself, but he needed to finish what he started, and he resolved to check in on her later, having picked up her details when he transferred the address for Agent Moretti, who he knew he could trust. *When this is all over, I'll make sure she's okay.*

Jens wasn't sure what he expected, but it wasn't a club with a massive pit filled with people. The floors cascaded up from the pit, each section looking like a labyrinth of tunnels leading through the underground club. In the center were three DJs pumping out electronic dance music through the whole building.

It wasn't the sort of place Jens expect to find a chief of the GIB hiding out. *Maybe that was the point?*

Moving through the crowd, Jens caught sight of more than a few dealers all pushing a new mind-meld drug, which would explain the free-moving kids all seeming to be lost in the music.

Jens could have had a field day with warrants, but these kids weren't why he was here. Scanning the room, he found what he was looking for, a large man of similar make and model to the one now passed out on the back stoop.

Unsure his arms could handle another conflict, Jens spotted a particularly intoxicated youth, and with a slight nudge watched as he toppled over into another group of partygoers.

Just as Jens hoped, the group did not take well to its new party guest and began to squabble, which brought the doorman over to intervene.

Jens made his move, swooping in and setting up the anti-lock mechanism on his Zen watch, allowing him to override the security system.

Slipping through the steel door as quietly as he could, he closed it behind him.

The hallway he found himself in now was eerily quiet, all the sounds from the club muffled to a dull hum. *Dammit!*

Sticking his ear up to the closest door, his fear was correct. *Soundproof!*

Looking down the hall, Jens figured there must be about twenty rooms: ten on either side along even intervals, and he had no way of knowing which one was the one he needed.

"Fuck it. Too late to turn back now."

He opened the first door and was shocked when he saw a large, balding man hung up by his feet wrapped in a black silicone suit, a ball lodged in his mouth. It wasn't the chief, and whoever he was waiting for hadn't arrived. Jens looked confused, but not as confused as the man, who'd started screaming noiselessly into the ball.

Jens didn't wait around for his companion, quickly shutting the door and continuing more cautiously down the hall. The next door he tried contained a large horse, but no Chief Daniels, and Jens really didn't want to see what was going to happen with the horse.

"Shit! I don't have time for this," Jens said, glancing back at the main door. *I needed to be smart, find him, and get the hell out.*

That's when Jens remember the GIB tracker on his phone. He'd had it approved for installation during a recent smuggling investigation he was working on in order to help track a supplier. He should have had it deactivated once the operation was finished, but he hadn't got around to it.

Jens knew that activating the device would break a number of rules, and it would mean the GIB would have a record of what he was using it for, but in this moment it felt worth it. *Future me can think of an excuse.*

Jens turned on the tracker, and sure enough a small blip appeared on the screen. *I have you now, you son of a bitch.*

The tracker led to a final set of two doors to choose from, when the sound of rhythmic thumping filled the hall, and Jens turned to see both a now conscious and rightfully pissed off security guard, and the doorman, step into the hallway.

Jens didn't want to stick around to see what the guard might do if he caught him, as Jens grabbed the door closest to him and slipped inside.

"Shit!" he said, cursing and seeing the room was also empty. Poking his head out the door, he realized that the two men still hadn't seen him, but the one he'd hit seemed ready to kill someone. *I have to get out of here. I need a plan that doesn't involve me dying.*

A soft click caught his attention as a tiny woman stepped into the room from a hidden door in the wall. She nearly jumped out of her skin when she saw him.

"Who are you? You're not supposed to be in here. Guard . . ." She began to call out, but Jens was faster, swooping in to place his hand over her mouth.

"Quiet! I'm with the GIB. I'm looking for someone," he said, trying to keep his voice as calm as he could manage under the circumstances. She stared at him defiantly.

"If I remove my hand, you promise not to scream?" She looked at him for a moment, her eyes darting around the room and eventually falling onto his Zen watch. She must have recognized it, as she nodded slowly. Jens slowly let her go and removed his hands from her and held them up in the air, doing his best not to appear threatening.

"I'm sorry for grabbing you," Jens said in a whisper, suddenly realizing he'd broken a cardinal rule for the GIB, and since this wasn't necessarily a sanctioned operation, he was spiralling into some dangerous territory.

But if she'd been bothered by the gesture, she didn't let it show, as she fell back into polite obedience. *What are they doing to you in here?*

"I'm Sergeant Jennings," he explained, trying to calm himself down.

"Amelia," she said softly before adding, "who are you looking for?"

"An asshole," Jens retorted, which received a smile from his new partner.

"You'll have to be more specific," Amelia said through a suppressed laugh. Pulling out his Zen watch, Jens uploaded a Halo image of Chief Daniels.

"Have you seen him? He should be near here."

She looked at the photo and took a step back, with a look of terror on her face.

"You recognize him?" he said optimistically.

"Yes," she said cautiously as she looked to his right, as if looking through the wall. The tracker was right; he went through the wrong door.

"Amelia, can you help me get to him? I need to be fast. The guys outside are looking for me," Jens said hopefully. She swallowed deeply.

"Please, you don't have to do anything. Just tell me where to go and how to get out of here. No one will know," Jens said, excited by the possibility of getting out of this in one piece.

She looked hesitantly at him. She likely had been told to trust people plenty of times, and for all that, this is where she landed. Jens couldn't blame her for hesitating.

"Please, he's a terrible person," Jens said, persisting, but from her reaction, she knew this already.

"Whatever he's done to you, I will stop him," Jens said firmly. He wanted to believe it himself, but at this point, he was riding blind. His proof was gone when he sent the little girl away. Since then, he'd been driven by raw anger.

After a couple of difficult seconds, she finally opened the doorway she'd been standing in.

"This is a service access. There is a door to the other room beside us. You can also follow it that way," she said, pointing down the long hallway. "It will take you to the back alley." Her voice was soft but resolute, uncaring if he was telling the truth.

"Thank you," Jens said, wishing he could take the girl with him. But if this didn't work, she could wind up dead right beside him, and even if she might prefer that, Jens couldn't put her at risk. *I'll come back and get her.*

But that thought still felt empty as she placed her arm on his.

"He has a guard, and . . . he may not be alone," she said with a sad expression. Jens recognized what she meant.

"Don't worry—I won't hurt whoever is in there."

"What about him?"

"Him . . . I might hurt," he said coldly, which received another smile from his new cohort.

Leaving Amelia in the empty room, Jens made his way through a dark corridor about five feet down the hallway to the next door, which he knew would lead him into the right room.

Pulling out his electro-pulse, he pressed the charge button, unsure of who was in the room. He knew he had to be careful.

Down the hall he spotted the escape stairwell. *Perfect, all I need is that bastard, and I can get the hell out of here without anyone knowing I was here. What could go wrong?*

With that in mind, Jens barged into the room, momentarily stunning everyone. Holding the electro-pulse in his hand, he scanned the room.

The room was small, containing only a large U-shaped couch and a table with two men sitting at it. Jens recognized one man immediately; the second he was less sure of, but that didn't matter.

On the table was a partially naked young woman stretched out. When she saw an unknown stranger enter, she screamed loudly and quickly attempted to cover herself up.

"Jennings?" Chief Daniels said in angry confusion after a moment, his eye adjusting to the scene. "What the hell are you doing here?"

Jens didn't waste time. Eventually someone else would come in; he needed to get out fast. He would figure out what to do with Chief Daniels later.

Firing his electro-pulse at the unknown man, he caught him in the chest, his body convulsing as the electric current shot through him and he collapsed to the floor.

"What the fuck are you doing, Jennings?" Chief Daniels shouted as Jens watched the partially nude dancer run out of the room screaming. *If they didn't know where I was before, they certainly do now.*

Without thinking, Jens reached across to Chief Daniels, who was sitting. The man put his arms up in defence. He might have been older than Jens, but he was not a weak man; it showed as he fought back.

"You're under arrest, Chief Daniels," Jens said, wishing his voice sounded a little more confident than it did.

Chief Daniels began to laugh.

"You don't know what the fuck you're doing!" he shouted.

His words sank in, and for a moment, Jens felt as if he were making a terrible mistake, but then his mind wandered to the little girl he had just saved, and all his anger flooded back.

Without a word, Jens grabbed his boss's head and smashed it into the table. The man cried out in pain, and when he sat up, he had blood draining from his nose, giving Jens a weird sense of satisfaction. Before he had time to retaliate, Jens was on him, slapping on a pair of mag cuffs. Jens was winging it now, as he pulled the big man up to his feet.

"Time to move," Jens said hurriedly.

"Do you know how royally fucked you are, Jennings?" Chief Daniels shouted as Jens pulled him into the back hallway. "I'm the fucking chief of the GIB. You have no right!" he said, spitting the words at Jens as fresh blood poured from his nose.

Jens watched as the large guard he'd knocked out entered the room, and to his surprise he checked on the man collapsed on the floor first rather than chase Jens. *Lucky for me.*

Moving quickly down the hall, he checked back periodically to see if they were being followed, but no one was there. Reaching a door, Jens pushed the chief's body into the handle; the man's head cracked off the door at the same time.

"Fuck!" he cried out. Then to Jens' surprise, he began to laugh. "Do you know who you just EP'd in there? Do you?"

Jens ignored the man; he didn't know, and right now he didn't care. All he cared about was getting down to the back exit. When he spotted a set of metal loading stairs ahead, he knew he must be close. *Two flights down and there should be a service area. I should be able to get out from here, hopefully.*

"You can kiss your job goodbye, you piece of shit. You'll never work again." Chief Daniels carried on speaking, obviously dissatisfied with Jens' silence.

"Move it," Jens said with a little push as he led him down the stairs to the first landing.

"You don't get it, do you? What do you think is going to happen here?" he said with an amused smile on his face.

Annoyed, Jens shoved him against the wall.

"You're going to jail, you sack of shit," Jens shouted, momentarily taken aback by the fit of laughter that ensued.

"You've got to be shitting me, Jennings. For what? Getting a dance? She was legal!"

"I know what you've been doing," Jens said, not wanting to back down.

"What's that, you prick?" Chief Daniels said, once again spittle and blood flying at Jens' face.

Taking a moment to wipe his face, Jens glared at the man.

"I know about the kids, you filthy, fuckin' bastard—that you lure them in off the streets, that you sell them!" Saying it out loud, Jens could feel the anger pulsing through his body, his hands wrapped tightly around the man's blue blazer.

"I don't know what the fuck you're on about, but . . . ," he began saying, but Jens cut him off.

"I have proof! Photos, records of your meetings and the girls. It's enough to put you away," Jens said coldly. But to Jens' surprise, Chief Daniels continued to laugh.

"You don't have a fuckin' clue. You have nothing. All you've done is assaulted two men in a bar."

"I have pictures . . . ," Jens started to shout.

"I don't give a fuck if you have my diary! I'm the goddamned chief of the GIB. Who do you think people are going to side with—you and your crackpot story? Or my illustrious fuckin' career! I'm untouchable, you dumb fuck!" The chief's voice rang through the stairwell, and he glanced up, as if expecting to be found any minute. Jens felt something snap as he watched the man's lips curl into a smile. In the chief's mind he'd already been freed, and the thought made Jens want to scream.

The chief's cocksureness began to weaken Jens' belief that he would go down for what he'd done. How could a man so evil possibly get away with this?

Glancing down the stairs, Jens understood that the only way out, was down. Staring the chief in the eyes, he said, "No one's untouchable," his voice quiet and cold as he grabbed his boss and kneed him in the testicles, then watched as he fell back in pain, all the way down the metal stairs.

Chief Daniels' body arched awkwardly as he tried unsuccessfully to free his hands in a desperate attempted to brace for impact.

Jens watched as Chief Daniels' body crumpled against the first stair. The momentum of the fall twisted the man's body in agony as he cried out in pain with each passing step. Jens watched, feeling cruel, but unable to stop it if he'd wanted to. The whole painful display took only seconds. Chief Daniels' body finally smacked the bottom floor with a dull whap.

Jens followed his victim down with a calm understanding that the man would most likely be dead when he arrived. To his surprise as he approached the motionless man, he noticed a weak breath from his lips. The sudden reality of the situation washed over Jens as he began to regret his actions, watching as the blood began to pool out of the man's prone body. *This isn't justice, it's vengeance.*

It had been a mistake; he'd tried to kill someone, and here he was still alive. Jens quickly unlocked the mag cuffs still shackling Daniels' hands together and then pulled up his Zen watch, calling in the med vac team. It wouldn't be long till it arrived.

To his surprise, one of the large men from the club began running down the stairs, his actions too late to make a difference. He glanced down at Jens, hovering over Chief Daniels, his Zen watch on display as he called in the med vac team.

Jens prepared to run. This man was clearly ready to kill. Jens had done his damage already, and soon the medical team would arrive, and either Chief Daniels would be dead or the team would help him.

But to his surprise, the guard stopped and returned wordlessly to where he'd come from.

Jens' focus remained steady on Ali as she sat patiently through the entire story.

"He had to suffer like everyone he hurt. I was prepared to lose everything to show him he wouldn't win," Jens said, hoping for a reaction, but when Ali remained silent, he continued. "No one was going to give those victims justice. So, I did. I had to make him pay."

Jens was pleading now, unsure if it was to Ali or himself. His eyes were bloodshot as he struggled to hold back his tears. Jens look desperately to Ali, but she only sat there, looking at him and waiting for more.

"But he woke up and didn't remember anything. There was no footage, and no one else was there to claim differently. I was placed on suspension and had a restraining order placed on me for his protection." Jens' head sank low into his chest.

"Do you regret it?" Ali asked.

"No. I would do it again."

"Easy to say when you got away with it."

"Maybe."

For a long while, the ECar remained silent as neither Jens nor Ali was able to speak.

"So, what, you want to push Angela Choi down a set of stairs?" Ali asked, her tone serious as she glared at him.

"No. Look at him," Jens said and pointed out the window to Chief Daniels in the kitchen. "What do you see?"

Ali looked out dispassionately.

"I see a guy cooking dinner," she said, and Jens nodded.

"I see a guy living a pretty good life, making dinner for his loving wife, in his nice house in a great community."

"What's your point?" Ali asked.

"My point is he's not suffering. He's not paying for what he did. He broke some bones, and now he gets this. He doesn't even know what

I did to him." Jens shook his head, remembering what he'd done.

"I was wrong. I was angry because he would get away with it, and I didn't think there was anything I could do. So, I did something stupid. And yes, I got away with it. I still have my job. But it's happening again, and I have a choice. Do what they want us to do and stand down, or fight for the justice those people deserve. No more pushing people downstairs," Jens said, the last bit receiving a welcomed smile from Ali.

"Look, I know I don't deserve it. I've been a shit partner. But I could really use your help here," Jens said, looking at Ali.

"Say I wanted to help, which is still a hard maybe. You've basically just told the two biggest companies in the West that we are looking into them. You think they won't find a way to cover their tracks?" Ali said, her arms folding across her chest.

"I admit it was a poor showing on my part . . ."

"You think?" Ali said, interrupting.

"But I think we can still find proof," Jens countered.

"How?" Ali asked Jens, still not sure she should trust him.

"There was a man in the lottery—I think he's the one who's been calling me. He knows something, and we just need to find him," Jens said, hoping this would be enough to persuade her.

"Great, who is he?" Ali asked.

"I don't know."

"Okay, where is he?"

"No idea." So far Jens was not off to a great start.

"So, let me get this straight. Your big idea is that you have a guy, but you don't who or where he is? How the hell is that a plan?" Ali asked incredulously.

"It's not. It's a starting point, and I could use your help." Jens pleaded with her. "You in?"

Ali looked out the window at Chief Daniels.

"A shit bag, eh?" she said.

"The worst."

"Fuck it, I'm in," she said after a moment.

Jens opted for a little smile, knowing that getting Ali on board was only step one.

Step two, however, would have to wait, as Jens felt a buzz on his Zen watch. He pulled up a data message from Granger.

"Where the hell is he, Jens? What did you do with Anton Preston?"

31

Granger's message hadn't become any clearer to Jens as he and Ali got back into the city, making their way to Memorial Hospital.

As for his relationship with Ali, the trip had been a minor success. Though Ali might not have been fully convinced, she was at least speaking with him again. *I'll take the win.*

"Jens, what the hell, man. Please. Please! Tell me you did not kidnap Anton Preston from the hospital? For the love of all things merciful, please tell me you don't have him." Granger's worried voice reached him, and Jens suddenly realized what had happened. The PPD had lost Anton from the hospital, and Granger believed Jens had something to do with it.

"You didn't, did you?" Ali asked.

"Come on, really?"

"I had to ask. Because none of this makes sense," Ali said, looking over her data pad.

"What are you looking at?" Jens said, his eyes narrowing in on Ali.

"According to the PPD, early this morning Anton Preston was taken from his guarded hospital bed. The constable watching him was knocked unconscious using a neurotoxin," Ali read from a PPD report, ignoring Jens' questions.

"How the hell do you have access to that?" Jens asked, eyeing Ali skeptically.

"I'm borrowing it."

"Who the hell would lend you their PPD data?" Jens said, and he noticed Ali started to blush.

"I wouldn't say she let me borrow it," Ali said, her face turning to a deeper shade of red at each question.

"Go on, then," Jens said, crossing his arms.

"What?"

"Well, I get flak from you for not following the rules, and here you are hacked into someone's data screen."

"Not hacked, borrowed," she said, putting a finger up in protest.

"Well, who are you borrowing this from?" he asked again. Ali still attempted to ignore the question, but Jens refused to back down.

"Dr. Nazari. She had her password written down at her house, and I thought we could use the information."

As Ali spoke, her eyes never left the data screen, but Jens caught the tiniest flicker in her eyes as he suddenly realized her attention had fully turned on him.

"How did you get . . ." Jens figured it out before he finished speaking, and Ali looked at him, slowly her face a full scarlet red.

"Right. Well, smart thinking. Anything else useful in there?"

Jens understood that it was hard enough for people to have relationships in the PPD and imagined Dr. Nazari would be pretty pissed to learn Ali was on her network. So, Jens understood the risk she was taking.

"Not really," Ali said, signing off the data pad. "Last update was fifteen minutes ago."

"What did it say?" Jens asked.

"Were you there last night?" she asked, looking to Jens. He was reluctant to say anything and seemed to be saved as his Zen watch vibrated from an unknown caller.

Jens looked over at Ali, and he placed the call on speaker. For a moment there was nothing on the other end. Jens could hear the breathing, though.

"Hello?" he said softly, not wanting to scare the other person.

"If you want to know about the lottery, meet me in Zone Eighty-Nine, Limestone Courtyard One hour, don't be late." Then the line went dead.

Jens looked over at Ali and smiled.

"Who was that?" Ali asked, as her mind tried to piece together what just happened.

"That was the inside man at the lottery. I found him yesterday when we were there," he said.

"You found him, and you didn't tell me?" she said, punching his arm. It was a friendly gesture, but Jens wasn't used to friends or gestures, so it surprised him.

"Ouch," he said instinctively.

"Suck it up. Why didn't you tell me?" Ali said, holding her hands up in frustration.

"Are you serious?" he said, pointing between the two of them as if to say this is the first time they've talked. Ali ignored him.

"We have to go, right?" Ali asked.

"We need to understand what those bastards are playing at," Jens agreed.

"We sure we want to know?" Ali said with an air of nervousness surrounding the words.

If Captain Rollins or Chief Furland found out they were investigating, it would undoubtedly mean a more permanent suspension. But if they didn't do it, no one else would.

"I understand if you want to wait. We could lose our jobs for good this time," Jens said.

"No," Ali said confidently. "It just means we can't get caught," she said. Her conviction was strong, making Jens respect her even more.

"Sounds good to me," Jens said, happy to see his partner excited by the chase.

"One more thing," Jens said. Ali turned to look at him, as she typed the new address into the ECar.

Jens' watch vibrated again. Seeing who it was, he put a finger to his lips to signal Ali to be quiet.

"Captain Rollins, miss me already?" Jens said with a smirk.

"Agent Jennings. It appears even on your leave you are still a pain in my ass. You want to tell me why I have a special writ, which has asked you to come in and answer for the disappearance of Anton Preston?" Captain Rollins sounded rightfully angry.

"Ma'am, it's great to hear from you . . . ," Jens began saying.

"Cut the crap, Jennings. Did you take Anton Preston from his hospital room? Yes or no? We know you saw him last night."

"Yes, I was there last night. I received an anonymous message saying he was in danger."

"You got an anonymous message about a suspect who might be in danger, and you didn't think to tell your superiors about it?" Her voice was full of contempt.

"In my defence, ma'am, technically, I was on . . ." He tried once again, getting shut down.

"Damn your technicalities, Jennings. You get your ass into head-quarters in the next forty-five minutes, or I will personally handwrite your release papers." The phone went dead before Jens had the chance to argue.

"Shit!" Jens said, slapping glove box.

"So . . . quite a bit of information in there you didn't share with me. Were you going to tell me all this?" Ali asked, crossing her arms.

"I was just going to tell you. I swear to God, but with everything that was going on, it just didn't seem as relevant," he said, trying to explain but failing horribly.

"Not relevant? The hell is wrong with you?" Ali said, punching his arm, only this time it was intended to hurt.

"Ouch. Okay, fair," he said, rubbing his broken arm. "It wouldn't matter—the number was encrypted. We can't trace it without GIB access."

"Or I can send the information to my friend up north? Ask them to do it. You ever think of that, dum-dum?" Ali said, pulling her arm back as if to punch him again. Jens flinched.

"Okay, I get it. Tell you things. But I swear that is the last of the information I know. Promise."

"You're sure?" Ali's arm was still cocked.

"Yes. No. Wait. Ms. Purchase is on the GLF board. Right now she is the link between the two companies. But that's all I know."

For a long moment Ali simply stared, judging Jens, likely trying to see if she should or could trust him.

"Good to know," she said, lowering her arm slightly.

"I punched out Zhang?" Jens added cautiously, as Ali tilted her head and narrowed her eyes.

"So, you're saying you're about to get fired . . . again."

"Not likely. At least not for that. I was technically a civilian, and he laid hands on me

first. That and the fact that it was in the bullpen in front of everyone, I'm willing to bet he drops the whole thing," Jens added. Ali dropped her arm and began to laugh.

"I've yet to determine how someone so smart can be so stupid," Ali said, laughing again. "Okay, fine. So, what do we do now? You can't be in two places at once." Jens dropped his head; she was right—he couldn't go back to the GIB and see their new informant.

"You go to the GIB. Figure out what the hell they want and not get fired. Let me go talk to the lottery person," Ali finally said. Jens hated to admit it was the only plan, although he strongly felt the need to be at the meeting with the informant.

"What if he gets spooked and doesn't show?" Jens said.

"What if you don't show up to see Captain Rollins? None of this matters if you're fired, Jens," Ali countered.

Jens knew she was right. *Dammit! One of the biggest cases of my life, and here I am giving a piece of the puzzle away.*

"Jens, I know you want to be there. But you brought me out here to show me why this matters to you. You can't just get my help when it's convenient for you. Either you trust me, or you don't. What's it going to be?" Ali said as if she could read his mind. It was a fair ultimatum. *Time to shit or get off the pot.*

"You're right. You take care of the informant. I'll head into the GIB and find out what they want. With any luck, by the end of the day, we will have a trace on that number, information on the lottery, and me not fired." He nodded slowly as he laid out his dark shopping list.

"Thank you," Ali said, leaning back in her chair and giving him a warm smile.

Soon, they would need to split up when they reached the city limits, and despite the surreal circumstances of the situation, Jens felt surprisingly comfortable.

"So," Jens said after a minute, "you want to tell me how you got Dr. Nazari's password from her house?" Jens said with a smile.

"Fuck off," Ali said, her smile turning into a laugh that soon rippled between the two of them.

32

Jens regretted saying he would go back to headquarters the moment he'd walked in. It was clear he wasn't the most popular person in the building; only now it wasn't limited to Zhang and his gang of half-wits.

It seemed everyone was a little bitter about smearing the name of GIB agents. The lottery was not something people usually went after, though Jens reminded himself that it wasn't the lottery per se; it was the people abusing their power, resulting in the deaths of innocent people.

Sometimes people forgot to dissociate the institution from the individual, often willing to blame whichever one suited their argument better.

Jens walked into Captain Rollins' office, realizing quickly he was not alone, and it was not a friendly visit. Chief Furland was standing in the corner typing away on a data pad. Jens was unsure if it was a good sign they were standing or a bad one. But when they noticed him walk in, Jens reckoned it was a bad one.

"When the hell were you going to tell us that you got a message from someone about a suspect, Jennings?" Captain Rollins' practically spit the words out at him.

"And no bullshit about not needing to tell us about it because you were on leave. You don't get that privilege, Jennings," Chief Furland added, only a little less threatening. Jens assumed that Chief Furland felt a little safer near the top, if only just a little. They were higher in the pecking order of who would get the heat if this all falls through.

A case such as this was usually seen as both untouchable and promotional, depending on how it played out. *A rising tide lifts all boats. But if the boat sinks, it needs to take only a few down with it.*

Jens needed to be smart. He had the opportunity to let them know what was going on, but he was under more pressure now that he wasn't technically a GIB agent.

He noticed there was no despondence coordinator present, which either meant he wasn't going to be relieved of duty at this exact moment, though that could easily change.

"This case is deeper than we could have imagined. The message about Anton Preston didn't seem real, and I didn't know who it came from. I figured it would be best to check it out myself first." Jens was getting pretty good at telling half-truths.

"What did it say?" Captain Rollins asked.

"Ma'am?"

"The damned message, Jennings! What exactly did it say?" she repeated, a little more condescendingly than normal.

"It said he was in danger, and I should check on him. I arrived and he was there, but no one else was. Other than the beating he took, he seemed fine. I assumed it was a concerned hacker friend who heard about what happened," Jens said, brushing off the idea with a shrug. He had no idea who would have sent him the message or how they got his number. But he was proud of himself for coming up with what seemed like a logical proposal.

"After I arrived, the senior constable for the PPD arrived, so I left it with them," he concluded, and Chief Furland did not look impressed, slamming their hand on the table.

"You mean to tell me that you, the man who brought us this

'information' on potential corruption, left our key witness with an organization you told us might be corrupt?!" Their voice was a low growl now.

Jens suddenly began to feel a little ridiculous about the whole thing. After all, it had been him who put this information in their heads, and they were trusting him to take care of it.

"I was asked to stand down. I assumed it was . . . ," Jens began to say.

Captain Rollins' face was beet red, and Jens swore he could see steam coming from her ears.

"Don't you give me that bullshit, Jennings," Captain Rollins said, hissing, before she unleashed on him. "You asked to be on this case, and you overstepped your limits when you infringed on the unspoken contract we have with society. You have no right to turn that around on me. Had you not had your head so far up your ass and told us what was going on, we might have been able to assist in some way. Now we've lost our only lead to connect the organizations together," she shouted, sweat beading from her forehead. She stood, met Jens' eyes, pounded her fist on the desk, then dropped back down in the chair, huffing.

Jens knew she had put her neck on the line, and he was not making it easy for her—which made what he was about to say far worse.

"Not our only lead, ma'am," Jens said calmly, the room returning to silence while they processed the information.

Chief Furland sat down in a small chair under the window while Captain Rollins tapped the window dampers shut, masking them from the rest of the bullpen, as some people were now struggling not to watch from their desks.

"Pardon me, Agent Jennings?" Captain Rollins said slowly. Jens assumed she was still deciding the best method of decapitation she would use on him.

"What I did was wrong, and I know that," Jens began, getting a *"get to the damned point"* look from his two superiors, "but one of the reasons I overstepped, breaking the social contract, was because I believe I had a silver bullet, something that linked the lottery and Stone Industries together."

"What?" Chief Furland asked.

"A whistleblower, Chief Furland," Jens said slowly.

"You mean to tell me you have proof from the inside linking the lottery to the death of Nigel Eriksen?"

"And Stone Industries," Jens said with confidence. "At least we think we do."

"Firstly, thinking isn't having. Also, who the hell is *we?*" Captain Rollins said, leaning in a little closer.

"Agent Hantsport has . . . is getting it now, ma'am," Jens said, trying to sound confident.

"So, you've been carrying out unsanctioned work?" Chief Furland asked, standing up and moving toward Jens.

"Not quite. I was approach by a mysterious caller about possible information within the charity. I tracked them down and was on my way to pick up the information when you asked me to come in," Jens said, struggling to decipher if what he was saying was good or bad to the room.

"And you sent Agent Hantsport? Alone? With no backup?" Chief Furland stood up. "Track her Zen watch, find out where she is, and have a team . . . no, Agent Jennings, you go and pick her up," they said, pointing to Jens now, their expression giving him a sudden bout of panic.

"Why, what's going on?" Jens asked, now more confused than ever.

"You say you tracked him down? If he has sensitive information on the lottery and we know the lottery is willing to kill to keep its secrets . . ." Chief Furland's words were precise, their logic slowly sinking into everyones collective minds.

It was Jens' turn to be upset with himself. How had he not thought of that, and now he was sending Ali potentially into a trap.

"Her Zen watch is up, and she is heading toward Zone Eighty-Nine," Captain Rollins said, getting up from her chair. "Dammit, she just went off-line."

"Ma'am, I'm sorry, but you have to let me go," Jens said, making his way toward the door, Captain Rollins looking to Jens then Chief Furland, but if they had agreed or not Jens didn't know as he was already out the door.

To his surprise, Captain Rollins was following close behind. It must have looked strange for anyone watching as the captain chased him through the bullpen, not bothering to stop to answer questions. Jens had his Zen watch out and was attempting to reach Ali, but it was dead. He reached the elevator, Jens' watch taking him to the main floor. He paused briefly to let Captain Rollins on before he headed down.

"Ma'am, I don't think . . . ," Jens began to say.

"Keep at it, then, Jennings, because it appears to me you haven't been doing a lot of that since I helped you get back in here," she said, not bothering to look at him. Jens felt more ashamed than ever. Once again, he had held back information, and again he was putting someone in danger because of it. *When am I going to learn?*

"Just do me a favour, Jennings. When we get Hantsport back, no more secrets. Either you tell me what you know, or you're gone. Got it?" she said, her eyes burning through him. The elevator doors opened, and she placed her arm across his chest.

"Got it?" she said again.

"Got it," Jens said before the two exited the elevator. Jens pulled out his Zen watch. Ali should be arriving at the meeting place at any minute and Jens and Captain Rollins were likely ten minutes out. With the GIB protocol on the ECar, they should be able to save a minute or two. Ali's Zen watch was dead. Jens cursed himself and hopped in the back of the ECar. Jens wondered if the meeting was taking place in a dead zone, it would have been smart offering protection to both the informant and Ali. Jens had to try his hardest not to imagine the alternative as Captain Rollings hopped in beside him as the ECar raced away.

It felt like a lifetime before they finally reached Zone eighty-nine. The intense silence the entire journey over didn't help Jens feel any better, either. Captain Rollins may have tried to say something, but Jens was too busy beating himself up for the stupidity of letting his partner be in this position. *How could I have been so naive?*

The more he thought about the events of the day, the more he realized the chance that Ms. Purchase or Derris had seen him with the guy in the office. There had been something else about their interaction at the lottery that he couldn't quite put his finger on.

It had been strange that they were even there. Ms. Purchase had said it was board related. *But why was Derris, the head of Mr. Stone's security, there?*

No, it seemed far more likely Ms. Purchase was there to see someone, and Jens suspected it was Mrs. Choi. She seemed far too interested in Mrs. Choi's well-being than Jens would have believed.

Something else strange about the whole interaction was nagging at Jens. *What was it? Or maybe I'm just trying not to think about the fact that Ali still isn't answering?*

Jens knew they would be getting to Zone eighty-nine soon, and Limestone Courtyard was programmed into the vehicle.

"When we get there," Captain Rollins said suddenly, "we need to be prepared. If something is going on, whoever it is will want to hide it. We need to be ready for anything."

"What did you have in mind, Captain?" Jens said, looking at her and hoping maybe she had a good plan up her sleeve. He was wrong. "Beats me. It seems the rate of people dying on this case is pretty high, so maybe let's just try not to die," she said, her tone a little too casual for the words. Jens didn't know if he should laugh or shake his head.

She wasn't wrong about that being the best plan, and Jens had to admit he admired her for putting herself in this situation with him. It wouldn't have been out of her station to send him with backup, but he thought it was a sign of her understanding and belief in them that she was there. At least he hoped that was the case.

Captain Rollins pulled up her Halo from her data pad, showing the area surrounding the building. Jens looked it over, assessing the building from both sides.

It looked like pretty tight quarters, but luckily the front of the building opened to a courtyard with a popular café patio in its core. This was probably where the informant would meet as it would provide them with easy cover and less likely for anyone to try anything stupid. It had been well thought out by whomever Ali was there to meet.

They also must be tech savvy to put a cover on the area to stop data signals. It wasn't uncommon for areas to have dead zones, as they were routinely checked, monitored, and rebooted to update signals.

The city attempted to keep people informed, but it was so routine, people just accepted it, and society tended to forgive the minor inconveniences.

Since no alarms had been triggered, this was a supervised blackout, and it was impossible to know if Ali was aware of it or not.

Jens tried to focus on the simple plan Captain Rollins had begun to lay out.

It was easy enough. Each would choose a crossroads, and both Jens and Captain Rollins who press in as they made way toward Limestone

Courtyard. Then they would scout the area and assess what to do next from a distance. With any luck, Ali was fine, and they could provide watch. If she seemed in trouble, they could step in.

Jens hopped out from the ECar first and rounded the bend, leaving Captain Rollins to get out on the next block. He was supposed to wait, but he would be damned if he would be doing that.

He quickly made his way down the street to the courtyard. It was packed with locals and tourists. The area was near one of the many rivers and was a great place for restaurants and bars, so was never short of people.

Jens glanced at his watch, five fifteen, and the dinner crowd would be getting in soon. He arrived at the courtyard and looked around. The café across from him was busy, and he couldn't make out anyone who looked like Ali. Maybe she was inside?

He scanned the area again. In the center of the courtyard was a large fountain where people would often throw survivor coins in it and make a wish. At one point, coins were used as currency. But since digital credits had become the primary currency of the West, coins were souvenirs, collectibles, and wish-making devices.

Jens looked out past the fountain, thinking maybe he could see Ali in the café sitting with a man at a table. Her back was to him, and he couldn't quite tell if it was her. He started to move toward the couple as the woman got up from the table and made her way toward the exit. Damn, why couldn't she just turn around?

He became more and more confident it had been Ali. Finally getting a glimpse of her face, he attempted to call her again, but they were still in a dead zone.

Ali was moving quickly toward the street, where Captain Rollins should be popping out any moment. Jens started to follow her. Where the hell was Rollins? She should be here by now.

Jens was squeezing through the bodies of people and was about fifteen meters away from Ali when he finally spotted Captain Rollins coming out of the street. He wanted to yell but thought better of it, thinking it wouldn't be good to draw very much attention to themselves.

Ali was moving right toward Captain Rollins. For a moment, Jens started to get nervous that he'd been following the wrong person. His suspicions were confirmed when Captain Rollins stepped up to the woman and proceeded right past her. Jens spun around, looking about frantically. *Maybe she was gone?*

"Jens?" a voice came from behind him. He turned, and he saw Ali smiling at him near the fountain. He headed toward her. *She's safe!*

That's when Jens watched helplessly as a hooded figured appeared from nowhere and plunged a knife into Ali's side. She winced in pain as her body slouched over, her knees collapsing as she tumbled to the ground. Her eyes were wide with surprise but changed to fear as the realization of what had happened sank in. The assailant was already off running.

"Stop!" Jens shouted as he pulled out his electro-pulse and pointed it at the hooded figure now darting through the busy crowd of people. Jens couldn't get a clean shot as bodies began to fan out around Ali's now-bleeding body.

"Jens, get them! I've got Ali," Captain Rollins called as she got down to the ground, laying Ali on her back. Jens knew all she could do was to shut the wound and wait for help. With any luck, it didn't hit anything serious, but Jens knew better than to hope.

Acting on instinct, Jens spotted Ali's attacker, who had made some distance between them and Jens. Though Jens knew it didn't matter how far away they were, he would stop at nothing to get them. Between the adrenaline pumping through his veins and his anger, Jens was ready for a fight, and this son of a bitch was about to get it.

The figure made their way for the narrow streets behind the café.

Jens, having just gone over the maps, knew where they were likely to come out.

Acting instinctively, Jens calculated the best route to intersect them. Typically, he would have his data pad up and guiding him in the right direction, but not only was it down, also he didn't have access to it. So, he would have to do this one old school.

He reached into his memory pulling up details, taking the first left heading down a side street. It was a gamble, but if the assailant took the left in the fork, they would pop out right where Jens would come out two blocks down. If not, Jens would have to act quickly to make up the difference.

It was worth the risk, as Jens popped out ten feet in front of the hooded figure. They noticed Jens, stopped and turned, but it was too late—Jens was on them.

Jens aimed the electro-pulse and waited, gaining a little more ground on the assailant until he was only a few feet behind. Jens pulled the trigger, firing the leads straight into their back and dropping them with fifty thousand volts. Their body dropped like a sack of potatoes and began to convulse. Normally one jolt would be enough, but Jens couldn't resist a second.

"For your sake, you better hope she's okay," Jens said, whispering into their ear. Jens pulled back the hood revealing what appeared to be a man who Jens had never seen before, but was unlikely to forget the man who stabbed his partner right in front of him. Rolling him over, Jens noticed the puddle of urine pooling up on the ground from where he had pissed himself. Jens couldn't help smiling as he put a set of mag cuffs on to restrain the guy's wrist and pulled him up shakily to his feet.

A crowd had gathered by the time Jens pulled the unknown man back to where Ali lay on the ground. Jens had attempted to get the guy's name, but he was still shaken up by the taser and wasn't able to say much. *Likely wouldn't talk, anyway.*

Jens watched as Captain Rollins, who had obtained the help of a friendly citizen to apply pressure while attempting to cauterize the wound, thought the real issue would be potential internal bleeding.

"I thought for sure you'd be passed out by now," Jens said to Ali on the ground, now struggling not to laugh. Jens supposed the captain would have hit her with a med shot. It was a quick fix that would allow nanobots into Ali's system to get started on the serious damage. It would also provide the medical team with data to better assess all the damage done.

The shot was painful, and Ali would be feeling it. Most people would have passed out by now. *Just another sign of Ali's strength.*

"What? And miss all the fun?" she said behind gritted teeth.

"This the asshole who stabbed me?" Ali asked, nodding to the guy Jens was holding up.

"He pissed himself," Jens noted, causing Ali to laugh once again, her body flinching at the pain it caused.

"Med Team should be here in under a minute. Then I'm going to need to bring him in for questioning," Captain Rollins said, turning to look at Jens and his new friend. "He's mine when they arrive," she added, her eyes narrowing in on the culprit before returning to assist with Ali. Jens knew what she was saying.

Jens was still on leave, and this little adventure didn't change that—which meant that when the Med Team arrived, Captain Rollins would need to take him back to headquarters. That didn't leave Jens much time. He pulled him away toward the fountain in the center of the square, a few feet from everyone else.

"Listen, you little shit bag. You're going to tell me who sent you to do this and why. Now!" Jens tried to keep his voice low so as not to raise suspicion, but he was finding it hard. His knuckles were white as they gripped the man's sweater.

"My family is safe. My family is safe," the man repeated like a mantra. Jens had assumed this was a confident murderer who'd tried to make a run at an agent, but Jens realized now that instead he was looking at a scared-shitless human just doing his best to survive. *But what was he trying to survive?*

"Who paid you to do this? Was it the lottery? Or Stone Industries?" Jens said, hissing through his teeth; the names gave the man a sickly laugh—one that turned Jens inside upside down.

"You don't understand, do you? There is nothing you can do," the man said in a moment of clarity before he returned to his mantra again.

"Who are you?" Jens said, trying to appear slightly more sympathetic as he released his hands from the man's sweater.

"I'm no one. Not anymore," he replied. Jens eyed him suspiciously. "I don't exist anymore. I've done my part." None of this was making a lick of sense to Jens, as he wished just once he could get a straight answer.

"You're going to pay for what you did," Jens said, but the man wasn't paying any attention. Instead, he was fiddling with something in his mouth. Jens couldn't make out what it was.

In the distance, Jens could see the Med Team pull up and start moving toward Ali. This meant Captain Rollins would be here soon. He needed to be quick.

"Was it Firefly?" Jens asked softly, remembering what Anton Preston had said in the interview room. The man stopped fiddling and looked at Jens. His eyes were welling up, and he began to cry.

"It's too late," he said through the tears.

"It's not too late. We can help you," Jens said, wanting to believe his own words, but they came out hollow. The man must have thought the same, because he began shaking his head and backing away slowly.

"I've played my part, and now they'll be left alone!" he said, almost shouting now but not at Jens. His eyes darted around the crowd as if trying to find someone who'd been watching them. Then his eyes were suddenly looking directly at Jens.

"I'm sorry," he said softly.

"What was your part?" Jens asked.

"To bring you down," he said, stepping into Jens. Just then, a loud shrieking pierced through Jens' ears as both Jens and the man began to scream.

All around him, people must have heard the ear-splitting sound, as they began to slowly collapse under its high frequency. It was too late by the time Jens realized what was going on. This sound was familiar, and something for which both the GIB and the PPD had trained. But training was different from life, and the excruciating pain in Jens' ears meant he was in the epicentre of it all.

Time seemed to slow as Jens looked around the courtyard, recognizing all the potential victims. There was no way to get himself or anyone else away in time.

The frequency was growing stronger, and Jens knew that in a few moments, it would stop, then the device would explode, sending an energy pulse that would destroy everything within fifteen feet of it and cause severe damage to everything within thirty feet.

Jens realized it must have been the detonator the man was playing with in his mouth early on. He kicked himself for being so blind. Jens knew the bomb must be on the man, which meant Jens wouldn't be able to get away, and the likelihood of his survival plummeted with every passing second. However, he could try to help as many people as possible, but that meant remembering his training.

An energy pulse couldn't be blocked. The device would detonate and fire off an energy pulse that would rip through everything it touched. It was an orb of destruction and was ruthless. This had been a suicide mission.

The hooded man was crying out in pain, feeling the momentum of the bomb. It was designed to build up energy around it until it hit a breaking point and ruptured. The sound was a high-frequency pitch, which crippled everyone around it. Jens' head felt as though it wanted to explode. The searing pain nestled into his mind and a throbbing behind his eyes, made it almost impossible to think.

He knew he needed to think back to his training, but his mind was a wasteland. All his energy was going into fighting the brutalizing surge of pain threatening to destroy him even before the final explosion.

The energy waves surged around them. Even the fountain was displacing tiny waves behind the hooded man. Jens watched the agony on the man's face as he screamed, and for a moment, Jens felt as though he was ready to succumb to the pain and let the blast take him away.

Then somewhere in the deep recesses of his mind, Jens retrieved a memory. He had only a couple of seconds, but maybe it would be enough. Moving as fast as his legs would carry him, he reached the hooded man and pushed.

The sudden jolt pulled the man from his torment as his legs hit the edge of the fountain and his momentum carried him backward toward the pool of water. As the man fell, Jens made one desperate attempt to get away. His body was reeling, and his skin felt as though at any moment it would melt from his body. His only chance to survive meant creating as much distance as he could in the short time he had.

Jens heard the muffled slap of the man's body as he hit the pool of water. He got one final step in before deafening silence. The energy had peaked.

In a last-ditch effort, Jens jumped away from the fountain, not knowing if it would be enough.

As he jumped, the silence felt like an eternity. All around him the world fell still, despite his body hurtling to the ground as the energy pulse finally detonated.

Jens felt his body fly through the air, his head erupting with pain, while his eyes felt as though they might rupture.

Every inch of his body suddenly exploded with a white-hot burning sensation, the pain so great that he barely felt the thud as his back collided into the metal light pole. Breath erupted from his lungs. Jens thrashed in pain, unsure of what to do. After what felt like an eternity, Jens rebooted, sucking in a fiery breath of air. His mind was unable to distinguish all the different types of pain he felt. But he was alive.

Jens wished he could go back to feeling nothing again. His head was fuzzy, and he couldn't tell whether his eyes were open or closed. The pain seared through his body, but he could move, albeit not well. After a few seconds, he managed to wiggle his fingers, eventually lifting them up to his numb face. His eyes began to clear, and he saw his bloodstained fingers, but was unclear where the blood was coming from. With all the pain he was feeling, he imagined the blood could be from anywhere.

Jens began to take stock of his injuries, knowing the explosion would have ruptured blood vessels in his eyes, nose, and ears—not to mention the energy burns on his body from the explosion.

It would take a few minutes for his senses to come back to full feeling, but he didn't have time. He needed to get up. He needed to check on Ali and the survivors. He attempted to move his legs, but the feeling had yet to return.

Jens sucked in a cumbersome breath, each one difficult but each seeming to get a little easier. The ringing in his ears was slowly replaced by the muffled sounds of the screams and groans around him.

He hadn't been the only one in the blast range, but he hoped the water would have dampened the power of the blast enough to limit the destruction. His being alive, given his proximity to the epicentre, was a hopeful sign. Jens looked to the fountain, which had been destroyed in the blast.

Tinted red water and debris flooded the courtyard, with the remains of the hooded man scattered throughout. *I wonder if this was worth it, if it was enough to save his family?*

Jens could sort that out later. For now, he needed to get up; he needed to know Ali and Captain Rollins were safe.

The effort it took for Jens to push himself up to a seated position was staggering. A tidal wave of pain rushed through his system as the energy burns felt as though they were ripping apart his skin. Each ruptured blood cell shocked his system, threatening to knock him out. He was sure he was about to pass out when a hand weakly grabbed his shoulder, slumping down beside him.

"Smart move on the fountain, Jennings," Captain Rollins said, appearing beside him. She'd been cut up from the blast but was on her feet and moving considerably better than Jens. When Jens tried to respond, he realized quickly his throat felt as though he were rubbing sandpaper together, and no sound came out.

"Ali is okay. She's in a lot of pain, and she will likely need some bed rest for a few days, but she is alive. So is everyone else. Thanks to you," she said, as if reading his mind, as she gave his shoulder a light squeeze. His body cried out in pain even at the light touch.

The energy burn flared up on the back of his body. He was sure when he got home, the exposed skin on his back would look like a cooked lobster.

"Sorry about that," the captain said, letting out a little laugh. Jens was so relieved he didn't know if he should laugh or cry. He was alive, again, despite another attempt from Firefly to kill him. He would have jumped for joy, but instead vomited up a combination of lunch and blood, missing the captain, but splashing himself.

"Right. Looks like you may need some assistance." The captain struggled to her feet and moved off to get help. Jens looked across the scene; his eyesight was finally coming back.

He noticed the blast radius had been reduced to only fifteen feet, limiting the damage, and was relieved his plan had worked. Jens looked around at the devastation. People had their Zen watches out videoing the scenes around them. *What was with people and their desire to share damage and destruction?*

A few could likely sell it to a news agency looking to post the video, no doubt highlighting it as a tragic, solo attempt to attack the GIB—no one fully able to believe the real story of a secret organization attempting to kill the agents looking into them.

Jens followed one young man as he recorded the scene around him, obviously narrating the events for posterity.

Then, Jens saw her. A middle-aged woman with a long jacket stood by one of the buildings behind the fountain with a clear view of Jens and was looking directly at him. Her long hair fluttered in the wind. He couldn't be sure, but he thought she was smiling at him.

She held a white hat in her left hand, and when she moved to put the hat on her head, Jens spotted it. The metallic black Zen watch, the same as the one he'd seen after the accident. *But is it really her?*

The idea spun in his mind as he realized where he'd gone wrong. He tried to call out, but only crackly air hissed out.

Jens was forced to watch as the woman turned to leave. He made another attempt to get up, to chase her. He managed to get to one knee before the pain overpowered him and flooded through him, and as he collapsed to the ground, the sweet surrender of nothingness washed over him.

33

The next time Jens woke up, he was tucked into a comfortable bed under soothing sheets, though his body was still in serious pain as he began to squirm around. The hazy image of the blast played in his mind as he tried desperately to bring it into focus. He felt trapped, he needed to get out, needed to find something.

"Easy, Jens, you're safe. We're at the Octavia Davis General in Zone Eighty-Nine. You were nearly blown up," said a familiar voice beside him. Ali sat in a cerebral chair at the foot of the bed, rolling around to the side where he could see her.

"You don't say." Jens croaked out the words, his vocal cords enflamed from the explosion.

"There's water beside you if you want it," Ali said, ignoring the sarcasm.

Jens reached over, grabbing the cup of water beside the bed, and took a gulp. He noticed his hand, which had been plastered with a thick cream, and glancing down, realized it covered his body. His face suddenly flushed red as he realized he was mostly naked.

"Organic burn cream," Ali said as she rolled up towards his bed, looking at the jar beside him. She shrugged.

"What?" Jens asked, seeing the odd look on Ali's face.

"Nothing," she said with a smile. "I guess I just didn't figure you for the natural healing type." She rolled closer and scanned his body, letting out a little snort of laughter. "But you, do you, Jens."

The cream was good; it meant he didn't have any internal burns, just energy rash. But it did nothing to hide his embarrassment.

"Cool chair," Jens said with a smirk, trying to change the topic. Ali's expression shifted to one of pure satisfaction.

"Like it?" she said as the chair began to spin in circles. "It's one of the new cerebral chairs," she said with excitement. When Jens remained blank, she added, "It means I can move it with my mind, dumbass."

"Ohhh! That explains the goofy headgear," Jens said, his eyes landing on the shiny graphene disk that rested on the top of Ali's head.

"If I could make it give you the finger, I would," Ali said jokingly.

"I'll have to take your word for it," Jens said, feeling a sudden burning across his abdomen. He winced in pain.

"What do you remember?" Ali asked, returning to the foot of the bed.

"The last thing I remember is lying on the ground in pain," he said slowly.

"Checks out," Ali said with a smile. "Quick thinking on using the fountain as a power dampener." She began rolling around the room, her mind obviously restless, and the headpiece was picking up on it.

Jens hated the idea of being paralyzed for any amount of time. The thought of being trapped with only his mind terrified him even more, no matter how cool the tech was.

"How are you feeling?"

Ali spun on him, coming to an abrupt stop. "Doctors say I was lucky to be just out of the blast radius—only some minor energy burns—and the seal over the wound stayed intact." She stared at him for a moment as if she wanted to say more.

As she was about to speak, Jens cut her off. "Well, I'm glad you're not dead," Jens said, trying to avoid the emotional stuff, and he felt that was where it might be heading. He was happy to have a partner he could trust, and he was happy she was alive, but he didn't need to talk about it.

Ali seemed happy to avoid it as well. If nothing else, they were now connected by something more than the GIB. They were in deep, and all they had was each other.

"Something tells me this won't be their only attempt," Ali said, returning to her mental pacing.

"Have you had any visits from any nice doctors?" Jens said, giving Ali a little smirk.

"If you're referring to Dr. Nazari..."

"I am."

"I think I understand why people don't share things with you Jens, you're annoying." Ali said rolling her eyes and then her chair away from him.

"Let me guess, full checkup and requested access to your file?"

"It was cute! She cares Jens."

"Yes, she a saint." Jens laughed, causing a ripple of pain across his body.

"I'm glad that hurt." Ali said.

"Have you seen Captain Rollins? How is she?" Jens asked.

"She's fine. Again, minor burns, but she was out of the blast radius as well. Only you and a couple of civilians got the full energy blast," Ali told him.

Jens looked down, feeling as though he were forgetting something important.

"But don't worry, they're all fine as well," Ali said after a moment. Jens nodded absently, feeling a little guilty he hadn't been thinking about the other people in the blast. He was too fixated on what he needed to find.

"The news is calling him a disgruntled employee," Ali said softly.

"Who?" Jens said, looking back at her confused.

"Gerald Williams. He's the man who, you know. Blew himself up." Her voice was flat.

"Disgruntled, my ass." Jens scoffed at the idea. "He knew what he was doing and why."

"What did he say to you?" Ali asked, puzzled, her eyes glancing subconsciously to her side.

"I can't remember much, and what I do remember isn't much. He kept saying his family would be safe," Jens said, trying to remember everything that happened. Things were coming back slowly, one of the reasons he avoided taking all the doctors' medications. They made him groggy, which he hated.

"He also called out to someone before he died . . ." Jens paused, playing his part back in his mind. "I think he was talking to someone there."

The explosion, the searing pain, Captain Rollins, and something else . . .

"A woman!" he cried out, his voice raspy and harsh. "A woman was there by the building watching. I think she was the one he was talking to." He began to cough.

"How can you be sure?" Ali said, rolling around to the other side of the bed. It was eerie how silently she moved.

"I'm not, but there was something about her that was different. I know it." Jens tried to think about what it was but couldn't recall what he saw. "Dammit!"

"Jens, it's fine. Normally, you'd have some mild memory loss, but it will come back soon. Besides, we can't leave here for at least twenty-four hours." Ali turned her chair around and began rolling around again as if mentally pacing.

"What are you talking about?" Jens asked as he tried to sit up. Pain ran through his body, but this time he didn't pass out. "Holy shit, that hurt."

"Easy, Jens, you're still not in good shape," Ali said, spinning back around at the sound of his grunting.

"Ali, what are you talking about?" Jens' voice was direct, and he could tell by her face she was uncomfortable.

"Okay, but don't get angry . . . ," she began saying.

Jens knew at that moment he was about to get very angry.

"Technically, you and I were never supposed to be there. We are civilians . . . ," she said, continuing.

"Civilians who stopped a murder and a bombing!" Jens shouted, wincing in pain.

"I said don't get angry," Ali said, staying silent, giving Jens a moment to calm down.

"Look, both Captain Rollins and Chief Furland know why we were there. But it doesn't justify our actions. They asked for some time to sort it out. Seeing as how we are stuck in the hospital, I didn't think it was that big a deal," Ali said, rolling back to his side.

"Your meeting? What did you learn?" Jens asked, ignoring her words completely.

"Jens, I just told you to take a break," she said, turning away from him.

"And I'm asking you to tell me what the hell we all nearly died for. You owe me that," Jens said. He spoke this last part softly, knowing Ali didn't really owe him anything; she'd been stabbed meeting someone he'd sent her to. It should have been him getting stabbed.

"Fine . . . ," Ali said after a moment.

"Wait," Jens said, the words surprising him, coming out almost unconsciously as he looked at her in her chair. She would heal, he knew that, but still.

"I'm sorry," Jens said after a moment, unable to look at her as he said it. He'd never really apologized to her yet.

"I put you in danger and now . . . ," Jens continued saying.

It was Ali's turn to cut him off. "I put myself in danger. I knew what the risks were before I went. Look, this is bigger than both of us. You can't do this alone, and honestly . . . I'm not sure we can do it, just the two of us." Ali's voice was a hushed whisper by the end.

"What did you find out?" Jens asked again. Ali looked at him cautiously before letting out a big sigh.

"It's bad, Jens. It's really bad." She shook her head. "The lottery's deception doesn't just go back fifty-five hundred days."

"What?"

"From what I was told, it goes back . . . ," Ali began to say, stopping as a nurse entered. She was tall with long, braided hair; her face was hidden behind a mask.

"We're fine in here," Jens said, annoyed to be cut off from Ali's update. But the woman ignored him, moving around the room toward Ali's cerebral chair.

"I said we're fine . . ." Jens stopped speaking as he watched the nurse place a hand on Ali's neck, a micro injector in her palm shooting what Jens hoped was only a sedative into Ali's artery, her head immediately going limp.

Jens went to let out a cry for help, but before he got a word out, the intruder was on him. Jens attempted to lift his arms, to fight back, but he was still too weak. Each movement made his skin feel as though it was cracking apart. *Was this really how it was going to end? Stuck in a damned bed?*

The woman was quick and surprisingly strong, but Jens, fought through the pain, his hand clawing at the woman's face, as he ripped off her mask.

"It's you. But . . . ?" was all Jens could say before the sudden pain of the micro needle punched into his neck, and for the third time in less than twenty-four hours, Jens' world went dark.

34

I should be dead.

It was all Jens could think of as he blinked himself awake, the white ceiling lights searing into his eyes. He was flat on his back in a bed, and when he tried to move, pain coursed through his body, and he could feel that his wrist had been bound tightly to a metal frame. He felt groggy, but his mind was racing.

The sudden sensory overload made him vomit. Whoever had taken him must have been prepared for this, having kindly left a bucket beside him. Jens respectfully declined, choosing instead to vomit on the floor. He wasn't about to accommodate the assholes who'd drugged and taken him.

"That's what the bucket was for," said a calm voice belonging to a figure standing in the entrance of what appeared to be a retrofitted hospital room. Jens could hear the steady beep of the monitor he'd been hooked up to.

"Where the hell is Ali?" Jens' voice came out in a growl instead of the shout he'd intended. "How long have I been out?"

His best guess was hours, judging by the healing of the energy burns. He appeared to have no additional wounds. They were at least taking care of him.

"She's safe. She is just getting treated for some of her wounds."

The figure stepped out from the darkened doorway into the lit room. Jens immediately recognized her.

"You," Jens said, recognizing the woman who'd drugged him as she pulled down her mask. "What do you want?"

"Justice, revenge. You can call it whatever you want. But mostly. . . I just want the truth." She stepped in and grabbed the analogue medical chart clipped to the foot of the bed.

"What are you doing?" Jens asked, wishing he'd been better prepared to decipher her plans. Frustrated with himself, he realized he'd been played, set up at some point along the way, and he wanted to know why. "Why am I here?" he asked.

"You'll find out soon enough, Senior Agent Adam Jennings. But right now, you need to rest. Your energy burns are healing nicely."

She put the document back in its little holder and turned to leave.

"Wait!" Jens called out to her. The tall woman stopped and turned to face him. She was beautiful. Her hair was shorter now, which made her appear a little different from the last time Jens had seen her, but there was no doubt in his mind this was her, the woman from the warehouse.

"Why did you drag me into this?" Jens said, praying he'd get a straight answer, as he watched her hover over him.

"It always had to be you," she said, her eyes lingering on him for a few beats. "I promise I will answer your questions in due time. But for right now you are safe—your partner is safe. You just need to rest and heal."

The woman turned and walked away.

"Wait, what the hell does that mean? Where are we? Where the hell is Ali?!" He was shouting as he began to compete with the rapid beeping sound coming from the machine beside him, and then sudden calm washed over him. Whatever injection had been flushed into his system lulled him back to sleep.

"You know a hell of a lot more about what's going on, and you're sure as shit not a reporter."

The words came out like molasses as he struggled and inevitably failed to keep his eyes from closing. Jens felt an unwanted echo of his earlier waking as he emerged from his forced sleep. At least this time when he woke up, he was no longer in any pain. Whatever ointment they had used on his energy burns had worked wonders. But as he sat up, he realized he was still restrained. *They might have wanted to heal me, but they didn't trust me . . . good call.*

Beside the bed was a woman possibly six hundred or so days younger than Jens.

"You're very beautiful," Jens said aloud. The drugs had made him a little too relaxed around his captors. But she was attractive to Jens, her short brown hair angled sharply across her face, and her skin was soft as she placed a hand on his forehead, in a soothing gesture to prevent him from moving.

"Easy now," she said in a soft Eastern accent. "You've healed tremendously, but you've been in stasis for a couple days, and your body might be a little disoriented."

Jens might have been more abrasive had it not been for the woman's warm smile and gentle touch. She was very calming until he'd finally clocked what she'd said.

"I've been here for how long?" Jens said, trying and failing to stay relaxed. He watched as she moved gracefully around the room checking the monitors, taking notes on the paper document at the foot of the bed.

"Forty-eight hours, at least that's how long you've been in my care." She continued to work as she answered his questions.

"Do you know why I'm here?" Jens asked, giving the doctor a nice chuckle as she once again placed her soft hands on his wrist taking his pulse.

"No. But if you're here, it means you're important to the cause," she said, her lips moving slowly as she silently counted. "A little high, but normal, I imagine, under the circumstances."

"The cause?" Jens said, ignoring what he hoped was a little joke, not at all enjoying the words "important to the cause."

"I should let Sonya explain it to you," she said, writing a few notes on his clipboard.

"Sonya? Was she the one I spoke with before?" Jens said, trying to remember when that might have been.

"All in good time," she said, placing the file back in its home at the foot of the bed and turning to leave.

"Wait!" Jens said frantically. "Who are you?"

"My name is Akela," she said gently.

"Beautiful name," Jens said, once again more aloud than he'd intended, but he couldn't help noticing her blush.

"I'll be back to check on you soon," Akela said, giggling as she left the room and passing a person with a familiar face that Jens would have liked to forget.

"Thank you, Doctor," the woman, who Jens knew now to be Sonya, said to Akela as she left. Sonya went to the folder at the foot of the bed and began to read.

"Looks like you'll make a full recovery," she said, smiling back at him. Jens wasn't sure if he was ready to let his guard down with her quite yet. As far as he was concerned, she'd kidnapped him and Ali.

"It's time you told me what's going on," Jens said demandingly. The time for pleasantries had passed. If Jens had really been here for forty-eight hours, surely someone would be looking for them.

"You're right. And you're not a prisoner here despite what you might think. We needed to stop you from harming any of us or yourself," she said, walking over and unlocking the handcuffs with an old-fashioned key.

Jens instinctively pulled his freed hand toward himself and rubbed the tender skin where the metal had been pressed against him. Sonya, moved to the desk at the side of the room, and opening one of the drawers, she tossed Jens a set of clothes.

"These should fit you. Get changed, and I'll show you around." She left the room before he could say anything. Jens had looked around for exits but found no windows, and the only other door seemed to lead to the bathroom. *Like I have a choice?*

It was in Jens' best interest to hear what she had to say. After all, whoever it was who had him, hadn't tried to kill him, which had been a nice change. But they did kidnap and lock him up, so he decided to err on the side of caution.

Jens was slow to get moving. Akela was right; his body was stiff as he swung his legs off the side of the bed and gently hopped off. But he was impressed with the lack of pain from the energy burns. Now on his feet, the first thing he noticed was how badly he needed to pee, and he tried to ignore how someone managed to assist with that while he was unconscious.

Jens put the supplied clothes on, the measurements extremely accurate. The suit itself was an interesting choice, as it was not his standard blue of the GIB but still a familiar-feeling earthen green. Finally dressed, he stepped outside, meeting Sonya by the door.

"Did you break into my apartment and steal my suit?" he asked skeptically.

"We went into your apartment and got you a fresh suit," she replied. "Besides, we asked for your permission. And you didn't say no."

"I don't remember saying yes."

"You're welcome," she said with a shrug. "We felt you looked better in the green. Hope you don't mind," she said, as she started down a long corridor, which looked a lot like an old hospital.

The rooms were being pumped with circulated air, making it stuffy, but at least it was cool. Fluorescent lights chattered to life as they walked through the hallways. This might have been a great facility once, but now it was on its last legs.

"What is this place?" Jens said, glancing into nearby rooms as they walked. Most were empty, but some had patients tucked into beds; others housed four or five people sitting around a table talking quietly. Every face looked more and more bothered to see him, which surprised Jens, who also didn't want to be there.

"It's a safe house. We use it when one of us is in danger or injured," Sonya said, ignoring all the people they passed.

"Are you terrorists?" Jens asked. Sonya ignored the question as she continued with her talk. Jens got the impression she wasn't used to getting so many questions.

"Dr. Akela, who you've had the pleasure to meet, is one of the team of doctors we recruited to help us." Sonya spoke as if she were giving a tour of a school campus.

"Right, but what are you?" Jens said, interrupting and giving Sonya pause. She let out a frustrated sigh.

"It's complicated," she said carefully.

"Uncomplicate it," Jens said forcefully.

"I can't," she shouted, pinching the rim of her nose, pausing for a moment. "Let me show you something," she said after a moment. Sonya walked ahead of him farther down the corridor until she got to a heavy-looking door, which had been propped open. She passed through it, and in the center of the room was a large hospital bed. Jens could see even more monitors hooked up to the resting body. Dr. Akela stood to the side, looking through notes as she examined the monitors.

"How is he today?" Sonya asked.

"Better, but he still isn't showing signs of waking. Whatever they did to him in there damaged him pretty badly. I've introduced a few nanobots into his brain to relieve the swelling and reconnect the damaged tissue. But it is a long course of action, and there is no guarantee it will work." Akela's eyes never left the person in the bed, and Jens could see her emotion as she spoke. Whoever was in the bed meant a lot to her.

Jens' curiosity got the better of him, and he moved in closer. He shouldn't have been surprised by the inhabitant: it was Anton Preston. After all, he thought, Anton had disappeared just before Jens himself had been kidnapped.

Anton Preston lay in the bed, his body unmoving, and the only sounds were being made by the machines beeping at his side.

"Where is Ali?" Jens asked. Seeing Anton made him realize his partner was still hurt and in danger. He needed to see her and know she was fine.

"I'm right here."

A voice came out from behind him at the doorway, a soft buzz from a motor echoing in the room. Turning to look, Jens saw Ali, sitting in the cerebral chair from the hospital. She was still in temporary paralysis, but she looked fine.

"Ali! You're okay?" Jens said, unsure what to do with himself, choosing to place a hand on her shoulder.

"I'm fine. All things considered, they have been very helpful." Her voice was calm, which made Jens uneasy.

"But you're out and moving around . . . why?" he asked.

Ali glanced around the room before looking back at Jens and shrugging. Jens was afraid of what she might say.

"Look at me," Ali said, gesturing her head at the chair she was embedded in. "I'm hardly a threat to anyone here," Ali said with a smile as she rolled up beside him. Jens sighed with relief, and it must have shown.

"Did you think I was part of this gang? Come on, Jens, I think I would have done better than getting stabbed to get you here," she said, laughing.

"I don't know what to think," Jens said quietly.

"Well, not that. Honestly, I'm allowed out only because they thought I would handle it better. You know you're not the most approachable person," Ali said, receiving a head shake and a small sympathy smile from Dr. Akela.

"I was concerned!" Jens retorted. "So, what have they told you?"

"Nothing," Ali said quietly. "They wanted to wait to tell us both," she added, looking over at Sonya. "Well, we're both here . . . what do you say you get some explaining in?" Ali said, getting a nod of approval from Jens.

"Follow me," Sonya said as she turned to leave the room. Ali followed, then Jens, who turned back to get one more look at Akela, finishing her checkup on Anton.

That's when Jens noticed her stroke his cheek, and he got the distinct impression Anton wasn't just her patient. As if sensing him, she met his eye, her distant smile leaving him with no doubt that she loved Anton.

The structure of the building was mazelike. Out of the medical wing, they moved into what looked like communal living quarters. Thirty or so people were scattered throughout the large space, talking, though they stopped speaking as Jens walked, and Ali rolled, by, but they all showed respect to Sonya as she passed.

"My name is Sonya Preston. Anton is my brother." She didn't look back at them to see if they were listening or following. Jens and Ali were, of course, doing both.

"Ash and Sun are two people?" Jens blurted out, silently berating himself for not making the connection sooner. Sonya nodded.

"So, you're the one who's been sending me updates?" Jens added.

"Sort of," Sonya said with a smile. "When this whole thing began, my brother and I wanted to expose the truth about Firefly to the people. It was just the two of us. But as we started to share our knowledge and learn more about the world they affected, we found more of us." She gestured around the space.

Jens took a better look around and realized each was tasked with different things. Everyone one of them running like a little hive of bees working to get their honey. *But what was the honey?*

"We thought that Ash and Sun could be anyone. So, we thought, why be a snake, when you could be a hydra?" she said.

Jens had to dig deep into the recesses of his childhood to remember the myth of the hydra. The story told of a beast that when its head was cut off, two more grew back.

"Isn't the hydra a bad thing?" Ali asked, rolling close behind Sonya, who smiled at the question.

"There is no good and bad. The more you look into the world, you realize this is a fact. Good people do bad things and vice versa. We think it's more like yin and yang." She hit them with yet another old world reference. Jens started to wonder if they were in the presence of a naturalist organization.

"And no, we're not Naturalist," she added, as if reading his mind. "Both my brother and I believe technology is the best way for humanity to move forward. However, basic understanding of Naturalist practices is an efficient way to operate underground without drawing unwanted suspicion," Sonya said as she passed through another doorway.

"So why the old world references?" Jens asked, unsure of what he should believe. It was one thing to be dragged into an underworld battle between two secret organizations and another to be tricked into a cult.

"Yin and yang?" Sonya asked.

Jens nodded.

"It's an understanding that one can't exist without the other. Night and day, good and evil. We exist because we must. We are not a good organization, but neither are we a bad one."

"Wait, you lost me," Jens said, jumping in. "You're not saying you're good?"

Sonya shook her head.

"What are you saying?" Ali asked her slowly.

"The lottery does wonderful things for the world. They help people in need. No one can dispute that. But there is an underside to that organization that doesn't help people. It destroys them. We have been working to try to figure out who is responsible and how they do that," Sonya said, leading them down another corridor into a similar common space as before.

"How do you know it exists?" Jens asked skeptically.

"They are good. They cover their tracks, but they have been doing it for so long that no one looks into them. They've got sloppy. Look at what you've uncovered in the past week," she said, turning to look at both Jens and Ali.

Jens didn't need a reminder of what had happened to him in the week. It had been a quick leap from deadbeat to pariah in the agency, not to mention the multiple attempts on his life.

"Everything we've found is disputable," Jens pointed out.

"Not to mention, someone told them we were looking into them," Ali said, shooting Jens a dirty look.

"Right, well, I did do that," Jens said.

Ali shook it off, giving him a smile.

"The man Ali met with before the explosion? We used the information he gave her to piece together some of the missing bits," Sonya said, Jens turning on Ali.

"You gave them our data?"

"I'm in a cerebral chair, dickhead," Ali said, scoffing. "What was I supposed to do?"

"I didn't even know you had anything," Jens said, looking around in confusion.

"My attacker wasn't the man I met," Ali said. "I was stopped before the fountain by a smaller man, and before you ask, no, he didn't say much other than 'You didn't get this from me.' He slipped the data drive into my pocket and left. That's when I looked up and saw you," she concluded.

"Okay, but did you at least find out what was on it?" Jens asked, turning now to Sonya.

"It might be easier if I show you," Sonya said, walking through the large room, which appeared to be a makeshift council room. Chairs were placed around the table with a Halo screen displayed in the center, giving everyone sitting around the table a version of the same image.

"You're pretty well funded," Jens remarked, looking at the data console in the middle of the table. He didn't know much about technology, but he knew this wasn't cheap.

"Like I said, we're not all good." She smiled and took a seat. Jens suddenly felt uncomfortable knowing he was sitting in a room with criminals who felt they could and should justify their actions.

It had always been black and white for him, but Sonya and Ash and Sun seemed to live in a universal gray area. So gray, in fact, that Jens wasn't ready to say it wasn't black. Although he was a prisoner, they'd saved his life. The least he could do was hear them out.

"What do you make of this?" Ali said quietly as she rolled up beside him.

"Not sure yet. But they don't seem to want to kill us, which is nice," he said, musing.

Ali smiled. "Not yet," she added.

This was a little too close to the bone for Jens, reminding himself they'd been kidnapped to get here. Despite their demeanor, he was not their friend. Not yet.

Sonya pulled out a data key and put it in the Halo. In front of them were hundreds of thousands of data logs.

"Global Lottery Foundation: Winners Records."

Jens read the top of the entry.

"Jesus Christ, there is no way anyone could go through this much data," Jens said, watching as the pages continued to pile up. "It must go back . . ."

"Three centuries," Sonya said. "It likely goes on for longer, but there seems to be enough information here to form a pattern," she said, finishing.

"What pattern might that be?" Jens ask skeptically.

Sonya shot him a look.

"Would you like to answer this one, Ms. Hantsport?" Sonya asked.

Ali shook her head. "I'm not entirely sure how it works myself. Let's just say he wasn't much of a chatter," she said.

"His name is Boris Lincoln, and it's not surprising he didn't chat, considering what he gave you—and considering that Mr. Eriksen had already been killed because of it. I would imagine Mr. Lincoln will be dead soon, too," Sonya said coldly.

"I could send a team to watch him," Jens suggested.

"It's too late. If they want him dead, they will get him. Our best hope is that they don't know it was him who did it," Sonya said matter-of-factly.

"Well, we can't sit here and do nothing." Jens smacked the table. "I don't understand your organization at all. You want to help, but you seem all too willing to let the people who help you die? What kind of people do that?"

"YOU DON'T UNDERSTAND WHO WE ARE DEALING WITH,"

Sonya snapped back, staring defiantly at Jens. She sucked in a long, calming, breath. "You don't get it, do you? Everything we do know we have only because people have dared to share it. Even then, we never get enough information to do anything. We are dealing with a labyrinth of secrets. We have no idea what they really do, how they do it, or why."

"So, what do you know?" Jens said demandingly.

"We know they are hiding something. We know they use the charity to mask it. We know they can hijack city waste-management trucks and run them into ECars." Sonya's eyes fell squarely on Jens now. "We know that whatever it is they are hiding, they have no problems killing anyone to keep it hidden."

"Dr. Atkins," Jens said quickly.

Sonya nodded gravely. Yet with everything Jens had seen and heard over the past few days, it all felt a little off.

Conspiracy theories always held an element of truth to them, which made them tantalizing to some people. Something skirting the realm of possibility kept the listener wanting more, the mystical underbelly always just out of reach. This was no different.

Looking at the desperation in Sonya's eyes, Jens was suddenly aware that she, Anton, and everyone aligned with Ash and Sun didn't have any real evidence to support their claims. If they did, why the hell would they need to drag him into it?

"Look, I appreciate you taking care of Ali and me, but we're out. This seems like a chance to chase our own tails, and I already feel as if I do that enough without your help. So, if we are allowed to leave, we will," Jens said, standing up from the table.

For a tense moment, Sonya stared back defiantly. Finally, she gave him a nod, and Jens turned to leave.

"Come on, Ali," Jens said as he walked away. "Ali, let's go," he said, surprised when she didn't move. "What? Is your head thing not working?"

"I'm not going," she said softly.

"Come on, you can't be serious," Jens said as Ali turned to face him.

"I haven't seen what's on the data card, remember. I can't leave. Not yet," she said calmly.

"What could possibly be so important that you want to stay in this shithole," Jens said, referring less to the building and more to the situation they were in.

Jens had been away long enough from the real world, and this little game that had hijacked his life was starting to get a little frustrating. He was an agent with the GIB and was currently inside an underground movement hell-bent on bringing down his world. It didn't make any sense.

"Three centuries," Sonya spoke softly. "That's how long the data goes back. The lottery has been funnelling credits in and out of it for three hundred years, at the least. When was the last time you have thought about anything in years? Aren't you a tiny bit curious to know why?"

Sonya and Ali faced Jens.

"No," Jens said after a long moment, turning and walking out of the room before anyone had a chance to say anything else. It didn't matter that he had no idea where he was or how he would get out; he was tired of being in that room.

In the past seven days, someone had tried to kill him twice, he'd discovered two underground organizations, got a partner, lost a partner, on repeat. Maybe he was just destined to be alone. *Why do people seem to think I want to change anything?*

Jens was happy with his life and was happy to serve the people. As far as he was concerned, people lived a pretty good life. *So why try to fuck that up because of a suspicion!*

"The lottery gives out millions to people in need on a daily basis, not to mention its thousands of assistance programs. If they were doing something illicit, could it really be so bad that they need to be stopped?" Jens mumbled to himself as he walked through the halls.

He hadn't been paying any attention to where he was going, and after a few minutes, he realized he was lost. A hand tapped his shoulder. He turned to find Dr. Akela behind him.

"Hi," she said softly. Jens noticed an injector needle in her hand.

"Here to kill me?" Jens asked, wishing it had sounded more like a joke. Dr. Akela followed his eyes down to the needle.

"God, no. No, I'm just here to knock you out. You'll wake up in your own bed tomorrow morning—if that's what you want," she said gently.

"How can I trust you?" Jens said, looking deeply into her eyes and wishing more than anything he could.

"Trust has to be earned. I likely haven't given you any reason to trust me yet. This is more of a leap of faith," she said.

Jens was unable resist her infectious smile.

"Fair enough," Jens said, watching as her eyes broke away. She seemed to be searching for the right words.

"Why do you want to leave?" she asked.

"All this doesn't seem to be my problem," he said, the words sounding empty when he said them out loud.

"You're right, it's not. It's no one's problem unless we make it our problem," she said.

"So why would anyone want to do that?" Jens asked, feeling the need to question everything.

"Everyone has their own reasons," she said. Her voice was soft and distant, as if thinking back on something painful.

"I'm sorry," Jens replied.

"For what? You're right—it's not your problem, and unless you're willing to find out what the issue is, it can never be your problem," she said. The words wrenched at him.

What's more, he hated that she wasn't wrong. It was the easiest thing to turn his back on everything and leave, go back to the way things were. *Ignorance is bliss.*

But this seed had been planted, and somewhere inside, he knew the only plan of action was to water it a little and see if it lived or died.

"Why are you here?" Jens asked, looking at Akela. For a moment, she didn't look at him, and Jens regretted asking her about it. *Here I am about to abandon them, and I still feel as if I deserve to know why others stay?*

"I'm sorry . . . ," he began to say.

"I'm here because of my father," she said at last. "I was born in Jaipur . . . named after my father, Aknon," she continued, looking at Jens expectantly. He understood immediately what that meant.

Jaipur was a city in the Eastern Star that still didn't offer state-assisted operations such as the one Akela would have needed.

"My father was supportive, but the funds he needed was more than we could afford, but together my parents managed to save the credits to support me," Akela said, her eyes beginning to gloss over.

"You . . . ," Jens began to say, but she raised her hand to stop him.

"We were managing fine, until my mother was attacked on her way home from work. She had eighteen thousand six hundred fifteen days remaining, and her loss destroyed my father. With only him paying off the debts, he couldn't manage it. I hadn't even passed three thousand days before all this." Her voice was quivering, and Jens hated himself for forcing her to relive her memories. "After she died, things started to seem pretty bleak. Then five hundred days after she died, an old man visited my father, offering to take on his debt and send me to one of the best private schools in the West under the condition I begin immediately. I didn't want to leave him, but he insisted, telling me it was what my mother would have wanted and that everything would be fine, that I would be taken care of. He promised me," she said softly. "But a month after I began attending school, I received news that my father had disappeared. He had eighteen thousand two hundred days left, and no one could explain to me where he'd gone, only that they had realized he was missing after he'd won the lottery and they'd tried to track him down. But they couldn't find him."

"And since you were the closest relative, you received his winnings?" Jens said thoughtfully, beginning to see where the connection was leading.

"Yes. But my father would have never left me. Not like that," Akela said, letting out a heavy sigh. "Everything that my dad did, he did for me. So that I could have the life I wanted. Whoever that man was, he wanted something. And he exploited my father's love for me to get it."

Jens had done everything in his power to remain quiet, but his mind was bursting with questions, none of which he felt comfortable asking Akela after she'd shared such an intimate story.

Instead, he replayed the weird coincidences between Akela's father and Natasha Lilford's brother, how he'd been saying similar things before he died—only her brother had turned up dead, and she was still poor. *What changed?*

"You think your father traded his life to win the lottery?" Jens asked.

"I'm not sure, but again, less than four thousand days later, I won the lottery, this time on my own. Twenty-five hundred days after that, when I'd decided to be a doctor, I was offered a full scholarship paid for by an anonymous donor. Pretty lucky coincidence for one person, isn't it?" Akela's brows tilted thoughtfully at Jens.

"But that's all it could be, a coincidence," Jens said, trying not to sound insensitive.

"You're right. And maybe I would have gone through all that thinking it was some sort of karma for losing my parents. It hadn't been for this," she said, taking out a white card from her pocket. It looked beaten up and some of the edges had frayed, but it seemed taken care of.

She handed it over to Jens. He opened it, and all it said in simple text was "I hope your life is a good one." Jens read it over twice before turning it over and seeing nothing on the other side but weathered white paper.

"This was delivered two thousand days after my father disappeared," Akela said, looking at Jens expectantly. "I think he was the one who sent it."

"You think your father is alive?" Jens asked skeptically.

"I think he was. But this was the first and only note I ever received," she said, taking the letter and putting it carefully back in her pocket. "It was enough for me to grow suspicious. I began looking into the lottery, since it was the only real connection I had. That's when I met Anton." His name brought a smile to the corner of her mouth. "He's special, incredibly talented, and was looking for answers, too. Everyone here is looking for answers. I've lived a full and blessed life. But I would trade it all to be with my father. We never got our days together, and if someone is trying to take that away from other people, wouldn't you want to stop that?" Akela said as she placed her hand on Jens'. Her touch was warm, and he desperately wanted to say yes to her.

She'd said it herself; her life was blessed. Yet she chose to be wrapped up in a game of underground chess in which people are not afraid to kill to win. *If someone were taking advantage of people, isn't it my job to do something about it?*

"What are you worried about?" Akela asked.

"I'm guess I'm trying to figure out if you're all Cappers or Dreamers," Jens said with a rare smile.

"What?"

302

"Never mind."

"No, tell me." Akela looked thoughtfully at him.

"It's just something my grandfather used to say, that our society has two types of people—people who wanted everything to be equal, no wealth gaps, all things are shared. He called those people Cappers."

"And the Dreamers?"

"That was people who saw competition within society as a positive thing, that we have a cycle of change that is possible only with progress."

"So, he thought people would get lazy?" she asked.

"Not at all, just that the lack of competition would stifle innovation. Imagine running a race, but you could only ever run ten kilometers an hour? You could train to be faster, but it wouldn't matter, because you would be capped. Maybe a majority of people would be content with this, that's okay, but what you lose is this rare gift that occurs in humanity—that one spark that, despite years of human genetics, can't be created. It has to be found. Those people who see limitations as a personal challenge to overcome, they are the reasons we have progress. They are the ones who dare to dream," Jens said, his face reddening as he realized Akela had been looking right at him. "Sorry. I don't think about my grandfather much."

"I think it's good to remember those who are gone, my father used to say similar things." Akela said, her own thoughts elsewhere. "So, which one are you?"

"I think the world is not without its struggles, but I don't think it is a terrible place to live," Jens said, unsure if that answered her question, though she seemed content with it.

"What do you think I am?" she asked, taking a step closer to him so that there was less than an arm's length between the pair.

"I'm not sure yet. But I like to think you're a Dreamer," Jens said, his voice soft.

"I guess you'll just have to find out."

"What am I supposed to do?" Jens said, his voice pleading to Akela for answers, wishing that he'd been forced to do desk work instead of being sent to investigate the damned warehouse fire.

"Hear them out. If you listen to the information they have, and you still want to leave, I promise I will stab you with this needle." She laughed hard at her own joke, a little snort sneaking its way in.

Jens smiled; she'd been honest with him, and he knew that couldn't have been easy. So far, she'd been the first person here he'd trusted; that should count for something.

"Deal?" she offered.

"That seems like a pretty shit deal," Jens said after a moment, then added with a smile, "but deal."

Akela smiled, capped the dart, and placed it back in her pocket. Her other hand moved to his shoulder.

"Right, well, where the hell are we, because I can honestly tell you I'm very lost," Jens said, looking around, all the walls and rooms of the building seeming to look the same.

"It's a maze, but I promise you it gets easier . . . if you stay, that is," Akela said, laughing once again as she led him down the hall.

"One thing at a time," Jens said as he followed her.

35

The conference room fell silent as Dr. Akela walked Jens back in. All eyes turned except for Ali, still confined in her chair. She had rotated as much as the thing would allow. She was the only one who greeted him with a smile when she saw him.

"You're back," Sonya said, her voice devoid of pleasantries. Her guarded nature and cold disposition seemed a useful protection for the work she did. It reminded Jens of pretty much every GIB retiree, which he would never say to her.

Unlike the rest of the world, people such as Jens and Sonya saw the crude underbelly of society, the unpleasantness of human nature that, despite generations of genetic modifications, always seemed to worm its way out like a thin layer of grime in the world.

Jens hadn't heard enough to know if the room he found himself in was filled with Cappers or Dreamers. Akela at least seemed to be a Dreamer. If she believed enough in Ash and Sun, Jens could at least hear them out.

"I wanted to hear what you learned," Jens said, taking a seat beside Ali. Her body paralysis must have been improving, as she managed to place her hand on top of his.

"I think you're doing the right thing," Ali whispered.

"Yeah, well, we'll see about that," Jens whispered back. Ali smiled at him all the same.

"So, what did you find?" he asked the room. Sonya looked at him and shook her head.

"Right, well, maybe it would be better for Ali to explain what we have, and we'll fill in the blanks. Ali?" Sonya said, looking at Ali, her face steadfast. Ali placed her other hand over her wounded stomach. Sonya was smart; it would be hard for Ali, but she knew it would be better for Jens to hear it from someone he trusted.

"Boris Lincoln has been working at the lottery for twenty-two years. He worked closely with Nigel Eriksen until his death. According to Boris, Eriksen had discovered some anomalies in the winners' records," Ali said, starting off slowly but quickly finding her rhythm as she looked at the data in front of her.

"It didn't seem like much," she continued saying, "but it appeared that on more than one occasion in the past ten years, some lottery winners went missing, presumed dead, shortly after their success. Their winnings were given to their families. To add to the suspicions, within five years, give or take, another member of the family would win again. In some cases, multiple family members won. It doesn't seem like much. But when the odds of this happening once are about one in a hundred million, it seemed strange for it to have happened five times in the fifteen-year record." Ali found her groove, sounding like a seasoned pro.

"According to Boris, who wrote us a rather detailed message in his notes, he advised Nigel not to show this to anyone," Ali said.

"Why would he do that?" Jens said, interrupting.

"According to him, these anomalies had been found before. When they were, two things happened. Either they were swept under the rug and forgotten . . . ," Ali said, her voice fading, unable to say what was next.

"Or?" Sonya said, pressing.

"Or whoever found them would turn up dead or missing," Ali said, letting the point sit a moment. "My guess would be Nigel Eriksen decided not to let it sit and took it to someone in charge, someone he likely thought he could trust."

"Angela Choi," Jens chimed in.

Ali nodded; it seemed most logical, as Choi oversaw his file and was senior enough to have the influence Eriksen would have liked.

"Boris came to me with documentation dating back three hundred years. He claimed the anomalies were hidden within the information, but they were there. The lottery had no reason to hide them, because who would ever look into a couple of hundred anomalies over that long a time frame?"

"He's right," Sonya said, jumping in. "Unless someone was overly suspicious of the lottery, no one would ever go after them. Besides, what's a couple of hundred anomalies when they help millions more?" This last line seemed to be added for Jens.

Jens had been ignoring Sonya, as his focus was drawn to a suddenly very quiet Akela in the corner. Jens knew her and her father to be one of those anomalies. Her father was gone, and she was taken care of. Jens assumed that if he and Ali were to investigate the families of those affected, they would likely find more cases like Akela's in which they'd been "very lucky."

"So, you want to bring down the lottery?" Jens said, returning Sonya's stare. She didn't flinch.

"No," she said, catching Jens by surprise. "We're not naive, Agent Jennings."

"Jens, please. You've kidnapped me and saved my life. I feel as if you're as close to a friend as I have," he said, trying to keep the sarcasm out of his voice.

"The lottery might have some hidden secrets to it, but that doesn't change the fact that they truly help millions every year. As far as we can tell, only these anomalies are different. Everything else they do is legitimate. But it doesn't change the fact that they are taking people under the pretense that their families will be taken care of. We need to know what they are doing and why they are doing it," Sonya said, pulling up the Halo screen which projected up, out of the center of the table so that each person around the table could see each other and the halo images.

It showed various webs of people, some of who Jens recognized, such as Allan Stone and Maggie Purchase, but most of them he didn't.

Jens was very surprised to see a face on the screen that he recognized but wasn't sure why or from where.

"Who are these people?" Ali asked. Jens was thankful he didn't have to.

"These are the people we believe to be in Firefly." Sonya said, "It has about fourteen names, and most of them are from the West. But we believe that Firefly is made up of people from around the globe. Because the lottery is a global entity, they use its reach to perform tasks around the world. Nigel Eriksen's credit theft wasn't all that was fabricated. According to some of the data we found, the lottery is moving credits into various accounts around the world. It doesn't look like much, but we believe they are safe accounts designed to pay people. We can't prove that yet, but it's the best theory we have," Sonya finished.

"Theory?" Jens decided to apply scrutiny, figuring if he were going to be subjective, he may as well hit them in the weak spots and see where they bleed.

"Unfortunately, they are very good at what they do. They also appear to be evolving and learning new ways of keeping themselves hidden," Sonya said, unfazed by Jens' jab.

"What's that mean?" he said, standing up and pacing along the side of the table. He hoped it appeared as if he were challenging them, which he was, but the real reason was to get a better look at the Halo and of the man on the other side of the table. He couldn't shake the feeling that he knew him.

"The records we got from Boris," Sonya said.

"Correction, we got," Jens said, pointing at Ali and himself.

"Fine. The information you got," Sonya said, continuing with a sigh. "Showed the lottery changing its tactics on how the credits are moved around. Every fifteen or so years, a new approach is made to cover up, double down, and press forward."

"It's brilliant," Ali said to herself, looking over the data. Clearly, she was better versed than Jens on these matters.

"So, they are evolving." It was meant to be a joke, but Jens' remarks didn't appear to sit well with Sonya, who was nervously scrolling through the data.

"You might think it's funny. But my brother and I are considered two of the best hackers in the world. We have a team of fifteen throughout the globe combing through data logs, and all we have been able to find is loose information connecting these fifteen people. For anyone to keep something like this so hidden would take . . . an unimaginable amount of time and credits," she said, her tone suggesting a hint of fear.

The room was silent as Sonya let that sink in.

"Who is this?" Jens finally asked about the man in front of him.

"Gunther Strasburg—he's a Central importer based in New Amsterdam. Do you know him?" Sonya asked skeptically. Jens shook his head.

"He looks familiar, but I've never been to New Amsterdam. What else do you know about him?" Jens asked. The name had been of little help to him.

"That's where things get weird," Sonya said.

"That's where they 'get' weird?" Ali said, musing.

"All these people seem to just pop up out of nowhere. They've been digitally scrubbed of all unnecessary information before being placed into a role of power. It's like each of them come out of nowhere," Sonya said.

"How can anyone come out of nowhere?" Jens asked.

"They can't," Sonya said with a worried look on her face.

"Not without a scary amount of tech," Ali said, jumping in.

Jens was starting to see why the whole thing was so worrisome. If there were indeed a group of people who could slot people into powerful positions from seemingly out of nowhere, there could be no limits to what they might do.

"Look, this is a lot to take in, and Ali, you still need to rest. Stay tonight and eat, and I promise to try to answer any questions you may have. Tomorrow, we will make sure you get home safely," Sonya said as she shut down the Halo screen.

Jens wasn't convinced he wanted to stay another night, but looking at Ali, with her hand still placed on her ribs, he knew Sonya was right.

"If you'll excuse me, I need to go check on my brother. We eat dinner in a few hours. Before then, feel free to walk around the facility. Akela has some time before her next rotation and can show you around," Sonya said, giving a nod to Akela, who smiled warmly before Sonya turned and walked out of the conference room.

Jens couldn't see Akela, who'd been hiding in the back of the room, but if she had been bothered by what she'd just heard, no one would've known it.

"What would you like to see first?" Akela said politely, leading them out of the room.

The facility was even larger than Jens and Ali had suspected, and the shock on their faces must have shown. Akela gave them some background.

"It's an abandoned military base that was used at the height of World War Three," Akela said, leading them down one of the narrow hallways that fed into a mammoth room.

"This is one of the many med bays in the bunker. Each bunker is self-sufficient and could support and feed up to two hundred thousand people," Akela continued saying.

"I heard about these bunkers. I didn't realize they were still around," Ali said as she peered around the space. "They acted as giant containment units for people with the virus?"

Akela nodded vaguely, each of them remembering the old stories.

"Every government had its own version of why its system had failed, but the most common one was people's selfishness. The world was full of people all too happy to lie and even bribe their way out of being sent to live down in the bunkers. Usually this was people in a position of power, unwilling to give up their privileged lives to live in a place they expected everyone else to go. But as is often the case, viruses don't see money and power, so eventually, their selfishness led to a complete system collapse. Right now we are in one of five connected compounds here. There are more hidden throughout the world. It truly is a remarkable place, despite its history," Akela said, as they moved into a large domed terrarium fit with a flourishing greenhouse and vegetation. The light in the room mimicked the light from the sun perfectly. At the center of the terrarium was a park complete with grass and trees, and they saw young children playing catch.

"It's incredible," Ali said softly.

"How many people live here now?" Jens asked, watching the kids run around in the park playing next to a surprisingly large river.

"In the compound we have roughly a thousand or so members at any given time, including their families," Akela said, gesturing at the kids.

"That many?" Jens said.

"You sound surprised," Akela said as she led them over a small bridge leading to a path that followed along the river.

"You could say that." Jens was trying to figure out just who in their right minds would drag their kids into this type of underground world. But he kept his mouth shut.

"This river," Ali asked as she rolled along beside them, nodding to the steady flow of water, "how is that possible?"

"It's actually quite impressive." Akela grinned. "The river generates the power needed to pump fresh water up here to us. This water flows into the atrium garden, the greenhouse, and all the apartments for personal use. Once it's used, it's sent down to the lower-level treatment facility and sanitized before the cycle repeats itself. It's entirely self-sufficient."

"Very cool," Ali said, watching as the river flowed through a series of mini-generators.

"Don't you get tired of being underground?" Jens asked, not bothering to hide his skepticism. "Wouldn't people go crazy cooped up down here?"

"Follow me," Akela said, leading them out through a large archway into a massive corridor. "This is only one of hundreds built across the country. When the virus hit, the plan was to contain it down here. Obviously, it didn't work, and often these areas were forced to house many more than two hundred thousand," Akela said.

Before Jens knew it, they had entered another large atrium, this one giving the illusion of outdoor woodlands.

"In theory these compounds were not evil, just abused by the fear of the masses. Every hundred meters we have a new atrium, with a constant supply of fresh water. Even the lights are designed to mimic the sun," Akela said, gesturing at the surrounding lights, which created a warm glow.

"Mimic being the operative word," Jens said bitterly.

Akela laughed.

"My point is with a thousand people, it's a pleasant place to live. We are protected here, and for some of the people staying with us, that means a lot."

Akela continued to walk through the atrium with Ali rolling along beside.

"It's not all bad, Jens," Ali said, smiling at him.

Jens desperately wanted to ask Akela more about the people who couldn't leave, but got the sense it would be ignored. Instead, he stared up at the fictitious bright sun and tried to ignore the pleasant scent of fresh oranges wafting in the air.

As Jens walked through the next archway, he was distracted by the carved lines etched into the side of the walls. Looking closer, he could see there were heights marked up on the old wall, the tiny initials of children who'd been forced to live down here during the outbreak and who likely died down here as well.

"Why would anyone choose to live down here?" Jens said to himself as his hand glided over the child-marked wall.

"You forget. Those people didn't choose to." Akela said as she turned left, ignoring the unlit corridor looming to her right.

"What's down there?" Jens asked, taking a step and watching as the motion sensors picked up his movement and began to light his way.

Akela sighed as she looked down the hall, her face filled with sadness.

"The crematorium," she said, exhaling. "No one goes down there anymore," she began saying—"at least not unless we have to." She spoke quietly as she turned to continue down the next corridor.

Jens moved to catch up with Akela and Ali as they made their way into the next atrium.

"I know you have your reservations about this place, but these facilities are perfect for housing self-sufficient societies," Akela said, turning to look back at Jens and Ali.

"You mean to tell me more people use these facilities?" Ali asked skeptically.

"They were built around the world to act as safeguards. To protect people, they were never marked on any maps. They remained completely separated from the outside world," Akela said.

Jens shook his head at the absurdity and the foolishness of the past.

"You have to understand people were ruled by fear of the unknown. They didn't have the resources we have to detect and contain new viruses. What takes us weeks to cure took them months, even years to discover. It was a completely different time," Akela said.

She saw Ali fussing with her side and handed her a pill.

"For the pain and the itchiness," she said with a wink.

Ali took the pill, and Jens saw her relax immediately.

"To answer your question, Ali, yes. These facilities are used throughout the world. Our organization uses a couple, but some people say there are entire colonies of people who still live down in the depths of the earth, who just decided never to come back up. They have been lost now for centuries, or the stories could be mere legends. But you could see how you could manage down here and not have it be so bad," she said, giggling at Jens' obvious distaste toward the idea.

"I'm sorry," Akela said, glancing down at her Zen watch, "but I have to go check on . . . I have to do my rounds."

Jens assumed she was talking about Anton, but for all he knew she had many patients. He'd not seen another doctor yet, and with a thousand people, she was bound to be busy.

"Thank you for showing us around," Ali said, no longer rubbing her side; whatever pill she'd been given seemed to be working.

"If you follow that corridor, your rooms will be on the left about halfway down," Akela said, pointing at the nearest tunnel.

Then unexpectedly, Akela placed her hand on Jens' arm. He turned to face her; Jens could have sworn she looked nervous.

"Thank you for staying," she said quietly, her eyes lingering for what felt like eternity, before she turned and left him alone with Ali, who sat there was grinning at him.

Thankfully Ali didn't say anything all the way to her room, and it wasn't until Jens turned to help her onto the bed that he noticed she was still smiling at him.

"You could try to make it less obvious that you're into her," Ali said teasingly as he lifted her up to the bed. Jens forced himself not to drop her to the floor.

"You could piss off," Jens retorted, causing Ali to laugh and then grab her side in pain.

"Ow Stop. You can't make me laugh," she said with a pained grin. Then, changing the subject, she said, "It's a pretty interesting place."

"What do you make of all of it?" Jens said quietly.

"Which part?" she said as Jens helped to pull the covers over her feet.

"All of it. The people, the place, the story," Jens said. "More importantly, aren't people going to be suspicious of where we've been the last couple of days?"

Ali's eyebrows lifted. It was a question that had been on Jens' mind since he'd opted to stay behind.

"Hard to deny what we've seen here," Ali said, "and apparently they took care of us being 'missing,' too."

"How?" Jens asked.

"I was discharged into the care of a house nurse. You're the asshole who discharged himself, likely wallowing in self-pity in his apartment, not talking with anyone because you've been suspended," Ali said.

Jens laughed loudly as he realized she was being serious.

"Wow, that is painfully accurate," he said, getting a smile from Ali. "What about Captain Rollins?"

"She's fine, just a couple of scrapes," Ali said.

"There is no way she'll believe any of that," Jens said, wishing he wasn't as predictable as Ash and Sun had suspected him to be.

"More likely she'll just be happy that we show up alive tomorrow," Ali said quietly.

"*If* we show up alive," Jens said, sitting back in a chair beside Ali's bed.

"You can't still think they're going to kill you?" Ali asked, getting a wan smile from Jens.

"No. Well, I don't know. This whole thing seems a little crazy. Don't you think?" Jens said, trying to keep his voice low, unsure if anyone was listening in.

"Doesn't mean they're not telling the truth," Ali said, her voice just above a whisper as she laid her head down on her pillow.

"That's more terrifying," Jens said, surprised when Ali began to laugh uncontrollably, even more surprised when he did the same.

Jens had laid his head back on the chair, finding it much more comfortable than it should have been, but he was tired. This was the first time he wasn't forced into sleep in a couple of days, and his body was eager for a rest. Beside him, Ali had already begun to doze off, and Jens quickly followed.

36

Jens woke with a start, for a moment forgetting where he was, but was happy to see Ali still resting peacefully beside him.

There were no clocks in the room, and Jens couldn't seem to get his Zen watch to work, wondering whether it was dead or disconnected in the bunker. Despite a little stiffness, he felt great, having had the first actual sleep in days. His only regret was not making it to a real bed. Giving his neck a light rub, he was confident it wouldn't be thanking him any time soon.

Jens could tell from Ali's monitors she was doing well. Likely she should be up and moving by the time she woke up. She would be tender, of course, but it could be worse.

Jens rubbed his own damaged arm. Letting out a yawn, he stood, deciding to find his own bed to try and maybe get a little more sleep. Quietly, he exited Ali's room, only to be confronted by the mazelike corridors. He assumed that his room must be close by, so he walked to the nearest door, hoping maybe to get lucky.

To his frustration, the first few doors were all locked, and as he continued down the corridor, he heard Sonya's voice coming closer.

The last thing Jens needed right now was to talk with her. There would be time enough for that once he'd had an appropriate amount of sleep. Scrambling, he hoped that one of the doors would be open as he manoeuvred down the hall.

Sonya seemed to be just around the next bend, and in a moment, she would spot him. He had one more door to try before she'd be on top of him. To his luck, it opened as he quietly slipped through the door just as Sonya rounded the corner.

Jens listened closely to Sonya and whoever she'd been talking with passed by the door. Letting out a breath, he hadn't realized he'd been holding it. He turned to examine the room he was in, hoping he would find an empty bed.

But when he turned to look, he noticed a hospital curtain pulled across the room and the sound of a woman crying as she whispered to herself or someone else.

Jens couldn't make out the words, but the whole thing seemed intimate. Jens wanted to leave as the whispering fell silent.

"I know you're in here," said the familiar soft voice of Akela from behind the curtain.

Jens didn't say anything as he moved quietly around the curtain.

"Oh, it's you," Akela said as she wiped the tears from her eyes. "I thought you were Sonya," she said, trying to smile.

Akela sat at the bedside of Anton holding his hand. Jens could see the wet bedsheets where Akela's tears had fallen, giving some insight to how long she'd been sitting there.

"I'm sorry," Jens said as he made his way awkwardly farther into the room, wishing he'd just turned and left when he had the chance. "I didn't mean to interrupt. I was just hiding from Sonya, and this door was . . . it doesn't matter, I should leave," he said, feeling even more stupid after each word.

"Wait," Akela said as she stood up. Her hand still clasped Anton's, but with her free hand raised as if to stop Jens from leaving. He knew he should go, but even as he was thinking it, he felt himself turning back around to look at her.

"I'm glad you're here," she said, gently placing Anton's hand down beside his resting body. Jens watched, remembering just how soft her hands had been.

"You are?" Jens said, trying to ignore the racing of his heart, hoping his face wasn't betraying how much he wanted to see her.

"Yes," she said, walking over to him. "I should run some tests on you to make sure you're okay."

Jens' heart sank; of course that was what she was talking about. She was a doctor, and he was her patient. *Why would she be interested in seeing me except to make sure I was okay?*

"The swelling in your head was pretty bad. I meant to check it, especially before you go to bed," she said.

Jens didn't want to tell her he'd just woken up from an indeterminate amount of sleep.

"How do you feel?" Akela said, placing a hand on his forehead, her touch just as soft as he remembered. For a moment his eyes closed, and he allowed himself to imagine things could be different, wishing he didn't have to open them, not wanting the feeling to go away.

Her other hand moved to wrap his wrist; her fingers were cold to the touch.

"A little fast," Akela said. Jens was happy she wasn't looking at him when his face flushed red with embarrassment, as he forced himself not to pull his hand away.

"Your hands are cold," Jens said, wishing he'd said nothing. Akela laughed, releasing his hand as she did.

"Sorry about that."

Jens wished he'd kept quiet and that her hands were still around his wrist.

Jens could barely believe she was real; he was so used to being alone he'd started to assume that would be the case forever.

"I mean I'm just not used to being touched," he blurted out. *Stop talking, you idiot!*

"Not while you're awake, at least," Akela said jokingly as she quickly turned away. Jens wondered if he'd imagined her blushing as she did.

"GIB agents don't get out a lot," Jens said, the words vomiting out of him now. "I mean I've dated people . . . in the past, I mean . . . not now . . ." He desperately wanted to stop, but the words kept falling out of him as if he hadn't ever talked with anyone ever before. "It's just touching people isn't really in the job description." *What the hell am I saying?*

"I understand," Akela said mercifully, cutting Jens off.

"You do?" Jens said, as he tried to laugh it off.

"Life's not exactly normal when you're part of an underground movement," Akela said with a laugh.

"But you and Anton?" Jens said, his eyes glancing to the comatose body of Anton. Akela's smile faded as she followed his gaze.

"Anton and I . . . it's complicated," she said, her eyes unmoving as she watched him sleep.

Jens wanted to know more, to ask questions, but he knew now was not the time for those questions.

Akela reached for a stethoscope hanging off the headboard of Anton's bed.

"Can you sit?" she said, taking a seat as she pulled over an extra chair.

Jens looked over at Anton lying on the bed.

"Don't worry," she said, "he won't care." She laughed at her own joke and patted the seat in front of her.

"Is he okay?" Jens said, taking the seat that faced both Akela and Anton. There was an abrupt feeling of guilt as he did.

"Don't know," she said quietly. "For all our advancements, we still don't understand everything about the human body. The brain is one of the most fascinating and complex organs in the world," Akela said, somehow managing to sound both captivated and disheartened at the same time.

"Can you lift up your shirt?" Akela asked, putting the stethoscope earbuds in. Jens looked at her confusedly. "I want to check your breathing."

"With that?" Jens looked skeptically at the tiny device dangling from Akela's neck. Normally a scanner would examine his body, giving a full reading.

"It's a stethoscope. I like some of the old tricks," she said, spotting Jens' apprehension.

"Seems a little . . . archaic," he said, laughing.

"It keeps my brain healthy, and I like the challenge. Now lift," she said with amusement. Smiling, Jens did as she asked, lifting his shirt.

"It might be cold," she said. As she placed the freezing-cold piece of metal against his chest, his body flinched.

"Cold, eh?" he said, shivering.

"Breathe in. And out," she said softly, the earbuds of the stethoscope pinched in her ears.

"So . . . are you two . . . together?" Jens tried and failed to make it sound casual.

Akela looked at him for a long moment, and for a second, Jens feared she couldn't hear him.

"We were," she said finally.

"Were?" Jens said, puzzled.

"It's complicated," she said, pulling the stethoscope off his chest.

"Anton wanted to speed up the plan. I disagreed. I thought he was being impatient," she said, stealing a glance at Anton when she thought Jens wasn't looking.

"Plan for what?" Jens asked. Akela gestured at the room around her.

"All this . . . bringing down Firefly," she said, placing the stethoscope on the table.

"You didn't want to?" Jens asked, trying to hide his surprise.

"I want to bring down Firefly as much as the rest of them. But the plan was rough. At best," she said, pulling herself up on the foot of Anton's bed, resting her hand on his feet.

"What was his plan?" Jens said, looking at Anton's impassive, sleeping face. He couldn't help remembering the lively man who sat across from him in the prison and wondered how he could have got here.

"You," Akela said, looking directly at Jens.

"Me?" Jens blurted out, trying hard not to laugh at the idea. "Why me?"

"Not sure. He was adamant about you being involved," she said, her tone serious.

"And he never told anyone why?" Jens asked. Wishing he didn't sound as desperate as he was.

"Anton was a little cautious of everyone. I guess it came with the territory. He wanted to be in control, and he understood the reach of Firefly. He was afraid they might learn what he knew," she said, reaching for Anton's resting hand.

Jens looked down at Anton, his mind racing with more questions than answers. *Had Anton known something about me that I don't? What made me so special, and why would he drag me into this shitstorm?*

"Smart plan, Anton," Jens said, standing up. "But Sonya is his sister. He must have trusted her?" Jens asked. Akela nodded her head.

"Sonya didn't like you being involved. But with the warehouse incident and you coming back to duty, Anton was convinced it was the right call. So, he acted before she could stop him, unofficially getting the ball rolling. Once it started, it was hard to stop," Akela said, her hand warmly rubbing Anton's.

"Anton mentioned he had left proof with someone he trusts, to prove who did all this. Does Sonya have it?" Jens asked, remembering his interaction with Anton.

"No," Akela said quietly after a moment, her eyes never leaving Anton. "I do." She pulled out a small data stick from her pocket and held it out in front of her.

"So, that's the proof?" Jens asked, amazed that such a small item could have such big ramifications for peoples' lives.

Akela simply shrugged.

"You haven't looked at it?" Jens asked in amazement.

Akela stayed silent.

"So, you don't know what's on it?" he asked.

Her head slowly shook side to side.

"Why?" Jens asked incredulously.

"He asked me not to," Akela said, handing the data key to Jens. "He said I would know when to give it to you."

"And that's now?" Jens asked confusedly, trying to ignore the data key, so dangerous that people would kill to keep it hidden.

"Anton's brain worked differently from everyone else's. He saw problems like puzzles. If he had a reason for not giving it to his sister or to you directly, I'm sure it was a good one," Akela said without a hint of hesitation.

"So why now?" Jens said, still unable to take the drive from Akela's outstretched hand. Once again it seemed all Akela could do was shrug. For someone holding a boatload of dangerous information, she certainly seemed clueless about it all.

"It feels right," she said with a laugh. "Besides, it's mine to give."

"What about before in the hall? I could have taken this to my captain, and all this would be over," Jens said, standing up and trying to play it over in his mind. "I could have ended all of it."

"What is on this drive is bigger than all of us. Our sliver of information is only the tip of the iceberg," Akela said as she stood from her chair and walked up to Jens.

"If Anton thought it would be enough to just catch the people involved, he wouldn't have turned himself in. He wouldn't have put his life in danger as he did. He would have released the video. But he didn't." She was standing in front of Jens now. Her body was so close. She smelled of fresh flowers, and her eyes widened as she met his own. For a brief second, he thought maybe he'd stopped breathing.

"He needed you." Akela's throat caught as she placed her hand on his chest, the metallic data drive an uncomfortable presence in her gentle hands. "He needed you to understand what was going on and discover the big picture for yourself."

Jens' hand met hers. She grabbed it, placing the data drive firmly in his grip. "You are important," she said gently.

They stared at each other for a long moment, their hands gripped together. Jens wished it could last forever. As his eyes locked on her, the connection between them felt tangible. A rush of emotions flooded his body, and he felt a desire to hold her and kiss her. But the timing was wrong. Her eyes may have been on him, but her heart was with Anton.

"But why?" Jens asked, wishing that for once he could have been somebody else, as she released her hand and pulled away from him.

"I'm not sure. But whatever his reason was, it's why you're here and he's there," Akela said, moving away from Jens and retaking her seat next to Anton, grabbing his hand.

"No pressure, then," Jens said, feeling the weight of the data key in his hand as he began tossing it up and down.

"I should get some rest," Jens said, turning to leave when he noticed Akela holding Anton's hand.

"For what it's worth, I believe him. You are special," Akela said.

Jens turned to meet her eyes one last time before smiling and walking out of the room. For a moment he stood in the hallway massaging the data key anxiously in his hand. He wasn't sure what the hell he had done to be dragged into this mess, but at least he had one less secret to deal with now that he had the data key.

Jens hurried off down the hall until he found an unlocked empty room. Taking a seat, he pulled out his ocular pads and placed them behind his ears.

He hadn't noticed he was sweating, but his clammy hands placed the data key into his watch.

A blank screen appeared, and after a moment, a request for a thumbprint flashed across the screen.

Jens slowly placed his finger on the Zen watch and was relieved when the file flashed green, showing access granted as two files were displayed in front of him. He tried not to think about how Anton might have obtained a digital copy of his thumbprint. He was too preoccupied with the files now displayed on the screen.

One simply said, "Data log_78377839," but the other was labelled "Senior Agent Adam Jennings."

Jens clicked on the one with his name on it. Anton Preston's face appeared on the screen.

"Senior Agent Adam Jennings. I assume if you're watching this, you've tracked down the rest of Ash and Sun and have met Akela."

Jens laughed at the use of the term "tracked down."

"You're probably wondering why I didn't just give you this video when I turned myself in. But as you could see, it implicates a lot of big names in our city." Anton must have assumed he'd watch the other file first.

"Something like this would put a dent in the system. But that's not my goal. If you're here, you must have learned there is something bigger at play, something . . ." Jens paused the video. If he were going to understand what Anton was talking about, he needed to know what was on the other file. He shut down Anton's video log and opened "Data log_78377839." It began to play.

The video was ten minutes, forty-six seconds long, but it took only one minute, thirteen seconds to realize just how truly damned his situation was.

37

It took a moment after the video had shut down for Jens to finally process everything in his mind. A part of him wished he'd simply gone to sleep and not watched the video, because there would be little chance of him sleeping now, not with the tornado of information in his brain.

The video certainly explained why Anton was so adamant on Jens' not seeing it earlier. The implications for the mayor and the PPD were almost too difficult to conceive. Jens struggled to remain seated as he watched, and instead paced throughout the room, unable to quiet his mind or his body.

Anton had been right; no one would believe this video existed, or why the subjects of the video were there in the first place. Even having watched it, Jens wasn't entirely sure he understood what was happening, and based on what Ash and Sun had told him, they were as much in the dark as everyone else, but at least they seemed to have a flashlight.

Jens needed to speak with Sonya again. She was the only one who might know what Anton was thinking. But if Akela was right, Anton hadn't shown Sonya the video, which didn't make any sense. *Why would he share it with me and not his own sister?*

Since sleeping was off the table, and his mind was abuzz with new information, Jens figured he would do some good old-fashioned sleuthing. Making his way back into the hallway, he realized he still had no idea where he was going in the massive compound, but he figured eventually he would run into someone and then start there. Hopefully by that time, he would have processed at least some of what he'd just seen.

The last few days had been overwhelming; usually he would have recharged his mind and processed his thoughts at the end of each day. But since he'd been blown up and kidnapped, he'd not really had the time to refresh himself.

The video had cast an interesting light on the night of the fire. Jens recognized one of the clips from the arrest video.

It was no doubt a shock when Constable Wilson and the PPD picked him up with that video. Wilson would have some explaining to do, and Jens made a mental note to speak with her first when he could. It must have taken a vast amount of people to pull this off. *She wasn't doing any of this alone.*

Jens would have to assume that everyone on-site when Anton was picked up was in on the cover-up. This, to Jens' regret, included Granger. He didn't want to think about that now. He would still need help, and Granger was his only in at the station.

Jens followed along the corridor, reaching one of the many large atriums. While most people were probably asleep, there were a few he did not recognize up and walking around—although, from their suspicious stares, they seemed to know who he was.

The only one not staring was a kid with likely little more than five thousand days on him sitting at a table. He didn't look up or seem to care about anything that was going on around him. He just focused on the book in front of him.

Jens watched a moment as the boy's finger traced down a page with remarkable efficiency before flipping it over and repeating the process.

It was weird to see anyone reading an actual book, let alone reading one as quickly as he was. Jens approached cautiously, looking over his shoulder at the book. He attempted to follow along, but the kid was fast, and before he managed the first quarter of a page, the kid had turned to the next.

"Can I help you?" the kid said, still not looking up from the pages.

"I'm looking for Sonya. Can you tell me where she is?" Jens said, watching the kid's finger stop briefly. *Had he heard my voice and figured out who I was?*

If it had thrown him off, he didn't let it show. He just pointed down one of the many halls.

"She'll be in the war room. Down that hall, second door on the left. Follow the green line," he said, his index finger once again working its way down the page.

Jens had noticed the coloured lines before, traced along the top of the walls. *That must be how they navigate the tunnels.*

Jens was about to leave when he realized this kid was the first person to talk with him other than Sonya and Akela. If he were going to learn more about the movement, this might be his only chance. Checking around the room, he noticed everyone still seemed to be keeping a close eye on him. Most people, it appeared, didn't like having him in the compound.

"Do you know who I am?" Jens asked, turning back around to the kid.

This time his finger didn't stop moving down the page. "Umm hum," he said with a dismissive nod.

"Then I'm at a disadvantage, because I don't know who you are," Jens said, taking the empty seat across from the kid. Once he sat down, Jens saw how tall the boy was, noticing his feet crossed as he stretched his legs out. The boy had curly red hair and deep-green eyes. He wasn't trying to hide his annoyance at having been distracted from his book. The boy looked cautiously around the room as if weighing what his options were.

"Collin," he said in a deeper voice than Jens would have thought for such a skinny kid. For the first time, Jens noticed the book he'd been reading.

"*The History of Advanced Physics?* Aren't you a little young to be learning that in school?" Jens asked, surprised when Collin began to laugh. "What?" Jens asked, not sure he got the joke.

"Nothing school could teach me that I can't teach myself," Collin said, shutting the book and placing it on the table.

It was thick, and certainly not the type of light reading Jens would have picked up.

"Why are you here?" Jens asked.

"None of your damn business," Collin shot back. He might be a genius, but that didn't necessarily make him friendly.

"Look, kid, I never wanted to be here. But I am now, and I'm here to help," Jens said, hoping his voice sounded friendlier than he was feeling.

"Maybe you are. But you're one of them. The way I see it, you've got to do a hell of a lot more than bring us some data to show us you're on our side," Collin said.

Jens wanted to ask how such a young kid knew as much as he did but refrained. He needed to stay focused.

"What side do you think I'm on?" Jens asked, feeling surprisingly small as the kid sized him up.

Collin shrugged and opened his book.

Jens wasn't used to being challenged especially by someone so young, and he was almost impressed despite his anger.

"Knowing what you know? I'm surprised you would need to think about what side you're on. Now piss off," Collin said, his finger going back to tracking along the page.

Jens got up from the table and started down the corridor. Clearly, he'd hoped for a more insightful talk; it was becoming clear that everyone in this building except for Anton, Akela, and Ali hated him. He was sure Sonya would have them all killed if she didn't think she could use them for more information. Jens was happy to oblige, seeing as he already had one group trying to kill him, and it would be against his better judgment to add a second. But Collin was right about one thing—sooner or later, Jens was going to have to pick a side.

Jens walked into the war room. It was the same room where Sonya had shown him the documents Ali had retrieved. Now it was only Sonya and an older man Jens had never seen before in the room whispering together. When they saw it was Jens at the door, the conversation stopped. No doubt they were discussing him, as everyone else seemed to be doing.

"Agent Jennings. You're awake?" said the older man. "I'm Conrad Jensen. It's a pleasure to meet you." He stood up and approached Jens with an open palm, a formal greeting that no one else had been inclined to offer.

Conrad was a large man with deep-set blue eyes and blond hair. He was sturdy for an older man, and his strength still showed as he gripped Jens' hand.

"Should I be saying, 'It's nice to meet you'?" Jens said, gripping the man's hand with a little extra force.

"You can say whatever you want. From what I hear, you've been a huge help to us." His smile was disarming. He spoke fast and directly. Jens got the impression he was a career politician.

"Ambassador Jensen was just leaving," Sonya said, giving him a curt nod as if to tell him not to speak with Jens, while also confirming Jens' suspicions about the man. Jensen returned the smile, unperturbed by Sonya's bluntness, and made his way to the door.

"Perhaps we'll meet again on the sunny side, Agent Jennings," Jensen said, turning back to give Jens another signature grin before leaving.

"Sunny side?" Jens asked, looking to Sonya.

"His joke for seeing people in the real world," Sonya said with an exhalation; it was clearly not her favourite expression.

"So does that mean you're going to let us go?" Jens asked as Sonya sat back down in the chair, all formalities gone from the room.

"We were never going to keep you here," she said as she pinched the bridge of her nose.

"That's good to know," Jens said, laughing as he took a seat across the table from her.

"We're not bad people, Agent Jennings," Sonya said, her voice sounding exhausted.

"Please call me Jens," Jens said.

"Okay, Jens. Are you going to turn us in when we let you go?" she asked as she leaned forward, her elbows resting on the table. She was trying her best to look brave, but Jens thought this possibility truly scared her.

"Does my answer change you letting me go?" he asked, partially kidding but knowing it could be a risk. For a long moment, Sonya just stared at him.

"No," she said, after a moment, "but it would ruin decades of research on a group of people set on controlling the known world," she said, leaning back and rocking in her chair.

"Why are you so sure they are evil?" Jens asked

"History," Sonya replied as if expecting the question.

"What the hell does history have to do with this?" Jens asked, puzzled.

"When, in the history of the human race, has there ever been an organization attempting to manipulate a mass group of people who aren't doing it for selfish reasons? If what they were doing was 'good,' why would they need to hide themselves?" Sonya said contemptuously.

It was a valid point; Jens could list more than a few societies that had been manipulated into believing their wills were free.

"What makes you believe they are doing anything?" Jens asked.

"Do you know what really scares me?" she said finally, her voice full of sincerity.

Jens appreciated her directness but couldn't shake the impression she was as good at controlling a room as any politician. She had an agenda, and Jens would be best to keep that in mind.

"What?" he replied.

"That we've been looking into them for years now. Some people in our ranks have been doing it for decades. But Firefly has been so good at covering their tracks that all we ever get are shadows. What you've given us is the first tangible evidence we've ever really had. Everything else? Firsthand accounts that can't be collaborated in any way. You've seen more information than most people in our group, and you still have trouble believing anything is going on," she said, her eyes never leaving his.

"So why does that scare you?" Jens asked after a moment.

"Because if they're so laced throughout our society that even when we see firsthand what they can do, our instincts are to brush it aside in disbelief," she said. Jens saw, for the first time, genuine fear in her eyes.

"Just imagine what they are capable of," Sonya said, leaning back in her chair. "You may not believe it yet, Agent Jennings, but it doesn't mean it isn't happening."

It became clear to Jens that Sonya was a true believer in the cause, whatever that may be. Jens still couldn't be sure. Whoever was behind this was willing to kill for what they wanted, but other than rigging the lottery in some capacity, Jens couldn't understand what their objective could be.

"It seems improbable that their only objective is to cheat the system," Jens said after a moment, "so what's the point of it all?"

"That's the real question. And the one we don't know the answer to," Sonya said.

"People cheat the system all the time, and sooner or later they always get caught," Jens argued.

"Three hundred years . . . that we know about. Even if we exposed this, do you honestly think it would change anything? Maybe a couple of people lose their positions? They help too many people in need every year—there is no denying they do good work," Sonya explained.

"Then what's the problem?" Jens asked.

"The problem is they do all of it devoid of accountability. They are judge, jury, and executioner. Who gave them the right?" Sonya said as a troubled expression streaked across her face.

Her brother had fallen victim to Firefly, and likely Jens would have to wait to discover more of her story; she wasn't doing this for no reason.

"What happens to the people taken?" Jens asked Sonya. She looked at him for a moment, maybe trying to weigh what to say.

"They die. At least that's what the story is," she said.

"But you don't believe that?" he asked.

"Would you?" she questioned. "If you were going to go to all the trouble of paying off someone's family, what good would they be to you dead?"

"Do the victims have anything in common?" Jens asked, getting up as he began to pace the room. It was time to start treating this like a case. Jens might not be buying the secret-society thing, but he was a good agent, and this was a case like any other. Things would have to add up somewhere.

"From what we've found?" Sonya pulled up the data screen in front of her. A list of a hundred or so names, some with faces, some without, appeared. "No," she said, scrolling through some of the more recent names.

"But keep in mind some of these names go back over three hundred years. Our data records aren't that good, and some of these people were like ghosts," Sonya said, watching as the images flashed across the screen.

"How can anyone alive be a ghost?" Jens asked, watching the files flicker past, his thoughts returning to Natasha and Ryan Lilford. They were not ghosts, by any means, but they were lost in the system.

"Society's children?" Jens said out loud, a smile flashing across Sonya's face.

"Ding, ding, ding. Obviously not all of them were. But we have found that most were at some time or another in the system. Society's children have been around for only the past century or so before that . . ."

"They were abandoned," Jens interjected.

"Basically. The system, in some places, was . . . less than kind to these kids," Sonya said, gentler than Jens had heard up till now.

"So, you have a group of people who grow up disenfranchised and alone, then what? They are offered a way out. But to do what? Who can make these kids disappear, and who can keep them hidden?" Jens said, his mind flooding with questions.

"You're finally asking the right questions," Sonya said, sitting back in her chair. "This is a rabbit hole with no end. Just when you think you're close to something . . ." Sonya smacked the table, startling Jens. "It's gone, and you're back to square one. Then you're just another person, two bricks shy of a full load. It's their greatest gift."

"You mean to tell me you believe they survive on the sole idea that society will keep their secret for fear of being seen as mad if they talk?" Jens said, trying and failing not to laugh at the absurdity of it all. Sonya shrugged and gestured at him.

"You've just seen the evidence. Are you ready to tell the world?" Sonya asked, gesturing to the faces on the data screen.

"No," Jens said, quietly looking at the data scroll in front of him. She wasn't wrong; Jens wasn't prepared to put this out there. But she wasn't right, either. It wasn't because he was afraid of appearing mad; it was because they needed more proof. *Or am I actually just afraid?*

"What if I'm not prepared to believe you?" Jens asked, looking to Sonya. "What if we're wrong and there is nothing more to find?"

Sonya took in a deep breath and thought for a moment.

"What if I told you the human race, as an entity, was inherently stupid?" Sonya said.

Jens laughed. "I'd be inclined to agree with you," he said.

"My brother and I believe humanity has never been good, just increasingly less bad. We're stuck in a cycle of ebbs and flows of good and evil, each moment in time trying to be better than the one before, and just when you think it's hit a climax of greatness," Sonya said, her voice devoid of humour, "an opportunist appears to take advantage of the people, and preys on the kindness and naivety of the masses. They rise to power on false claims and spread lies to divide the people, and then the cycle begins again."

"That's a pretty depressing way of looking at it," Jens said.

"Maybe, but it's been true of every era before us. We naively think we are smarter than previous generations, and, in many ways, maybe we are. But in the most important way, we're not." Sonya got up from her chair, pacing slowly around the room. "We forget that our enemies are also getting smarter, and, that unlike us, they rarely play by the rules. They're patient and take advantage of society's collective highs and exploit the lows. People in power slowly manipulate the system, and the vast population never sees it happening," Sonya said, her voice distant.

"So why me? I'm a senior agent with the Global Investigation Bureau who's tasked to bring down people like you. So why would your brother bring me in?" Jens asked, hoping she might be able to provide him with some of the missing pieces.

"Honestly? I'm not sure," Sonya said as she returned to her chair and shut down the Halo in front of them. The two sat quietly for a moment.

"He's your brother? How could you not know anything?" Jens said, more than a little annoyed at her lack of knowledge.

"My brother has been tracking you for a little over seven hundred days," Sonya said. "He was less than forthcoming with the why," she added, having recognized shock on Jens' face.

"How in the hell did he manage that?" Jens said, trying to figure out just how hard that would have been before his suspension.

"Don't underestimate how good we are at what we do, Jens," Sonya said with a knowing smile. "All I know is that Anton said he had a plan and that he learned something."

"What?" Jens said demandingly. Sonya shook her head.

"He never told anyone," she said, sighing deeply. "Anton is my twin brother. When we were kids, our parents died in a terrorist attack on one of the data labs in Charlotte—some organization pissed off about privacy or something," Sonya said quietly.

Jens remembered the attack. He was young, not even in the PPD yet when it happened. But it was big news—killed seventeen people and injured thirty-seven more.

"Wait, I thought your parents committed suicide, something about the lottery and a false winning?" Jens said, remembering what Captain Rollins had managed to pull up on Anton.

"That is all a sack of lies," Sonya said, pressing a button as a new Halo appeared in front of them. It showed a young couple and a news article headlined "Attack strikes deep" alongside a picture of two young siblings.

"You and Anton?" Jens asked.

"They tried to take our story from us, but we fight to keep it alive. I remember walking with Anton. We were supposed to meet our parents who were working in the data center. We left school and were about to go into the building when there was a loud bang and then nothing. I woke up screaming in pain to find Anton pulling me out of a fire. I saw his face, his nose bleeding, cuts all across his body. Tears were pouring down his face, and I thought they were because he was hurt. But that's when the pain hit me." Sonya pressed a pad on her ear and a Halo sleeve retracted from around her face, revealing the burn scar tissue on one side of her face.

"The doctors said I was fortunate that it didn't burn my eye. Unfortunately, at the time they said they couldn't do anything, as our parents' bodies hadn't been found and our insurance wouldn't cover the skin grafts. By the time our parents' bodies were discovered, the nanobots had healed my face to this," she said, touching her cheek softly.

"Couldn't they repair it after?" Jens questioned.

"I refused. It became a reminder of what I needed to do," Sonya answered defiantly.

"What was that?" asked Jens.

"Bring down anyone who would want to bring harm to others," Sonya said fiercely.

Jens could respect that; it was one reason he wanted to be a GIB agent, although he couldn't help feeling they were on opposite sides of the same coin.

"Anton has always felt as though he let me down, that he didn't protect me when he should have. My scar is my courage, but it's his shame," she said as her mind appeared to flood with thoughts of her brother.

338

"Is that why you cover it up with the Halo sleeve?" Jens asked, honestly hoping he wasn't crossing any lines with the question. To his surprise, Sonya almost laughed.

"No. In our line of work, it doesn't help to be recognized, and unfortunately this," she said, sliding her hand down her scarred face, "is recognizable. Don't get me wrong, when this fight is over, I will proudly display my scars, but for now I keep them for me."

Jens thought he should be happy Sonya was opening up to him by telling him all this, but there was still something that didn't make sense.

"I'm truly sorry for what happened to you both. No one should have to go through that. But what does this have to do with me?" he asked, hoping he wasn't sounding very rude.

"I told you, I'm not sure," she said, her anger slipping through. Jens got the impression she disliked being in the dark as much as he did.

"But if I had to guess?" Sonya began to say. "If Anton kept what he found about you a secret from me, it was because whatever he found, he considered it too dangerous to tell me about," she said, and her eyes locked on Jens.

"So, Agent Jennings? The question is what are you hiding from all of us?" Sonya asked, the palms of her hands resting on the table as she leaned in closer. Jens could feel the determination of this woman even from across the table.

"My brother is lying in a hospital bed because he believes you needed to work this case. You wouldn't believe his excitement when he discovered the timing of it all. Your suspension coming to an end, he thought it was fate."

Jens could feel the hate in Sonya's words, but he didn't know if it was for him or for her brother's secrets.

Jens was sympathetic toward Anton's situation, but Jens couldn't forget that thanks to him, he'd been in a car crash, broken an arm, and been blown up—all because Anton didn't want to share the damned information he had.

"I'm sorry about your brother, but he's in the situation because of himself," Jens said, bluntly, hoping he wasn't very harsh. "From what I've gathered, Anton was a smart guy, and if he were doing all this, it was because he thought it was the right thing to do."

"You don't know jack shit about my brother," Sonya shouted.

"I know he has a video of the warehouse fire. I know that it incriminates a lot of powerful people," Jens said, trying to gauge Sonya's reaction to the news.

"You've seen it? All of it?" she asked. Jens guessed she must have at least known of the video but was surprised Jens had seen it.

"He knowingly turned himself into the PPD with evidence showing corruption in the PPD. Frankly, I'm having trouble deciding if your brother thinks he's a martyr or an idiot," Jens said jokingly.

"Don't you dare call my brother an idiot." Sonya slammed her fist on the table. Obviously, he'd struck a nerve.

"Anton knew what he was doing, and this was part of the risk. All so that you, Agent Jennings, would be able to witness the dark underside of your system."

"Why the hell would he do that?" Jens shouted.

"You tell me? Because my brother was no fool, so, it begs the question what the hell are you going to do that he couldn't?" She emphasised her words with a jabbing finger, pointing at Jens.

"I hate to break it to you, but your brother might have been a touch delusional," Jens said hotly.

Sonya looked around the room as if searching for something to beat or kill him with.

He continued before she could do anything.

"I have absolutely no idea what is going on here. I am a GIB agent, and if you have evidence, it's my job to take that seriously. If he'd shown me this before, I could have . . . ," Jens began to say as Sonya cut him off.

"You still don't get it, do you?" Sonya said, waiting patiently for an answer, which Jens was unable to give her. "That's what I wanted him to do. Give it to you. Let you handle it. Start actually exposing these bastards. But he wouldn't. It wasn't the right move. No, he needed to convince you, and that seems to be going over well," she said, collapsing into her chair, her body exhausted.

"I'm going to give you what you want. I'll take what you've told me and think on it," Jens said.

Sonya gave him a regretful smile.

"It's no use—my brother was right. It's going to do nothing. Look at you, all this information laid out in front of you, and you still don't believe it, do you?" Sonya said as she shook her head at Jens' absent response.

Jens believed something was going on, but he couldn't be sure what. There had to be a logical explanation for all of it.

Was Jens being played again? Sonya still seemed to think he was hiding something from her, that Jens had some idea what it was her brother knew about him.

Sonya looked defeated, and Jens hated that his first thoughts were he was being manipulated. For too long he'd been given half-truths and partial information.

Was this a ploy to make him feel guilty about what happened to her and her brother as children? What she couldn't possibly understand was that Jens had absolutely no idea what could be so interesting about his life that Anton would feel the need to keep tabs on him. In fact, at this moment, he resented Anton for pulling him into this mess altogether.

But if this were the game, it was time to stop being the pawn and start taking control of the game.

Jens stared at Sonya for a moment and then got up without saying a word and left the room. *If I'm going to play this game, I need to get the hell out of this place and attack the problem from my world, on my terms.*

38

By some miracle, Jens was able to find Ali's room. She was still asleep, and what he really wanted was to march in and tell her they had to get the hell out of there. But seeing her lying there, he decided it might be best to let her finish her sleep; after all, she had been stabbed for him.

It was unlikely Jens would get any sleep, so he nestled into the only chair in the room and attached his ocular pads and began to rewatch the video from the night of the fire, hoping maybe he would see something he missed.

He watched the Halo in front of him as he played through it trying to catalog all the faces and markings. He could attempt to figure out who was all there. Each pass displayed a truly messed-up scene.

All in all, he cataloged eight people, including a semi-conscious Nigel Eriksen and fully alive Ryan Lilford. It was clear that something was going on, but unfortunately the video was too far away to capture the audio. He figured this would be enough to take to Captain Rollins in the morning. Then it would be someone else's problem.

After a couple of more passes, Jens could feel his eyes growing heavy, and as he leaned back into his chair, he once again dozed off.

"Jens? Wake up," Ali said, gave him a light shake.

"I'm up," he replied, trying not to appear as scattered as he felt. "Back on your feet?" he added, noticing Ali hovering over him.

"You see, that's what happens when you take the time to actually let your body heal," Ali said with a wink as she walked away. Despite her bravado, she still seemed a little unsteady on her feet.

"Clearly," Jens said with a laugh as he stood from the chair.

"I was still stabbed, you jackass," Ali said, putting on her jacket.

"Are we at all concerned that they managed to get our clothes from our units?" she said with a nervous smile.

"At this point? That would be one of the things I'm least concerned about," Jens said, his arms stretching back wide, before turning back to look at Ali.

Ali looked a little confused, for which Jens couldn't blame her. She'd missed most of the activities from the night before. The berating from Sonya, the video from Anton . . . he needed to catch her up.

"I've got a lot to tell you," he said, putting a finger to his lips as he waved for her to follow him.

"I see sleep hasn't made you any less weird," Ali said, joking, but Jens signalled for her to be quiet.

The one thing the night before hadn't done was improve his sense of direction. However, Jens had discovered at least one trick, which was to follow the coloured wall markers that seemed to be placed strategically around the complex.

At the very least, Jens felt as though he could lead them away from the main atrium where they could talk unheard by anyone who might try listening.

After a couple of turns, Jens finally managed to find what he had been looking for.

"Where the hell are we going?" Ali asked skeptically.

"I told you we need to talk," Jens said again as he entered the darkened hallway, the lights flickering on as they move along.

"And we couldn't do it in my room?" Ali inquired.

"No," Jens said bluntly. "I think we're being monitored in the rooms."

"So, why are you leading me through these scary tunnels?" Ali said, musing, as Jens stopped to face her.

"I've got something to tell you," he said softly.

"You said that already," Ali said, looking around the old space. "What? You just wanted to make sure we're good and lost before you told me?" she said with a smile.

"We're not lost," Jens said, trying to sound confident. He wasn't *lost*, although he also didn't know where they were.

"Sure," Ali said, "and we're not in a building with an underground secret society hell-bent on discovering what another secret society is up to," Ali said, musing, although the way she said it made the whole thing sound absurd. But sadly, she wasn't wrong; it was the premise of what they were trying to do.

"Right, well, it doesn't mean we're lost," Jens said.

"So, what's so damned important that can't wait?" Ali said, looking around. She was obviously confident that no one was there.

Jens took a deep sigh; he'd already decided she should know what he'd seen, and when opportunity allowed, he would show her the actual video. After all, she'd been stabbed because of it, and although she was outside the blast radius, she was still nearly blown up, too. She deserved to know why.

"Something happened last night."

"Bad dreams?" she said with a laugh.

Ali stopped laughing when she saw the concern in Jens' face, and she began to understand why as he proceeded to walk her through it all. He told her of his encounter with Akela, of her relationship with Anton, her giving him the video from Anton, of his watching the full video of the night of the fire, and finally of his little impromptu conversation with Sonya. When he finished, he paused to let it all sink in with Ali and to give her a minute to mull it over.

Ali's face was devoid of emotion, but Jens watched as her eyes seemed to be dancing. He imagined her playing the scenarios in her mind. Jens hoped she'd end up at the same conclusions as he did.

"You have to show me that video," she said quietly after a moment.

"I will, just not here," Jens promised. Ali gave him an understanding nod.

Jens found so much comfort in her trust, and despite their short time together, he found it hard to imagine not having her here.

It was clear what they had to do next, but just then, they heard footsteps around the corner.

Jens instinctively reached for his confiscated electro-pulse.

"Who's there?" Jens called out, hoping whoever it was hadn't just heard their whole discussion. Jens wasn't sure how much anyone really knew in this place, and he wasn't about to give up his video without a fight.

The mystery person remained silent, giving Jens a bad feeling; they needed a plan. Luckily Ali seemed to have one, nodding at him as she pressed her back tightly against the concrete wall, preparing to grab whoever it was as Jens lured them out.

With Ali in position and the footsteps seeming close enough to the corner, Jens popped out, startling them as Ali rolled off the wall and grabbed the hooded figure before they could run.

"The hell do you want!" Jens shouted, trying his best to sound intimidating. But as he pulled back the hood, it revealed someone who was neither intimidated nor scared but annoyed.

"Collin?" Jens asked, recognizing the kid from the night before. He was holding a book in one hand, his ocular pads pressed on listening to something.

"What the hell!" Collin shouted. Ali was still unsure what to do, looking to Jens, who signalled her to let him go. "What the hell was that for?"

"Sorry, Collin, we called out . . . ," Jens began saying. Collin pulled off the ocular pads.

"I was listening to music," he shouted, waving the ocular pads in Ali's and Jens' faces. "I didn't realize that was a crime, Mr. GIB."

"It's not. We just . . . ," Jens said, his words unsuccessful in calming the situation.

"Look, I don't care. Dr. Akela and Sonya sent me to find you. I found you—which, by the way, wasn't easy when you're just aimlessly walking around the facility," he said, gesturing to the random location.

"How did you know we were here?" Ali asked as her eye brows pinching together suspiciously.

"I didn't," Collin snapped back.

"But you found us," Ali asked, surprised.

"You think this was the first place I checked?" he said, looking at them as if they were stupid. "It's a simple algorithm I designed to maximise habitual walking patterns and use that to efficiently scan the complex."

It was Jens' turn to look confused. This kid was either messing with them, or he was actually incredibly smart.

"Why would you need that algorithm?" Jens asked. "Lose people often?"

"No," Collin said bluntly. "You're the first idiots we've brought down here who would wander this far from the center." Collin laughed at his own joke.

"But you have an algorithm?" Jens asked.

"No, dummy. I made the algorithm like . . ." Collin looked at a timepiece on his arm "thirty-six minutes ago."

Jens and Ali looked at each other, unsure of what to make of this kid, until spotting the advanced geometry book in his hand.

"Impressive," Ali said, which received a snort from Collin. "We're sorry," she added, her voice more tender than Jens had heard in the past.

"Whatever. Just come with me," Collin said, not waiting to see if they were following. He opened his book back up and started to walk.

Jens and Ali followed him quietly, making a couple of turns before they arrived at the war room. Collin didn't bother looking up; he just pointed at the room and then continued reading his book.

"Weird kid," Ali said as he walked away.

"Maybe," Jens said, watching him leave. "But he might also be the smartest person in the building."

Ali gave him a pat on the back.

"He's just a kid," Ali said with a smile as she and Jens entered the war room.

Inside, at the table were Akela; Sonya; Conrad Jensen, who Jens recognized from the night before; and a few other people. Only Akela smiled at them as they entered.

"Time for you to be gone," Sonya said matter-of-factly. "We can't risk keeping you here any longer."

Sonya nodded to the people off to the side, who slid Ali and Jens gear across the table to them.

"May I?" Akela asked as she approached Ali, waiting for permission to look at her wound.

"Of course," Ali said.

Akela pulled up Ali's shirt, revealing a deep-purple scar on her stomach. It was the first time Jens had seen it, and although it had healed well, she would likely have a scar there for life without any body modifications.

"It looks good, but be careful. It will be prone to tears for the next two to three days," Akela said, lowering Ali's shirt and giving another warm smile.

"Thank you, Akela," Ali said, giving her hand a gentle squeeze. Jens wished she would have a reason to come over to him, but he had been given the "all clear" the night before. Whatever moment they'd had,

Jens knew she still cared for Anton; it likely didn't help that his sister was in the room.

Or so he told himself as he was forced to settle for a small smile.

"I'll be taking you out. I'm Conrad Jensen," Conrad said, looking at Ali as he offered her a handshake. "Nice to meet you."

"Ali Hantsport," Ali said in her official-sounding voice as she took his hand, receiving a politician's smile from Conrad.

"I hope you don't mind, but . . ." Sonya threw them black hoods, which Jens snatched out of the air.

"Put these on," she said as she stood, obviously ready to see them gone.

"Is this necessary?" Ali asked.

"We could always drug you again?" Sonya said it with a smile that hinted if she had her way, that's what she would be doing.

"What's next?" Jens said, looking directly at Sonya.

"I think that's up to you, Agent Jennings," Sonya said, her eyes narrowing in on him. In that moment, Jens got a feeling of dread that they would be as likely to kill them as free them once the hoods were on.

He resigned himself to the belief that if they'd wanted them dead, they would have done it already. No, they were hedging their bets.

Jens and Ali might not have been their allies yet, but for now, they were still useful. Sonya had been right when she said it was up to them to figure out just how useful they could be. With that in mind, Jens lifted the hood and placed it over his head, and once again his world went black.

Jens was grateful when they finally let him take off his hood—for one, his face was beginning to sweat and it was irritating him, and secondly, when the hood came off, he realized he had a general idea of where in the city they were.

Jens and Ali stood beside each other; their travel companion, or whoever had brought them here, was gone—likely disappeared in an ECar and was off to do more work for Ash and Sun.

"I wonder if bringing us here was a sign of trust or a punishment," Jens said, looking toward Ali, and she couldn't help laughing.

Looking around, Jens felt a familiarity with his surroundings, yet there was no doubt that so much had changed in the past three days.

"Funny how a murder and arson can lead to an underground society and blindfolding," Ali said, laughing as she tossed the hood in the nearest bin.

"Don't forget being blown up and stabbed," Jens said, laughing along with his friend, happy they were both able to do so.

"What now?" Ali asked when the laughter finally faded.

"I have no idea," Jens said honestly. He still had tons of unanswered questions, such as how was he involved or was he? Maybe Anton had been wrong. All Jens knew was that he'd had enough of playing their games.

At some point, whatever had been blocking their Zen watches had turned off, and now Jens felt a steady flow of vibrations coming from it.

Looking at the barrage of messages from Captain Rollins, Jens wondered if their plan had been as good as they thought. "Where the hell are you" and "I swear if you're not in my office by ten a.m., I will end you."

However, despite the initial messages, Jens realized they had been fairly accurate with their assumptions of how people would respond to his "habits," and he was unsure whether he should be impressed or disappointed.

Ali had also been bombarded with messages, and she was scrolling through. Jens imagined she had more heartfelt messages from people wishing her well.

"Shit!" she cried out suddenly. "Shit! Shit! Shit!" She started frantically scrolling through her messages and then typing away as fast as she could.

"What's wrong? You get fired?" Jens said, immediately regretting the bad joke as Ali shot him a quick glare. Jens had forgotten he had nearly got her fired once already.

"No, it's just . . ." She began looking over at him. "Never mind."

"What?" Jens tried to peek over to see what she was writing, but Ali had a blocker on her Zen watch. *Worth a try.*

"Come on, you can't burst out like that and not tell me. It's just . . . rude," Jens said playfully.

"It's personal," Ali said, shrugging off the comment.

"Like Dr. Nazari personal?" Jens asked, not needing her to say anything, as her face said it all.

"Trouble in paradise?" he added jokingly, which wasn't well received by Ali.

"Let me guess, she . . . found out you hacked into her medical account, and now she's super pissed off and hates you," Jens said as Ali continued to ignore him.

"Am I close?" he asked.

"Worse," Ali said, shaking her head as she read through the messages.

"What could be worse than a crime?" Jens asked.

"It wasn't a crime! I was borrowing it," Ali retorted.

"So, what happened?" Jens asked, setting the jokes aside.

"Well, it appears the all-powerful Ash and Sun did in fact cover the trail with the GIB," Ali said after a moment, still not looking up from her frantic typing, "but didn't tell my girlfriend, who now thinks I've been avoiding her for three days!"

"How is that worse?" Jens asked, surprised.

"Jesus, you really don't have a clue, do you?" Ali said, looking at him as if he were an idiot. Jens shrugged. "Not everyone is happy to just be alone forever, Jens. Some of us would like to spend time with another person."

"Ouch, I'd like to do that, too . . . at some point," Jens said. Ali started to laugh hysterically.

"Right," she added sarcastically.

"What? I'm a realist. How do we have time for anyone right now?" Jens said, gesturing to their surroundings.

Ali shook her head. "Relationships are like anything else. If you don't practice, you'll just be terrible at them," she said, giving Jens a sad smile.

"So, you're saying I should practice?" he asked, more than a little confused.

"I'm saying it couldn't hurt."

"What do you think I'm doing with you?" Jens said. The comment received another audible laugh from his partner.

"I'd hardly say being forced into a partnership is a great way to start a relationship," Ali said between bouts of laughter. "Not to mention since I became your partner, I've been stabbed, blown up, kidnapped, drugged, and put on suspension." She put her finger to her chin as if she were about to say more.

"I get it," Jens said, looking at his Zen watch. "Well, you won't have to worry about any more of that."

"The hell does that mean?" Ali asked as she stopped writing to meet his eye.

"It means I'm done," Jens said simply.

"The hell does *that* mean?" Ali shouted, her voice hitting a higher level of condescension.

"Look, I've got the video. I have all the proof I need to put some bad people away. I don't need a crusade," Jens said. A weird sense of relief and dread came as he said it out loud.

"You can't just forget what we've learned," Ali snapped back.

"I think I can," Jens said, musing.

"But you can't," Ali said. Jens heard the disappointment in her voice. Jens never wanted to have this conversation with Ali. He knew this was the right thing to do.

"You're right," Jens said softly. "Look at everything that happened to you since you became my partner. It has to stop."

"That's bullshit, Jens. You don't get to decide when we're done."

Ali's face was red now as she continued to shout. "What about Nigel Eriksen, Ryan Lilford, all the others!"

"We have enough to give them justice," Jens said.

"You're a lot of things, but I never figured you for a quitter, Jens."

Ali's words hit harder than the explosion.

"Look, I've made up my mind. This fight? Isn't my problem."

"What do you mean it's not your problem?" Ali asked. "You're just going to let this all go away?"

"What do you expect me to do?" Jens insisted.

"I don't know. Step up. Bring down the people responsible."

"What do you think I have been trying to do? And the last so-called criminal I went after? He lives in his big house with his loving wife."

"At least you tried!"

"I committed a crime!" Jens cried out. It was his turn to be upset. "I put a guy in the hospital, and my one saving grace is he doesn't remember it. Without that, I would be screwed!"

"You did the right thing."

"How can you say that?"

"Because the system is broken," Ali said angrily.

Jens was taken aback by the comment. He hadn't been prepared for any of this and had expected Ali to be on his side . . . not this.

"We are the system," Jens said slowly, suddenly worried about the direction of the conversation.

"And maybe that's why we're here?" Ali said calmly, as she shut down her Zen watch, whatever message she was sending before seeming unimportant. "The work we do, the good we think we provide. What if it's all for nothing? What if we're just good little robots doing our jobs and someone else is pulling the strings?" Ali's words felt like a punch in the stomach. She was talking about his whole existence and how it may not matter.

"I can't believe that," Jens said after a moment.

"I don't want to, either! I've given up everything to be where I am. But I have to know if it means something, don't you?" Ali's words hung in the air.

For a long moment, Jens simply stared at Ali ,unable to speak. He felt for her. Like him, she'd made sacrifices, giving up parts of her life to protect society. But it was the lot they chose. It didn't mean they had to like it.

"What I did to Chief Daniels was selfish. Just because I didn't think I was going to get the outcome I wanted, I tried to take it for myself," Jens said. "At least this way someone will go down for what happened."

"That isn't enough, Jens."

"What if what Firefly is doing is right? That their big picture does more good than bad?"

"You can't mean that, Jens."

"If we do this, Ali, we would have done our jobs," Jens said softly.

"Maybe sometimes doing our jobs just isn't enough?" Ali said, shaking her head. "Maybe that's the whole damn reason we are even here." she said as an ECar arrived.

"Take the win, Ali," Jens said as he hopped inside. "You coming?" he asked, but the door slamming behind him said it all.

39

It felt as if the ride to the GIB headquarters was an eternity, Jens still unsure if he were doing the right thing. But his mind was fixed on getting his old life back. Maybe then he could go back to being happy. Well, maybe not happy. Inside he'd always felt as if maybe he was never meant for happiness, but he would settle for contentment. *Why should I waste another one of my twenty-nine thousand two hundred days on some underground war?*

Jens had always had one goal in life, and that was to follow in the footsteps of the only man who'd ever really watched out for him, his grandfather.

He'd done it right, served his time, and then eventually started a family. Jens didn't know about the family part, but he had, up until two hundred and twenty-five days ago, been doing great with the service part. *But was that all there was to the man? After all, Jens was only a boy when his grandfather passed away. How much of his life did he really know about? Was there something he was missing? How in the hell did I ever get in this situation? One name, Anton Preston.*

From the moment he had mentioned Ryan Lilford, Jens had been running around in his little game, ignoring his own reservations about it all.

Jens looked down at his wrist, noticing the slight discolouration from a fresh scar on his forearm, just above his Zen watch—his dark navy blue watch he'd been given on his entrance into the GIB to match the suit.

So, who gets a matte-black Zen watch?

So much had happened, Jens had completely forgotten about what he'd seen in the car after the accident. Someone had wanted either him or Dr. Atkins dead. *Would I have been just collateral damage?*

"Display photos, military technology show last year," Jens said, suddenly remembering something about a black Zen watch.

"Display all references to matte-black, military-grade Zen watches," Jens said as four images popped up, but only one caught Jens' eye.

"Who makes this model?" Jens said, tapping on the image.

"Designer is unknown," the voice came back.

"What do you know about the Zen watch?"

"A prototype, depicted as the watch of tomorrow, valued at one million credits, though the design would never be approved, as many of its functions are against numerous society agreements."

"Why would anyone design a watch that can't be used?"

"Watches such as these are typically designed to show advanced capabilities and updated design features. They are strictly experimental."

"Well, it seemed like someone no longer wanted them to be experimental. Add information to thought board for future use," Jens said, shutting down his watch.

He wasn't quite sure why he would need to save this information; in a few hours he would be off the case, and it would be someone else's problem.

Jens' mind was set; he would go to Captain Rollins and wash his hands of all this. Whoever was after him had tried to kill him twice. Why risk a third time? It was better to survive and bring down the people who killed Ryan Lilford and Nigel Eriksen. At least some justice would be served.

Jens arrived at the GIB headquarters alone, resolved to his plan. He had everything he needed to bring in the people responsible. He made his way into the building, up the elevator to the bullpen. But as he reached the thirty-sixth floor and prepared to get off the elevator to meet Captain Rollins, he asked himself: *Am I doing the right thing?* A sudden pang of guilt lurched in his stomach; he knew that wasn't the question he needed to answer. He couldn't understand it, but he got the distinct feeling he wasn't where he was supposed to be.

It was weak, settled somewhere in the pit of his stomach, but it was there. He might have had half a mind to turn and run if there hadn't been the misfortune of Captain Rollins walking out of her office and locking eyes with him.

"Agent Jennings. My office, now," she shouted across the room, but her tone was even, so he held on to the hope that maybe he wouldn't be in very much trouble.

She didn't wait to see if he was coming; she simply turned on her heel and marched into her office. Anyone who hadn't seen him surely knew he was there now, including Agent Zhang, who was leaning back in his chair. Jens was too far away to be certain, but he could have sworn he saw a hint of purple under his eye from where Jens had punched him.

"Looking good, Zhang," Jens said as he casually rubbed his middle finger under his eye mockingly. It was a juvenile gesture, but it didn't mean it didn't feel good. It was made all the sweeter as he watched Zhang's face go from smug to anger in a flash.

"What's that? Three dead now on your watch?" Zhang said, spitting out the words and making a show of counting his fingers thoughtfully. Obviously, the rumours had still been spreading, or this was Zhang's attempt to start one. Either way, it was frustrating.

"Where's Agent Hantsport?" he added. "Stab her in the back like you usually do, Jens? Should I make that four?" he said, pinching his fourth finger with an evil smile.

Jens didn't want to admit just how much that hurt. Ali might not be dead, but he shouldn't have left it as he did, after everything she had done for him. She should be here with him. *Or do I just think that because it would mean I was doing the right thing?*

Looking over at the pure hatred in Zhang's eyes, Jens found it hard to believe that they had ever been partners, though that felt like forever ago now.

Like Ali, Jens had refused his assignment to work with Zhang. Up till then, only Agent Moretti had been comfortable with Jens being a little younger and a little more experienced than most. But despite their initial rocky beginnings, they had actually worked well together.

That was until Jens discovered that Chief Daniels had been connected to illegal trafficking.

At the time Jens, still hadn't known how bad it was, only that he was using his power to keep it all under wraps and taking some credits for his efforts. Jens took it to Zhang, thinking he would help him investigate, but Zhang, always the loyalist, couldn't betray their chief.

Needless to say, he'd been less than impressed when he discovered Jens hadn't given up on the case and seemed to take the entire pursuit as a personal insult.

In the end, despite Jens' managing to convince almost everyone that he had been at the club with Chief Daniels to protect him, Zhang refused to believe his story.

Maybe one day they could see eye to eye again; at least Jens was confident that his old partner would agree with his current action. *Maybe one day Ali will, too?*

40

"Where the hell have you been?" Captain Rollins said harshly as she turned on him from the window of her office. Jens shut the door as the windows switched modes, but not before Jens noticed more than a few glares from the other agents in the bullpen.

"And don't give me that bullshit about needing time. You might be an asshole, but you're not that big an asshole," she said. "Leaving after what just happened?" Her voice rang throughout the room, and Jens wondered if he heard a hint of worry in there as well.

"I've been away," he said, unsure if he could even explain the past couple of days if he'd wanted to.

"No shit, Sherlock, I want to know where and why," Captain Rollins said as she turned on him.

"You may want to sit down," Jens said calmly. Rollins stopped, giving Jens a calculated stare.

"You may want to get on with it, agent," she said, her contempt spilling into each word. Jens admired her gusto, but not even she had a clue what she was about to hear.

"Where's Chief Furland?" Jens asked. He'd assumed after their last meeting that they would want to be here.

"Would you be surprised to learn they are trying to distance themselves from you? I, on the other hand, have the privilege to see this this through." Her voice was thick with sarcasm. "And after our little impulse explosion . . . let's just say people started to ask questions wondering about our ability to handle the situation."

"What's that supposed to mean?"

"I see you need me to spell it out for you," she said, "Fine, some people are wondering if you are a liability." *No wonder Chief Furland cut ties and ran!*

Jens tried to ignore the irony that he was in some way about to do the same thing.

"But you're still here?" Jens asked evenly, watching as Captain Rollins let out a massive sigh before meeting his eyes once again.

"You're a lot of things, including a liability. But you're not afraid to ask the hard questions, and someone has to," she said quietly, a hint of fear in her voice. *At least I still have some friends.*

"So," she continued, "you going to tell me what the hell is happening?"

Clearly Captain Rollins was under immense pressure to fire Jens and bury this whole matter, which only made what he was about to tell her so much worse.

Captain Rollins stared unwaveringly at Jens as he took a seat across from her desk. He let out a long slow breath as Captain Rollins turned to face out her window as she normally did. Jens was almost curious enough to ask why but figured now wasn't the best time.

He walked her through the last seventy-two hours since the explosion. The kidnapping by Ash and Sun, being held in their underground bunker. Making sure to mention that they took great care in rehabilitating Ali, who was now up and running. If she had been interested in knowing why Ali wasn't with him now, she didn't say, and Jens opted to leave that out. A pathetic attempt to delay the inevitable.

"The whole thing felt surreal, and if I'm honest, I haven't figured out how I feel about it all," Jens said, concluding his breakdown of events. Captain Rollins remained remarkably quiet as she continued to stare out the window.

"You're not telling me everything, are you?" she asked quietly after a long pause, still not turning to face him. This had been lucky for Jens, as she didn't see the look of shock on his face.

Up till now, Jens had remained quiet about the video of the night of the fire, wanting to wait and gauge Captain Rollins' reaction first.

"No," Jens answered solemnly. The past seventy-two hours had seemed almost fantastical as, for a brief time, Jens and Ali essentially had their lives stripped away. As much as he wanted to, he wasn't prepared to share everything. Not yet.

"Where's Ali now?" Captain Rollins seemed to accept Jens' decision not to share everything right away. *I don't deserve that sort of trust, not after everything I've done.*

"She had some personal matters to attend to," Jens said, lying. Truthfully, he had no idea where she was. "After all, we're technically still civilians," he added, catching an eye roll from the captain in the reflection of the glass.

"Don't give me that crap. You're GIB," she said sternly. Jens opened his Zen watch, making an elaborate show of trying to get his GIB access code, receiving a red "Permission denied" sprawled across the Halo.

Captain Rollins' eyes rolled again as she opened her own Zen watch and typed away for a moment before a buzz and a green "Access granted" message displayed on Jens' watch.

"Happy?" she said, shutting down her own Halo.

"Ali, too?" he asked.

Captain Rollins sighed as she redisplayed her watch and began typing away on the Halo and sending off another access pass. He had no way of knowing if she really had, but he chose to take her word.

"What about the tribunal?" Jens asked, suddenly remembering his disciplinary tribunal, which must have occurred while he was with Ash and Sun.

"You were cleared, fined four hundred credits, which was struck from your pay and donated to the lottery at the request of Angela Choi," she said dismissively.

Jens smiled. All in all, that was a fair judgment, although he wasn't sure if he should be pleased or terrified. He had expected Firefly to come down hard on him; after all, he was trying to expose them.

"I saw the video, Jennings. It was a rookie mistake stepping into her like that. I expect better from you," she said disapprovingly.

"I admit it was not my finest moment, and I know, moving forward, I have to find a way to keep my impulses in check."

"What makes you think you're moving forward?" she said, lifting her brow. "Lucky for you a video of the explosion was leaked, showing you risking your life to save all those people. It was a smart play by Ash and Sun," she said with a smile, turning to see the genuine look of confusion on Jens' face.

"Ash and Sun never released that video," Jens replied. It was Captain Rollins' turn to be confused.

"It had to be them—who else would have?"

"I'm not sure, but I can confidently say if they did release it, they did it without telling me," Jens said, thinking back to his time in the bunker. *Would they have done it and not told me?*

"Well, regardless of who it was, it saved your ass," Captain Rollins added, clearly unfazed by the anonymity of it all.

Jens, on the other hand, needed to know. Whoever had released that video did it for a reason.

"Do you have the video?" he asked, trying to hide the concern in his voice.

"It's uploaded so anyone can view it," Captain Rollins said, reaching for her data pad and projecting the video Halo in front of them.

Although the image was shaky, Jens could still vividly remember the scenes from the day. He grimaced as the explosion went off, watching as the energy wave erupted, the blast sending his body flying back through the air along with anyone unfortunate enough to be near the fountain, the man's voice echoing in his mind as he released the pressure: *I've done what you've asked.* The headline read, "Lone Terrorist."

"Why do they think he was acting alone?" Jens asked.

"According to the investigation, he had no affiliates or any known group. He was an isolated case," she said. "Why?"

"Because he wasn't alone. There was a woman there," Jens said, scanning the scene. "She was the one he called out to, the one he was afraid of."

"He never called out to anyone?" she said.

"Fast forward a bit," Jens said, ignoring her unease. Captain Rollins moved the dial ahead, the images passing by Jens slowly, waiting to see it.

"What are you . . ."

"Stop!" Jens shouted, pointing at a blank space on the screen.

"Where is she?" he exclaimed. He'd known she was standing there. The image of her had been seared into his memory like the person who broke the doctor's neck.

"Who?" Captain Rollins asked suspiciously.

"There was a woman right here, watching me after the explosion. I think she was the one he was calling to."

"Calling to?" she asked. Jens had a sudden moment of panic.

"Rewind the video to right before he activates the bomb."

She did what he asked, and he peered at the screen.

"There!"

She stopped and pressed play; the audio on the recording started to play.

"I've done what you asked," the man's voice said clearly.

"You see, he was calling out to someone, letting them know that he was compliant," Jens insisted.

"Or was he yelling at you trying to trick you into coming closer?" she asked.

"I know what I saw," Jens said defiantly.

"Right, well, this video shows something different. Maybe you just . . ."

"Videos can be altered," Jens cut in. Suddenly he was aware of the reason he'd come in the first place.

If this video could be altered, so could the footage of the fire. He'd come under the assumption that what he had in his possession was a legitimate video of the event of the night of the murder. This video proved that not everything seen is necessarily the truth. People can manipulate the images on screen.

"What do you mean altered?" Captain Rollins asked him.

If what he saw proved videos could be altered, then how could he take the video to Captain Rollins and convince her the woman from the explosion was real? If anything, he would be damning himself.

He'd already been through this once before, and he got lucky. If he were going to do this again, he needed some real proof claiming the video was true. He needed someone who was there, someone who could verify the video was real. One name jumped out at Jens. *But would she confess to a crime?*

"Is everything all right, Jennings?" the captain asked.

Jens' face must have betrayed him more than he'd hoped it would.

"Fine, ma'am," he said, trying to regain his composure. She stared at him for a moment, plotting her next words carefully.

"Are you going to share with me what's going on?" she asked slowly.

"For the moment, I think it's best if I get a little more information," Jens said. "May I be excused, ma'am?"

Captain Rollins nodded as Jens got up from his chair and made his way toward the door, knowing what he needed to do. "Jennings, please don't do anything stupid," she added before he had a chance to open the door.

"I'll try," he said as he exited the room.

Walking across the bullpen, Jens ignored the eyes around him. *How the hell did I end up here?* Jens was having a difficult time knowing what and who he should trust. Someone had to be lying to him, but whether that was Ash and Sun or Firefly, he couldn't be sure. *Perhaps they both were?* For a brief moment, Jens toyed with the idea of dropping everything altogether and bailing. But he couldn't do that now. *But what if you are still just being manipulated? I should do this now-leave it and move on.*

The existential crisis faded quickly as he put some pieces of the puzzle together, and it all started with Constable Wilson.

Entering the elevator, he placed on his ocular pads and made a call.

"Zone Fifty-Six, Constable Mullen speaking. How may I direct your call?" said a familiar voice on the other end of the line. Jens was suddenly thankful for his brief encounter with Constable Mullen the last time he'd been at the station visiting Anton.

She'd been helpful while he was there, although he also knew she was predisposed to gossip, which meant he'd have to play this coolly.

"Hi, it's Senior Agent Adam Jennings from the GIB. We met last week," Jens said, trying to remain natural.

"Right, yes, Agent Jennings, what can I do for you?" she replied, her tone respectful but annoyed by this seemingly disregard for the main line.

Typically, agents would reach out personally, but Jens didn't have Constable Wilson's details and had no way of getting them without giving away his plan. Jens was hit with a sudden dash of inspiration.

"I was wondering if Constable Granger is still in the building. I tried to ping him, but it didn't show up." Jens could have pinged Constable Wilson; this would have given him a rough idea of where she was. All constables could be reached that way for emergencies, but he couldn't be bothered to rummage through all the Wilsons in the directory.

"That checks out with Granger," the voice said on the other end of the line. Jens was happy his assumption paid off; now he just needed to finesse this next part.

"He mentioned he would be at the station till . . ." Jens looked at his watch. Christ, it had been a long day, "sixish. Said he'd be with Constable Wilson?"

Jens was surprised to hear laughter from the other end of the phone.

"I bet he did," Constable Mullen said.

"Sorry?" Jens asked; he hadn't meant for it to sound intense, but it must have unnerved Mullens on the other line, because she quickly began backpedaling as she remembered with who she was speaking.

"Sorry, sir. It's just . . . never mind. I'm not sure about Constable Granger, but actually hold on one moment."

The line went silent. He waited for a moment before the line picked back up.

"Constable Wilson is here," she said. "Agent Jennings, are you there?"

Jens could have cheered had he not been who he was. He couldn't believe his luck; the only catch now was what to do next as Constable Mullen had already patched him through to Constable Wilson.

"Wilson, I have Agent Jennings on the line for you," Constable Mullen said formally.

"Hi, Constable Wilson. How are you?" he said slowly, trying and failing to play it cool. Jens noticed a slight buzz on the line, which meant the call had not been fully transferred and that Constable

Mullen was still on the line.

"Good, sir, I hear you're looking for Craig . . . Constable Granger, I mean," Constable Wilson said, sounding nervous.

"Yes. Well, actually I was hoping I might speak with you, while I have you. It's about the Anton Preston case. He's gone missing." This wouldn't likely be news to her, but he needed to get Constable Mullen off the line.

"I heard, but . . . ," she began saying.

"Could we speak privately?" Jens asked, trying to sound more confident than he felt. The whole flying-by-the-seat-of-his-pants thing was not his specialty.

He would have preferred to speak to her in person, and if he managed to hop in an ECar, he knew he'd be there in under ten minutes. He just needed to stall her and keep her on the line.

"Absolutely, sir," said Constable Mullen sheepishly as Jens heard the line drop from the call, leaving just Constable Wilson and him alone.

"Can I ask what this is about?" asked Constable Wilson.

"I have a lead on his whereabouts," Jens said, lying, but it felt like more of an obscured truth, as he'd just spent the last seventy-two hours in the same complex as Anton, but Jens couldn't tell her that or where it was, even if he'd wanted to.

"Really?" she asked, sounding hopeful.

"We believe he has been taken by Ash and Sun."

"But he is Ash and Sun, sir."

"We don't think he is. We think he is just one part of a larger organization, albeit he's a large part." Jens was scrambling now, realizing he'd somehow have to explain himself.

"Really? What makes you say that?" she said.

Maybe I've overestimated just how much she knows?

"We received messages from Ash and Sun while he was in the hospital, so either he has magic powers, or he isn't acting alone."

Jens knew he needed to toe the line here; he checked his ECar, eight minutes out.

"I guess that makes sense why it had been so hard to track him down in the first place."

"You'd looked for him before?"

"Not me, but other PPD units had tried."

"Why?" Jens questioned.

"He's a hacker, sir—it's kind of our job." She gave a slight laugh from the other side of the line.

"Makes sense. So, you had been familiar with him before this?"

"Yes, sir."

"So, you must have been excited when you brought him in," Jens said looking at the ECar "6 minutes" out. All he needed to do was keep her on the line a little longer.

"We brought him in, sir. It was a team effort. If it hadn't been for your tip, sir, we might never have found him."

"Yeah, the whole thing was fortunate. Much like the body of Ryan Lilford."

"Who?"

"The boy from the river—I noticed you were the officer on-site for that as well."

"It was a simple suicide, sir, not much to investigate."

"You don't believe the information from that live feed?" Jens asked.

"Just a bunch of altered information and facts to fit a new narrative. I'm confident we did the right thing." Wilson said trying her best to sound confident, though Jens could sense otherwise.

"Still, between bringing in Anton Preston and a missing person, you seemed to be having a busy week."

"So did you, sir. But I'm not sure I fully understand what you're asking me."

"I'm just trying to get an understanding of the great work you did."

"Thank you, sir. But to be honest, I played only a part. But it was Craig, I mean Constable Granger, who brought me in."

"What?" Jens said with a gasp.

"Sir?" Wilson asked.

All this time Jens had assumed it was Wilson who'd brought everyone in.

"You were the constable on-site, no? You picked up Ryan Lilford."

"Yes, but . . . sir, can I ask why any of this matters?" she asked, her voice sounding more and more suspicious.

Jens was now totally confused. How in the hell was he supposed to understand who was lying to him when everyone around him seemed to be lying? He decided to play the only card he knew he had left.

"I know about the video."

"What?" Her voice came out a soft whisper; even so, there was no hiding the fear in her voice. Jens glanced at the time, only three minutes out.

"I know about the video, the one Anton Preston brought in, the one you had destroyed."

"I didn't . . ."

"Don't insult me by trying to lie." Jens could hear heavy breathing on the other end of the line, so he decided to double down. "Do you think someone like Anton would go into the police station without a second copy? A plan B?" Jens let the words sink in a moment. "You must have been pretty happy when you saw the footage of you on there—so many important people counting on you to get rid of it."

"You're bluffing."

"Why do you think he was so calm? Even after he saw it was you bringing him in. He'd planned this out well beyond our little raid. He's as brilliant as we give him credit for."

"He's dead."

"No, he's very much alive."

"That's impossible," she said, her voice shaking now.

"Is it?" Jens asked accusingly. Only one minute out now.

That's when the line went dead, not that it mattered. There was nowhere she could run to now. Jens had successfully rattled her cage, and when he finally picked her up, he hoped she would finally enlighten him on what the hell was going on. At least that was what was supposed to happen.

41

Jens ran in through the main doors, having jumped out of the ECar upon arrival. Quickly, he found Constable Mullen sitting at the front desk.

"Where is Constable Wilson?" Jens asked, skipping the pleasantries. He could feel his heart pounding in his chest.

"What did you say to her?" Constable Mullen said sharply, Jens momentarily taken aback by the cold tone of her voice.

"This is important. I need to find Constable Wilson. Now!" Jens slammed his palm on the desk, something he picked up from Captain Rollins.

It seemed to do the trick, for Constable Mullen, although she still seemed very much confused, pointed to the elevator.

"She shot up to the top floor."

"What's on the top floor?"

"Normally just a few offices, but it's under renovation" Constable Mullens said with a shrug.

"Why would she go up there?" Jens asked suspiciously.

"Get some air. It's the only place in the building you can get access to the roof. Not the first time someone in this building needed . . ."

"Shit!" Jens ran over to the elevator and, setting his GIB Zen watch up to the reader, a moment later the doors slid open, and Jens stepped in.

She's fine, the uncomfortable thought replaying in Jens' mind as he resisted the sudden urge to vomit in the elevator. He would have liked to know more, but right now it was more important to find Wilson and make sure she came with him.

She was the only one who could verify in person that the video he had was real and not fake. There was something suspicious about the way she was reacting as well that made him uneasy. *If she were going to run, why stay in the building and why go to the roof?*

Sadly, he knew there was only one logical explanation—in which case, he couldn't waste any time.

Jens reached the top floor. It was dark; the power for the floor must have been disabled, and the only light coming in was from the windows. It took a moment for his eyes to adjust to the space, and when they did, he quickly manoeuvred around the room looking for a stairway up to the roof.

Fortunately, Jens recognized the layout from similar government buildings and thanked the city's boring yet tactical decision to make them all so familiar. However, most buildings didn't have hallways filled with wood and tools that jetted out in weird directions. After whacking his shins for a third time, he remembered the flashlight on his watch.

He silently cursed himself as another lone pipe thudded into him before he managed to adjust the light for the hallway.

When he got to the top of the stairs, he pushed opened the door, and the flashlight did nothing to prepare his eyes for the sudden surge of sunlight that burst through the doorway, burning his eyes.

Instinctively, he threw his hands up to shield his eyes, and after a moment, his eyes adjusted to the sunlight, revealing the image he'd been most afraid of.

Constable Wilson stood in the distance; her face was filled with terror, as tears streamed down her face, and she peered over the edge of the tall building, one foot braced on the edge as if readying herself to jump.

Jens quickly steadied himself as he tried not to cry out, afraid he would scare her. She hadn't noticed him yet, and to Jens' surprise, she wasn't alone on the roof. Constable Granger stood about six feet from her, his palm up, as he appeared to be talking her down.

"I can't do it," Jens heard her say quietly through the tears.

"Yes, you can. It's easy . . . ," Granger began to say, his voice even. He noticed Jens a second after Wilson, his presence startling her, causing her to slip a little and forcing her to lean closer to the edge. Granger looked at Jens, his face awash with emotion, but his eyes betrayed his nervousness.

"You! You did this!" Wilson said, her voice catching as she shouted at Jens.

"Jens, stay there," Granger said calmly.

"Constable Wilson. Please, I can help you. You just need to trust me," Jens said in a voice so calm he surprised himself. He could feel his heart pounding; this was not what he had wanted.

"You don't understand!" Wilson said, sounding already defeated.

"Help me understand, then," Jens called back.

"I can't," she said quietly.

"Vikki, please. You know what you have to do," Granger said to her before leaning in to whisper something that Jens couldn't make out.

Whatever he said seemed to break the woman, as more tears began to flow while Jens watched Granger move closer to her. But the movement only caused her to flinch away as she began to shake her head fiercely.

"Think of your family," Granger said, stepping closer. For a moment, it looked as though she would step off the ledge, but Jens knew from experience that in these situations, most people wanted to live. With such a short time on this earth, it was rarely the desired outcome in the end. But something was off about the mention of her family; rather than hope, Jens thought he saw remorse.

Her face went blank, and before anyone could intervene, Jens watched as Constable Wilson stepped up and off the ledge of Station House Fifty-four.

Both Jens and Granger closed the gaps quickly between them and the edge of the building, Granger reaching it first, his eyes wide in shock.

Jens' eyes were fixed on the silent body of Victoria Wilson as she plummeted from the hundred-storey building.

For a brief moment, Jens felt as though time stopped as he watched her body fall to the ground. The distance did nothing to diminish the horrific sound of her body colliding with the ground.

The body hit the pavement just outside the east entrance of the building. Like tiny ants, onlookers stopped and gaped in horror while they realized what exactly they were looking at.

Some began screaming and running off. Jens stood silently; selfishly, he realized he lost the only witness he had to authenticate the video, while beside him, his friend was in tears as he just watched a woman he loved kill herself. It was the worst moment of Jens' life.

"What did you say to her?" Jens asked, his voice barely above a whisper, but Granger had heard him. Granger's face was red, and his eyes were puffed up; he opened his mouth as if to speak, but nothing seemed to come out. Finally, he sucked in a heavy breath.

"It doesn't matter. It didn't work," he said, his voice breaking with each word.

It was hours before both Jens and Granger were able to be released from the scene, and only after the PPD was satisfied with their stories. There had been data cams on the roof, which help paint a fuller picture of the event, although the investigators were less than satisfied with Jens' reasons for wanting to talk with Constable Wilson in the first place.

He couldn't simply say he thought she, along with the current mayor and the largest organization in the world, was part of a wider cover-up to mask the murders of certain individuals. No matter how much he wanted to.

No, that avenue had been closed, and it died with Constable Wilson. Without her around to collaborate the video, Jens couldn't imagine anyone believing him.

Jens felt haggard as he stepped out of the interview room; his body was weak from exhaustion. All he wanted to do was sleep. But when he saw Granger standing on his own peering out the window, his face a mix of torment and sadness, he knew he wasn't the one truly hurting.

Jens approached his unmoving friend as he placed a hand on his shoulder. If Jens' presence startled him at all, Granger didn't show it.

"You look like you could use a drink," Jens said softly. His friend didn't say anything as his head slowly dropped to his chest and as he tried to wipe away a tear from his face.

It didn't take much convincing for the two of them to end up at their local spot. However, neither one felt the need to say much for the first couple of rounds. What they needed was company, not conversation.

There wasn't much either one could do to help the other, not unless Jens could bring back Constable Wilson or Granger could confirm he was at the meeting Anton had caught on video, which would not only incriminate him in a large-scale crime, but would also mean the end of his career. So, neither seemed bound to happen, and frankly, it wasn't a conversation Jens was eager to bring up, at least not right now.

"You cared about her, didn't you?" Jens finally asked after the second round of drinks had been finished, with a third on its way.

For a long moment, Granger just sat there staring at the nearly empty glass, the remaining swigs swirling around as he rocked it back and forth. Eventually he let out a big sigh.

"Yeah, I mean I guess I didn't realize just how much until . . . now," he said, the words struggling to come out.

"How did you meet?" Jens said, finishing his drink just in time for the server to swing in and replace it with a full one.

"We did ops together awhile back. I was told . . . I brought her in because she is . . . was good." Granger took a large gulp from his fresh beer. "It wasn't long after that that we started, you know," he said, giving Jens a sad smile.

Jens had never been good at connecting with people, but he certainly wasn't void of human emotion. His friend was hurting, and he could see that.

Jens wished he could respect that, but unfortunately, he was out of options now, and he was forced to cling to one final hope of getting answers—even if that meant hurting his friend more, telling himself it was for the greater good, even though Jens was having a hard time believing it.

"Do you know why she was on the roof?" Jens asked, unsure of how much Granger knew.

"No," he said, shaking his head slowly. "I saw her heading up. She looked upset, so I thought I would check on her," Granger said with a sigh. "Clearly she was."

"So, she never told you I spoke with her?" Jens asked softly.

"She may have mentioned it, but, honestly, it's all a little fuzzy. Same as I told the incident specialist," Granger said, shaking his head.

Jens didn't like making him relive it, but he needed some answers.

"I need to ask you something, and I need you to answer honestly," Jens said, lowering his voice as if someone could be listening. Granger simply stared at him, unmoving. Jens decided to take his silence as approval to continue.

"The day you brought in Anton Preston, did you see anything . . . suspicious?" Jens knew Granger must have known something when his eyes dropped down to his drink at the mention of the arrest. "You did, didn't you?"

"I know about the deleted files," Granger said quietly. Jens had figured as much, but it still didn't feel good to hear him say it.

"Why didn't you say anything?"

"Why does it matter? She's dead now," he said coldly.

"The video she erased had some pretty serious information on it—information I need." Jens was surprised when his friend began to laugh. It was an eerie, hollow laugh as he slammed his drink on the table and glared at Jens.

"You can't just leave it alone, can you? Wilson jumped off a roof to avoid talking with you, and you still can't give it up?" Granger's words were harsh.

"People don't like you, Jens. I like you. Maybe that new partner of yours does, too," Granger said. "But you drive people away because you can't just leave it alone. You're always trying to be some sort of hero." He let out an exaggerated laugh.

"You know more about the deleted drives, don't you?" Jens said, ignoring Granger's ramblings.

"I know enough to tell you that you're wrong. Whatever you think is going on here, you're wrong." Granger downed the full beer in front of him. "And unless you're careful, you'll be next."

Granger turned to leave, but Jens grabbed his wrist.

"I can help you," Jens said, his voice filled with concern for his friend.

Granger scoffed. "Wow. You know, for a smart guy, you really can be an ignorant piece of shit." With that, Granger pulled his hand away, leaving Jens alone at the bar.

Jens sat still for a moment trying to understand what had just happened; as per usual, Jens was hoping for some answers, and now all he had was more questions. One thing was for certain—Granger knew more about this than he would admit.

Jens couldn't help wondering just how much his friend had known. Clearly, he'd been lying to him, and Jens had gone to him for help. *Had I put my faith in the wrong person?*

A good constable was dead, and the only proof of why she'd killed herself was a video of the acting mayor of the city watching as an innocent man was killed. To make matters worse, Jens still had no idea why any of this was happening, and the one person who might have helped may have just threatened his life.

For the first time, Jens felt hopeless and defeated. Maybe he would have been better off never coming back after his suspension. Life was certainly less complicated before, and he'd found a pleasant way of dealing with the mundane of it all.

With that spark in his mind, he finished his beer and made for home. He wasn't sure what tomorrow would bring, but tonight he would forget it all. Ash and Sun, Firefly, Constable Wilson, Dr. Atkins, Ryan Lilford, and the numerous other dead bodies that had piled up in Jens' world in the past week.

Jens could hardly believe just how quickly his life had begun to unravel, and it all happened the day he pushed Chief Daniels down the stairs. *Is Granger right? Am I ruining people's lives because I'm trying to be some sort of hero?*

Jens had never thought of himself that way; he'd always just tried to do what was right. *No. I try to do what I think is right.*

There was a difference. He didn't decide what was right; that's why there is a society in which the people decide. *Is that still true if Firefly is real? Are they pulling the strings and I'm simply here to enforce it?*

Jens hated this paradox—the continuous loop of mind games in which he was stuck. He desperately wanted it all to go away and for the emptiness to replace his rattled thoughts.

Arriving back at his apartment, Jens made his way into his bedroom, the calming thoughts so close to him now he could cry.

The walk home had only made it worse. The pressure in his head felt as though it would explode. Reaching into his dresser, he pulled out the familiar tin; he opened it up and found the purple vial resting inside.

It was only a matter of seconds now, and the sweet release would finally come. His body shuddered as he lifted the sealed vial up to his nose. He made to break the casement and release the neurotoxins held within, just as a familiar buzz from his Zen watch went off and stopped him.

42

The feeling startled him at first, and he nearly dropped the small glass vial containing the purple sands of Enzo. Jens felt his body consumed with anger at the delay of his release.

"Outside." Jens read the message twice before opening the front-door data cam. Sure enough, Ali stood waving at the cam, holding a small bag.

Jens thought about ignoring the alert. In a moment he could be relieved of all his thoughts rather than answering the door and bringing them all back around. His head began to throb at the idea.

"I know you're here, dickhead," Ali said, now staring up at the cam.

With a heavy sigh, Jens set the vial in the tin and placed it on the bedside table. *With any luck, I can send her away quickly and get back to my peaceful nothingness.*

If he thought it would be easy to be rid of Ali, he was wrong, as she barged in right past him as he opened the door.

"We're drinking this," she said, pulling a nice bottle of whiskey out of the bag she'd been carrying it in and placing it on his living room table.

"I was actually about to . . . ," Jens began to say but was cut off.

"Listen, dickhead. You and I have some things to talk about, so stop being a baby and get two glasses," Ali said, plopping herself down on the couch.

Jens glanced over at his room, remembering the vial on the bedside table. Ali followed his glance, but if she recognized the tin on the dresser, she didn't say anything.

"Unless, of course, you had other plans?" Ali said, letting the bottle drop to her side, her eyes glancing toward the bedroom. Jens took another look at the vial on the bedside table, then back at his partner. With a sigh, Jens went to the kitchen, grabbing two glasses, and returned to the couch, placing the glasses on the table before taking a seat beside his friend.

"What do we have to talk about?" Jens said as Ali picked up the bottle and opened it. Wordlessly, she began pouring two small glasses and handed one to him.

"Cheers," she said before draining the whiskey in one quick gulp. Staring at him, she waited until he followed her lead and finished his drink.

The liquid burned as it went down his throat, and he couldn't help thinking about the three pints he'd had earlier and what this would mean for him tomorrow.

"How about how fucked up this week has been," Ali said as she refilled the glasses. "I heard about what happened to you at the PPD. You all right?" she asked, unable to hide the worry in her eyes.

"I'm fine," Jens said, trying to relieve his friend, who once again glanced into his room. "Honestly."

"You want to talk about it?" she said as she leaned back and sipped on the slightly larger second pour. Jens hadn't wanted to laugh, but he found he couldn't help himself as he reached for his newly filled glass.

"I think I've had enough talking for one day, thanks."

Thankful his friend had decided to sip her new drink, he followed suit, sipping from his fresh glass. When Ali still looked confused, Jens continued.

"After the incident, I went to have drinks with Granger. I hoped he could shed some light on the video. As it turns out, he might know a little more about all this stuff than I thought."

"No surprise there," Ali said matter-of-factly. It was Jens' turn to be surprised.

"What? You think Constable Wilson could have pulled all this off on her own?" she said; her confidence in the statement couldn't help making Jens feel a little ridiculous.

"Look, I didn't know either, but when you know the truth, it's hard to feel as if it wasn't obvious all along," she said, clearly noticing the pained expression on Jens' face.

"Everything about this makes me angry," Jens said, shaking his head. "How are we supposed to know what to believe? I can't help feeling as if I've been played this whole time."

The room was silent for a long moment while the two of them sipped their drinks.

"So why don't we take back a little control?" Ali said, breaking the silence.

"In case you forgot, I tried, and there is no one left who would possibly confirm that the video is real," Jens replied.

"Who cares?" she said bluntly.

"Hard to convict the mayor with a video that we know can be altered," Jens countered.

"How do you know it can be altered?"

"let's just say our friends in Firefly made sure I got that message."

"Maybe they did. But not everyone knows that. Who says we have to be the ones to bring it into the GIB?"

Ali's enthusiasm began to build as the plan began to form. Jens was slow to catch up, but eventually he figured out where she was going.

"We can't," he said sharply. "We can't release the video."

"Of course, we can! No one knows we have it. At least not anyone who can risk saying anything about it," she said passionately. "No one else seems to want to play by the rules. I mean we've nearly been killed like . . . three times this week. We can't just sit back and take punches. We need to start throwing a couple of our own—get ahead of them."

Jens was thinking about it now, and he couldn't fault her logic; after all, no one really knew they had the videos.

"Say we do this," Jens began saying slowly. "How would we do it? It can't come back on us, for obvious reasons."

Ali thought for a moment before snapping her fingers.

"My friend in Tkaronto. I can send them the file, and they can make sure it can't get back to us," she said confidently.

"You trust this person that much?" Jens asked hesitantly. "I wasn't kidding about the consequences of getting caught."

"I trust them with my life," Ali said without hesitation.

Jens looked at her for a long moment before he got up and went into his room. A moment later, he returned with the data drive.

"Let's do it," he said with a big smile.

Ali got up and took the drive from Jens and walked over to the Halo at Jens' kitchen table. She plugged the drive in and began going through the folder and quickly noticed the second file.

"What's this?" Ali asked, her hand hovering over the file.

Jens had been so caught up in the in the video linking Mayor Stone to the deaths at the warehouse that he'd completely forgot about the second video that Anton had left him.

"It's a message from Anton explaining the video. But this is the video you want," Jens said, pointing to the larger of the two files.

Ali clicked on the file, and Anton's video of the night of the warehouse fire began to play. With the click of a couple of keys, Ali had the back door of the data file opened up.

"What are you doing?" Jens asked, trying not to sound surprised at his partner's computer skills.

"I'm just scrubbing any information that they might be able to link it to us. It won't be perfect, but it will make it easier for my friend to clean up later," Ali said, a determined look on her face.

"Where in the hell did you learn all this?" Jens asked as he tried and failed to follow the screens flashing around in front of him.

"I've always enjoyed computers. I was even going to join Tkaronto's cybercrimes unit," Ali said as she scanned the page in front of her, tweaking it slightly.

"Why didn't you? You're obviously good," Jens said as he shook his head in amazement. Ali stopped her work and gave Jens a big smile.

"And miss being in the field?" Ali laughed and continued to work. "I like it, but it gets boring."

Jens could appreciate that, knowing how he couldn't handle being stuck behind a desk; it would kill him.

"If you're so good with computers, why do we need your friend in Tkaronto? Wouldn't it be better to keep this to ourselves?" Jens asked, a sudden rush of nerves hitting him. Ali gave him another big smile, which did little to calm his nerves.

"Trust me. If we don't want any of this traced back to us, we need them to release it," Ali said confidently.

"And you trust them?" Jens asked slowly.

"With every part of my being," she said, looking Jens square in the eyes.

Jens nodded slowly. Even if he didn't trust Ali's friend, he would trust her.

Typing a few more lines of script, Ali stepped back from the Halo.

"Done!" Ali said, sounding far more excited than Jens felt.

"So, we're really going to release this video?" Jens said, his voice little more than a whisper.

"All you have to do is press Send, and it will be uploaded first thing in the morning," Ali said, gesturing to the green Send icon on the Halo.

"You press that button, and everyone in the world will know what happened that night," Ali said proudly.

"It's not justice," Jens said hesitantly.

"Maybe not," Ali said, her voice solemn, "but at least it's the truth. That has to count for something."

Jens found himself nodding at her words, then despite it all, the emotions of the past week began pouring out of him in slowly building laughter.

"Why are you laughing?" Ali said, her brow creased.

"Because earlier today, I wanted this all to end. I was prepared to toss in the towel. Now here I am one click away from betraying the system I'm supposed to protect. It feels as though I'm free diving into a massive pile of shit," Jens said, his eyes not leaving the Halo.

"Then I say it's time to get messy," Ali said with a grin, as she clicked the Send button before Jens had a chance to argue. In the blink of an eye, the message was gone.

Jens turned sharply toward Ali.

Still with a smile on her face, she placed a gentle hand on Jens' shoulder.

"We're not here to protect the system, Jens. We're here to protect people," Ali said sweetly.

Jens nodded slowly.

"I need a drink," he said stiffly as he turned to walk back into the living room. He grabbed the bottle of whiskey and poured two heavy glasses. He handed one over to Ali.

"Here's to getting messy," Jens said with a cool smile. Ali clinked her glass with his.

"Here's to getting messy," she replied before both taking a big swig.

43

Ali and Jens sat together on the couch, the mostly drunk bottle of whiskey between them. Jens could feel his eyes beginning to droop as he sat contentedly on his couch. Tomorrow he would have hell to pay, but tonight had been about celebrating.

"Jens?" Ali said softly from beside him, her voice sounding as though she were ready for sleep as well.

"Yeah?" Jens said, shifting his body slightly to turn and look at her.

"I've been thinking about the second video," she said, her head turning to face him.

"What video?" Jens said, a confused expression on his face.

"Anton's second video. What did it say?" she asked as she sat up, leaning toward him. "It must have said something?"

Jens had completely forgot about the second video; with everything that was going on, he obviously didn't find it as important as the warehouse video. He'd just assumed it was Anton explaining his side of the story.

"You watched it?" Ali continued saying; her voice was slurred slightly from the drinking. Jens' own mind was moving uncomfortably slow. Before he answered, he thought for a long moment about the night he watched the video.

"Not all of it," Jens said after a moment.

Ali didn't bother waiting. She got up and stumbled over to the Halo on the counter. The data key was still plugged in, and with a couple of quick keystrokes, she had the file up and playing before Jens had even got up from the couch.

The video began to play with the familiar opening Jens had watched in the bunker, only this time he wasn't alone.

"Senior Agent Adam Jennings. I assume if you're watching this, you've tracked down the rest of Ash and Sun and have met Akela. You're probably wondering why I didn't just give you this video when I turned myself in," Anton said.

"But as you could see, it implicates a lot of big names in our city. Something like this would put a dent in the system. But that's not my goal," he added. "If you're here, you must have learned there is something bigger at play, something you may even now have a hard time believing . . . Firefly."

Jens and Ali were on high alert hearing the word *Firefly*.

"That is one of the names they have gone by. But for all we know, which sadly isn't a lot, they have many names. They have been slowly pulling the strings of our society for so long it is difficult to know exactly where their influence stops. I suspect it doesn't. Their very existence is woven into the fabric of the global society," Anton continued to say.

"You must have so many questions, and regrettably I don't have the answers for most of them. But one has probably bothered you the most—why did I choose you?"

Jens had secretly hoped that this information would come up ever since Akela had told him about Anton's obsession with him since his suspension.

"Honestly, I'm not entirely sure yet. All I know is you are important to them. Your involvement in the Chief Daniels investigation seemed to disrupt them. Yet you are still alive. That was when I started to track you closely. I wish I could explain just how rare it is to be alive once you've crossed them," Anton said.

"My best guess is that it has something to do with your grandfather, and I hope knowing this will trigger something in you and make it clear. I don't believe he was everything you believed him to be. I think he was a member of Firefly."

Ali looked at him expectantly, but Jens only shook his head. This information had completely set him back. Out of all the reasons Jens had believed he would be tied up in all this, he never once believed it had anything to do with his grandfather. He'd been a simple man who kept to himself, and except for seeing Jens, the man had been a relative recluse in his final days. He'd always told Jens he'd wanted to travel, but he never did, and, on his Death Day, not even Jens' parents had bothered to show up. How could a man like that have anything to do with Firefly?

"I know none of this may seem helpful, and I hope that I get the chance to explain myself to you one day," Anton said, "but in case I might be dead, there is only one piece of information that truly has value to you."

Ali, who had remained silent throughout the video, perked up at this. Jens was also excited as he listened intently.

"He remembers," Anton said after a long pause. "He remembers everything."

The words meant nothing to Ali, who had noticeably deflated. But Jens knew exactly what he'd meant, and his mind began to flood once again with unanswered questions as the screen in front of them went dark.

"Who remembers what?" Ali asked a moment later. But Jens didn't have the words to explain to her just yet.

"I need to go," Jens said stiffly.

"What?" Ali said, noticeably confused. "Why?"

"Look. I can't explain it right now. Can you get home all right?"

"Yes, but . . . ," she began to protest, but he stopped her.

"I promise I will tell you everything, but right now I have to go."

"Now? It's nearly eleven p.m.?" she said, looking at her Zen watch.

"You can stay here—make sure the video goes out," he said, pleading with her.

"Sure. But . . . ," Ali said, nodding, and if she'd been planning on protesting further, Jens wouldn't be around to hear it, because he was out the door, his Zen watch resting on the kitchen counter. *It's time I finally get some answers.*

It had taken well over an hour to get there without his Zen watch, but Jens finally arrived at his destination. He remained the legally required one hundred yards as he stood and stared at the home of Chief Daniels.

He knew from the moment he took another step forward that his Zen watch would have informed the police, and they would have arrived within ten minutes to take him away.

But with no watch, he had no tracker, which meant no one would stop him before he got the answers he'd come for.

As he approached the front door, Jens was surprised by the doubt he felt. His mind had been so focused on getting here that he'd not thought a lot about the practicality of what he was about to do.

The man had a wife, and what was Jens going to do? He wasn't in the habit of breaking the law, and yet here he was breaking numerous laws all on the whim of a criminal.

Jens had been led on numerous wild-goose chases this week, and for all he knew, this was just another.

Jens' heart was racing as he approached the door to Chief Daniels' home. It had been a long time since he'd been invited into the man's house, and it seemed as though it would be sometime longer, if ever he would be. Instead, he would be forced to break in.

However, as he moved in to check the lock, he was surprised to find the door was open. *Cocky little prick.*

The house was dark, but Jens heard the sounds coming from a room down the hall and saw the light glow of a Halo screen.

Slowly Jens tiptoed down the hall. Reaching the doorway, he peered in and was surprised to see Chief Daniels sitting on a couch with a mostly empty bottle of whiskey in front of him.

The man slowly looked up and glared at Jens without a hint of surprise on his face.

"Whiskey?" he said, slurring a little.

Jens stepped farther in, not saying anything to the man, more than a little shocked by his calm presence in the room.

"Suit yourself," the man said, draining his current glass, and poured in the remainder of the bottle. "You have till I finish this glass," he said smugly before taking a rather large gulp and smacking his lips together. "Better get moving."

"How did you know I would be here?" was all Jens could think to say as he strode into the room.

Chief Daniels began to laugh.

"I was hoping you could clear that up for me," he said as he pulled out a small slip of paper from his pocket. Opening it up, the man cleared his throat theatrically before he began to read.

"He knows," he said, letting out another hearty laugh. "That's it! All they wrote. Slipped under my front door a couple of days ago." He crumpled up the paper and tossed it across the room.

"Where's your . . . ," Jens began to say.

"Suggested she go to her sister's. Don't you worry, Jennings, we're all alone. Just you and me," Chief Daniels said.

"You've just been waiting for me?" Jens asked.

"Haven't really been sleeping much these days. This helps," he said, waving to the now-empty bottle of whiskey. "Enough pleasantries," he said, leaning forward. "How'd you figure it out?"

"So, it's true?" Jens said, unable to hide the shock in his voice. Chief Daniels began to laugh again as he tapped his nose knowingly.

"Anton Preston told me," Jens said after a moment.

"How did that sneaky little bastard . . . never mind. Doesn't matter now, I guess."

The words began to fade. He fumbled around the cushions before pulling up a gun from the side of the couch and pointing it at Jens as he crinkled his nose and shut one eye. Jens stuttered back, reflexively waiting for the shot. But it never came. When he looked over, the man had an evil smile.

"Phew!" he said playfully as he began to laugh again. "I told you. You have till I finish my drink," he said, taking another sip of whiskey.

"You filthy piece of shit . . ." Jens, his eyes filled with rage, took a step closer to him, but was stopped by the gun waving in his direction.

"Aww-aww-aww," Chief Daniels said calmly. "This time I have the upper hand, Jennings, and my hands aren't cuffed," the chief said, giving Jens a knowing wink.

"What the fuck is this all about?" Jens spat out each word.

"Wow, I would have thought you knew a little bit more," he said, taking another drink from his glass and letting out a long sigh. "Tick-tick-tick."

"Were you trafficking those kids?" Jens said, unable to think properly. He'd been so thrown off by the sudden change in positions he hardly knew where to start. He had millions of questions. This question, however, received a large groan from his former chief as he began to hit his fist, still gripping the gun in his hand, against his head.

"This again! Tell me you didn't come here about this stupid . . . yes, okay, I took advantage of my position and some people, I was letting a few things slide and taking a smidge off the top. Blah-blah-blah, you pushed me down a large metal staircase, happy?" Jens wasn't, but he didn't say anything. Instead, he let his mind settle on the one question he knew the man was waiting for.

"Who or what is Firefly?" Jens asked.

"That's the question, isn't it?" the chief said with a big swig from his drink.

Jens saw this meant the depletion of his allotted timeline. He assumed that would be when the man started shooting at him, and he was wary of his appointment with death.

"So? Do you know?" Jens asked again.

"A little. I guess. Only a few people really know what Firefly is."

"So, you don't know?" Jens said, prodding.

"I didn't say that." He paused for a moment before adding, "It's complicated."

"So uncomplicate it?" Jens was starting to get annoyed. He wasn't sure why he was here; apparently the man's crimes meant nothing to him, and now Jens wasn't sure if he knew anything—just the ramblings of a drunken man.

"They recruit people . . . like me—people in some positions of power who they can leverage."

"People like Constable Wilson? Constable Granger?" Jens added. Secretly he'd hoped his friend wasn't involved. But what little optimism he had vanished at his former boss's shrug.

"Heard about Wilson, shame. As for Granger, yeah. Always good to have a couple of people on the ground to help . . . settle the dust," he said nonchalantly. He must have seen the pained expression on Jens' face, because he added, "Don't take it personally. You have no idea how big a reach these people have."

"I know they have people in the lottery," Jens said confidently as Chief Daniels began to laugh.

"In? They *are* the lottery," he said passively. "Where do you think the credits come from? They have . . . trillions of credits at their disposal. Just let that sink in," he said, taking a tiny sip from his glass as he examined the remaining contents.

"They control everything, and your little gang of data junkies can't do anything about it," he said, smiling as he recognized the look of surprise on Jens' face. "Oh, yeah, we know about Ash and Sun and their little hodgepodge of 'freedom' fighters."

Jens was beginning to grow wary of the gun in the man's hand as he swirled the contents of the glass around. He figured he had only a few questions left before he had to start dodging bullets, and he wanted to make them count.

"Was my grandfather a member of Firefly?" Jens asked. Chief Daniels stopped swirling his glass and looked Jens in the eye with a pained expression.

"He was the one who introduced me," he said sadly.

"Introduced you to who?" Jens hoped he could get a little more information out of the man before he ran. He had no intention of staying around for the man to finish his drink. As soon as he got the answer, he would be gone.

For a long moment, Chief Daniels sat staring at his drink before he began to cry.

"The Doctor," he said, his voice barely a whisper.

"Who's the Doctor?" Jens asked, but Chief Daniels simply began to shake his head.

"They are a ghost. They have no name and no face," Chief Daniels said so quietly that Jens had to strain his ears to make it out. The sudden shift in the man's demeanour reminded Jens of a little boy who was lost, and for a brief moment, Jens felt sorry for the man.

"I can help you," Jens said softly. "We can bring them in, if you help me." Against his better judgment, Jens took a step closer and put out his hand, extending it for his ex-boss to grab.

Chief Daniels looked up through blurry eyes at Jens and began to shake his head.

"You don't understand yet," a sad smile forming on his tear-soaked face. "We're already dead." Then he took the final drink from his glass.

"All done," he said, his voice cold and empty as he lifted the gun.

Jens had nowhere to go, and he cursed himself for being so exposed. All he could do was jump and hope the man's aim was off with his obvious intoxication.

Diving for the floor, Jens heard the shot fired from the gun. He hit the floor with a thud, thankful he hadn't been hit. Knowing the second shot would be coming any second, he rolled quickly to one side, making his way to his knee.

But the second shot never fired, and when Jens turned to see his assailant, he found the man sitting on his couch, the gun resting weightlessly in his hand beside him. Blood covered the wall behind the couch, along with some of the remnants of the man's brains from where the bullet had launched itself out the other side.

Jens moved slowly to the lifeless body of the man he'd once tried to kill, and despite knowing, pressed his hands against the man's wrist and felt nothing. Chief Daniels had killed himself.

As had been the case from the beginning of this investigation, Jens felt as though every answer only created more questions. The only consolation in his mind was now he had a name for his enemy, the Doctor.

Taking in the scene around him, he felt the walls beginning to close in on him as he glanced down at the man's wrist; his metallic gold Zen watch, a gift for his GIB retirement, read six thousand five hundred and two days. That's how many days the man had left before he should have died, and yet whatever power Firefly held had caused two people in a single day to end their lives.

The chilling final words of Chief Daniels replayed in Jens' mind: "We're already dead." Jens couldn't be sure what he meant by that, nor did he have any time to ponder the words as he noticed something else on the man's Zen watch, an emergency call notice flashing red across its face.

The bastard had sent an emergency alarm to the PPD before he'd shot himself, and Jens was standing in the middle of a crime scene.

That's when Jens heard the unmistakable sounds of sirens in the distance.

THE END

Acknowledgment

First of all I would like to thank you, the reader. If you have managed to get to this point in the book then it means you have finished it. I truly hope you enjoyed reading Ash and Sun as much as I enjoyed writing it!

If you did enjoy it please feel free to share this story with your friends, review it online or sign up for my email list for upcoming book releases and stories on my website www.jonnyonthepage.com.

Ash and Sun is my debut novel which I began writing during the COVID-19 pandemic after I discovered how possible it had become to self-publish a book. I have always had stories in my head and have written a few plays and screenplays. The concept of putting work out into the world by publishing it myself was intriguing. All it would take is writing it.

As it turns out writing a book when it's been in your mind for so long isn't as hard as I thought. All it took was hours of sitting down and committing to putting words on a page. Fortunately, I had the advantage of time on my hands and the story in my mind. All I needed to do was commit.

The true difficulty has been the editing process which I can honestly say could not have been done without the help of so many people. There are a few of these people that I would like to thank now. The first is my Mum, who has read and edited roughly seven drafts of this story and has been such a big supporter of me beginning my writing journey and I would be remiss if I didn't thank her immensely for everything she has done (She will likely also edit this Acknowledgment page as well so even more thanks for that.)

I would also like to thank my partner Hilary for all of her support while I have been working through this first book, she's been incredible with reading early drafts, giving me suggestions, and all around being a source of positivity during the last couple of years it's taken me to do this. Thank you, my love.

Then there is my family who has always been very supportive of me while I have tried to take on all of these creative endeavours in my life. Particularly my Dad who I'm not entirely sure has ever truly understood exactly what I am doing at any one time but none the less has supported me unconditionally through it all. I truly have been fortunate to have been born into a family that offers up so much love and support and it is all because of both my Mum and my Dad. So, thank you both for everything you continue to do for me.

There have also been many people who are not my direct family who have helped make this book possible and I would like to take this moment to thank them as well. Laura, who was one of my first editors on this project. Her attention to detail and her willingness to discuss the choices in the story helped make it stronger and I appreciate everything you did. Leighton, who helped proofread the story and fix all of the little mistakes I missed along the way, I thank you. I have always said, I am a writer and not a speller. So truly this book would be in shambles without the hard work of the editors who assisted me along the way.

I would also like to thank Robyn, who helped design the cover art for the book. As is the theme with this first novel she is also my amazing sister-in-law and a gifted artist who passes her time as an architect, a mother and somehow still found time to develop and design this beautiful cover art. The cover is what catches your eye first and I am sure that more than one reader was compelled by Robyn's art to give the book a try. Robyn, you are a talent! Thank you.

Lastly, I would like to thank you the reader, once again. A book is not a book without people who want to read it. I hope that it has provided you with some joy and possibly some entertainment. I do not plan to stop writing and I have a few additional works nearly finished and I look forward to sharing those with you all soon.

Ash and Sun was developed in my mind as a trilogy and I have already started outlining Book two. Although I have a few other projects I've been working on completing, I will be continuing the second installment very soon, but if you liked this book and are eager for book two, send me an email and let me know Jonny@jonnyonthepage.com and I'll work to make it happen. Jens and Ali have a lot more ahead of them and I look forward to sharing that journey with you all soon!

Until next time,

Jonny Thompson

About the Author

Jonny Thompson is a writer and performer living in Ponamogoat-itjg/Dartmouth, NS with his partner Hilary and their delightfully entertaining dog Henry. Jonny was born in England and grew up in the traditional lands of the Anishinabewaki and Attiwonderonk nations now St. Marys, Ontario. Jonny attended Dalhousie University, where he received a BA in Theatre. He's worked professionally for over 12 years, including 5 years performing young audience puppet shows worldwide with Mermaid Theatre of NS. He's also worked on various stage and television productions and has written and directed a couple of short films. Over the past few years, Jonny has been exploring the world of novel writing and he is excited to share with you some of the stories he's been developing. Thank you for reading!

You can connect with me on:

🌐 https://www.jonnyonthepage.com

CPSIA information can be obtained
at www.ICGtesting.com
Printed in the USA
LVHW112049161022
730833LV00001B/150

9 781738 666003